LINKED ACROSS TIME

LINKED ACROSS TIME

VOLUME ONE

DAWN BROWER

MONARCHAL GLENN PRESS

"When I fall in love, it will be forever."

— JANE AUSTEN, SENSE AND
SENSIBILITY

CONTENTS

SAVED BY MY BLACKGUARD

LINKED ACROSS TIME ONE

DAWN BROWER

Dawn Brower

SAVED
BY MY
Blackguard

Linked Across Time

"You may delay, but time will not."

— BENJAMIN FRANKLIN

AUTHOR'S NOTE

Thank you to everyone who read my books and keeps asking for more. You're the reason I continue to write and develop new stories. This is the start of a new adventure I hope you all enjoy as much as I did. Before you ask (because I have beta readers that liked him despite his naughtiness). Yes Captain Jack will get his own book. You just might have to wait a while to get it. He was a surprise I didn't expect or plan on initially, but I had a lot of fun with him.

CHAPTER 1

New York, August 18, 1987

PAUL DEWITT TAPPED HIS FINGERS ON THE ARM of the chair. The starkness of the doctor's office was blinding and he couldn't focus on any one thing. The waiting was driving him insane. As the hands on the clock ticked by he could hear parts of his life fall out of existence. What was wrong with him? Why had he passed out? He needed answers and the damned doctor better come and give them to him soon. He wasn't ready to die. There was so much he had yet to accomplish.

The doctor rushed in, sat behind his desk and laid a manila folder on it. He studied Paul with his fingers steepled together in concentration. After a long drawn out silence he sighed and opened the file. He pulled out a sheet of paper and handed it to Paul.

"We've run all the necessary tests and we've come to one conclusion." The doctor paused and stared into Paul's eyes. "You're working yourself to an early grave. If you don't slow down you won't see your thirtieth birthday."

"What is wrong with me?" Paul glanced at the sheet of paper, but it was all gibberish to him. "Explain what all these numbers mean."

"The short answer is you are too stressed. Your heart is working too hard and you don't sleep enough. Your body is exhausted and fighting itself. It gave in when you wanted to push it past its limits." The doctor grabbed the paper and put it back in the file and closed it. "Despite what you believe, Paul, you're not limitless. You need to take better care of yourself. The best advice I can give you is to take a vacation. Delegate some of your duties and take a step back from your business. From your own admission you work over 80 hours a week. At that pace, you won't live to do anything with the money you're accumulating. Medically speaking, I can only do so much for you."

The good doctor could stick his advice someplace rather unpleasant and twist it like a sharp blade. He couldn't afford a vacation. His company was on the brink of a major takeover of a computer software firm. They held the necessary patents he needed to launch his personal computers on the market. His product would be more affordable to the average family and all the market research showed they would be a high profit margin for his company. Being sick wasn't something he could afford at such a critical time in his family's company. He was the only one who could make sure the takeover went through. His brother was a dismal failure at business and preferred to party rather than taking any responsibility. If he didn't handle everything who would?

"I can't take a vacation." He snorted. "The very idea is ludicrous."

The doctor shrugged. "Ultimately it is your decision. What is more important to you? Your company or your health? I can't make those decisions for you. My job is to point out to you the ramifications of those decisions."

Paul hated to admit the doctor was right. Exhaustion swept through him leaving him drained. He rubbed his eyes, hoping it would help keep him focused. If only he could make it through the next month to see the takeover through... They had to slowly buy up stock using a few different dummy corporations before they could seize control. It would be bad to have the SEC on their backs. He could do some of the work from home if needed. The office and day-to-day business could get by on its own. That was why he had an administrative assistant for. And she was damned good at her job.

"How long?"

"Pardon?" The doctor raised an eyebrow. "How long for what?"

"How long of a vacation do you recommend I take?"

"A month—"

"Is too long," Paul interrupted him. "There's no way I could take a month off from the company. I would end up destitute leaving it for that long."

The doctor shook his head and sighed. "I doubt it would come to that. A week then. Do you think you could manage that?"

Paul tilted his head and considered it. He might be able to manage a week. He could leave detailed instructions with Christy. She knew how he liked things handled and he could depend on her to keep the machine running while he frolicked on the beach. He almost snorted at the absurdity of him lounging on the sand while waves crashed to shore. It wouldn't take him but a day to go mad with boredom. Maybe the doctor was right and he needed to slow down, but to do nothing? That was a fate worse than death. He didn't know how to live a carefree life. It wasn't in his genetic makeup.

"I might be able to take a week, if I have a week to prepare the company for my departure."

The doctor frowned, and then said. "That might be detrimental. Do you need a whole week?"

"Yes," he said, emphatically. "I handle a lot of the details of the company every day. I need time to prepare them for my absence. I know you believe I need this vacation, and you know I disagree. I can't in good conscience leave without doing my due diligence as CEO."

"Fine, but I want you to come by my office in a few days for a stress test. I'm afraid if you push too hard you will have a heart attack before the end of the week."

Was his heart really that overworked? He was tired, but surely the doctor was overreacting. He'd only passed out the once...

"I will have my assistant set up an appointment. I'm not sure when I have a time open."

The doctor nodded. "It really is for the best. When you get back from your vacation I also suggest you cut your work hours by at least a third. Find something else to fill your time with."

"What could I possibly do other than work?" Paul rolled his eyes. "I don't like people and I have no hobbies. Work is all I know."

"I don't know—try dating, find someone to love. Get married, have a family."

Paul almost snorted at his words. He may have been his doctor since he was a small boy, but that didn't mean he had to follow his relationship advice. Women were only good for one thing, and he didn't need one in his life full time to get that. He had no desire to find love. It wasn't in the cards for him and he was all right with that fate. As far as kids, his sister had a couple that could inherit the company. He didn't need any progeny to pass it down to.

"Thanks, but I will have to pass on your sage advice. A family is the last thing I need. You already said I'm stressed, what do you think a wife and kids would do to me?"

"Just slow down. The rest of your life will fall in place once you do. Enjoy your vacation."

Enjoy? Somehow he believed that was the last thing he would do. It didn't matter. If he had to sleep in and be lazy for a week to help heal his heart he would do it. The rest of the doctor's advice wasn't even an option. He didn't need or want someone to nag him for the rest of his life. He was perfectly content the way things were.

"I suppose I can try to anyway. Do you have any recommendations for a vacation spot?"

The doctor shook his head. "No and it doesn't matter as long as you relax wherever it is. You can stay home if you like, just don't go into the office."

"Right." He doubted he would be able to resist the urge to go into the office if he stayed home. So an island getaway it was. He'd have his assistant book his vacation for him. It didn't matter where as long as it was nice and relaxing just as the doctor ordered. "I suppose I will be going. Thanks for the advice."

Paul stood up and left the doctor's office. He had to get back to Dewitt Enterprises and start the plans necessary for his impromptu vacation.

PORT ROYAL, AUGUST 28, 1987

The heat of the sun poured over Paul as he lounged on the beach, and the waves crashed on the shore. He pulled his sunglasses off his face and wiped the sweat off his forehead. The forced vacation was already driving him mad.

Sure, Port Royal was amazing and beautiful. There were plenty of stunning sights around him, including the sexy brunette who kept giving him come-hither looks as she strolled down the beach in her tiny white bikini. He couldn't even muster the smallest amount of interest in her—even if she was sexy. The desire wasn't there for him. He'd been on the island two days and he was going stir crazy. He had to do something more than lounge on the beach staring into the sea-green water. At least, he could be thankful he didn't take the doctor's original advice for a month long vacation. That would have been torture he never would have survived through.

Paul sighed. He glanced over his shoulder and an idea took root. There was a lot on this island to see and maybe it was time he started to explore it. The hotel was nice and had every luxury known to man, but he wasn't used to taking advantage of it. His father made sure he understood what was important. The family fortune rested squarely on his shoulders. It was his responsibility to ensure the rest of them lived in the style they'd become accustomed to. The Dewitts came from old money, well as old as an American could come from money anyway. They founded their business early on in the history of the country and managed to hold onto their fortune by sheer will and grit.

If only dad had instilled the same values in his worthless brother and debutante sister.

Paul stood up and headed toward the lush vegetation on the island. A hike along the mountain ridge might be what he needed to loosen up. Sitting around and being lazy didn't suit him, but he could get behind some good old-fashioned exercise. He put his sunglasses back on and started the long trek up the Blue Mountains of Jamaica. He'd meander up a bit, check them out and then head back to the hotel for dinner.

After a short while he stopped at the edge of a cave and looked out at the ocean. It was quite a view. Overhead he saw some cloud formations that had an angry gray appearance. A storm must be heading toward the island. He should head back toward the hotel before he got caught up in a torrential downfall. He started to walk back when he saw a shadow out of the corner of his eye. He turned, startled, as a woman raced ahead of him. Her dress was something from another time. He'd seen enough old pictures to know it wasn't normal to see a woman prancing around in clothing straight out of the eighteenth century. She had long golden blonde hair that fell down her back in waves. Paul was instantly intrigued.

"Wait up, you shouldn't be out here alone. There is a storm coming in."

She ignored him and kept running. The fear in her eyes alarmed him when she glanced over her shoulder. He raced after her as lightning crashed and a thunderous boom followed. Paul had to help her. If he left her alone in the storm he would be the worst cad ever.

"Miss, don't run. I can help you."

Maybe she couldn't hear him. The thunder was rather loud and getting closer with each rumble. The rain began to fall in waves. After a while, he couldn't see two feet in front of him and he'd lost sight of the blonde. He slowly made his way to where he last sighted her. A huge blast of lightning blinded him as a gust of wind blew over him. He scrambled to find his balance, but soon lost it and fell forward. Pain shot through his head and he began to lose consciousness. His arms flailed out as he plummeted toward the bottom of the mountain. His mouth fell open with a silent scream.

So much for being a good samaritan, next time, if he lived through this, he'd leave the woman to her own fate...

CHAPTER 2

St. Kitts, August 18, 1722

LADY EVELYN BECKETT FINISHED DRESSING IN A light muslin gown. The summer heat on the island didn't leave many options for a lady, and she was dying in the sweltering heat. Her long golden blonde curls were drenched with sweat. She sat down and began the tedious process of plaiting them and wrapping them into a tight chignon. Even the smallest loose strand would lead to unwanted warmth on her already overheated skin.

"Lady Evelyn," a maid said. She curtsied quickly before speaking again. "Pardon my interruption, but your father requests your presence in his study."

Her father, the Earl of Ashland, owned the plantation they currently resided in. She'd lived in England during her formative years, but when her mother died he packed them up and started a new life in the West Indies. Evelyn hated every moment of her time on the island and looked forward to returning to the cooler climate of England. Maybe this was the moment she'd been waiting for. Her betrothed, the Duke of Southington, might have finally summoned her for their wedding.

"Tell him I will be down in a moment." She hid her excitement. It wouldn't do to show her emotions. Her father frowned upon a lady doing anything untoward. "I need to finish my coiffure."

Her father had very strict ideas of what a lady should and should not do. He took being overprotective to extreme lengths. She had a footman, or rather a guard as she thought of the man, who followed her everywhere she went. He denied her a personal maid forcing her to learn how to dress herself properly and see to her own needs. It was supposed to teach her humility. The entire household watched her every move. She couldn't sneeze without someone reporting it to him.

After feeling her hair and glancing over her dress, she was satisfied that she would be presentable and made her way to her father's study. A servant stood outside his door. Evelyn glanced up at him and asked, "Is he available?"

She learned early on not to barge into her father's study. The one and only time she did it her bottom had burned for a week from the whipping he'd given her. It was a mistake she never made again. If there was one thing she did right it was never to repeat the same mistake twice. Living on the island and without a mother's guidance oftentimes left her at a disadvantage—her parents were as different as night and day. Her mother had been loving, kind, and nurturing. She sheltered her from most of her father's darker proclivities. Once she was gone, she saw him for the man he really was. A monster she couldn't wait to escape.

He nodded. "Lord Ashland is expecting you."

She steeled herself to deal with her father and walked stiffly into his study. Gray hair flopped forward, shadowing his face as he bent over his desk and studied a document. She folded her hands in front of her and patiently waited for him to acknowledge her presence and give her leave to sit down. After a few moments he glanced up and gestured her forward. "Evelyn, come in girl. Don't dawdle."

She repressed the urge to roll her eyes. Insolence was forbidden. "Yes, Father."

"Sit. We have much to discuss."

He stood and walked over to a nearby window. The sunlight illuminated him. He was a sturdy man and he'd worked hard to build his fortune in the West Indies. It was starting to take a toll on him. New wrinkles were forming on his forehead and around his eyes every day. Evelyn didn't doubt the stress he put himself under would put him in an early grave. Sadly, she doubted she would miss him once he was gone. He made her life hell.

She sat, waiting for him to tell her why he summoned her. His lack of conversation was making her nervous. Why wouldn't he get it out and tell her what she'd done wrong this time? If it was the duke summoning her for their wedding he'd have already said it. This had to be bad if he left her wallowing in misery.

"I've tried to do my best by you. Raise you right and humble," he began. "I know you must think me evil, but I truly have your best interests at heart."

This wasn't good. He was gearing up to a lecture she wouldn't leave unscathed from.

"Yes, father, I mean no"—she shook her head ardently—"I don't think you're evil." He really was. "I know you only want to make sure I have a good life." As long as she followed his rules and didn't deviate from them in any way.

He laughed. "Don't try and dupe me, girl. I am well aware of what you truly believe." Her father waved a hand dismissively. "It doesn't matter. It's not why I summoned you. I received a letter from the Duke of Southington. It's time for you to return to England for your wedding. It isn't a good time for me to leave the plantation so I'm sending you with a maid as a chaperone. He expects you in England in six weeks for the wedding."

Evelyn gulped. "I understand."

She wanted to jump for joy. Surely the duke would be better than living under her father's care. Six weeks and she'd be the Duchess of Southington, she could hardly wait.

He nodded. "I've already ordered your trunks packed. You're leaving on a ship this evening."

"So soon?" The words were out before she could stop them. She bit her lip and awaited her punishment. It was usually a slap in the face for daring to question him. When no reprimand came, she slowly opened her eyes and was surprised at the expression on her father's face. He looked contrite.

"I've made a lot of mistakes. I won't apologize for them, it's the only way I knew how to raise you.

Sometimes I wish..." He shook his head. "It doesn't matter what I wish. If your mother were here she'd be better at this. I'm going to miss you, Evelyn. It's harder to say goodbye than I thought it would be."

This was a side of her father she'd never seen. She had no map to guide her. How was she supposed to respond to this sudden change? If she took a wrong move she could end up regretting it. So she said nothing and waited for him to continue. When there were no adequate words it was better to wait her father out, another lesson she'd learned the hard way. There were too many to count.

"What are you waiting for?" He shooed his hands at her. "Go prepare to leave."

So much for sentimentality, it was nice to see, no matter how brief it was. It showed her that for a small moment in time her father had a heart. He kept it buried too deep for the world to see. In the grand scheme of things it didn't matter. She still wanted to be as far away from him as possible. Surely there was something greater and more meaningful for her life than to be the daughter of an autocratic earl.

So she left him alone in his study, the way he preferred, and went to prepare for her new life.

OUT AT SEA, AUGUST 21, 1722

Evelyn had been aboard the ship for days. For too long they didn't move because there was no wind to guide the sails. The journey was going to take forever at the rate they were traveling. The waves rocked the ship and made her stomach queasy. The daily walks on the deck did nothing to ease her discomfort. Sailing never had been something she enjoyed. The trek from England to St. Kitts had been equally as horrible.

"Lady Evelyn."

Abby's voice broke through her melancholy.

Evelyn turned toward the maid her father assigned to her for her journey and said, "Yes?"

"Perhaps it's time we take shelter in your cabin. Your cheeks are getting red from too much sun."

Evelyn had no desire to be cooped up in her sweltering cabin. She didn't care if her cheeks burned under the sun's heat. It was a blessing to breathe the fresh salt air. She was about to tell Abby that when a shout echoed on the breeze from above.

"Jolly Roger, ahoy!" A sailor called down from the crow's nest.

The first mate scrambled forward, shouting, "All hands hoay!"

Chaos ensued as everyone hurried to get on

deck. They forgot about Evelyn in the process and she got shoved against one of the masts. Her head hit it hard and she crumpled to the ground. She stared off into the distance, dazed for several hectic moments.

"Lady Evelyn." Her maid shook her. "You need to get up. Pirates are attacking the ship."

"What?" The words were not registering. "Who is attacking?"

"Have you taken leave of your senses?" Abby shrieked. "Get up now and go to your cabin where you'll be safe."

Abby grabbed her arm and yanked hard. Evelyn barely moved. She shook her head to clear it. What had Abby said? Oh yes, pirates. The words finally started to penetrate her mind and she got up. Her movements were sluggish and she swayed with each step she took.

"Keep moving," Abby urged.

A blast hit the hull of the ship lurching her forward. Her knees hit the deck hard and took the brunt of her fall. She would have bruises all over her body before this day was done. She scrambled back to her feet feeling her way toward the entrance to get below deck and the safety of her cabin. The cannons fired again and another explosion rocked the hull.

Vibrations rolled across her fingers as she moved against the side of the ship.

"Hurry. For the love of God, make haste. We're going to die at this slow pace." Her maid's voice was filled with terror. "Why did I let the earl talk me into joining you on this voyage back to England? I'd be safe in my bed on the island if not for you."

A part of Evelyn knew Abby didn't like her. This was all the confirmation she needed. "If I am such a burden you can leave me alone."

She'd probably be better off without her maid tagging along behind her, spying on her. She didn't doubt Abby would report her every move back to her father. Soon he would have no control over her life. A new man would have that honor. She had only met the duke once when she was a small girl. He'd seemed so foreboding then, but not unkind. Evelyn hoped her original assessment wasn't wrong. It was easy to fool a girl, but as a woman she would see through any façade he presented her. Under her father's tutelage she'd been trained for any possibility. She'd had to grow strong and able to withstand anything because of his unruly temper and exact expectations.

Abby stuck her chin in the air defiantly. "Good

riddance too. I'm sure the pirates will find you lovely."

She scooted past Evelyn and headed down to the cabin. It took every bit of strength she had to fight back the tears threatening to fall. Abby had the right of it. Good riddance to her spy and task master. Her life would be inherently easier without having to deal with the maid dictating to her in her father's absence. Maybe the pirates would be a better choice.

"Prepare to be boarded," a pirate called out.

The pounding of feet on the deck filled her ears. Shouts and screams joined the bombardment of noise. Strange men shifted from one side of the ship to the other as they fought for control. The pirates filled the ship and before long they seized power of the vessel. Evelyn wanted to crawl into a hole and seek cover, but the time for hiding had passed.

"What do we have here?"

A husky voice as rich as the Scottish whisky her father preferred filled her ears. Something she shouldn't know much about, but out of curiosity she'd sneaked a taste or two of the amber liquor. Evelyn looked up and stared straight into eyes the exact shade of the Caribbean Sea. The pirate's golden-blond hair shimmered in the sunlight. He was perhaps one of the most beautiful men she'd ever gazed upon. She'd heard pirates were a dirty lot, but this one was surely a different breed altogether.

"Who are you?"

He studied her for a moment and then his lips tilted into a wicked smile. It made him intrinsically more appealing. The sexy beast was too gorgeous for his own good. He would be devastating to the female population if he were unleashed upon them.

"Captain Jack Morgan at your service." He bowed to her. "Percy, come help the Lady board the Siren Song. She's going to join our crew as my mistress."

"But Capt..." The pirate stammered.

"Are you refusing to follow a direct order?" Captain Morgan glared at him.

"No, Captain." He bowed his head in submission. He leaned in and said with a loud whisper, "Women are a curse on board a ship."

"I don't bow down to superstition. This woman is mine and I intend to keep her." The captain waved a hand dismissing the other pirate. "Now, do what I ordered."

Evelyn turned her head back and forth between the two. Did the pirate captain say she was going to be his mistress? Over her dead body... She was meant to be a duchess and she'd be damned if she let that man lay a hand on her. He might be astoundingly striking, but her father hadn't raised a fool.

"I am no man's mistress," she spat out, finally finding her voice, and the spine she'd grown dealing with her father's tyranny.

"Of course not, you're Captain Morgan's and he's no mere man."

Evelyn's gaze flew toward the pirate who'd cowed before his captain. "I don't recognize him as someone in need of worship. He might be a god to you, but he's nothing to me."

Captain Morgan laughed. "Let her be for now. She'll come around in time. They all do."

A cocky smile filled his dazzling visage. Evelyn wanted to wipe it permanently off his face. He was so damned sure of himself. How many women had fallen at his feet? She would not be among them. "You can wait till the end of time. I will not be changing my mind."

"We'll see, love." His grin widened and he traced her jaw with the tip of his finger. "I've been told I have a magic touch."

She shivered involuntarily. Why did he have to be so bloody handsome? "I wouldn't know. You do nothing for me."

He chuckled lightly. "I like this one. She has

spirit. We're going to have a lot of fun together." He turned toward the other pirate. "Take her aboard the ship now." He gestured his arms toward the ship Evelyn had been sailing on before they attacked. "As for this one, scuttle it."

Percy yanked her toward the gangway and hauled her across it toward their ship.

"What did the captain mean by scuttle it?"

"He means to sink the ship." Percy didn't even bother to look at her. He kept pulling her toward a cabin on the ship. He shoved her inside and locked it from the outside.

"You can't murder everyone on the ship." She banged on the door.

The last thing she thought she heard him say was, "Not your call to make."

Then there was nothing but silence, leaving Evelyn alone with her own dreary thoughts. There was no saving her from the fate she found herself in. She had only herself to rely on. Jack Morgan believed she'd willingly fall into his arms. He didn't know her or her resolve. As long as he didn't force her she could withstand his advances. She took a deep breath and forced herself to relax. She would need her strength for the upcoming battle.

CHAPTER 3

Out at Sea, August 28, 1722

Evelyn had somehow managed to avoid Captain Jack Morgan's advances for a week. It was by sheer will she'd been able to tell him no when he turned on the charm. He was overwhelming every one of her senses. His very presence was a lure of seduction that was proving almost irresistible. She had to get off the Siren Song before she willingly gave herself to the handsome devil.

Why, oh why does he have to be so charismatic and fun? It was a question she asked herself several times every day she'd been forced to be in his company. She let out a relieved breath every time he left the cabin. He, at least, refused to take her as long as she was unwilling. For that alone he earned her respect. Most men in his situation would have taken her and not bothered to seek permission. It was a horrible fate to suffer and she was thankful for that small favor. Still, he let his wishes known to her at every meeting.

Soon he would seek a kiss and she'd be at a loss to stop him. A part of her wanted him to. The part that knew she deserved better prevented her from giving in to him. She had a future to protect and it wasn't with a too handsome pirate. Besides, while he refused to be with her without her consent he still gave the orders to murder everyone on the ship she'd been sailing on. Ironic that Abby had wanted to be separated from her to obtain her own safety and she still ended up finding her death at the bottom of the sea. She should feel sadness, and a part of her did, but a larger part of her didn't. Abby had made it clear how she felt about her. Evelyn had never wanted her maid to die though. She'd never wish that on any person.

"How is the lovely Lady Evelyn this afternoon?"

She looked up and almost got lost in his beautiful sea-green eyes. He wasn't for her. The Duke of

Southington would not marry a woman with a sullied reputation. He still might not once he realized she'd been kidnapped by pirates. As long as she remained true to herself, it would all work out as it was supposed to. She had faith in her destiny. Jack Morgan was not her future.

"I would be better if I could leave this cabin."

He smiled. "I can arrange that. But you would owe me a boon."

She tilted her head and studied him. This was a trick, she was sure of it. She'd gotten to know him over the last week. Instead of falling headfirst into his scheme she decided to change the subject.

"Where are you taking me?"

He laughed and folded his arms across his burly chest. She pushed her heathen thoughts out of her head and stared him in the eyes. It wouldn't do to get caught ogling him like a prize.

"We're headed to the pirates' den." He raised an eyebrow mockingly. "Why, are you hoping you'll get a better offer at Port Royal?"

She snorted and then covered her mouth and nose with her hand. It was a reflex. Snorting was unladylike and her father would have slapped her for such a rude gesture. Evelyn shook her head slowly.

"No, I don't want anything another scalawag has to offer. I'd rather you took me to England. My betrothed is expecting me."

The captain frowned and shook his head. "I'm afraid I can't accommodate you. If I get anywhere near England it would be the hangman's noose for me. I rather enjoy breathing and having an intact neck."

She'd been afraid that would be his answer. How was she ever going to get back to England and marry the duke? "There must be a way for you to send me home."

He shrugged. "I rather like having you around. In time you won't mind the pirate life. It has its benefits." Captain Jack wiggled his eyebrows suggestively.

Oh, he was so stubborn. Why couldn't he see reason? She stomped her foot with frustration. "I don't want to live this life. Did you ever once stop to think what this would do to me? My reputation is in tatters. No respectable man will have anything to do with me. I'm impure just by being alone with you."

His smile widened as he gazed at her. Wickedness poured out of him as he glanced over her. "Then I don't understand why you're fighting what is between us. Surely you feel what I do."

"Lust?" She raised an eyebrow. "There is more to life than giving into your baser instincts. I will not lay with you no matter how prettily you wrap up the package. It is not something I want or will condone."

"Then we're at an impasse, love." He leaned down and whispered in her ear, "But you should know pleasure beyond your wildest imagination, and I can give that to you."

She sucked in a breath. His promises were so tempting, if she wanted that from him. He was gorgeous but she didn't want to be anything more than friends with him. Evelyn mentally counted to ten to regain control. Dealing with Jack was akin to reasoning with a small child.

He took a step back and smiled down at her. "I have decided to give you something you want without compensation."

What game was he playing now? She scrunched her eyebrows together with disbelief. "What are you after?"

"Oh, what I want has been clear all along, love." His grin grew wider on his face. "I want every inch of you naked and spread out willingly for me on my bed. I plan to feast on. Say the word and I'll make it happen."

"No." Her mouth formed a firm flat line. "Quit teasing me."

He sighed. "Have it your way. Instead I'm going to give you the freedom you seek. My men know to leave you alone or to suffer the consequence. Go roam the ship."

She was afraid to step out of the cabin. What if she did and he expected something she was not willing to give him? She had to know exactly what she was getting into before she took him for his word.

"And you don't expect me to pay for this gift later?"

He lifted his hand and did a crisscross motion over his heart. "I promise. This is something I want you to have. If I show you some generosity maybe you won't see me for the evil man you believe me to be."

Of course he had an ulterior motive. That didn't surprise her one iota. She wouldn't turn down his offer though. Evelyn was desperate to get out of the cabin. The only thing she was surprised about was him caving into her desire.

"How long until we get to this pirates' den you told me about?"

"Making plans, are you?" He laughed. "Don't

worry I will protect you. The other pirates won't touch what belongs to me."

"I am not yours," she replied. "I belong to no man."

Maybe this was for the best. Her father had ruled her life. She needed this space to breathe. Captain Jack wasn't for her, but she could weave her own path.

He saluted her. "I do enjoy these chats. To answer your question we should be there within the hour."

No wonder he was allowing her on deck. The ship would be docking soon. If they were going to the pirates' den she'd be reluctant to leave the ship. Pirates were an untrustworthy lot. What Captain Jack had planned for her she did not know. He could be a hard man to read at times. She fidgeted under his stare. "Can I go on deck now?"

"Of course, would you like me to escort you?"

That was the last thing she wanted. She needed some space between them. Over the long week she had started to like him, but that didn't mean she would give him her innocence. A bit of an epiphany hit her during their conversation. She had more freedom than to stroll on the deck. For the first time in her life she had options, and one of them was to marry for love.

"Can I go by myself?"

"Yes," he replied. "Enjoy your stroll. If you change your mind you know where to find me."

She spun on her heels and faced him. Perhaps she should mess with him a little bit. Give a little tit for tat. Evelyn sashayed over to him, lifted her hand and twinkled her fingers up his chest all the way to his lips. She traced them with the tip of her finger. "Jack, darling, please I beg you..." She leaned in close and whispered, "I need something only you can give me."

"Tell me?" His voice took on a husky tone as he leaned in closer to her.

Evelyn stepped back and grinned. "Space. All I need is what you've already granted me, freedom to explore the ship and the same once we dock in Port Royal."

It had been too easy to suck him in. Perhaps he did desire her in truth. Evelyn wanted more than the pirate had to offer. She wanted love and stability. He gave off a menacing aura. Jack was a pirate—a fact of life—but she rather liked him. He lived by his own code of ethics and she respected him. He wasn't the man she needed in her life though.

"You're a wicked lass messing with a man." He shook his head. "Where did an innocent learn such a trick?"

She shrugged. "I'm a quick study."

"I do love your wit and quick thinking." He chuckled. "I will give you that. Go explore the ship. We'll continue this discussion later."

Evelyn nodded and headed out of the cabin. None of the pirates stopped to ask her what she was doing. As she walked across the deck she could see land in the distance. Captain Jack hadn't lied. They would be sailing into a harbor soon. She went to the railing and tilted her head back, basking in the sun's warmth. A rumble of thunder echoed through her ears. Her eyes fluttered open and she caught sight of dark clouds heading toward the ship. A bolt of lightning struck the water. The wind began to pick up and waves crashed against the ship's hull. Where had this sudden storm come from?

"Batten down the hatches," a call came down from the crow's nest. "Storm is heading our way."

"Raise the masts," Captain Morgan shouted. "We need to try to beat the storm and anchor in Port Royal before it hits."

Evelyn stared at them all in shock. She was still confused how the storm had managed to sneak up on them. It came out of nowhere. The wind whipped against her as she watched the pirates gear the ship for a different kind of battle. The sea could be more devastating than an angry adversary. The wind was strong and they managed to use it to their advantage as they closed the distance between them and the island. They would make it. Evelyn had to remain patient and not give into her worry.

"You," an angry voice said from behind her. "This is your fault. I told the captain it was bad luck to bring a woman on board. Maybe if I sacrifice you to Davy Jones's locker the fate's will forgive us and let the Siren Song make it to shore."

"What?" Evelyn turned, baffled, at the sight of Percy. "I didn't do this."

Superstitious men couldn't be reasoned with though. He shoved her hard and she tumbled over board. The waves sucked her under and she swallowed sea water. For the first time in her life she was thankful for her father's tutelage. It was at his instance she had learned how to swim. She pulled up her billowing skirts and wrapped them as best she could into the ribbon around her waist as she kicked to remain afloat. Then she swam toward shore, letting the waves carry her when she could to save her strength. Thank God, they were close to shore otherwise she wouldn't stand a chance.

Evelyn got into the shallower water of the beach and floated the waves to shore. She crawled onto the beach spitting out salt water. The storm raged on and grew in strength as she lay on the beach trying to get enough energy to find shelter. If Percy had shoved her off the boat any later she wouldn't have made it. The waves were getting higher and higher as they headed toward the beach.

This was a bad storm and she might still die if she didn't get off the beach. Evelyn tried to push herself to her feet, but it was futile. The swim to shore had drained her. Her skirts had come lose and were falling again around her ankles. They were soaked through and heavy. Think Evelyn, think. What could she do? Where could she go?

"There you are. Why didn't you stop?"

She looked up into the blue eyes of a man she'd never seen before. He had an odd accent, that she couldn't place and his clothes were equally peculiar. His pants had been sheared up to his thighs, and he wore a white unbuttoned shirt over another under-shirt. She should be scandalized, but she was too tired to bother. "What?" she asked baffled.

He winced and held his head between his hands.

The man appeared to be in excruciating pain as he rubbed his temples. "I called for you. You kept running." He lowered his hands and looked around him. It was his turn to appear confused. "How did I end up on the beach again? Where is the hotel? How far did I wander on my hike?"

"Are you lost?"

That was all she needed, a man who didn't know where he was. What good would he do? They needed shelter from the storm that was growing in intensity with each passing minute.

"I might be, but I think we have more pressing problems."

She glared at him and said, "Thanks for stating the obvious."

He laughed. "I think I like you. Come, I will help you up. I know where there is a cave we can take shelter from the storm."

She lifted her arm and placed her hand in his. Maybe she wouldn't die this day after all. Someone was looking out for her. The man wrapped his arm around her waist and supported her as they rushed into the lush jungle toward the cave.

"I'm Paul, by the way."

"Just Paul?"

He grinned. She sucked in a breath. She'd

thought Captain Jack handsome, but this man beat him in every way. His dark hair and light blue eyes stole her attention. It was the first time she truly looked at him and his striking exterior. Before that moment, survival was her foremost concern. What was it with handsome men falling into her life? Was this some kind of test and she had no idea what she needed to do to pass?

"Paul Dewitt," he replied. "I am on vacation. I live in New York. From your accent I assume you're English. What should I call you?"

They hadn't been formally introduced so she shouldn't technically be speaking to him at all. But she could forgive him that slight considering their dire circumstances. "I'm Lady Evelyn Beckett."

"One of those aristocrats?" He shrugged. "I thought they were a dying breed."

Evelyn frowned. She didn't have a clue what he was referring to. "I wouldn't know. Can we find this cave now? I need to rest."

He nodded and pushed forward. The wind whipped around them growing in strength. Each movement was a struggle as they fought their way against the wind force. Soon the cave's opening was in front of them, and not a moment too soon. They entered and he helped her sit down.

"Relax, Lady Evelyn," he said in the darkness. "I think we're going to be here a while, waiting out this storm."

She was very much afraid he was right. But at least she was safe and alive. With a sigh, she laid down and let her exhaustion take over. Her eyes closed on their own accord and all thoughts left her mind as she gave into her need to sleep.

CHAPTER 4

Paul scrubbed his hands over his face. It had grown dark as the storm raged outside the cave. He couldn't see anything around him. If he only he had some kind of light so he could look at his watch—he was dying to know how long they'd already been stuck inside the cavern. Lady Evelyn hadn't said a word in what felt like hours. He could hear her uneven breathing, and her breath hitched every so often when her body shivered from the cold. If they didn't find any warmth soon she might get hypothermia. The cold was starting to bother him too. He rubbed his hands together trying to warm them, and then gave up. They were practically numb so he shoved them inside his short's pocket. His fingers hit an object he'd forgotten about—a matchbook from the hotel he'd snatched earlier in the day. How had its existence slipped from his mind? Those little babies might save them both. Only one problem stood in his way. Something to use to build a fire with... He moved toward the front of the cave and what little light entered it. There was some brush and sticks at the mouth. He gathered up what he could, along with some small stones to make a fire pit. It wouldn't last long, but it was a start. It would give him some light to work by too. Maybe he could find some larger pieces of dry wood if his luck held out.

His fingers shook as he lit one of the matches to light the brush and small sticks he located. The brush lit quickly and the sticks weren't far behind. Warmth started to fill the cavern. Not enough to erase the chill, but still nice after the constant cold the wind brought into the cavern.

Paul stared down at the fire, satisfied it would stay burning he went to gather more small sticks to throw on the fire as it died down. Paul made several trips and had a stockpile of sticks near the fire to use as needed. He looked over at Evelyn. Her dress was still soaking wet and she continued to shiver. It left him with little choice. The dress had to be removed or she'd never get warm.

He began the long process of unlacing her gown. Why was she wearing the infernal thing to begin with? It had to be uncomfortable. Women and their fashion choices always baffled him. The desire to wear an old-fashioned gown didn't make any kind of sense to him. There were garments that were more comfortable and could still be feminine. She didn't need to wear something so archaic to feel like a woman. Maybe there had been some kind of period reenactment drama or party going on. He didn't explore much of the island and hadn't looked past the beach and his hotel room since he arrived.

The dress finally came loose. Evelyn moaned as he pushed the bodice down. He had to lift her up so he could take it completely off. Her head lopped backward onto his shoulder. Poor thing was completely exhausted. He felt like a cad undressing her while she was unconscious. It couldn't be helped though. She'd freeze if he didn't get the wet clothes off her. Once he removed the dress he laid her back down. His undershirt was a little wet, but it would dry fast. He took his other shirt off and draped it over her sleeping form. It was thin, but would offer a small amount of warmth. She had too many clothes on. What was with all the underclothes she had on? Everything she wore was still damp and prevented her from getting warm. He laid her dress on the other side of the cave near the fire to dry.

Evelyn moaned again. Paul turned around to check on her. She shook uncontrollably. He had to do something to help warm her. He rushed over to her side and picked her up, then carried her closer to the fire. With her nestled in his arms he sat down with her directly in front of him. Her head fell back and rested against his shoulder. Paul wrapped his arms around her and used the combination of their body heat and the fire to warm her.

"Easy sweetheart, it won't take long for you to get warm," he whispered. He hoped and prayed she made it through the storm. He wouldn't know what to do if she died on him... he didn't even want to think about.

He picked up a few more sticks and tossed them into the fire while he studied it. After a few moments after making sure it would burn for a while so he rested his head against the cavern wall and let his eyes close. He could use a bit of sleep himself.

She was finally warm. The cold had gotten so bad it seemed to seep into her bones and made itself a home. Evelyn's eyes fluttered open. It took a few moments for them to clear from the haze of sleep. A small fire was in front of her, probably adding to her warmth. Awareness filled her senses in slow degrees. She took in her surroundings, all the sounds, and sights. It was then she realized she was wrapped in someone's arms and screamed.

"Was that really necessary?" A droll voice uttered from behind her.

Evelyn leaped from his arms and almost fell into the fire. Her arms swung outward to help gain her balance. It would be disastrous to add burns to her already bruised body.

"Easy, sweetheart. I didn't work so hard to save you for you to die of self-inflicted burns."

"Who are you?" She scooted to the other side of the cavern and crossed her arms over her chest, after she realized she no longer wore her muslin gown. "Did you undress me?"

She could barely make out his features in the firelight. He was handsome and familiar, but she couldn't place him. How did she know him? Her body warmed as she perused him. It tingled in places it never had before. The man was gorgeous, but clearly a blackguard for taking advantage of her while she slept.

"Relax, I'm not going to attack you." He rubbed his face with his hands. "It's been a long day, and it is well into the night. I don't know how long this storm is going to last, and I'd rather not deal with a histrionic female."

"I will have you know I by no means ever give into hysteria." She held her chin up in defiance. Her father never would have allowed it. She was to be a proper lady at all times, with a calm and cool demeanor. "But I will not stand for a man I'm not remotely acquainted with seeing me in my shift. What did you do with my gown?"

"I already introduced myself if you recall. We're on a first name basis." He folded his arms across his chest. "Look Evie, I don't know how I came to find you. The last thing I remember before I saw you on the beach was falling to my death outside this cave. It's why I knew where to find it. Nothing has made sense since I stumbled upon you. All I want to do is ride out this storm and book the first flight home. This vacation has to be the worst one ever recorded."

She tilted her head and studied him. Was he insane? That made things a little different. She would have to give him a wide berth. It was hard to tell what someone who'd lost their mind might do. Book a flight? How did he expect to fly anywhere?

Everyone knew that was impossible. Clearly he'd taken leave of his senses. She might be able to forgive him taking liberties with her person—but she doubted it.

"Have you escaped from an asylum?" She glared at him. "And my name is not Evie."

"All right. But since you don't recall my name let me remind you. I'm Paul Dewitt." He shrugged and laughed. "Explain this nonsense you are spouting? Are you insinuating I'm insane?"

How dare he mock her? She wasn't the one losing her mind.

"Everyone knows you can't fly. If you want to get anywhere it has to be by horse, carriage, or ship."

He fell over in uproarious laughter. What had she said that was so bloody funny? She wasn't the ridiculous one. She didn't suggest they could fly anywhere.

"I don't know why you are laughing, but I'm tired of it. If you can't have a reasonable and normal conversation at least stop rolling around as if you heard a joke. I don't find any of this funny."

"Oh sweetheart, you wouldn't." He wiped the corners of his eye. "Please tell me you've seen a plane. They are more than capable of flying us anywhere we want to go."

She had no idea what he was referring to. "You're serious?"

"Lady, it's 1987. Planes have been a reality since the Wright brothers first flew at Kitty Hawk in 1903." He shrugged. "They've come a long way since that first flight, but they are commonplace these days. How have you not seen one?"

She opened her mouth and closed it several times. How does one respond to that? He clearly had a very active imagination. Whoever these Wright brothers were, they must be geniuses to build such a contraption. What was she thinking entertaining his delusions? She shook her head to clear that rubbish away. He thought it was 1987 and these brothers flew in 1903. She had to tell him he was misinformed.

"You're wrong."

"I assure you I'm not."

She shook her head. "No, it's not 1987. It's not even close to 1903. Why would you believe it was?"

"Because I was born in 1958 and I will be 30 in less than 3 months. I flew over here on one of those planes because my doctor ordered me to take a vacation or I'd have a heart attack before my birthday. I agreed to humor him since he is a family friend."

His delusion went further than she thought. The

poor man. "I'm afraid I must inform you it is in fact, the year of our lord, 1722."

He started to chuckle so hard he had trouble breathing. His penchant for laughter was starting to irritate her. Why did he find everything she said so damned funny.

"It all makes sense now," he spat out. "Your dress, the storm, and even not remembering how I ended up on the beach. I've died and this is my hell."

"I seriously doubt God would punish us both with the same hell. I don't even know you, or how you ended up here, but I can assure you we are both very much alive. I didn't fight so hard to make it to land to give in now."

"Why do you believe it is 1722?"

"Because I was born at the start of the century on December 17, 1700. My father is the Earl of Ashland and owns a plantation on St. Kitts. I was sailing, with my maid, back to England to marry the Duke of Southington when our ship was attacked by pirates. When the storm hit, one of them thought I had caused it and threw me overboard. If we'd not been so close to shore I wouldn't have survived."

It was his turn to open and close his mouth. He stared at her with a baffled expression on his face. He stayed silent for several minutes, picking up a few sticks and tossing them on the fire.

"I can prove I'm from 1987. Can you prove you're from 1722?"

"Other than my clothing I have nothing," she replied. "What do you have that would prove you're not from my time?"

He lifted his hand and tapped at something on his wrist. "This is a Rolex. Do you know what that is?"

She shook her head. Part of it was shiny and glinted in the firelight. The other part wrapped around his wrist, the band was perhaps leather. "I don't believe so."

"These weren't even available until 1905. It is a watch, a fancy one. This doesn't prove that I'm from 1987, but it does prove I'm not from 1722. I have one other thing that will aid my case."

She wanted to look closer at his watch. It looked fascinating, but she didn't ask. What other proof did he have? This was all rather fascinating. "What?"

Paul reached into his pocket and pulled something out. He leaned over and handed it to her. "Don't drop this. It is one of the things we need to survive through this storm. The other is food and water. When the storm lessens I will look for something to eat or drink."

"What is it?" She rubbed her fingertips across the little square.

"It's a matchbook. You might have had something like it in 1722. I'm not sure when the first matches were invented. It's what is stamped on the front that proves my case. Can you read?"

She snorted. "Of course. I've been well-educated."

How dare he imply she was ignorant?

"Flip it over and read it, but remember do not drop it in the fire."

She rolled her eyes. How many times did he have to tell her not to drop the infernal thing? Evelyn leaned closer to the fire and read the inscription, Port Royal Hotel and Suites, 75th anniversary, 1912-1987. "How can this be?"

"It seems one of us has done a bit of time travel, and I'm afraid it might be me."

That couldn't be good news... What was going to happen to them and was any of what he said possible? Evelyn couldn't wait for the storm to pass so they could investigate and uncover the truth.

CHAPTER 5

PAUL PUSHED THROUGH THE WET VEGETATION IN search of food. They'd been holed up inside the cavern for a couple of days as the storm passed over them. What they were experiencing could be the eye of the storm. If it was, he was afraid the storm was far from over. It wasn't as bad as a full blown hurricane from what he understood of the storm surges, but it was still a devastating tropical one. He needed to get supplies and fast. He didn't know how much time they had before the second part of the storm hit.

"Ouch," he shouted as his foot hit something on the ground. He looked to see what had caused his injury and smiled.

The intense wind speed of the storm had knocked some coconuts from the trees. He grabbed as many as he could carry and headed back to the cavern. He'd make a couple of trips to gather a few more. Not a diverse diet, but they would provide them the sustenance they needed to survive. They could drink the coconut water and eat the nut meat. The shells could be used to keep the fire going. It was a life-saving find. The good news was he had his Swiss army knife in his pocket too. He'd held back from showing it to Evelyn. He hadn't wanted to frighten her. She was already too skittish. The knife would make it easier to break the tough shell open.

"Honey, I'm home," he called out as he entered the cave. He rather enjoyed teasing Evelyn. She reacted differently each time he did and he awaited each response with an inner glee.

"Did you hit your head while you were out?"

Paul smiled. He'd gotten to know her rather well over the past few days. She was prickly by nature. The more he discovered the more he liked. She had a backbone and didn't put up with anything he dished out. Under different circumstances he might consider dating her.

"I found some food. I'm going to get more before the storm starts again."

She picked up one of the coconuts and studied it. "What is this? Are you sure they are edible?"

He frowned. "Have you never seen a coconut before?"

"Why would I have?" She frowned. "I don't prepare any food. That is why we had servants for. I have seen these weird brown objects, but I didn't know what they were. If you say we can eat them I will take your word for it."

"Right. You are one of those aristocrats I learned about in history classes." He shrugged. "I'm going to get more. I will explain how fabulous these little babies are when I get back. Don't go outside the cave. The storm could start up again at anytime. I'm pretty sure we are in the eye."

"What is the eye?" She furrowed her eyebrows together. "Some of the things you say are so confusing."

"It is a term for the lull in the storm. It is similar to a cyclone. In the middle of it there is dead silence as the wind whips around. Once the eye passes we get the wind and rain hitting us at every angle again."

"Oh." She chewed on her bottom lip. "I'm so hungry. Can't I eat one of these while you're out?"

He laughed. "Do you know how to break it open?"

"No, but I think I'm intelligent enough to ascertain how to do it."

She was precious and she'd fit right in with the women's lib movement from the seventies. He wanted to squeeze her and keep her safe. Somehow he doubted she'd willingly let him though. If they had more time... He shook his head. There wasn't any time. He didn't know what was going on or if he was truly in 1722. All he knew was that he'd do anything to survive and make sure she did as well.

"Sweetheart, I'm sure with the right tools you could do anything." He smiled. "Trust me you don't have them. Wait until I get back and I will make sure you have something to eat and drink."

"All right." She sighed. "I can manage to wait for a little while longer."

"I promise I won't be long. I want to make a couple more trips to grab a few more so we have plenty to eat if the storm lasts longer than I think it will."

"I understand," she said solemnly. "Be safe."

He nodded at her and left the cave. As fast as he could he retraced his steps and gathered a few more coconuts and headed back. Without a word he dumped them inside and headed back out again. The rain started to pour and the wind picked up as he trekked back to the coconut trees. He hauled a few more into his arms and raced back. As he entered the cave again the wind howled loudly and a torrential downpour fell from the sky.

Thunder boomed outside as he dropped the coconuts on the ground. Evelyn jumped from the noise. "Easy. It was going to happen at some point. I will break open one of these coconuts now. Some food might help to ease your nerves."

"Yes, and how are we going to open these infernal things? I know you said we would need some kind of tool, but I thought you were lying to me. I admit I tried to open one while you were out and was not successful in the least."

He had a feeling she'd try. Hunger was a powerful motivator. He reached into his pocket and pulled out his knife.

"You carry a coconut tool on your person at all time?" She raised an eyebrow. "How does one know when they might need such a thing?"

He laughed. "This isn't a coconut tool. It's just a tool, period. It can be used for many things." Paul opened up several parts of it. "This here is a knife. This is a screwdriver, and this is scissors."

"That is fascinating. What else is on it?" She reached over attempting to grab it. "Let me see it."

"Not right now. Later I will let you examine it.

For now let's poke a hole in a coconut and drink the water inside."

He pushed the other parts back in, leaving the screwdriver out, and then grabbed a rock. Using the rock as a hammer he pounded into the tough shell. After several tries he managed to poke a hole through it.

"Here, put the hole near your mouth and drink its contents."

She wrinkled her nose up as she studied it. "Are you sure?"

"Yes. The coconut water will hydrate you and satisfy your hunger. After you drink it all I will break it open so you can eat the nutty flesh."

She studied it for a few moments and then did as he instructed. "It's not bad, but it's not good either. At this point though I'm grateful to have anything—it feels so good going down my throat." Evelyn drank the coconut dry and handed it back to him.

He broke open the coconut using the rock and his knife. It was a long tedious process but worth it. The white flesh scooped out easily enough with his knife. She ate one side and he ate the other. Later he'd poke a hole in another one and drink the coconut water. After they consumed it he tossed the shells in the fire.

"They smell heavenly, it's the best fire I've ever had." Evelyn smiled. "If I ever go back to St. Kitts I'm going to order the servants to burn the shells on cold nights."

"I aim to please." He bowed. "We should get comfortable. It's going to be a long night again."

She nodded. "Thank you for taking care of me."

He opened his mouth and then closed it. It was on the tip of his tongue to say it was his pleasure. What had happened to him in the past few days? If he didn't know better he'd swear she'd bewitched him. When he sat in the doctor's office he'd sworn off women, relationships, and especially love. Why was he picturing a future with Lady Evelyn Beckett? He must have hit his head to deviate from his normal thought process. He had to get her out of his system so he would be able to move on. There was no other choice. If, and when, he got back to 1987 he'd be leaving her behind. As much as he liked her he knew it couldn't work between them. They were as different as night and day. She was perfect in every way. If he were to fall in love she would be every-thing he wanted in a woman. Evelyn was resilient, kind, intelligent, and she didn't get hysterical. He liked that she had a cool head on her shoulders.

It also amused him that she'd gotten comfortable

in his presence. She didn't even bother with modesty any more. She left her dress lying on the cavern floor to dry and walked proudly around in only her shift. Paul didn't mention he'd seen women parade themselves around in a lot less. He liked that she didn't flaunt her body.

He swallowed a lump in his throat as he realized he wanted to keep her by his side forever. There had to be a way to make it happen. Even if he had to remain in 1722 with no prospects and no true way to see to her comfort—somehow, some way he'd keep them together. He just had to convince her of it.

Paul chuckled.

"What's so funny?"

"I remembered something the doctor said to me before I left New York."

"Oh?" she raised an eyebrow. "Do you care to share?"

He found that he did want to tell her everything. "Yes, but let's sit down in front of the fire first."

He sat down and Evelyn joined him. She leaned her head back against him and curled her body alongside his. This had been their standard arrangement since the first night. She soon realized how important sharing body heat was. After the initial shock she saw reason and sat in front of him to keep warm. It was these moments he relished. She was relaxed and safe, wrapped inside his arms.

"You said your doctor ordered you to take a vacation. You don't appear ill. Why did he tell you to rest?"

He sighed. "I'm the CEO of my family's company."

"What is that?" she asked.

"I am in control of it and I make sure it keeps running. Basically, I am responsible for seeing the family doesn't lose all of its assets and continues to live in the lifestyle they've become accustomed to."

Evelyn leaned her head further back into his shoulder in an attempt to look at him. "How has this made you ill?"

He wanted to lean down and place his lips on hers. The urge was so strong he gave into it. The kiss was light and sweet. A quick peck of his lips against hers, at a much later time he wanted to explore her mouth fully. Paul knew he'd have to ease her into it. She was too innocent and he wouldn't take advantage of her.

She ran her fingers over her lips. "Why did you do that?"

"It seemed like a good idea." He smiled. She looked adorable. "To answer your earlier question I was putting too much stress on my heart. I passed out in my office and my family ordered me to see the doctor to have some tests run. The simple answer is I'm working myself to an early grave. There was no choice. It was either slow down or die. As much as I wanted to continue working I thought perhaps giving in and having a small vacation was a compromise I'd willingly take."

"Do you regret it?"

Did he? No, if he hadn't gone to Port Royal he'd never have met Evelyn. Sometimes things happened over which you had no control, but they changed your life in the best possible ways. Evelyn did that for him. He started to see how she could make his life better.

"I don't. I might even start to listen to all of the doctor's advice. Turns out he might know a little bit more than I do."

He smiled to himself. Who knew he'd be fool enough to willingly leap into a relationship with a woman, and if his luck held out he might even find love too.

"If it means anything to you I'm glad you're here too." She snuggled closer into him. "And I don't mean that because you're keeping me safe and fed. I like you and I wouldn't want to be stranded on this island with anyone else."

Paul had never been happier in his life.

"Go to sleep, sweetheart. Maybe the storm will pass by morning and we can look for civilization."

He leaned his head back and closed his eyes. Sleep didn't find him for a long time. Holding Evelyn was a highlight he wanted to bask in for as long as possible. Soon they'd leave the cave and reality would sink in. Paul had always been a smart man, and with time running out he made sure to appreciate what little time they might have left.

CHAPTER 6

Evelyn leaned against Paul's chest. She didn't want to move. The warmth of his body offered as much comfort as could be gained inside the cave. It had nothing to do with how much she loved being in his arms. All right, maybe it did... a tiny bit. She had to be honest with herself. How could she have thought him to be a blackguard? He was so far from being an evil man it was ridiculous she'd believed him to be one. His actions proved how good he was. Not once over the past several days had he done something that wasn't for their benefit. Every step he took was to ensure they survived and would have a chance after the storm passed.

"I think it's safe to leave the cave now."

"Do we really have to?" She wasn't looking forward to facing the real world. As soon as they left the cabin their idyllic time would come to a close. "I am not looking forward to walking anywhere."

If only they could stay in their little haven forever. She wondered if it was possible to live off coconuts. Although that diet might get old rather fast —they weren't bad, but they weren't her favorite food by any means. She didn't want to leave Paul. What if he had really come from another time? What would she do without him? After Captain Jack kidnapped her she started to consider her options. Marrying the Duke of Southington didn't sit well with her. It hurt to think about being with anyone other than the man holding her. There had to be a way for them to stay together. Fate threw them together for a reason. She firmly believed it and would follow him no matter where life sent them. As long as they were together that was all that mattered to her.

"I'm not relishing it either. We've been inactive for days now. Our muscles are sure to protest, but we can't stay here forever."

She sighed. "I know you're right."

Evelyn stood up and stretched her arms. Her muscles were achy and it felt good to move around a bit. She turned and saw Paul staring at her. What was he thinking? Did he feel the same things she did? As much as she wanted to ask she was equally afraid to discover the answers. For all she knew he had a love back home.

"I don't know this island and I'm unsure what direction we should take."

"I'm afraid I won't be any help. Even on St. Kitts I wasn't allowed to do anything on my own. Your guess is as good as mine."

"I realized that when you reminded me you depended on servants for food." He nodded and gestured toward her dress. "You probably should put that back on. If we run into anyone else they might get the wrong idea."

She knew he was right. Society would immediately demand he marry her. In truth they would regardless. They'd spent too much time alone together for any other result. It still amazed her she'd gotten so comfortable around him to forego the dress for days. Evelyn strolled over and picked it up. Her dress was still slightly damp. The cave was dark, and without much sunlight it hadn't given it a chance to fully dry. Without thinking too much about what their next steps were she slid the dress on. She wouldn't be able to do all the laces herself though.

"Can you do up the back for me?"

Without a word he did as she asked. The feel of his hands against the bare flesh of her back sent shivers down her spine. She wanted to turn around and beg him to hold her, to never leave her, but most importantly to love her. Evelyn was afraid it was too late for her heart. It had taken one giant leap willingly and gave itself to him to have for always. She couldn't look past the moment they were in. The future was too scary and unknown.

"There, you're presentable now."

She ran her hand through her hair. "Well, as presentable as I can manage."

He smiled. "You're beautiful."

Evelyn's lips tilted into a small smile at his words. "I'm glad you think so. It's always nice to hear, even though I know how much of a mess I must look like."

He lifted his hand and ran his fingers over her hair. Then he lifted his other hand and cupped her cheek. "You'll always be beautiful to me."

A stab of pain pierced her heart. His words hurt as much as they gave her joy. Why did everything have to be so complicated? She was tired of all the drama in her life. It would be nice for once to have something come easy. She fidgeted under his gaze

69

and looked down. She didn't know how to respond to his words. Did she admit she found him handsome? Maybe she should tell him how much he'd come to mean to her. This was uncharted territory for her, a situation she'd never found herself in before. One she couldn't help but hoped she never found herself in again. Paul was the only man she wanted.

"Evelyn." He brushed her cheek with one of his fingers. "Look at me."

Slowly she lifted her head and let her gaze meet his. She sucked in a deep breath at the fire in his eyes. Was she reading him right? Her mouth fell open in anticipation. She didn't know how she knew it, but she believed he was going to kiss her. The first time he did it had taken her by surprise. It was over before it had ever begun. A light sweet kiss that had left her wanting more, she'd enjoyed it and wanted to explore the feel of his lips against hers.

He leaned down and pressed his lips on hers. Heat filled her in places she didn't know existed. They burned with each roll of his mouth over hers, and when he pushed his tongue inside her mouth she moaned in pleasure. The touch of his tongue on hers was simply bliss. She wrapped her arms around his waist and pulled him closer to her. The more she experienced the more she desired. Their kiss could go on forever and she still wouldn't have enough. If she'd known a kiss could make her feel so much she'd have demanded he do it sooner.

He pulled back and stared down at her. His breath was uneven and his eyes alight with something she couldn't identify. She wanted to hold him tight and never let go. So she did the next best thing, she leaned her head against him and sighed with contentment. Once they left the cave there was no turning back. She wanted to burn this memory into her mind so she'd never forget it.

"We need to go now."

"I know." She stepped back and smiled. "Let's get off this island and figure out where and when we are."

He pulled her hand in his and led her out of the cave.

PAUL WISHED THEY COULD HAVE STAYED IN THE cave forever. He knew it wasn't possible or even realistic, but he was afraid of what the real world might offer for them. They walked together, hand in hand toward the beach. He figured it was the best place to start. He could get a better idea of where they were from what he remembered of his brief stay on the island.

When they reached the beach they both stopped short, staring, stunned at the devastation that surrounded them. All they could see for the entire length of the beach was debris washed in from the ocean. Seaweed littered the beach from one end to the other. A tree had been uprooted near the edge of the forest and lay across the sand, stripped bare of any leaves. The wind had wreaked havoc on the area and the ocean hadn't been any kinder. Seashells were mixed in with the vegetation and foliage that spread across the sand.

"I have never seen something so…" Evelyn paused and shook her head. "I have no words for this. It is horrible."

There was no doubt in his mind what century he was in. If this were his time the debris would be much worse. The beach wouldn't be this—clean—for lack of a better word. He didn't need to go any further to know and accept he'd somehow traveled through time. When the doctor ordered him to take a vacation he was pretty sure this wasn't what he had in mind. A person didn't generally time travel to get away from their problems. There were much easier ways to get away from the day to day grind.

"It could be worse." Paul sighed. "This beach is littered with natural debris. There isn't anything man made to add to it. In 1987, and with the pollution that came with that time, it would be littered with items careless people throw into the ocean. There is also the possibility of boats being lifted out of the area they are docked in and finding a new home on a beach or road. The winds of a hurricane or tropical storm are not forgiving, no one or anything is safe from them. We're lucky to have escaped with our lives."

"I can't picture what it must be like for you. To live so far in the future, there must be many wondrous things that you could tell me about."

Paul wanted to tell her anything she wished to know. He wasn't so sure it was prudent to fill her head with tales of the twentieth century. There had been too many advances made and it would take too long to explain them all. If she came back with him then he could show her everything and give her books to educate herself with.

He was already thinking of what he could do for her if she came with him. It wasn't a foregone conclusion, but he wanted it to be. If they got back to 1987, after he figured out how to get there, he knew how to get her the proper paperwork to live in his time. It was to their benefit he was so filthy rich and had a wide array of contacts. Once they got all the little details out of the way, then they could get married and truly begin their life together.

"One day I will share it all with you. For now, I think we have bigger problems."

"I know. We have to find a way off this island."

She wasn't wrong. They did need to get off the island as fast as they possibly could. For more reasons than he dared to count. They couldn't live on the island for long without going crazy. What kind of life would they have? They had other issues to deal with as well. One being the band of pirates that seemed to be heading in their general direction and Paul had no urge to deal with the blood thirsty lot.

"You're right, sweetheart. But for now, I think we need to go back and hide in our cave."

"Why?" She lifted an eyebrow. "I thought we needed to find civilization."

"We do." He nodded. "But I think that I figured out what happened to the pirate ship you were on."

"You did?"

He spun her around and pointed. The pirate ship appeared to have been run aground on the other side of the island. The masts were visible over the trees. At least two miles in the distance he could see people walking toward them. It had to be some of the pirates who survived the storm.

"Oh my." Her hand flew to her mouth. "Captain Jack was trying to use the wind to make it into the harbor before the storm hit. It looks like it didn't work. I hope he made it."

He squashed down the instant jealousy that flooded him at her words. Why did she have sympathy for a pirate who'd kidnapped her? She should wish him dead. It wasn't the time to argue about it, and he didn't really want to hear what she thought of the pirate captain. As far as he was concerned, she should never mention the man's name again.

"I don't want to find out one way or the other. Let's move toward the cave. I don't want them to realize where we are or what direction we took. From what little I know of pirates they aren't the most congenial sort."

"They aren't very nice," she agreed.

He laughed. "That's putting things mildly."

He reached over and placed her hand in his and led her back into the forest. The lush vegetation would give them enough cover. He hoped the pirates hadn't noticed them on the beach. If their luck held, they'd remain safe until they passed by them again. It would also give him a little bit more time to figure out how he'd traveled through time. If he could recreate the scenario and take them both back to 1987, they'd be safe from any harm.

CHAPTER 7

THEY HAD BEEN BACK IN THE CAVE FOR A FEW days. Paul handed Evelyn a coconut. She took a drink from the tiny hole he drilled into it with his tool. They'd settled back into the cave without much ado. It had become a home for them over the past week. Afraid the smoke might attract the pirates, Paul hadn't lit a fire. At least she was no longer cold. Her clothes were dry and didn't add to the chill air. The wind had died down somewhat, but the sky was still cloudy. The temperature had yet to rise to the normal temperature of a tropical island.

She handed him the coconut and he took a quick drink, and then gave it back to her. He was always doing that. Making sure she had her fill first. But, as idyllic as their time had been, she was starting to get irritable. Her skin itched, and her hair was too dirty to describe.

"I really wish I could take a bath. I'm so grimy from sand and salt water. I miss home."

He glanced at her. He wasn't looking any better than she felt. Perhaps they both could use a good washing. Too bad they didn't have anything to bathe with. She missed her rose scented bath soap.

"I saw a waterfall when I was out earlier. At the base of it is a large pool. It is probably safe enough to go use it. I didn't see any signs of the pirates. Tomorrow I think we should leave the cave for good."

One more night without facing the real world, she was relieved. They could get to the business of resuming their lives. It was terrifying, but she knew they couldn't remain where they were forever. It was time to move on and see how they interacted with each other without the safety of their self-made paradise. "Can we? I would love to at least rinse the salt and sand out of my hair."

"Yes. We can go now if you'd like."

She nodded. "Yes, please."

He held out his hand for her. She placed hers in his and he helped her to her feet. She couldn't wait to take a swim in the pool. It didn't matter that it was inappropriate. She didn't doubt he had feelings for her. Perhaps she was a bit mad for presuming he wanted to be with her forever, but she believed it with her whole heart. Actions spoke louder than words. When he was ready, he'd tell her how much he loved her. She could be patient.

"It isn't far from the cave."

They walked for a few moments until they reached the pool he'd told her about. It was beautiful. There were flowers twisting down in vines down the cliff and the pool was crystal clear. She could see down to the bottom. It didn't appear to be too deep. The waterfall wasn't large. It flowed enough to keep feeding the pool with fresh water. She wanted to stand under it and let the spray wash over her.

"It's beautiful."

"It is," he agreed. His voice had a whimsical tone to it.

She turned to look at him. His gaze wasn't focused on the waterfall. It was fixated on her. Her breath hitched a bit at his heat-filled stare. She wanted everything it was offering to her. All she had to do was reach out and take it. Take him. Then they would belong together forever. Did she dare do it? Deep down, she knew it wouldn't take much for him to give in and make love to her. She wanted it more than anything. He was trying to be as gentlemanly as possible and for that she respected him, but it was time to let that go and be together in every way. An idea formed in her mind... It was time to be brave and take a chance. Paul wouldn't let her down. She wasn't a seductress by any means. For him, she'd take any chance and do what was needed to erase all barriers between them.

Evelyn turned around and lifted her hair over her shoulder. "Can you unlace my dress?"

He pulled at the laces and loosened them enough for her to step out of it. Nervous, she kept her back to him and let her long blonde tresses cover her back again. They were the only shield she was going to allow herself. She set the gown carefully on a rock near the pool. Then she lowered her shift and stood before him without a stitch of clothes on. After she set the rest of her clothing on the rock with her dress she glanced over her shoulder and said, "Are you going to join me in the pool?'

Her question was met with silence. She took that as a good sign. He didn't deny or affirm his intentions. Paul would consider all options before making a decision. That was who he was. She'd gotten to know him rather well over the past several days. She didn't doubt he'd join her in the pool. She headed toward it knowing he'd soon follow her.

The pool in the water was warm. She'd been afraid it would be cold, almost hoped it would be. Her body was heated with desire, and was covered by the water of the pool. She dipped her head back and soaked her head completely. Once it was submerged she lifted her hands and rubbed at her scalp. She moaned with pleasure. The itching had started to drive her mad.

"Let me help."

Her eyes fluttered opened and met Paul's gaze. His blue eyes were a mixture of fire and ice. He lifted his hands and finished what she started with her hair. It felt even better with him doing the massaging. His large body dwarfed hers as he stood behind her. Need pooled in her belly. How to ask him for what she wanted? Her innocence was not helping her to seduce the man she loved.

"I want to stand under the waterfall."

"Then we shall do that. Let's swim over there." He kissed her neck from behind her. "You go first. I will be right behind you."

Evelyn swam over to the waterfall. Her body was still mostly covered by the pool of water. It was a little shallower near the falls. Her bosom was uncovered as she stepped onto a rock and went under the falls. The spray was light and seemed to float down the small cliff. The shower whispered over her, massaging her skin. It was the most amazing thing she'd ever experienced in her life. She moaned in pleasure as it washed over her. The only thing that would make it better was if Paul were with her.

She looked over her shoulder and realized he hadn't yet joined her. He appeared to be rooted in the spot she'd left him. His gaze remained fixed on her. She started to call for him, but he had already begun moving toward her. Good he should enjoy the wondrous falls too.

EVELYN WAS A SIREN SONG. HE STILL COULDN'T believe she had stripped bare in front of him. He didn't know what she'd do next. When she stood under the falls and exposed herself further he about lost it. Her breasts were beautiful and he wanted to cup them in the palm of his hands. For what seemed like an eternity he stared at her transfixed by her beauty. Once he snapped out of his stupor he realized he had to have her. He wanted to wait and woo her properly as she deserved. But if she was willing then he'd take her now under the magic of the water-fall. He swam to her side and stopped in front of her.

"You like it?" he asked.

"It's perfect." She smiled. "You took too long getting here. I was lonely."

When had she turned into a seductress? How did he ever think he'd be able to resist her? She was everything he didn't know he wanted. Now that he found her he wasn't ever letting her go. He pulled her into his arms and brought his lips down on hers. Their passion ignited within him and burnt him from the inside out. He couldn't get enough of her mouth. Their kiss went on and on bringing him to the brink of exploding.

He wrapped an arm around her and pulled her closer. With his free hand he lifted it and placing his hand over one of her breasts, kneaded it. She moaned and rubbed herself against him. They couldn't stay in the pool. They'd not get very far and Paul was dying to be inside her. He had to make sure she was ready for him. She was a virgin and he couldn't rush their first time.

Paul pulled back and stared down at her. "Wrap your legs around me, sweetheart."

She did as he asked. He walked further under the waterfall and set her on the edge of a cliff filled with lush vegetation. He kissed her again to distract her. With care he reached down and cupped her between her thighs. She moaned louder as he caressed her tender flesh with his fingers. He pushed one inside her as he continued to rub her clit with another finger. She thrashed in his arms. He trailed kisses down her neck and stopped at her breasts. He licked one nipple, and then sucked it into his mouth. Evelyn moaned louder. Her breath was constant heavy pants. He pushed another finger inside her as he rubbed her clit again. Later, when they were more comfortable, he'd taste her and make her scream as he sucked her clit in his mouth. For now this would have to do. She screamed as her climax hit her.

"I thought the waterfall was the best thing I'd ever felt. That has to be... I don't know how to describe it. We must do it again."

Paul laughed. "We're not done."

"There's more?"

"I promise you there is so much more that we won't get to it all today."

He had so many things he wanted to do with her. This was only the beginning of their time together. He wanted forever and he would have it with her. She was his everything. He didn't know he would fall in love as fast as he did, but he had never met anyone like Evelyn before.

She lay back languidly on top of the rock. "I'm waiting."

Who was he to deny her? Paul crawled up on the cliff and joined her, pulling her back into his arms, and kissed her senseless. Evelyn's legs opened wide as he caressed her tender flesh once again. Once she melted in his arms again he started to push himself into her warm heat. He moved slowly letting her adjust to his size. With every kiss, he would enter her a little bit more until he was fully seated inside her tight channel.

"Are you all right?"

"I'm perfect."

He agreed. She was perfect. Paul moved in and out of her in slow agonizing thrusts. This was the first time they would ever make love and he wanted it to be as special as he could make it. It had to be something they would always remember. There was no reason to rush and every reason to relish in the feel of their bodies joined together as one. The closer they came to an orgasm the faster his pace became. At a certain point neither one of them could hold back their passion. Her breath hitched as her release was at the point of spiraling out of control. She screamed when it hit its peak. Her channel rippled over him sending him into the best release he'd ever had. There were no words to describe how amazing it was.

Making love, not just sex, was so much better. He'd thought all that was nonsense. How wrong he'd been. He sent a silent prayer up to whoever sent him back in time to find the love of his life. He owed them so much. When he got back to his time, to New York, he'd also stop in to see the doctor who demanded he take a vacation. He was the one who'd sent Paul on this path. If he hadn't followed his advice he wouldn't be holding the greatest treasure he'd ever find in his arms. The doctor deserved personal thanks for that alone.

"Paul."

"Yes, sweetheart?"

She lifted her hand and cupped his cheek. "When can we do that again?"

He laughed. She was precious and too adorable for words. "I need a little recovery time, but soon. I don't think I will ever get enough of you."

She sighed. "I agree. This is the best day of my life. We will have to do this often."

He leaned down and placed a light kiss on her lips. "I love you."

She grinned. "I love you too."

The pool, the waterfall, making love... it had all been amazing. So much so he wanted to stay in there and bask in its glory as long as possible. He was realistic though. He knew that they couldn't stay there. They had to get back to the real world. He had finally remembered what happened to him and how he fell back in time. The storm had played a huge part in it. The wind had picked him up and pushed him over the edge near the cave. He'd fallen, literally, through a time hole with the help of the storm surge.

He didn't know how they could use that to their advantage to return to 1987, but he had to figure out a way. They would be safer and happier in his time.

"I think we need to get dressed and head back to the cave. It's going to get dark soon."

"I know you're right." She sighed. "It's been so wonderful here I don't want to leave."

He kissed her nose. "Come, let's get dressed. I will start a fire tonight. I'm sure the pirates are long gone."

With her wet hair he didn't want her to catch a chill. For her he would risk anything, even the wrath of pirates. He hoped he was right and they were already on the other side of the island. They swam to the edge of the pool and stepped out. Paul dressed quickly, and then helped Evelyn tie the laces of her dress.

They headed back to the cave. He lifted her hand to his mouth and kissed the palm. Nothing would come between them. Life was as fantastic as it was ever going to be.

CHAPTER 8

Paul leaned down and kissed the top of Evelyn's head. They'd spent a good part of the day making love over and over again. It was their way of putting off the inevitable. He was aware they should leave and figure out what to do next, but he was reluctant to move. All he wanted to do was to hold the woman wrapped in his arms and forget about all of their problems. Unfortunately for them both they couldn't ignore their situation any longer.

"It's time," he said.

Evelyn reached up and ran her hand over his hair. "Must we?"

"I want to be with you forever. I don't see that we have any other choice."

He'd thought about their situation all night long.

Sleep had evaded him, and he was forced to face many truths. It was likely he was stuck in 1722. If that was the case they had to move on and start a life in another place. The best location for them to go was the Colonies. They were not yet the United States, but they were still a place where they could disappear. It hadn't become the land of opportunities for no reason. He could start from nothing and rebuild his whole life. They would marry and start their life together. They only had to find a way to get there.

"All right. I suppose we should get dressed and figure out how to get to the pirates' den Captain Jack mentioned. Maybe if we're lucky we can get one of them to help us."

Paul snorted. "I like that you're optimistic sweetheart, but that plan isn't likely to come to fruition."

She sat up and glared at him. "What do you suggest we do? I'm willing to listen to whatever you propose."

He stared at her and said nothing. As a man used to solving any problem he didn't know how to tell the woman he loved he had no idea how to save them. Their fate was up in the air without any support to see them through.

"I don't know." He scrubbed his face with both

of his hands. "I wish I had the answers but I'm lost. I've never felt so useless in my life."

"Don't be so hard on yourself." She reached up and cupped his cheek. "We'll figure it out. I have faith in us and our destiny. We didn't come together only to be pulled apart. Let's begin with Port Royal and see where it takes us."

Since he didn't have any better ideas he was forced to agree with her suggestion. He wished there was something else, anything that they could do instead. The idea of walking in with her among a group of men with little to no morals made his stomach clench up with dread. They were on the verge of signing their own death warrants, or worse. He didn't want to think what they might do to Evelyn if they killed him. She'd be easy prey for their lecherous intentions.

"All right." He pulled her into his arms. "But before we get dressed I want something from you."

"What?" she asked.

"This..."

He leaned down and captured her mouth with his. A kiss filled with promise and love. If they were about to walk into the den of iniquity then he wanted her taste to remain on his lips every step of the way. Evelyn pulled back with a sigh.

"I love your kisses. Promise me you will kiss me often for the rest of our lives."

He chuckled. "That is a promise I can keep."

Evelyn stood up and pulled on her shift. It was a sign he should follow her example and dress too, but he was entranced. She was graceful and beautiful. He loved watching her. Soon, she'd need him to help her tie up the laces of her dress. Paul reached for his clothes and put them on quickly. When he turned around she'd already pulled her dress up and awaited his attention.

"I'm ready for you to do my laces."

It always took her longer to get dressed. She had so many clothes to put on. His were simple shorts and a shirt. He leaned down and kissed her shoulder.

"None of that or we'll never get out of here," she chastised him.

"Yes, love."

He tied up her laces and spun her around into his embrace. The lure of her lips was hard to resist. The taste of her was starting to fade from his mouth and he needed another fix. He captured her lips with his and pushed his tongue inside her mouth. The kiss was different from the last one... it had a different promise. It told her that she was his always and he'd go to the ends of the earth to keep her at his side. He wasn't going to give up. It was time to release the defeatist attitude he'd let simmer at the bottom of his gut. Their love would see them through and they would find a way. He just had to believe. Paul took a step back and gazed down into her beautiful blue eyes. The languor of their time in the cave would remain with him always, but he was ready to see what the real world offered them. He had Evelyn and that was enough for him.

"Let's get out of here."

She placed her hand in his and they exited the cave. They stopped in front of the opening and stared out at the lush vegetation. The island had a lot of beauty to rival the dangers they faced. He leaned down and kissed her quickly. A flash of lightning followed by a rumble of thunder caught his attention. He glanced up at the sky and saw dark clouds filling it. They'd waited too long to leave and now another storm was rolling in.

Wait—this could be what they needed. A storm had sent him back in time, perhaps this one could push them both forward. This was where he was when it hit. He'd seen Evelyn running. It couldn't have been her. Perhaps it was an image of what was yet to come.

"Why if it isn't Lady Evelyn," a voice called out,

"I'm glad to see you alive. I was afraid you had perished in the storm."

Paul pushed her behind his back and turned to face the man who'd called out her name. If he knew who she was that could only mean one thing. He was one of the pirates who'd kidnapped her. He wouldn't let them get anywhere near her. It was his job to protect her.

"No thanks to you." Paul glared at him. "I won't let you hurt her. Leave us be and there won't be any trouble."

"Who said anything about harming anyone?" He waved a hand dismissively. "As to trouble...I rather like a little bit from time to time. It keeps things interesting." His lips tilted into a cocky smile.

"Jack?" Evelyn peeked around Paul. "I'm glad to see you made it too."

"See the lady likes me." Captain Jack waved at her. "You don't need to protect her from me. I would never hurt a hair on her pretty head. As to other things..." He wiggled his eyebrows. "That's entirely up to her."

Paul punched him in the face. He wouldn't, couldn't stand for him to speak about her in such a derogatory manner. She was special and wasn't to be the object of any man's lust. Well except for his, but that was different. He loved her.

"Was that necessary?" Captain Jack held his hand over his nose. "I didn't say I was going to do anything. If she wanted me she had ample opportunity to sample my charms. She turned me down." He shrugged. "It's her loss."

Evelyn giggled... Actually giggled. He wanted to punch the captain again. She'd not laughed so lightly in his presence. Paul saw red and wanted to dismantle every inch of the pirate. He didn't like it one bit that the woman he loved, was so devoted to, might be even remotely besotted with another man.

"Jack, quit teasing him. He doesn't have your sense of humor."

Paul glared at Jack, inspecting every inch of him. So, he appeared to be good-looking, and he could grudgingly admit he could see why a woman might find him attractive, but that didn't mean he had to like it. He was an irritating fellow. Why couldn't something pick him up and carry him someplace far away. That would please him immensely.

"Very well if you insist, love." He bowed. "For you I will cease baiting the man. But first you must tell me what happened to you. I tried to find you when the ship went aground but you were nowhere to be found."

Evelyn opened her mouth; no doubt to tell him how one of his crew shoved her overboard but the man responsible beat her to the punch.

"It's the witch!"

Captain Jack turned around. "What nonsense is this, Percy?"

"It's her fault. The storm and the destruction of the Siren Song. We'd have made it to port if you hadn't insisted on bring her on board."

Paul rolled his eyes. There was one thing to be grateful for being from the twentieth century. Witch burning and blaming them for the world's problems had gone out of style. This man wanted to blame Evelyn for something his tiny mind didn't understand.

"There is no such thing as witches. At least not in the sense you're spouting."

Percy rushed forward and poked Paul in the chest. "You're only saying that because you're under her spell. She did the same to the Captain. He's never taken a lady on board before her."

"She has done no such thing." Captain Jack shook his head. "I've never liked one on sight before.

Lady Evelyn is a treasure and I wanted her for my own. That doesn't make her a witch."

Percy got even more erratic at the captain's words. "You're wrong. It's why I pushed her overboard. If she's not a witch how did she survive? Everyone knows a witch floats and can survive a storm of her own making. The proof is standing right in front of you. She is alive and well so surely she must be a witch. Can't you see it?"

"You pushed her overboard?" The captain's voice was cold and filled with menace as he turned on his crew member. "You knew what she meant to me and that she was not to be harmed and you took it upon yourself to dispose of her, because you got some nonsense inside your head. You must have a death wish."

The captain's hand rested on the cutlass at his side. Paul was waiting for him to unsheathe it and skewer the man for daring to go against his orders. He wondered what was holding him back.

"I had to. You must see that." He waved his hands at the sky. "She's working her magic again. Another storm is going to hit. We must kill her if we want to save ourselves."

"The man is insane. Evelyn is not a witch." Paul

had to make the captain see reason. "No one has the power to control the weather."

"I don't blame Evelyn," Captain Jack paused and looked up at Paul, "I know what must be done."

Before the captain could react, Percy pushed past him and rushed at Evelyn. She screamed and ran away from him.

"Evelyn!" Paul shouted.

Paul's heart stopped at the familiar sight. This is how he'd seen her before. The vision that appeared to him before he fell back in time and in an instant he knew why he was there. It was to save her. That was why he'd seen her before he fell and passed out.

Evelyn stepped out of Percy's reach and spun around, heading back toward Paul. She tripped and fell as Percy lunged for her. Paul reacted and yanked him away from her before he could do her any permanent harm. The pirate fell back toward Captain Jack. He shook in fear as he glanced between Paul and Jack.

"She must die. You both know it. You're just afraid. Look past her charms and you'll see the truth."

Paul looked Jack in the eyes and said, "Kill him or I will with my bare hands."

"It will be my pleasure." Captain Jack's smile

looked menacing as he stalked toward Percy.

Evelyn stood and ran toward Paul. He opened his arms and held her close. The wind picked up. It was familiar to Paul. The storm was going to send him back. He knew it deep down. He didn't want to let her go. If he held on tight perhaps she could come back with him.

Captain Jack held up his cutlass. As he was about to strike Percy, his crew member reached out and tripped him. His cutlass tumbled to the ground landing near Percy. The wind spun around him and lifted Jack. Paul's mouth held open in shock as the captain disappeared before them. Where had he gone? Was he in 1987? Had the storm taken him instead of Paul?

Percy picked up the cutlass and stalked toward them.

"You're not going to hurt her." Paul held Evelyn tight in his embrace.

"I will and once she's dead you'll see her for what she is."

Paul stepped back, continuing to hold Evelyn in his embrace. Percy lunged forward. The wind picked up again spinning around them. Percy fought it to get to Evelyn and Paul. He tripped trying to get to them. The cutlass slid into his thigh spurting blood in every direction. From the amount of blood coming out of Percy's thigh Paul assumed he'd hit his femoral artery. There was too much blood to believe anything else. Percy wasn't going to live through such a devastating injury.

The strong wind knocked the breath right out of Paul. Through it all he never let go of Evelyn. It pushed at them until he couldn't see anything anymore. If he was about to die at least he got to do it with the love of his life. It was his last thought before he thought no more.

THE SUN BURNED. HE DIDN'T WANT TO OPEN HIS eyes. What had he had to drink? There had to be an explanation for the infernal beating inside his head. The last time he'd felt this bad was the one and only time he'd gotten hammered.

Then he remembered and leaped forward. "Evelyn!"

"Don't shout. You're hurting my head."

He looked over and saw her lying in the sand next to him, her hands wrapped around her head. Time travel didn't appear to agree with either one of them. It gave him a whopping headache and by her body language he'd guess she was experiencing something similar. He glanced across the beach and realized they were in his time, at the hotel he was staying at on the island.

He stood up and helped her to her feet. "Do you know where we are?"

She looked around. Her eyes widened as she caught sight of the large hotel behind her. It was massive and as lavish as Port Royal had to offer. His assistant made sure he had the best of the best for his vacation, including his own suite and every amenity available.

"Are we where I think we are?" She raised an eyebrow.

"If you mean my time then you're correct."

He couldn't wait to show her everything and start their life together. He wished and wished he could bring her back with him. Now he had her where he wanted her. They'd escaped death and he wasn't about to take the gift he'd been given for granted.

"I love you."

He'd never loved anyone before. Not in the way he did Evelyn. Something he couldn't get enough of or fully believe.

"I love you too," she said.

He only had one question left for her.

"Will you marry me?"

Evelyn stared down at him. Her mouth set in a firm line. She tapped her chin as she considered his question. If she didn't answer him soon he'd go crazy. The wench was doing it on purpose to make him think she could say no. Surely she wouldn't do that do them. He knew she loved him and the next step was marriage.

"I will on one condition."

He grinned, how had he ever doubted she might say no? "Anything"

"Please tell me you can take me somewhere I can have a proper bath. I'm done with roughing it. I wasn't made for the hard life."

He laughed and pulled her into his arms. She had no idea what luxuries he had in store for her. She'd never want for anything ever again. They'd get married before they left. He just had to make a few phone calls to get her legal paperwork. They couldn't travel until she had proper identification. Once they got to back to New York he didn't want anything getting between them.

"That's a promise I can keep."

And he did, Paul kept every promise he ever made her.

EPILOGUE

Five years later...

EVELYN STARED DOWN AT HER BEAUTIFUL infant daughter and sighed with contentment. Her life with Paul had been perfect from the moment they met. Being in his world only made their love shine brighter. Not once since they woke up on that beach did she regret falling in love with him. There was no other man that could make her feel the way he did.

"Mommy, can I hold her?"

She gazed down at her other daughter with just as much love. Alys's green eyes twinkled with delight as she stared into her sister's crib. Her blonde curls were falling around her shoulders. Her blue dress complimented her porcelain skin and rosy cheeks.

"Not now, dear."

Alys's tiny bottom lip pushed out into a full pout. "Why not?"

Evelyn patted her head lovingly. "She's asleep and we shouldn't disturb her rest. There will be plenty of time later to hold her at her christening."

A private ceremony was scheduled for later that evening. Only the closest of friends and family were to attend. Regina was to be christened and officially welcomed into the Dewitt family. She was the blessing they didn't think they'd ever have.

Evelyn didn't have much to do with her time other than take care of their two little girls. Before she had them she volunteered at a local children's hospital. One day a baby had been brought into the pediatric intensive care unit, having been abandoned in the emergency room. That little girl was Alys. She'd fallen in love with her the moment she'd laid eyes on her. She knew that she belonged with her and Paul. She begged Paul to pull whatever strings he could so they could adopt her. It had taken nearly a year, but finally she legally was their daughter. Alys had been the daughter of their hearts from the start. For a while she'd been the biggest blessing in their lives as it appeared they'd not be blessed with any other children.

They made love as often as any healthy couple, but she never became pregnant. She'd started to believe she was barren. It was a fact she'd have been forced to accept in her time. Paul encouraged her to see a doctor and after some treatment she'd been able to conceive. Her pregnancy had been hard, but every moment was worth it when she finally gave birth. Regina was their second blessing, and Evelyn didn't take any of those for granted.

Alys stomped her foot. "I want to hold my sister now."

At four going on five Alys wasn't used to not getting her way. Evelyn leaned down and kissed the top of her blonde head. "How about we have a snack instead?"

She needed to distract Alys before she woke the baby up. She wasn't too proud to use something that she knew the little girl craved more than her baby sister's attention.

She tilted her head and studied her mother. "A cookie?"

Evelyn didn't usually allow a treat in the morning. Alys was too smart for her own good and already learned what battles to fight. If she couldn't hold her sister, then she'd take the next best thing in her little mind.

"Only one," Evelyn replied.

Alys tilted her head and appeared to consider her options. After a moment she held up some fingers on her hand and said. "Three."

Let the bargaining begin... Alys took every answer and made it into a debate. Sometimes Evelyn wondered if her daughter was bound for political office. She could sweet-talk anyone into or out of anything. How her mind worked was scary at times.

"Three is too many. I will give you two."

"Okay." Alys said and skipped toward the kitchen.

Evelyn followed behind her, thankful she hadn't thrown a temper tantrum. There hadn't been one in a while, but that didn't mean one wouldn't come at any time. Alys was both headstrong and loving. She knew what she wanted and set out to get it. Evelyn didn't doubt she'd go far and do great things with her life. Sometimes it saddened her that her biological mother had abandoned her. She didn't know what she was missing. Evelyn was happy to pick up her slack and give the little girl all the love she could.

She pulled the cookie jar into the middle of the counter and pulled two out. She leaned down and handed both to Alys. "Go sit at the table. I will bring you some milk and a napkin."

Alys snatched both and ran to the table. Evelyn laughed at her. She shook her head and took a cup out of the cupboard and filled it with milk. She set it along with a napkin on the table for Alys. After Alys finished her snack Evelyn had her lay down for a nap. They had a long evening planned and she'd never make it through it all without one.

"I don't want a nap." Alys pouted. "I'm getting too old for one."

Evelyn leaned down and kissed her daughters forehead. "How about a bedtime story to help you sleep?"

"Yes, please."

Evelyn weaved a tale of adventure involving Alys's favorite pirate captain, who also happened to be Evelyn's as well. She didn't know what happened to Captain Jack Morgan and this was her way of keeping him alive. One day she might write down their adventures so that everyone would know about the dashing pirate. She knew his intentions hadn't been honorable when he took her, but in the end he'd been willing to protect her at all costs. For that she'd always be grateful to him. She might not have the life she had with Paul and their girls if not for him.

After she finished the story she gazed down at her sleeping daughter. She was so innocent and beautiful. When she was asleep it was hard to tell she could be a terror. She leaned down and kissed her forehead. Now that both girls were asleep she had other plans.

She had a desire to see her husband. Lucky for her, he'd cut down his hours dramatically and was home more than he was in the office. The downside was he had a home office for when he had urgent work to do.

That is where she found him. Hunched over a computer plugging away at the keys engrossed in whatever was on the screen. She shut the door with a soft click and turned the lock. They had time for something special and much needed alone time.

"Do you have time for a break?"

"I'm trying to get these reports done before the christening. I'm almost done." He chewed on his bottom lip. His dark hair flopped over his forehead. He worked too hard.

She'd have to distract him. His work was important, but not more important than his health. The doctor warned him long ago against doing too much.

It was her job to see he didn't overdo it. Paul was to live a long and happy life with her and their daughters. She'd accept nothing less.

"I can't convince you to take a small break?" She danced her fingers across his neck, and leaned down to whisper in his ear. "I'm not wearing any drawers."

She'd purposely left her undergarments off when she dressed for this reason. His eyes met hers and heated. His hands trailed up her thigh and under her dress. He found her slick center and caressed her heated flesh. Her desire amplified under his ministrations. She loved how her husband touched her and brought her pleasure. It always amazed her how wonderful it felt to be loved by him.

"You're a naughty girl, sweetheart," He pulled her into his lap. "But I rather like this side of you."

She rather liked that side of him too. Their life had been full of adventure. Evelyn wouldn't change one thing. Whatever force brought them together had forever earned her gratitude.

"I thought you might." She smiled coyly. Evelyn licked her lips and ran her fingers through his hair. She pulled on a few strands and tugged his head closer to hers. "Now would you rather finish that report or have some wicked fun with me?"

Paul pulled her into his arms and kissed her

senseless. His report was forgotten as he made sweet love to her. Evelyn was indeed the luckiest woman alive, and she vowed never to take it for granted.

SEARCHING FOR MY ROGUE

LINKED ACROSS TIME TWO

DAWN BROWER

Dawn Brower

SEARCHING
FOR MY
Rogue

Linked Across Time

"Time is an illusion."

— ALBERT EINSTEIN

CHAPTER 1

September 5, 2015

"Aly, have you seen my shoes?"

Alys Dewitt rolled her eyes. "Did you check under the bed?" Her younger sister, Regina, was constantly losing something. They both sat in Regina's chamber wearing their undergarments covered by a silk robe. If it wasn't one thing, her sister would make something up so the attention would fall back to where she believed it belonged—on her.

Alys plopped down into one of the fancy retro chairs next to the window and pulled a nail file from her overstuffed purse. She slid it across her nails to even them out. Maybe she would get lucky and Regina would find her shoes without asking for help.

"You can help me, you know," Regina whined. "You *are* my maid of honor."

No such luck...

With a sigh, she dropped the nail file back in her purse. She should have known better. Regina couldn't do anything on her own. Drama queen? Her sister put the very idea to shame. Men loved her though. They weren't able to look past her perfect frame and flawless heart-shaped face. That Regina's face was draped with platinum blonde hair and aquamarine eyes didn't hurt and was enough to give Alys a complex. Her perfect sister...

In truth, Alys was tired of people comparing them. She was content with how she looked and her life choices. So what if she was still single and her sister appeared to have found the man of her dreams. Someday, she'd find a man worth spending the rest of her life with, and if she didn't, well, that was perfectly fine too.

At least that's what she kept telling herself. *Complex—ugh—okay, I may have one.*

"I'm more than aware of my status in your wedding." The person in charge of making sure she showed up and radiated her perceived perfectness. Just because she organized things down to the last detail didn't mean she should have to do it. Her sister was lucky she loved her. She pasted a bright smile on her face and turned toward Regina. "I can't wait to watch you walk down the aisle and marry Trenton."

Alys couldn't wait for this wedding to be over with.

She loved her sister. Honestly. But her attitude grated on her nerves. Regina's spoiled princess demeanor drove her insane. Alys could only spend so much time with her before she felt her fingers start to twitch. A desire to wrap them around her sister's neck and squeeze filled her, and it took all of her self control not to act on it.

"You don't look very happy about it. Don't you want to be part of my wedding?" Regina pouted. "Your fists are clenched at your side, and you've been bitchier than usual."

Alys tilted her head heavenward, silently praying for patience. She turned her attention to her over-wrought sister. "I promise I want to be part of your big day." She crossed her heart and blew her a kiss. "Now think, where was the last place you saw your shoes?" *For once, please remember...* So she wouldn't have to mess up her own hair digging around for her sister's shoes.

Regina bit her lip and a small tear slid down her cheek. "I don't know."

Alys took a deep breath and braced herself for the stream of tears about to descend. "It will be fine, Gina. Let me take a look. I'm sure they're here." She crossed the room and patted her on the back. Alys turned and scanned the room. No, her shoes weren't any place obvious. It appeared as if she'd have to do some serious searching.

"Thank you," Regina's voice wobbled. "You are the best sister, truly."

That's what she was to everyone: the one they could always depend on. What would they do if she suddenly disappeared? Maybe she should. Teach them all they would have to learn to do for themselves sometimes. Alys couldn't really do it though. Meanness, along with selfishness, wasn't her go-to attitude. That was what made people lean on her so much. She was an easy target to get roped into doing everything. She walked around the room and looked under the furniture. No shoes. There was only one place left to check. Alys headed toward the closet.

Alys sat down in the walk-in closet and rifled through a pile of clothes. She tossed them to the other side in an effort to reach the bottom. Of course, lying in the middle of it all was a pair of white stilettos with clear crystals decorating the toes and along the side. Regina loved shoes and allowed everyone to choose their own style for the wedding. Alys had a similar pair; a bridesmaid gift from her sister. Her reasoning for the modern footwear was no one would see them under their long gowns. Everything else was Regency period accurate for the wedding.

She couldn't believe how careless Regina was being with her wedding attire. If it were her wedding, she'd have taken better care of her shoes. Looking perfect for her big day would top her list, along with meeting her intended in front of everyone and saying her vows. Regina tended to be a tad unorganized. Why would she need to keep track of her belongings when she had everyone else doing it for her?

"Found them," she called out from the back of the closet. "You hid them from yourself under a pile of clothes." Alys grabbed the shoes and stood. She left the closet and found her sister sitting on the edge of the bed, a forlorn expression on her face.

"Hey, are you all right?" Alys rubbed her shoulder. "What's bothering you?"

"Do you think I'm making a mistake?"

"Oh, honey, it's not my place to say." Was her sister having doubts? Didn't all brides on some level?

How could she make it better for her? "You love Trenton, don't you?"

"I do..."

Good, that gave her something to work with. "Then what's the real issue?"

"I always jump in without thinking. When he proposed, I said yes before he finished asking me. I was so excited and could already see how our future would go, but now..." Regina bit her lip. "I think I may have feelings for somebody else."

Oh dear...

"Who?" Alys waved her hand, dismissing her question. "Never mind, I don't want to know. Let me put it like this. When you close your eyes, who do you picture as the man you want to grow old with, build a family with, and wake up each day to their face lying next to yours?"

Regina closed her eyes. Her face remained calm and unmoving, lips parted as she breathed in and out. "Trenton." A soft smile formed on her beautiful face. "I see him with me each day."

"Then you don't need to worry about your choice. You've already made it."

Thank God... If Regina cancelled the wedding— Alys didn't want to think about the backlash from it. Her mother, bless her heart, would be apoplectic.

Crisis diverted, she needed Regina to finish dressing for her upcoming nuptials.

"I'm sorry I'm such a mess."

Alys smiled. "From what I understand these feelings are quite normal." She sat on the bed next to her sister and pulled her into a hug. "Now, I think we need to fix your makeup and get you into that lovely gown you picked out."

Regina rested her head on Alys's shoulder. "I know, you're right, but can we sit here for a minute?"

Alys wanted to give her whatever she desired, but they couldn't stay in their current position for very long. The wedding was scheduled to start in a half-hour. If they were going to be ready on time, they would have to start moving.

"Of course." Alys rubbed her arm. "Only a moment though. Mama will come barreling in any minute and go a little cray cray at the sight of us. Neither of us is ready."

Regina sighed. "Let's get me ready."

Alys stood up and held her hand out to her sister. "Come on, go sit at your vanity. Time to make you even more beautiful than you already are."

Regina sat and started fixing her face. Alys went to the closet and grabbed both of their dresses and laid them across the bed. She settled herself next to

Regina at the vanity, watching her apply her makeup. Her hair had been arranged earlier in a perfect chignon with curls framing her face. After more than thirty minutes, her sister sighed and set down her makeup brush and turned toward her.

Alys shrugged. At least her sister hadn't taken as long as she usually did to put on makeup. This maid of honor thing was not something she wanted to experience ever again. Regina was her only sister, so chances of it happening again were slim.

"I'm ready to get dressed now," Regina stated.

"Good. I have your dress right here."

Alys held up the Regency inspired wedding gown. Her sister had decided on a themed wedding. They were all to wear period dresses or suits—even the guests. Alys loved her dress. It had a high empire waist with lace along the edge of the bodice and intricate beading at the base of the skirt. The fabric was silky and shown in a brilliant, pure white. The bridesmaid dresses were similar, but in varied shades. Alys's dress was a brilliant emerald. Regina wanted to dress Alys in a color to match her eyes—and she approved of the choice. When she tried it on, complete bliss overtook her.

Alys helped her sister into her gown and helped her tie the sash around the front. It all had to be historically accurate. No zippers for any of the wedding party. Lucky for Alys, hers slipped on and only had a few ties under the bodice. A complicated dress would have made getting out of it rather difficult considering she didn't have a groom to help her out of it at the end of the evening.

"All ready." Alys smiled. "It's time to go downstairs."

Regina nodded and wound her arm around Alys's. They left the room and descended the stairs. Their father awaited them at the bottom, along with the best man, Bradford Kendall, the current Duke of Weston. He also happened to be Trenton's stepbrother. The wedding was taking place on his estate in Kent. Alys sucked in a breath at the sight of him in his period attire. The man was gorgeous. There was no other word for it. His jet-black hair was brushed back, and his dark blue eyes shot upward as he watched them walk down. To be accurate, he watched Regina. Could he be the other man her sister had feelings for?

They reached the bottom. Their father kissed them each on the cheek. "You both look lovely." He looped his arm around theirs, one of them on each side of him. "You ready for a wedding?"

"I am." Regina giggled.

Bradford joined them, his gaze never leaving Regina's face. "It's a beautiful day for one. Every seat is filled."

"I can't wait to marry Trenton."

Alys watched Bradford. He sucked in a harsh breath at her sister's words. The duke had feelings for Regina. That would make for some awkward family dinners. She frowned. It was too bad really. The man could have any woman he wanted—except Regina—and now, well, her. Alys didn't want a man besotted with her sister.

"Yes, but you should let Bradford and I go on before you. Why don't you spend a few minutes with Daddy while we walk to the church?" Alys wanted to put some distance between the two of them. If Bradford was given an inch, he'd try to talk Regina out of marrying his brother. She couldn't allow him to destroy her sister's wedding. "We will be patiently waiting to see you walk down the aisle."

"I don't..." Bradford started to say, but stopped when Alys pinched his side, hard.

He glared at her, his eyes promising retribution.

"Leave Regina alone," Alys whispered. "She needs some quality time with our father. We have other things to take care of." She looped her arm around his and raised an eyebrow. "What are you waiting for? You're to escort me down the aisle, right?"

"Archaic," he grumbled. "I can't fathom why she wanted such an old-fashioned wedding."

They exited the house and headed toward the church located on the estate.

Alys shrugged. "I don't know. I find it rather charming."

"You would," he replied, sarcasm in his voice.

Alys stopped in her tracks and stared up at him. "What's that supposed to mean?"

He tucked a stray curl behind her ear. "You have a romantic heart. Probably comes from all that whimsical romance you bury yourself in."

Heat filled her cheeks. "So, what you're saying is because I read romance novels I have unhealthy expectations?" How *dare* he? He didn't even know her. They were barely acquaintances. To think she'd thought he was handsome when they first met. Way to ruin her fantasies... She should thank him for the wakeup call. For a brief moment she'd considered him a possibility. Rogues were all fine and good in romance novels. In real life they were such a letdown. Only in make believe were they redeemable. This man left a bad taste in her mouth.

So what if she'd been searching for a rogue of her

own for some time now...It was time to wake up and realize she'd never find one worth fighting for.

"Your words, not mine." He shrugged. "I think we need to keep moving."

What an ass.

"Because I want a man to *love me* doesn't mean I have unreasonable expectations." She wanted to punch him and break his perfect nose.

"Love is for fools."

Wait... That meant he didn't love her sister.

"So what about your feelings for Regina?"

A deep throated chuckle filled the air. "Oh, sweetheart, that's not love. It's lust, pure and simple."

He needed to be taken down a peg or three... "Someday you will meet someone who takes your breath away. Your very existence moot without them by your side—every breath, every heartbeat, will be only for them. If you're lucky enough, they will feel the same. Either way, I hope I'm around to see you fall. It will be a damned beautiful sight. The great Duke of Weston on his knees before a mere woman."

He pinned her in place with a scathing look. Such striking blue eyes... "Not bloody likely."

Alys smirked. "Maybe not, still, it would be amusing to watch."

Bradford stared down at her with condescension.

He tilted his head to the side as he studied her. His lips twitched and formed one of his cocky smiles. Whatever light bulb had gone off inside of his head, Alys did not know, but she didn't like how he was looking at her.

"Tell me, Alys, have you ever been in the gallery on my estate?"

Where was he going with this? "No, I've only been here since yesterday. Not a lot of time for a tour. You do have a very large home."

"Pity." He glanced down at her through hooded eyes. "You might have seen something interesting in there."

Like what? Bradford was confusing her. He wasn't flirting, but he wasn't exactly being stand-offish either. Alys didn't know what game he was playing and didn't really care either. She was putting a stop to it before it went any further. "I'm sure it has a lot of lovely art, but I'm not generally drawn to pretty pictures." Books, on the other hand, were a craving she couldn't kick.

"Oh, it isn't a bunch of pretty pictures. Most of them are of my family."

The man was talking foolishness. Why would she care about portraits of his family? Alys shrugged. "I'm failing to follow your logic."

His lips tilted into an evil grin. "You remind me of someone in the portraits. Uncanny really. Remind me later, and maybe I will take the time to show you."

Was this his version of *"let me show you my etchings?"* Alys wasn't going to fall for his plans of seduction. She wasn't born yesterday. "No thanks. I won't be staying long enough to bother."

They had stopped just outside the church. The walk over had been enlightening. As far as Alys was concerned she wouldn't be repeating it. Bradford was a conundrum she didn't want to figure out. Soon Regina would be married to his step-brother. Alys wouldn't have to deal with him, but she hoped her sister knew what she was getting into. Bradford might just come between her and Trenton. He didn't seem like the type of man to step aside willingly.

"Suit yourself." He opened the church door and led her inside.

"Is Regina on her way?" Her mother rushed to their side. "It's time to start."

"Yes, she's coming over with Daddy. She should be here any minute. Go ahead and let them begin. Bradford and I can head down now."

Her mother didn't say a word and left them at the end of the aisle. The music started as Regina and her father entered the church. Bradford wound her arm around his, and together they marched down the aisle. They took their places and waited for the bride.

Regina came down the aisle with their father, tears falling down her cheeks as she approached Trenton. They said their vows—all of it a blur. Soon the wedding came to an end, and they were leaving the church. A reception was scheduled to immediately follow the nuptials.

Alys shook her head. For some reason, everything swam before her. A hammer seemed to pound against her skull—something wasn't right. She needed her purse. She'd have something in there to help whatever was going on. If she could get through the day, she could spend a week in bed if necessary. *Please, let me see Regina's wedding until the end...*

Alys followed everyone out blindly. She wanted a few minutes to herself. Maybe she could take a breath and find that time inside the manor. The people around her suffocated her, and she still couldn't get over Bradford's attitude. He would have ruined Regina's wedding for a brief affair. Who was this man? How had he come to discard love so easily? Jaded, cynical, and one of the current rogues in England—Dover, to be more precise—Bradford did what he wanted and didn't give it a second thought.

Alys shouldn't have been surprised at his words, yet she couldn't help feeling disappointed at the same time.

He was right about one thing. Alys did read a lot. She loved romance novels and had a soft spot for the rogues written on the pages. She wanted a rogue of her own, provided he left his scandalous past behind and promised to love her forever. That's part of what had attracted her to Bradford. He'd reminded her of a romantic hero. Too bad he turned out to be a bad seed all around and in love with her sister. He claimed he only lusted after her, but Alys didn't believe it was just that. The duke had protested too much. Bradford wasn't the rogue for her.

Maybe someday she would get her wish and find the rogue meant only for her. Doubtful...

She walked up to her room and grabbed her heavy purse, sliding the strap over her shoulder. It had everything she could possibly need in it. If she could have taken it down the aisle with her, she would have. It relieved her to have it with her. Alys liked to be in control as much as possible. She hated to be unprepared for anything. So she carried a purse filled with items that could potentially solve any problem that might arise. Not everything was so easily fixed, she knew that, but it didn't stop her from trying. Her purse was a kind of security blanket. It made her feel like she could do anything. Plus, it had one very important item inside: her reading tablet.

I better get down to the reception before someone misses me.

Once outside, she breathed in the fresh air. The cliffs alongside the large manor were breathtaking. Maybe she could take a minute to enjoy the sea before returning to the party. She made a beeline toward the cliff's edge. When she got there, she stopped and absorbed the view. So beautiful... As much as she loved it though, she had obligations she needed to see to. Her sister would never forgive her if she bailed on the rest of her big day. Alys turned, took two steps and stopped.

Was that a white rabbit at the edge? The poor thing was going to fall off. Maybe she should shoo it away. Alys, dazed, stumbled toward it. It was so blurred... *Why did everything suddenly look so hazy?*

That was the last thought she had before the wind was knocked out of her. Her feet slipped and her arms flailed against the breeze, desperate for something to grab onto. She kept falling and falling... Only one thing going through her mind—*Damn rabbit's fault.* She was about to die.

CHAPTER 2

September 5, 1815

MOONLIGHT ACTED AS HIS GUIDE AS THE BOAT moved across the English Channel. The trip home both grueling and exhausting, James couldn't get there soon enough. A deep burn filled his gut as he stretched. The wound on his side ached with each movement.

Bloody hell...

In the distance, he could see the shoreline. Soon, he'd be able to crawl into his own bed. France could go to the devil. The battle at Waterloo had left its mark on his soul. If he wanted a reminder, all he would have to do is look down on the jagged protruding scar on his abdomen. The images swam before his eyes—all the death, blood, and agony screaming through his mind.

If only he could forget...

To think many considered him lucky. The battle hadn't ended for him when the cease-fire had been called. It began when a saber slid into him, leaving a trail of blood and pain in its wake. The sawbones hadn't thought he'd make it through the night, but James had a mind of his own. He hadn't wanted his life to end on a dirty cot in the middle of a foreign countryside. For the first month, fever had raced through him as his body fought off the infection raging through his body. He'd finally been able to sit up and feed himself when news of his brother's death reached him—his presence was demanded back in England.

His boat hit the beach along the cove. James jumped out and attempted to pull it farther onto the beach. He fell backward, hitting the sand with a hard thud.

"Bloody rotten piece of..."

James stopped short of wishing it to fall into oblivion. It wasn't the boat's fault he wasn't at full strength. He'd leave it where it was and have a servant deal with it once he returned to Weston Manor.

With a deep breath in, then out again, James calmed himself.

"No time like the present to go home." And fall into a warm comfortable bed and sleep for a week. Crossing through France to get home had been treacherous even though Napoleon had been defeated at Waterloo. Smugglers still used the channel to import illegal goods and most of them didn't have any qualms about dispatching witnesses into the great beyond.

James took several steps along the sandy beach, stopped, and stared down the path leading to the caves built into the cliff. Someone was sprawled across the ground outside the entrance. Weary, and mistrustful, James took slow steps toward the entrance. He wouldn't put it past someone to be lying in wait to accost him before he made it home.

He closed in and kneeled before the person lying before him. Why, it was a woman... James placed his fingers at the base of her neck—a steady pulse beat against his skin. She was alive at least.

Her eyes fluttered open. "Bradford?"

Who the hell was Bradford? Was he responsible for the lady's condition? What kind of bastard would abandon a lady on the beach for anyone to find? James would have to take her up to Weston Manor.

"Miss, do you think you can walk?"

Please be able to walk... James wanted to help her, but his strength wasn't what it should be. He'd only had six weeks of healing before he'd been summoned home. The trip left him weaker than he'd like.

"I don't know... Where am I?" she mumbled, her eyes drifting closed. "Help me."

He nodded, though she didn't see him. "I will. Tell me who can I contact to let them know you're all right?"

"Weston." The word was barely coherent.

James stumbled back, startled at her words. Did she know his brother? Was she in search of him? Had she actually said, Edward, not Bradford? Her words were so garbled he could have heard her wrong. She couldn't be looking for *him*; James had never set eyes on her before.

"Miss..." James shook her. Her eyes opened into tiny slits. "What's your name? Do you know my brother, Edward?"

Her eyes fluttered closed, but not before she muttered, "Alys"

She didn't deny knowing Edward, but she hadn't admitted it either. "Well, Alys, I will make sure you get up to the manor. We can sort this out later."

He glanced around the area. A pair of shoes like he'd never seen before lay near her feet. They had spikes at least three inches long on the end. *How can she walk in those?* She probably couldn't, and that's why they laid near her feet instead of on them. A bag was lying across her mid-section, the straps across her shoulder. Was she running away from something? He picked up the shoes and put them inside her bag. He couldn't make out the contents in the dark. Perhaps he would take a look inside later. There might be some clues as to her identity and what she was after inside. When she was conscious he would question her further.

James stared down at her. He dreaded carrying her up through the tunnels to Weston Manor. The burning in his side intensified with each movement. It would only get worse if he were to lift her and carry her on the long trek up the cliff, but he couldn't leave her on the beach. He wrenched his arms underneath her lush frame and gathered her tightly against him. Her head fell onto his shoulder, cradling nicely in his embrace; it felt so...intimate.

Her eyes fluttered open and met his. They were a deep, rich green that seared his soul. "Thank you. Maybe you're not so bad after all." Her head lopped down on his shoulder, a long sigh escaping from her pretty pink lips. "Thought I was dead—maybe I am."

Who the hell was she speaking of? The lady was clearly delusional. Perhaps she'd hit her head and was seeing things. James pushed it out of his mind. He would deal with it all later. He needed to get her up to the manor and fetch a doctor to take a look at her. She must have been injured.

The hike up the side of the cliff through the tunnels was grueling on a good day. On a dark night, with no lantern guiding him and a heavy parcel, it was ten times worse. Once he breached the top and pushed through the hidden entrance he had to set Alys down to catch his breath. Sweat poured down his face and his arms shook from the exertion. His goal was clear in his sight. The manor nearly glowed in the moonlight. He merely needed to get himself, and Alys, a little bit farther. James took a deep breath and picked her up again.

"Almost there, sweetheart."

"You're so warm. Don't leave me here."

James groaned. *Poor thing—abandoned and cold on the beach.* "Stay with me. I will fetch a doctor to look you over once we're back at Weston Manor."

"Because you want to show me the infamous

gallery of Weston Manor, Your Grace?" Her lips tilted into a soft smile. "I'm not so easily seduced."

James sucked in a breath. She was so lovely, but she wasn't for him. James wasn't in the market for a wife. She *must* have known Edward, and he didn't want a woman already taken by his deceased brother. He'd see her taken care of and leave her alone. It was all he could offer her.

And why did she mention the gallery? She was talking nonsense again. Why would she want to look at the family portraits? James kept moving. He made it to the entrance and pounded on the door. It flew open and his gaze landed on the head butler. "Wilson, help me."

"Yes, Your Grace." He nodded. "How may I be of assistance?"

"The lady was on the beach." James gestured toward the woman in his arms. "I need to get her settled. What room is immediately available?"

Wilson tilted his head. "There are only two chambers unoccupied and prepared."

James raised an eyebrow. "She's not as light as she looks, man. Which ones?"

"Yours and..."

James groaned. "Wilson, please, have mercy."

"The other chamber is for the future Duchess of Weston. Your brother ordered it readied before he..."

"Say no more," James stopped him. "I know where you're going. It will have to do for now. I will take the young miss there. Send for a doctor to have her looked over."

James carried her up the stairs and past the ducal chambers. He kicked open the door and strolled over to the bed. He laid her on top of the coverlet. A lantern would need to be lit so the doctor would have light to examine her. He located one on the table by the door. Once it was lit, a soft glow filled the room. James carried it over to the bed and set it on the night-stand. He stared down at Alys. His brother always did have good taste. Luxurious honey gold hair, soft pink lips, cheeks flushed with a rosy glow—Alys was simply exquisite. Too bad she could never be for him...

"Your Grace, I sent a footman for the doctor. Is there anything else I can do for you before he arrives?"

It was going to take a bit longer before he became used to his new title. Damn it, Edward, why did you have to go and get yourself killed? James didn't want to be the bloody Duke of Weston. It came with way too many responsibilities. The second son wasn't supposed to be tied down with the duties of the dukedom. With the death of his brother, he'd been left with little choice. His commission as a cavalry officer had to be resigned, and he headed home to take up the mantle his brother left for him.

"Have a bath set up for me in my chamber. I need to wash off the grit of the journey home." He paused to regain some momentum. He was so tired. "Have my belongings been transferred? Oh, and before I forget, my boat is on the beach. Send someone down to anchor it."

Wilson nodded. "Yes, Your Grace."

"What about a valet?" He'd had no use for one in battle, but as the Duke of Weston he would need one. "Is there someone here who can take over the duties for me?"

"Your brother's valet is still in residence. Would you like me to wake him to attend to your needs?"

James shook his head. "No, don't bother him tonight. Let him know I will need his services in the morning. Tonight, I only want to bathe and rest." The last thing he needed to deal with was a well-meaning servant. He was more than capable of washing himself and dressing for bed. The valet would simply deal with taking care of his discarded clothes and organizing his belongings.

"Very well, Your Grace." Wilson turned to leave. He halted in the doorway. "I will await the doctor in the parlor. One of the maids will bring up the hot water for your bath. I will instruct them to let you know when it's fully prepared."

James slumped down in a chair near the bed. "All right. I will wait here for now. I don't want to leave her alone."

"You should know that Rosanna is in residence. She arrived from London earlier this morning."

James gaze flew to Wilson's. He didn't want to deal with his sister, but it looked like he didn't have a choice. She was being sent off to finishing school the last time he saw her. "I take it she hasn't found a suitor yet."

"I wouldn't presume to know, Your Grace. Perhaps it's something she wants to discuss with you."

James scrubbed his hands over his face. One more thing he'd never thought to deal with. His life was falling apart before his eyes—or at least the life he'd planned for himself. "Very well, Wilson. Do me a favor and don't tell her I've arrived yet. I will deal with her once I'm fully rested."

"As you wish." Wilson inclined his head. "I will

leave you with the young miss to await the doctor's arrival."

James shouldn't be left alone with Alys. It wasn't proper at all. The gossipmongers would shred them to pieces if they ever found out. Who was she? Would her family descend on him and demand he marry her? Hell, he should offer to do it. It was the right thing to do, but fool that he was, he wanted to pick his own wife. This lovely lady wasn't meant for him—she already cared for another, and it wasn't him.

Alys sighed and clutched her bag at her waist. Perhaps he should remove it. It couldn't be comfortable wrapped around her petite frame. James stood and hobbled over to the bed. His side itched and burned with each movement. He hissed as pain shot through him, but ignored it as best he could. Alys rolled over, making it easier for him to untangle the bag from her shoulder. He yanked it and stumbled backward. The bag hit the floor, some of the contents spilling out. The strange shoes, a weird tube, and a set of keys—Alys moaned loudly diverting his attention so he shoved it all back inside.

Alys moaned again.

James rushed to her side. "Alys?"

Her sea-green eyes met his. "You're a beautiful

man. Have I ever told you that? No, why would I?" She cupped his cheek with the palm of her hand. "Tell me, do you still believe love is for fools?"

James sucked in a breath. "Yes, I do." How had she known?

"Love is a dream—a whimsical journey constantly surprising you. It's not meant for fools. At least, not in the way you believe. True love is a journey you willingly leap into." She sighed. "You'll see one day. I will help you."

She pulled his head down and touched his lips to hers. Fire spread through him, lighting him up, burning him from the inside out—he had to stop her. He stumbled backward, putting distance between them. When he looked back down at her, her eyes were closed again.

"What kind of madness is she driving me to?"

"Your Grace, the doctor is here." Wilson called from the entrance.

"Very well. I will be in my chambers if you need me."

James hurried out of the room. His breathing heavy and tapered with each step he took. That had been way too close. What was the chit after? Was she truly mad, or did she believe he was his brother? An easy mistake to make—they were identical twins.

Oh, Edward, why did you have to die?

James punched the wall. He slid to the floor and cradled his head in his hands. Tears he hadn't allowed himself before fell down his cheeks. His body shook, he groaned as agony overtook him. So much loss, too much responsibility, and not enough of him to go around—weariness set through him.

A bath was suddenly too much for him to bear. He told the maid to leave it until morning. He needed to rest. James's life had just become inherently more difficult. He lusted after the woman he believed loved his brother. James could not, would not, give in to those urges.

He would take care of Alys, but he would not give her his heart. If he did, she'd own him. They hadn't even had a real conversation—he doubted she'd even seen him when she opened her eyes. Whoever she had seen, he couldn't live up to those expectations. She was wrong... Love, indeed, was for fools, and James would never play the fool.

Clanking wood against wood filled the room. A light breeze blew over her, spreading a few strands of hair across her face to tickle her nose. Alys wiped them away with the back of her hand.

Who had opened the damn window?

Alys rolled onto her side and groaned. The ache burned through her shoulders and hips. Her head had needles being pounded deep inside with a sledge hammer. *Kill me now.* She stretched her arms above her head to get the kinks out. Every muscle in her body screamed in protest. What had she done at Regina's wedding?

Alys bolted upward. "Oh my God... Regina's going to murder me."

"Miss, you really should lie down. You had quite an adventure from what I've been told."

Alys turned her head—a mistake, as the sledge-hammer hit the base of her skull harder than a ton of bricks. Her hand flew to her temple and she winced in pain. She needed her purse. Inside, she would find a bottle of pain pills. A couple—or ten—would dull what could only be a headache.

A flash of memory floated through her mind. Had she kissed Bradford? Lord help her, the ass would hold that over her head for sure. When had she managed to imbibe so much alcohol? At least Regina didn't have her destination wedding in Vegas.

With Alys's luck, she'd have somehow managed to do more than merely kiss Bradford.

This was so embarrassing...

Through hooded eyelids, she gazed over at the woman who had spoken. "Who are you?"

More importantly, why was she dressed in a uniform maids wore two hundred years ago? Regina had taken things a bit far with her themed wedding. Having the hired help wearing period accurate clothing was a tad ridiculous.

The woman curtsied. "You can call me Bessie."

"Right." Seriously? "Bessie, have you seen my purse?"

What if she was a thief? Since when do maids traipse into private quarters? They were taking this role playing to extremes. Alys scanned the room and sucked in a deep breath. This was *not* her room. Whose room was she in? And what had she done? She patted her side and groaned, again. The only clothing she wore was her panties—what had happened to her bra? How far had things gone with Bradford?

Please, please, let the answer be "not very far."

"Purse?" Bessie scrunched her eyebrows up, puzzled. "I'm not certain what you mean."

"A large purple bag about this wide." Alys held her hands out a foot apart. "And equally as long. There is a bunch of small crystals decorating the flap."

"Oh yes, I know where that is. It's in the armoire." Bessie pointed to a tall piece of furniture against the wall near the doorway. "Your dress is inside as well. I am a bit confused about your under-garments. Where is your shift?"

Alys gasped. "You undressed me?"

"Yes, miss." She nodded. "It was necessary for the doctor to get a good look at you. That was a nasty fall you took."

Her mouth fell open at the maid's words. Bessie

acted as if undressing her was normal. It was so... wrong. It took several seconds for all of what she said to register in her mind. Aly's gaze flew to hers. This invasive servant had a lot to account for. First things first, what had actually happened?

"Fall?" Alys raised an eyebrow questioningly.

"On the beach. His Grace found you last night and carried you inside."

Alys vaguely remembered falling, but that couldn't be right. If she fell off the cliff she would be dead, not just badly bruised. Bradford found her there though—she would have to apologize and thank him. She'd thought he was nothing but a lecherous rogue. Apparently he had a good heart if he was willing to carry her such a distance.

"I'm sorry...Bessie, was it? Did you say a doctor looked at me?"

"He did. He said you needed some rest." She inclined her head, briefly. "Are you hungry? I can have a tray sent up."

"Oh, that would be lovely, and would you please bring me my bag?" she repeated, hoping she would retrieve it as she'd previously asked. "I need it."

Pain relief was required...sooner rather than later. Rest was good and all, but it wouldn't make the unrelenting ache go away. She had some ibuprofen in her bag that would help with the inflammation and ease her discomfort.

"Certainly" The maid rushed over to the armoire and opened it. She lifted the purse out, carried it over to Alys, and set it on the bed beside her. "Here you go, miss. I will go and see to your breakfast."

"Wait," Alys called out to her.

Bessie stopped. "Yes?"

"Where is my suitcase?" She needed to get dressed. Alys did not want to don the bridesmaid dress again. She'd kill for a pair of comfy yoga pants and a loose T-shirt. "I need something to wear."

She dipped her head. "Do you wish to dress for the day?"

Was she simple-minded? Alys stared at her, at a loss on how to proceed. Bessie appeared to be really into her role. Maybe it was just best to play along. "Yes, can you retrieve my stuff? I can't lounge in bed all day. I have to get home."

Alys had a plane to catch. She could convalesce at her leisure in her own apartment in Baltimore. Who was she kidding? It wasn't in her nature to take it easy. She'd be running off to work as soon as she set foot back in Maryland. Her sister's wedding had derailed her life long enough. Alys only had a few more months left of her residency at Johns

Hopkins—she'd been promised a fellowship if she finished.

"I'm sorry, miss. I don't know where your," she paused and studied her a few seconds, "stuff is. All you came with was the bag you are holding and the clothes you wore. If you'd like help dressing, I can assist you."

What? She had to be joking. Her carry-on bag was in another room. Alys sighed. She would have to put on the stupid dress and go in search of it. "No," she waved her hand, dismissing her, "I don't need help putting the dress on. Thank you for the offer though."

Bessie curtsied, again. Why was this woman being so formal? Alys stopped short of rolling her eyes. The game was getting old. It had to end at some point. "I will be back shortly so you can break your fast. May I ask if you'd prefer chocolate or tea?"

Chocolate? For breakfast? "Do you have coffee?"

"I don't believe so..."

They didn't have coffee? How barbaric, and so, so wrong. But this was the English for you. They sure did love their damned tea. Good thing she didn't mind it. "I will take tea—very strong tea. Please don't bring up any weak or tepid stuff."

The maid nodded and hurried out of the room.

When she got dressed, she'd track Bradford down and give him a piece of her mind. How could he not have coffee? She'd go easy on him—but only a little bit. He did save her after all. Alys could forgive him for not having something proper to drink in the morning, though she'd much rather wish him to hell.

Alys opened her purse and laughed. Why had she put her shoes inside? Well at least she hadn't lost them—they'd cost a fortune. A pair of three thousand dollar Christian Louboutin, crystal-encrusted, shark tooth pattern shoes; she'd fallen in love with them immediately. The price tag hadn't mattered since they were a gift. Seemed a bit fitting too—she wanted to take a bite out of her sister's hide, but had to rein in her sharp teeth. Alys set the shoes aside, she didn't know if she was up to wearing them yet. Pills, she needed them.

She rummaged through her purse and found her bottle of ibuprofen. The sooner she swallowed the pill, the quicker her body aches would lessen. Alys tossed the bottle back inside and shoved it across the bed. At least she could get dressed in private. Bessie had said her clothing was in the armoire—lucky for her it was. She picked up her mint green bra and winced as she clicked the back closed. With the straps in place she let out a deep breath.

"Well, the hard part is done—now for the damned dress." Alys pulled the emerald green dress out of the closet and slipped it on. She tied the ribbons at the bodice closed.

Now to find Bradford...

Only one problem—without shoes, her dress dragged on the floor. Alys bit her lip and looked over at the bed, her pretty shoes sparkling in a stream of sunlight. Why did she have to be so damned short? As much as her body ached, she couldn't risk wearing them. It was better to leave her dress dragging. Besides, what did she care if she ruined it? Not like she planned on wearing it again—ever.

Alys opened the door to hunt down the lord of the manor. He had a lot of explaining to do. Like what happened to her when he found her on the beach—and if he had a part in her ending up there. When she stepped into the hall she stopped short.

Why does this look so different?

There was no modern lighting. Candle holders sat on tables, and sconces had unlit candles on the wall. How had she missed that before? She should pay better attention to her surroundings. Everything looked so strange to her now—out of place—or maybe out of time. She shook her head, what a silly idea. Out of time—how would one get lost in time anyway? The furnishings were rather antique looking though. To think Bradford had called Regina's wedding theme archaic when he kept such outdated lighting in this part of his home.

Alys's immediate question—where was he hiding in this mausoleum he called home?

She took a few steps and stopped at the next room. The door was ajar, so she peeked inside. It was a more masculine version of her chambers. A large four-poster bed sat in the middle, draped in deep red coverlets embellished in an antique gold. She scanned the area, but no one seemed to be inside. Alys couldn't help but wonder if perhaps it was Bradford's private quarters. Maybe that's why she ended up in a different room. He'd wanted to dispose of her immediately and go to his in peace. Would make sense, Bradford, in her experience leaned toward self-serving. If it benefited him, he might be willing to offer his assistance.

Alys strolled farther inside, drawn to the large window on the other side of the quarters. She halted in front of it and skimmed her hand against the lush curtains. They matched the bed's coverlet. Whoever decorated the bedroom had exquisite taste.

"What are you doing in here?" A deep masculine voice echoed through the chamber.

Alys spun on her heels and met Bradford's gaze. "I was looking for you."

He frowned. "Were you now?"

"Yes, I think we need to talk."

Why was he looking at her like that? Wait, why was he still wearing his wedding attire? Well, actually he'd lost some of it. All he wore was a billowy white shirt, open at the nape and tucked into his breeches. He looked—different. Something was off, but Alys couldn't pinpoint it. She would worry about it later though.

"This isn't the place for a lady, but you're correct. We should have a discussion." He gestured to the door. "Perhaps we can continue this conversation in the sitting room. You had a horrible ordeal, and I'm sure it's stressful to be out of bed. Please, come with me where you can sit comfortably."

"Why are you being so...stuffy?" She stared into his eyes. "And proper, you are never proper."

His whole body stiffened at her words. "I don't know what you mean."

"You're acting like we've never met. I've never known you to be so damned formal before." She tilted her head and studied him. "What happened to you?"

Alys studied him trying to figure out why he

seemed so different. It was his clothes. They *were* different. Not at all what he was wearing at the wedding...but similar. Why would he change into more period like attire? He had called Regina's penchant for a Regency themed wedding archaic. What was she missing?

"Miss, you are mistaking me for someone else." The duke's words dripped with disdain and his icy blue eyes added to the contempt he lorded over her. "I promise you, we've never laid eyes on each other before."

No, no, no, no... What was this? She was not losing her mind, she wasn't. Was she?

"Don't be silly. We met several months ago." Alys flicked her wrist nonchalantly. Why was Bradford pretending not to know her? This ducal demeanor of his was starting to piss her off. If he didn't knock it off, she'd forget about thanking him for rescuing her and punch him in his perfect face.

He continued to stare down at her. Several seconds ticked by without a word from him. Alys fidgeted as she waited for him to admit what she already knew. The arrogant jerk had to drop the pretense at some point. He knew full well they were already acquainted. His mouth formed a grim line as he studied her. Alys began to understand what a bug under a microscope must feel like. She didn't appreciate the scrutiny she was now experiencing under his direct gaze.

Bradford shook his head and stated firmly, "No. We did not."

"Yes, we did. You're the Duke of Weston. Your brother—"

He interrupted her, "My brother is dead."

"What?" Alys didn't know what was going on, but it couldn't be true. "What happened to him?"

"This isn't the place for this discussion. Please follow me."

He turned to leave, clearly expecting her to follow him out of the room. His words penetrated her brain and left her reeling with shock. Alys stood staring off in the distance. Trenton couldn't be dead. Regina must be devastated. No wonder Bradford acted so strange. She crumpled to the ground as the news fully hit her.

The duke turned around and rushed back to her side.

"I'm sorry." He kneeled beside her. "I know you cared for him."

Her gaze shot upward, meeting his. She shook her head. "Not me. My sister."

As selfish as Regina may be, right now, her whole

life must be falling apart before her eyes. She had to find her, help her through the pain. No wonder Bradford hadn't changed his clothing. The whole family must all still be in shock. She could forgive him his rude behavior—everything—she'd be losing her mind too if her sister died. What the hell had happened at the wedding?

Alys shot to her feet and ran past Bradford. Her sister needed her.

"Alys, wait—"

She ignored him and kept running down the hall. Nothing was going to stop her from finding Regina. Not even Bradford's good intentions. Family meant the world to her, even when they drove her to the brink of insanity.

CHAPTER 4

"Alys wait..." She either didn't hear him bellowing or she ignored him. He didn't know which it was, but it was clear he had to go after her. James bolted down the hall following the path she'd taken.

The poor thing was confused. He had to catch her before she hurt herself further. He'd summon the doctor again. She'd need something the calm her down, perhaps he'd know better how to care for her malady.

Alys stopped at the top of the stairs, resting her hand on the balustrade. Her breathing was ragged. Her gaze fell on his when she glanced briefly behind her—then she skipped down the steps two at a time. Right before she reached the bottom, she tripped over her skirts and tumbled over the remaining few steps.

Bloody hell. The chit was going to be the death of him. James quickly followed her down and kneeled before her. "Are you all right?"

"Damned skirt is too long," she muttered. Alys turned onto her side and glared up at him. "Of course I'm not all right, but nothing is broken. I'm sure I will have more bruises on top of the ones I already have."

"Let me help you up." James held out his hand to her.

"Thanks, I've got this." Alys rolled onto her knees and hopped up to her feet. She turned to him and asked, "Where have you stashed Regina?"

"Pardon me?" James had no clue who this Regina was.

"My sister." Alys rolled her eyes. "Where is she?"

James studied her for several seconds. She had mentioned something about her sister being devastated about Edward's death. Perhaps she had been on her way to meet up with Regina for their wedding —not hers, as James previously assumed. Where her sibling was, though, he had no idea.

"I'm not acquainted with you or any of your family members."

"I'm not in the mood for games, Bradford." Her lips pursed up in displeasure. "Don't make me hurt you. I'm well versed in all the areas to do the most damage to a person's body."

James rocked back on his heels. Both statements had him reeling. What order of woman was this standing before him? She threatened his person and didn't have a clue who he was. This Bradford again—he hadn't misheard her before—was clearly someone she didn't like very much.

"My name is *not* Bradford." He looked her up and down; trying to understand how a little slip of a woman could possibly do him any harm. "How do you propose to overpower me enough to impart any sort of damage to me?"

Her mouth fell open. Silence reigned throughout the room. James took advantage of her surprise and scooped her into his arms. Alys reached up quickly to wrap her arms around his neck, a reflex to catch her balance. "Put me down you big oaf," she demanded.

"Wilson, fetch the doctor at once," James bellowed. He switched his attention back to Alys and explained, "You require rest. The doctor left explicit directions. The maid I assigned to your room should not have allowed you to leave your bed, let alone get dressed and run around in your condition."

James spun around and began to ascend the stairs once again. The lady was going back to her bed, whether she liked it or not. James sensed the harridan in his arms was about to give him hell for his high-handedness. It really was for her benefit. He'd deal with her wrath once he had her back in her bed.

"My condition?" She raised an eyebrow. "What condition is this? I can assure you I'm fine. Just a tad banged up."

"Banged up?" James frowned. "You speak so strangely sometimes."

"Kettle? Black? You're acting out of character a bit." She snorted. "Since when are you not Bradford? What are you going by today? Decided you needed a little change in your life?"

"I've never been, nor will I ever be, called Bradford."

Alys was so peculiar, but something about her drew him. Her gaze held barely repressed anger and her cheeks flushed red. Her blonde hair fell around her face in waves. She must have been quite desperate to find her sister to leave without having the maid dress her hair properly. James rather like seeing her in such dishabille... He couldn't help wondering how she'd look after being well loved.

James mentally sighed. He couldn't hold onto such lecherous thoughts. Even if they were entertaining... Alys wouldn't be enthused to know he wanted to strip her naked and have his wicked way with her. Her nails bit into his shoulder, and he winced from the pinprick of pain they left behind. Unfortunately it led his imagination even further down the sea of lust. The woman in his arms didn't know what dangerous game she played.

"Oh?" She chewed on her bottom lip. "How should I address you?"

James stopped at the top of the stairs and looked down at her through a hooded gaze. She was so beautiful. All he could think about was kissing her pretty pink lips. He needed to put some distance between them. Barriers, the building blocks of the aristocracy, would ensure she knew her place in his life. Never had he wanted the title now bestowed upon him, but damned if he wasn't about to use it to his advantage.

"Your Grace."

"Seriously?" Alys's fist slammed into his shoulder. The harridan knew how to hit. Someone had taught her well. Maybe her earlier words were not a boast. "I think we are well past formalities. You're such a conceited ass. You make me want to scream. Put me down now."

"I will set you down once we reach your chambers." James wanted to rub his shoulder to relieve the ache, but he had more important priorities. "Not a moment before. Insulting me will not get you your way."

Alys's bottom lip popped out into a pout as James continued down the hall. She was damned near adorable, but the look in her eyes scared him a bit. What was she plotting?

"Well, *Your Grace*," Alys replied scathingly. "Challenge accepted."

Before he could respond to her words, she dropped her hands from around his neck and used her dead weight against him. When he was struggling to regain his equilibrium, she reached down and squeezed his manhood with her hand. The pain shot right up through him and he fell before he had a chance to catch himself from hitting the ground hard. He found himself sprawled out on the floor with her sprawled on top of him. Breathing became even more difficult, but James was used to excruciating pain. One tiny woman would not kill him when the French couldn't even manage to do it.

Alys rolled off him and hopped to her feet. She

raised her skirt, revealing a very trim ankle—and bare feet. She placed her foot on his neck and pressed down. "If I put all of my weight down, what little breath you're managing right now will diminish. You'll gasp until you can't get any air into your lungs. It will burn, and you'll become so desperate you'd beg me to let up if you could manage words." She pressed down a little bit, telling him with her actions she meant her words. "How about we start this day all over again and you start answering my questions. I'm not an empty-headed female incapable of understanding what is going on around me. Let's try some little words to start with and make our way from there. What's. Your. Fucking. Name."

She removed her foot and took several steps back. James turned onto his side and leaned against the wall. He'd seriously underestimated her. He glared up at her. Not for the first time, he wondered who she was. "I am James Kendall, Fifth Duke of Weston. Now, how about you tell me who you are and why you're in my home."

Alys gasped. "You said the *fifth* Duke of Weston —that can't be right." She paced up and down the hall. Her hands shook more and more with each stride.

James got to his feet. "I assure you, as much as it pains me, I am now the duke."

She stopped, spun around, and faced him. "Now? As in you weren't before?"

James bent his head and stared at her. "You didn't know my brother, did you?"

She shook her head. "I'm beginning to think I don't know anyone here."

Good, at least she was ready to be reasonable. "Who is Bradford?"

It was time for her to start giving him answers. She'd assaulted his person and insulted him more than he'd ever allowed from another individual. James wanted to know what her purpose was so he could start figuring out what to do with her. She had skills that scared him senseless.

"First, I need to know something."

Alys best be prepared to start telling him everything. He had not survived the bloody war to be done in by a tiny woman with deadly skills. Maybe she was a spy sent to finish him off. He had been instrumental in the battle that ended the war. An enemy might be seeking some sort of revenge against him or his family. "That's not how this works. This is my home. You attempted to harm me. You will tell me what I want to know."

"I can't tell you anything, not until I understand what is going on here," she explained. "Tell me, James, what is the date?"

What did that have to do with anything? He almost didn't answer her, but he was curious to know what game she was playing. James would humor her and see what path she planned on taking. "It is the sixth day of September."

"The year. What is the year?"

She was getting more and more intriguing with every question. He tilted his head and studied her for a second before answering, "1815."

She gasped and hit the floor. Her hands covered her face. "Oh, God! How did this happen?"

James kneeled before her. He didn't know what the date meant to her. Why did it upset her so much? He brushed one of her blonde locks behind her ear.

"Perhaps I can help you if you explain what is going on," he said, soothingly. "I've been told I'm good to have around in a crisis."

Alys shook her head. Her cheeks were soaked with tears. "You can't help me with this. I'm afraid of the very thing that could possibly return me to where I belong. I don't like heights..."

"It can't possibly be as bad as you think it is." James was perplexed. She was making even less sense with each statement she uttered. He'd thought Alys mad, but perhaps she was simply lost. James could help her return to her home. Her accent seemed familiar. "You're one of those colonials, aren't you?"

"Yeah?" She stared at him. "I don't see your point."

"We may have been at war not that long ago with them, but I'm sure I can find a ship to return you home."

Alys started to laugh wildly. She fell down to the ground holding her midsection between her arms. It echoed down the halls and irritated him. What was so funny? Why did the idea of putting her on a ship drive her to hysteria?

"I fail to understand why this is so humorous."

Alys gasped for breath. "Boat, oh that's rich. A freaking boat." She laughed again. "To think, when I woke, the first thing that crossed my mind was I had a plane to catch."

James opened his mouth to speak, but closed it. He didn't even know what to ask her. What was a plane and why did she have to catch it? Peculiar didn't even begin to describe Alys. He frowned. "I think you need to start telling me what's going on."

She stopped laughing, her face stone-still. Her

gaze landed on him. "You don't know how right you are, but I'm not sure how much I should tell you."

James had a feeling he wasn't going to like what she had to say. By the look on her face there was a lot going on—much more than he even realized. She didn't look happy, in fact, she looked even more frightened than before. Something happened that had devastated Alys all the way to her core. Her eyes were devoid of any jovial emotion, and seriousness, even in the face of her laughter, was rocking her emotions.

"Before I begin, you need to understand one very important thing."

"Proceed," he encouraged. "I'm listening."

"I'm not insane. You try to lock me up in Bedlam, and I will make you pay for it. I know how this century dealt with the people they believed mad. I have not lost my mind."

James smiled. He had thought perhaps that was the case at first, but now he didn't believe it. He saw intelligence in her eyes. Depending on her answers, he'd decide how to proceed. Alys might not be mad, but she might have other nefarious plans. "I will not have you placed anywhere. It will be up to you where you go from here."

If she was someone out to harm him or his family

she'd be in a far worse place than Bedlam. She might find herself in prison or deported. Her answers better satisfy him.

Alys nodded. "My name is Alys Dewitt," She paused, stared him in the eye, and dropped her news on him. "I was born on October 31, 1988."

His mouth gaped open, shock racked his mind. James could not have heard her correctly. She did not just say she was born almost one hundred and seventy-three years in the future. He'd assured her he believed her sane, but those words made him rethink his assessment. Something was off, and James didn't know what it was. He couldn't make a sound decision until he had all the facts.

"Please continue," he urged. "I need all the information.

Alys explained everything, and with each word, he realized he didn't understand anything. How did she fall off the cliff and end up on the beach where he found her? He remembered her strange shoes and stuffing them into her bag. James had meant to look inside to see if there were any clues to her identity, but in the chaos of bringing her home and having her looked at by the doctor, he'd forgotten. Perhaps he should investigate further. Alys could be delusional and only believed she was from the future. The tale she wove was too farfetched to take at her word. He needed something...tangible to accept that she traveled from another time.

"So, you see, I don't belong here," Alys finished.

"I can certainly understand why you don't think you do," he conceded. "However, I'm not sure I can believe such an outrageous tale."

Alys opened her mouth and closed it several times. James had a hard time wrapping his brain around the idea that she could possibly be from the future. These things didn't happen every day—or at all. It was a fantastical tale. He had never heard of something so extraordinary occurring. How was he to accept it had happened to Alys? It had to be pure nonsense she'd made up to explain why she was on his estate. Perhaps it was time for him to come to terms with her evident madness.

"I can prove it." She jumped up and ran into her chambers.

James followed her inside. She dumped her bag onto the bed and waved her hands over the contents. He scanned all the strange items. He didn't know what any of it was.

"What are these ojects? I am not familiar with any of it."

She opened a tiny leather pouch and pulled out a

rectangle object and thrust in his face. "Here look at this. It's my driver's license. My picture, date of birth, and address are all displayed on it."

James snatched it from her hand and examined it. He fell backward into a chair next to the bed. The object was so thin and made out of a material he'd never seen before. Her portrait was on the tiny card and her information typeset upon it. According to this little correspondence, Alys was from Baltimore, Maryland and was indeed born in a year far into the future.

"How did you create such a wondrous object?" James flipped it over and read the back of it. She volunteered to be a donor. What was she giving away? How had they managed to put all this information onto such a small card? "I've never seen anything like it before."

"I doubt you ever will again," Alys explained. "I can show you the other items in my bag. They all are things you wouldn't find in this century, and some not even in the next..."

James shook his head. It was all too much to take in. She appeared to be telling the truth. His examined the bed and perused over the items. Some were brightly colored, and they were in various shapes and sizes. When he had more time, he'd ask to look over it all again and have her explain what it all was. For now he needed time to think and figure out what to do next.

"Not now..." he paused and looked her in the eyes. "Perhaps later."

She nodded and placed all of the items back into her purple bag. "Just let me know when you're ready to discuss it further."

It was all confusing, and at the same time, everything finally made sense. She'd been a conundrum ever since he found her. Now that he knew her situation fully, he had one problem...what the bloody hell was he going to do about it?

Alys was alone and without family. There was no one to protect her, and he had no idea how to return her to her own time. There was no way around it; he'd have to marry her to protect her. It was the only way he knew to make sure she remained safe. She was right to worry about being placed in Bedlam. The mental hospital was stuffed full of individuals believed insane. If anyone came across Alys and her unbelievable tale, she'd be made a permanent resident there. Without a powerful ally and a name to protect her, nothing would prevent it from happening.

James stood, nodded to her, and said, "I have to

go to London. I will make some arrangements for you before I leave. When I return, we will discuss this further. Don't do anything rash beforehand."

He strode to his room to prepare for his journey. There was much to be done and not a moment to lose. The more he thought about it, the more resolved he became.

James never planned to marry. He'd left that to his brother. Edward was supposed to continue the line and have children. Fate had something else in mind for them both. Now he had a reason to get married. He would have had to find a lady to marry at some point. Now he didn't have to look and had time to acclimate himself to the idea. Alys would do as well as any other woman. At least she would make an interesting duchess. Hopefully, she wouldn't fight him too much on it. She'd fought him on everything since the moment she had awoken. James wouldn't be surprised if that was a hint for what he should expect the rest of his days. Alys was strong willed and didn't think twice about carrying out her threats. She'd come around and realize this was the best choice, the only decision, they could make. This *was* for the best—for them both.

CHAPTER 5

ALYS STILL COULDN'T BELIEVE SHE WAS STUCK two hundred years in the past. How could it have happened? She didn't fully comprehend what had happened to her, but James's reaction baffled her even more. He'd jumped up and barked orders, then promptly disappeared from her presence.

Had he believed her?

Alys shook her head. Why would he? If they reversed positions, she'd never have believed him. The whole situation was crazy. Maybe she had lost her mind...

She was in Regency England. It was beyond bizarre. It could all have been an elaborate joke... Yet Alys believed it for several reasons. After James left, she'd explored the house a little bit. What she did remember of Weston Manor...nothing of what she was currently viewing remained the same. All of the furniture was antique, or rather it would be in her time. It appeared—new in this version of the ducal estate. She found more staff as she explored. All of them regarded her the same way the maid Bessie had. After looking over several rooms she retreated to her chambers. She'd seen enough to acclimate herself to her new fate.

Now that she accepted her situation, she knew what had happened. Somehow, when she'd fallen off the cliff, it had transported her through time. There was some sort of time warp, a hole, whatever it was called over the cliffs. What made it work, Alys was uncertain of—but she couldn't deny that it did. Jumping off the same cliff, in the same spot, could very well end up in her death. A risk she wasn't willing to take—never mind her niggling fear of heights.

The cliffs were beautiful and she liked them, as long as she didn't have to actually look down. She could stand on the edge of the tallest mountain and be all right, even go so far as to say thrilled, until she looked down and imagined what the plummet to the ground would do to her. She was stuck firmly in the past.

So where did that really leave her?

She stared out the window. Everything appeared familiar, yet she was looking at a past version of what she'd remembered. Her career as a surgeon would go nowhere. In this time, women were not taken seriously. They'd never allow her to care for another person. Besides, she didn't have some of the necessary tools to practice her craft. A lot of the medicines readily available in her time hadn't even been invented in the one she found herself in. Alexander Fleming wouldn't discover the benefits of penicillin for another one hundred and thirteen years. How could she work, knowing what she did, with her hands tied? People were skeptical until something was proven, and even then they were not always apt to believe it. 1815, God help her, was not a time to be a progressive woman.

"Excuse me, miss, but the doctor has arrived."

Alys turned toward the sound of the maid's voice. Doctor? Oh yeah, James had one summoned when he still believed she needed to be examined. She closed her eyes and prayed for patience. She would need it if she had to deal with a doctor from this time period.

"Tell him his services are no longer required."

"It's not really your call to make," a man said as

he pushed his way into the room. "You are not a trained physician."

Alys laughed. If only he knew. "I'm willing to bet I know more about the human body than you do. Care to place a wager?"

"Consider yourself to be somewhat of a bluestocking, do you? No matter, you can read all the books you want. It doesn't replace real training and experience." The doctor set down a bag on a nearby table and opened it. He pulled out a small jar and set it next to him. "I think if you allow me to help, you'll feel better in no time at all."

Aly's mouth flew open at the sight of the jar. Did he really believe she'd allow him to put that disgusting specimen he carried around anywhere near her? What if he already had when he examined her previously? Bile rose up to her mouth and she managed to swallow it back down. This doctor was not touching her. "You are sadly mistaken if you think you are getting anywhere near me. Now put that thing away and leave."

"His Grace summoned me. It's not your place to dismiss me."

Alys swiped a metal letter opener off the desk near the window, held it up, and sashayed over to the doctor. She stood mere inches in front of him and placed it against the left side of his neck, rubbed it against the carotid, poking it enough for a small cut.

"Doctor, I apologize. I don't know your name," she said, absentmindedly. "It doesn't matter though. Do you know where I have this letter opener pressing?"

The doctor lost all color from his face, but he nodded slowly.

"Good, I see you understand. Now, I took an oath to help people, but let me make something very very clear. I would so hate for us to have a misunderstanding." She took a step closer and whispered in his ear. "Not at any time, ever, will you put a blood-sucking leech on me. It *will not* heal whatever ails me. Besides the fact I am *not* sick, all it will do is make me anemic over time. You do not have the skills to heal an insect, let alone a human being. Do not ever step foot in this residence again."

Alys took a step back. He touched his neck. He lifted his hand away and stared down at a drop of blood on his finger tips. He paled even further at the sight. Alys snorted. If he was afraid of a little blood, how dare he call himself a doctor.

His gaze locked with hers. Alys lifted her hand and wiggled her fingers at him in a little wave. He picked up his specimen and stuffed it inside his bag.

Then the doctor scrambled in retreat out of the room. A small smile formed on her face. *That was almost fun.*

Too bad she still had a headache. It had been hours since she took the ibuprofen. Maybe it was time for another dose. Where had she left her purse?

Clapping filled the room. Alys spun around to see who made the noise. "That was brilliant. You must teach me how to do that."

A pretty girl with ebony hair and brilliant blue eyes stood in front of her.

Alys raised an eyebrow. "Hold someone at knife point—well it doesn't have quite the same sound as saying letter opener point..."

She laughed. "It was brave. I do so want to be courageous. I'm Rosanna. Who are you?"

Someone with a blinding headache and no time for inquisitive young ladies.

Alys spotted her purse near the armoire. She strode over, grabbed it, and dug through the contents. The pain pills had to be inside somewhere, and she didn't feel like searching for them. *Ah, there they are.* She opened the bottle, dumped a couple pills into her hand, and then popped them in her mouth.

"What is that you have?"

Crap. She'd forgotten the young woman who'd

come into her room. Stupid headaches made her do dumb things. "Nothing to concern yourself with."

"Are you going to introduce yourself?"

Alys scowled. "Isn't it frowned upon to introduce yourself to stranger?"

"You are in my home—in the duchess's suite, no less. I'd say we're about to be family." She shrugged. "I'm sure James would have gotten around to introducing me to his intended at some point, but I'm rather impatient. Besides, he left, and I'm not going to hide in my room for days waiting for him to do it."

The girl did have a valid point. Drat that James for not having the foresight to think those who lived in the manor might find her curious.

"Wait...did you say this was the duchess's chambers?"

Rosanna nodded. "You didn't know that?"

No, she most definitely had not. Why had he put her in these rooms?

"How do you know James?"

"My, my, he certainly has been remiss." Her smile made her even lovelier. "I am Lady Rosanna Kendall, daughter of the third Duke of Weston, and sister to the fourth and now the fifth."

Ah, James mentioned his brother died. So, he hadn't been meant to inherit the dukedom. How heartbreaking. To only have the title because one's family member passed on? He'd looked so sad when he departed the news.

"Did your other brother die recently?" Alys had to know.

"Edward died a couple months ago. It's why I came home. I couldn't abide the ton while I was in mourning—so dreary. I was supposed to find a husband, but it's not easy weeding through the rakes and penniless lords. One wants my body and the other only my money...none wants the woman behind them."

Rosanna sat down in a nearby chair. Her skirts billowed around her. Everything about her seemed perfect. Her gown, her well-groomed hair, and even her flawless complexion—many women probably envied her the position she was in. Alys did not. It had to be quite difficult to deal with the obligations of being the daughter of a duke.

"I understand. Why marry anyone at all?"

Rosanna laughed. "How quaint. I can't remain single. That, my dear, is a fate worse than death—to be put up on a shelf and never have a family of my own. No, that won't do. I need to find someone who will take me as I am, but sadly I won't have a chance until the family is out of mourning."

"You can't get married while you're in mourning?" Seemed like there should be a work around for them to get past that little rule... Alys wished she knew more about the aristocracy. She'd never really cared. What little she knew she'd garnered from romance novels. *I wonder how much of it was fact and what was fiction?*

"No, but it looks like James might plan on doing that and not giving a fig about what society thinks. He's always made his own path in the world. It's why he fought in the war. He never could sit still for long. It doesn't surprise me he chose a woman equally as brave for his wife," she paused, inclining her head to study Alys, and continued, "You never did tell me your name. Am I to call you Miss or Your Grace?"

Alys laughed. "I'm not married to your brother. So no to Your Gracing me now or ever."

"So, Miss it is then." Rosanna nodded.

"You can call me Aly. All my family does." She smiled. "But if you want to know my name, it's Alys Dewitt."

Rosanna stood up and walked over to her. "It's nice to meet you, Aly. Please, call me Rose." She pulled Alys into a hug. "It's going to be nice having a sister.

Alys pulled back. "You're mistaken. James and I are not getting married."

"Oh?" Rosanna frowned. "I swear I heard him tell Wilson he's going to London for a special license. That could only mean he plans on getting married."

James couldn't possibly think she was going to marry him. He hadn't even asked her. Why would he think she'd jump into a marriage without discussing it first? Alys didn't plan on marrying anyone unless she was deeply in love with them. She barely knew him.

"I don't know what that means."

"It means, Aly dear, my brother saw you, wants you, and plans on staking a claim in the most permanent of ways." Rosanna laughed. "It's so like him. I'm sure you will know all once he returns."

"If he thinks I'm marrying him because he orders it, he's in for a rude awakening." How dare he plan her life without consulting her? Heat filled her cheeks as anger raged through her.

"You say the strangest things." Rosanna frowned. "Are these colloquialisms you're uttering something normal for Americans?"

Alys smiled. She had no idea... "You know where I'm from?"

"Another thing I overheard them talking about.

I'm also supposed to supply you with some of my gowns until a seamstress can be sent for. Apparently you lost your luggage in a carriage accident or something."

Ah, James had thought of everything, except to include her in on his plans. They would discuss that oversight upon his return. "Yeah. I am not sure what happened to my trunks. I came ahead of them." Way ahead of them—or was it behind them? Alys's head hurt just thinking about it.

"James is having a seamstress return with him from London. I asked my maid to pull out a few dresses and bring them here. She is talented with a needle and can alter them to fit you."

"Wonderful. I can't wait to start."

"She'll be here soon. I will leave you in her care." Rosanna stood to leave. "Before I go, can you give me a little hint of what those little brown objects were you swallowed?"

Alys groaned. Rosanna was not going to let it go. "Headache, or body ache, medicine."

"Really?" Rosanna smiled. "When you have time you will have to tell me more. That is quite fascinating."

With those words, she strolled out of the room. Rosanna and James were going to drive her mad—

both of them had their own agendas. Alys should be used to people who were not forthcoming with what they had planned. Her family had been doing it for years. She'd have to prepare herself for a siege when James got home. He'd find out that Alys was not someone to trifle with.

CHAPTER 6

It took a day for James to reach London. He hadn't wanted to tire his horse, so he took his time and stopped at an inn overnight. His first stop was to procure a special license to marry Alys. The Archbishop didn't allocate a special license often. James did everything he could to convince him to grant his request. The amount of funds he'd donated to the church to get the license should ensure his application was approved. No matter what, he would marry Alys. It was the only solution to her problem. All he could do was wait to see if the special license would be delivered to his townhouse.

He wanted to get back to Weston Manor as fast as possible, so hopefully it would go as planned. The townhouse owned by his estate rarely got used.

There was a skeleton staff kept in residence for upkeep and the occasional trip. James stabled his horse and entered through the front door.

"Your Grace." Timmons bowed. "Can I get anything for you?"

"No," James said. "I trust my room is prepared."

"Yes, as always. Should I inform Cook you will be home for the evening meal?"

"No. I'm going to my club. I'm expecting a messenger. If they come, put the documents on my desk in the library. If all goes well, I will leave in the morning. Have her plan for a light meal before I depart. If that changes, I will inform you upon my return."

"Very well, Your Grace." Timmons walked off.

James skipped up the stairs two at a time and went up to his chambers. His visit with the Archbishop had seemed to go well. If he granted him his special license, it would be delivered by the end of the day. He didn't foresee any issues. The Archbishop liked to wield his power of thinking it over. The problem was Alys wasn't of English blood and had no family around to speak for her. Luckily, she was of age and didn't need parental consent. He'd just fudged the year of her birth a little bit with the request. If he said she was from the future they'd have hauled him off for Bedlam. After he was finished, he strolled down the stairs and headed out the door. He could use some time at his club—it had been a long time since he'd been able to relax.

As soon as James strolled into his club, he was greeted by one of the patrons. "Good evening, Your Grace."

"Good evening," James nodded. "Anything interesting going on in the betting books?"

"Always, Your Grace. Would you like to look?"

Did he? He wouldn't have time to deal with any wagers. He shook his head. "No, not today. I think I will make my way to the back."

He walked to the back room and found a group of gentlemen engrossed in a game of whist. Any other time he might have considered joining them. He was beginning to wonder why he'd bothered coming to his club. Everything felt wrong. His first instinct was to bolt, return home, to Alys. He wanted to learn more about her. She must have so many fascinating things to talk about. The knowledge she must hold... Alys was intelligent and beautiful. He looked forward to their future together.

"James, bloody hell, didn't think you'd come to London to save your life."

He turned around and met the gaze of his best

friend, Dominic Rossington, the Marquess of Seabrook.

"Dom, good to see you." James nodded. "Are you here to find a game?"

"No," he shook his head. "I saw you walking back here and followed you. Do you want in on a game?"

"I don't know what I want. I'm at cross purposes."

Dominic nodded. "I see. Is something troubling you?"

How did he explain what was going on in his life? So much had happened in a short time. Dominic was one of his closest friends, yet even with his friend he had trouble opening up. The horrors of war had taken its toll. Never would he be the same again—he'd been inherently changed from the inside out.

"No, everything is fine." James waved his hand.

The patrons of White's bustled around them. James had always liked the atmosphere of the club. It was one of the few places he could come to and relax. Having a trusted friend with him made it that much better.

"So, what brings you to London?" Dominic asked.

"I came to obtain a special license from the Arch-bishop of Canterbury."

Dominic's mouth fell open. He stared at James in shock for several seconds. "Pardon me. I couldn't have heard you correctly. Did you say you went to obtain a special license?"

James frowned. "Why are you so shocked?"

Dominic's bark of laughter echoed through the room. Several gentlemen stopped and stared at them both. "Oh, that's rich. Do you want me to repeat your vehemence against the state of matrimony on previous conversations?"

Dom did have a point. His friend knew him rather well. James had stated on more than one occa-sion he wouldn't get married. He'd had no reason to. Things changed though with Edward's death. The ducal estate fell to his care. It was now up to him to carry on the ancestral line. So it shouldn't really be a surprise he would marry. Instead, it had become a matter of when. If he hadn't met Alys, he'd probably have put it off as long as possible. His plans had changed when she crashed into his life. It surprised him how much he accepted her place at his side. He actually looked forward to spending the rest of his life with her.

James rolled his eyes and grabbed Dominic's

arm. "Come, let's get a drink, and we can discuss it further."

"You want to get out of earshot of London's most notorious gamblers. Before you know it, your name will be in the betting books. The wagers will all be on who your intended is and why you feel the need to rush into marriage."

Dom was correct, as usual. They would all be out in droves trying to figure out what was going on in his life. The new Duke of Weston was speculated upon daily in the gossip sheets. They all wanted to know when, or if, he'd take a wife. Edward had been taking steps to marry, but never did before he died. Now, it was up to James, he had a duty he never expected to have.

Dominic followed him out of the card room. They settled into a private chamber and ordered drinks. James knew Dom was waiting for more information, but he didn't know how to explain Alys to his friend. She defied words—she just was.

"So are you going to tell me?" Dominic asked.

"What do you want to know?" Time to get it out. Dominic wouldn't let it go easily.

"Who is the lady who's stolen your heart?"

James snorted. "That's a little much don't you think?"

"No," Dominic said. He leaned on the table and stared James in the eyes. "If you're obtaining a special license it's one of two things: you compromised her, or you've fallen madly in love. Which is it?"

James tilted his head. He hadn't thought about it in quite those terms. In a sense, he had compromised Alys. They had been alone on several occasions, but that wasn't why he was marrying her. James wasn't in love, didn't believe in it, but he did believe in loyalty and protecting the innocent. He'd do right by Alys. Even if he could not give her his heart.

"I don't love her."

"I see. She must be a very lovely chit." Dom smirked. "Does she give out her wares easily? If you want, I can take her off your hands and find her a new protector."

James's fist slammed into Dom's face before he had time to think. "You will not talk about her in those terms. Ever."

"Damned, James." Dom held his nose as blood spurted out. He grabbed a handkerchief out of his pocket and held it against his broken nose. "You could have used your words. I'd have gotten the point."

"This was more effective."

Dominic glared at him. "Since when? You never used to act first and think later."

James sighed. Dark images floated through his mind. The screams of agony, the injured and dying, all swam behind his eyes. "Sometimes you don't have time to stop and think. Reflex or instinct is what saved me."

Dominic was quiet as he stared at James. After a few moments he spoke. "I heard it was bad. I didn't realize how much. For what it's worth, I'm glad you made it out—even if you are a lot harder than I remember."

"Yes, I don't think I will ever forget what I've seen."

Dominic nodded. "Nor should you. It's part of who you are now."

James closed his eyes and took a deep breath. "I'm sorry I punched you, but I don't appreciate you speaking about Alys like some common doxy."

"I didn't really believe you planned on marrying her. In my mind, I kept thinking you were having fun at my expense. You said so many times how you never planned on marrying... and you said you didn't love the girl." Dominic's eyes were filled with remorse. "I'd like to make it up to you. When do you plan on having the wedding?"

"First, I need to get the license. I'm hoping when I return to the townhouse it will be waiting there for me. The Archbishop said he'd consider my request. He didn't believe the urgency warranted a special license." James frowned. "I doubled the fee so he'd reconsider and send it by later on in the day. He agreed he might have been hasty in his assessment and would let me know before the night was out."

Dominic whistled. "Doubling it didn't get it for you immediately? What was his real objection?"

"Alys is American."

"I see." his friend frowned. "How did you get attached to one of those bloody upstarts?"

"Dom," James warned.

The marquess held up his hands. "I surrender, please no more, Your Grace. My face is too pretty for you to mark it up with those bricks you call fists."

James laughed. The ladies often described his friend as more beautiful than handsome. He had golden blond hair and honey colored eyes. James had heard them whispering about the Golden God. Whenever Dom was described in those terms, he rolled his eyes and walked in the opposite direction. It had given Dom quite an ego and a reputation as a veritable rake. He was pursued by the ladies of London—he never had to work for female companionship. It would serve him right to fall for a woman who wasn't fooled by his easy charm.

"It might make you more interesting. Think about it. All the ladies would fawn over you and kiss your scars to make them all better." James smiled. "I can see it now. You'd have a new one following you around each day."

"You are just jealous they always loved me better than you," Dominic retorted. "No reason to mar perfection simply because they follow me around like lost puppies in need of sustenance."

James rolled his eyes. "I'm sure it's a need only you can provide too."

"That's correct." Dominic said, with a cocky smile fast forming on his too perfect face. "I believe in delivering whatever they need—and they do need a lot. Pleasure, my friend, is one of life's greatest gifts. You deny yourself too much."

"I'll pass." James shrugged. "I'd much rather have pleasures that last a lifetime than fleeting moments that never amount to anything real."

"Your loss." Dominic smirked. "My gain."

"All in how you look at it." James sat back and took a swig of his brandy. "I'm content with my choices."

"Speaking of your choice—tell me about Alys."

James considered his words carefully. He didn't want to peak Dom's interest too much. He'd dig deeper if James hinted there was a mystery to solve. "She has pretty blonde hair and eyes that sparkle brighter than emeralds."

Dominic yawned. "Sounds ordinary—and boring. What's she like? You describe her beauty, but to be honest you appear mildly interested by that mundane description."

James tapped his fingers lightly on the table. Then he picked up his drink and swallowed it down. He hadn't wanted to get into any details. Dom was well known as a rake. He didn't want to encourage him. What if Alys preferred his friend? The Marquess of Seabrook was even less likely to settle down than he had been. Dom wouldn't stand by her. James knew his friend enjoyed pursuing ladies and remaining unencumbered. The idea of her choosing Dom over him left a bad taste in his mouth. So he did the only thing he could think of. He downplayed her attributes and made her sound as ordinary as possible. James sighed. "She's outspoken, a harridan, intelligent...and can drop a man to his knees in less than a minute."

"Now, I have to meet her." Dominic's grin spread wide. "When do you go back to Weston Manor?"

Bloody hell... Exactly what he didn't want. He couldn't tell his friend he forbade him from meeting Alys. That would make things even worse.

"Probably early in the morning. Depends on the Archbishop."

Dominic raised an eyebrow. "Do you really doubt he didn't grant you the license?"

"No," James said. "I fully expect to find it waiting for me when I return to my townhouse."

"Good. I will meet you at dawn to start the journey to Dover. This Alys must be amazing if you're giving up your freedom to spend the rest of your life with her." Dominic stood and gazed down at James. "And man, you need to consider how you feel about her. A man doesn't describe a woman like you did Alys and not feel anything for her."

With those words Dominic strolled out of the room. James's mouth fell open as his words sank in. What did he feel for Alys? He couldn't really say. Dominic did make a valid argument—protection aside, he did admire the lady. Maybe he should figure out what it meant. No, it didn't matter. He was going to marry her and give her the protection of his name. Wasn't that enough? Most marriages were based on far less.

CHAPTER 7

"Alys, how do you feel about going for a stroll with me?" Rosanna practically bounced into her room. "I'm finding it difficult to sit still. Please, say you'll come with me."

Alys shrugged. What else did she have to do? The maid had altered a couple of dresses for her so she had appropriate attire. Besides, she was bored, so spending some time with Rosanna appealed to her. Country life was not for her. She was used to action, and since she'd fallen through time it was sadly lacking in that department.

"Sure, why not?" Alys hopped to her feet. "Lead the way, Lady Rosanna."

"Rose, please." She grinned, cheekily. "I've told

you we're not to be so formal. We're to be sisters after all."

Alys rolled her eyes. "I'm not having this argument with you again."

"You'll see. James will be back any day, and he will verify my prediction." A gamine smiled filled her heart-shaped face. Her violet eyes nearly twinkled in excitement. "I know my brother rather well. Trust me, he intends to make you his duchess."

"Again…" Alys glared. "I'm not discussing this. Let's go outside for that walk you wanted. The sun is shining and it appears to be a lovely day. Let's go enjoy it."

Rosanna laughed and fluttered out the door. Alys followed behind her. When they reached the staircase, Rosanna skipped down the stairs in an unladylike fashion. Alys wished she could follow suit, but knew better. If she hopped down the stairs she'd end up on her backside. Skirts and slippers were not her friends. She tripped over them every time—if only she could get away with jeans or even a short skirt. Why had she thought this time to be romantic? The reality of it was anything but.

"Must you go so fast?"

Rosanna's giggles echoed through the hall. "Oh,

don't be so stodgy. You need a little fun, and I am going to see you get some." She grabbed her hand and pulled her along out the door. Alys almost tripped over her own feet several times in the process.

"Please, I'm not used to moving at such a fast pace in a skirt."

The girl paused and studied her. "That implies you are used to it in something other than a skirt."

Damn it. She'd dug a hole for herself. Alys had managed to downplay the ibuprofen by answering her questions with non-answers. Rosanna had wanted to sample them. It took every ounce of her intelligence to talk her out of it. Still, if given the opportunity, she didn't doubt Rosanna would nab them and give them a go. As long as she didn't take too many she'd be fine—but Alys wasn't about to risk her health on a maybe. She hoped Rosanna heeded her warnings.

"You caught me. I've worn pants in the past. They are so—freeing. Much easier to get around in."

"You're so progressive. I wish I was as brave as you." Rosanna stared off, a dreamy expression filling her face.

"You can be if you wish too. Sometimes being

brave is just accepting who you are and not changing it to fit a mold someone else set for you." Alys studied Rosanna. "I like to think I broke it and tossed it into a hole so deep no one will ever be able to find it. You have to forge your own path."

Rosanna nodded. "Is that what you did?"

"In a sense. My mother expected me to be the usual debutante. Find a husband, run charities, have the required amount of children. You know a predictable, dull, life." She looked Rosanna in the eyes. "It's not a bad life if it's what you want. I wanted so much more."

Regina was content to be that. Being a Dewitt had requirements. They were as blue blood as Americans could get. The Dewitts were old money and had the snobbishness to carry it off too. Alys, being the black sheep of the family, had chosen to study medicine. Her life would have a purpose, much to her mother's discontent.

"You don't want to marry and have children?"

Alys shook her head. "Not right away. I'd like to have a husband, a family, I wanted my life to have meaning first. I wanted to leave my mark on the world, so people would remember my name." She smiled softly. "So when I was gone from it they would know I was here. Everything I did would be so profound that when they uttered, 'Alys,' it would be with awe and respect." Her smile faded. "I doubt it will happen now. I've lost that opportunity by coming here. As long as I'm relegated to the status of wife and mother, a mere duchess, my name will mean nothing in the grand scheme of things."

"That's...sad." Rosanna frowned. "You don't believe in love? That it is what would make it all worthwhile?"

Alys stopped and considered the young woman's question. How should she explain her thought process? Rosanna grew up in a different era. How she was raised was different. They were worlds apart in comparison. Bradford had scoffed at the idea of love and appeared so cynical. Alys wasn't in the same league, but at the same time she wasn't so naïve either. Love, as much as some liked to believe, didn't make everything better. It helped, certainly. It just didn't cure all the ills or evil that surrounded them. It didn't stop her from craving a love of her own. To feel wrapped up in its warmth. Love was something she sought and hoped to one day have.

"Oh, I do. I absolutely do. Love is beautiful, profound, and all-encompassing." Alys nodded. "I want it so much my chest tightens at the very thought. If I could find someone to love me as much as I love them, it would be a dream come true. But merely having love in your life isn't enough for a happy ending. There is no such thing. To have true happiness, you need to look beyond finding a man to fill that void. You need a purpose. Love is only one aspect in getting that fulfillment."

Rosanna chewed on her bottom lip, contemplating her words. "I think I understand. You want love, but you also want your life to have meaning beyond that. You don't think you could have that with James?"

They started walking again. Could she have something more with James? How was she supposed to know that answer so soon? She had so many questions. He wasn't here to answer any of them. The foolish man had galloped away without discussing anything with her. Men were quick to make decisions and just thought a woman would follow blindly along. Alys was not one of those women. James He would see that upon his return. If she was truly stuck in the past, she'd have to figure out what to do. Marrying James shouldn't be her only option.

Alys shook her head and stared off in the distance. She continued toward the cliff. They'd been strolling for several minutes and were now almost to the edge of the cliff. In the very spot she'd been standing after her sister's wedding. Ironic that she was thinking about everything she'd wanted out of life and how it hadn't seemed possible then. Standing at the perimeter of what sent her tumbling through time made anything seem achievable, and also very much plausible. What it all meant though was lost to Alys. Why had she ended up there? What was she supposed to do? She'd never been so confused in her life.

"James is...nice. Very handsome and even chival-rous," Alys began. "But I barely know him. How am I to know if I could love him when I've only had a couple of conversations with him? One of them doesn't even count. I wasn't coherent and I believed him to be someone else."

"Many marriages have been built on less."

Alys laughed. "I suppose that is true. I want more than that." She shook her head. "No, I won't marry James. It wouldn't be fair to me or him."

"I wish you would reconsider." Rosanna pulled Alys's hand into hers. "James is a good man, and he would treat you well. He could use someone like you in his life. He's not had an easy one. Being the second born, Father ignored him."

Alys could relate to that a little bit. Her mother

doted on Regina, called her *princess*. It gave her sister a big head and built up her selfishness to extraordinary heights. It was one of the reasons why she had decided to do more with her life. She didn't want to be selfish; all right, she could be when warranted, but for the most part she did her best to give back. Being two hundred years in the past, she'd have to re-evaluate that goal and find a new purpose. Whatever that might be, she would be ready for it. Fates—*challenge accepted*—do your worst.

Alys chuckled under her breath. Not too long ago she'd uttered those words to James. He'd learned not to take her at face value. No one who spent time with her long did. She was a peacekeeper most of the time, until she was pushed too far. Sometimes snapping was the only course of action left. That's when all hell broke loose and all the inner crazy being bottled up exploded. She tried not to let it loose to often—the world had to forgive her though. This was not a normal situation, and holding it back would be worse.

She turned to Rosanna. "Is there a way to get down to the beach below?"

"Oh, yes," she nodded. "There are some caves that wind down to the bottom. Would you like to see them?"

That must be how James got her from the beach to the manor. Alys had wondered how he'd managed it. She never did get around to asking him for details. The beach was vague in her recollection.

"Please, show me."

Rosanna grabbed her hand and lead the way. "Now be careful where you step and follow my every step. The caves are crude. They were cut to deal with the French if they happened to attack by way of Calais. It is also a smuggler haven. I know Edward had problems with smugglers before he died."

How interesting...

"So there are a lot of smugglers around here?"

She nodded. "I suppose so. I don't know much. The little I know I overheard Edward talking about with Dominic, The Marquess of Seabrook." She paused and turned to face Rosanna. "Do you know him?"

Alys didn't know anyone in her current time period, but she couldn't tell Rosanna that. "No, I'm not acquainted with him."

"Oh! He's James's best friend. I'm sure you'll meet him."

Something in her tone made Alys wonder if she was smitten with him. Her cheeks pinkened a little bit when she said his name. "Do you have feelings for him?"

"What?" She waved her hand and started walking again, dragging Alys with her. "Don't be silly, of course not."

"I see." Alys stumbled. "Rosanna, slow down, I'm having trouble keeping up."

"Right, sorry. I get rather excited sometimes."

Alys figured that much out on her own. "Anyway. Tell me what you overheard."

They got to the end of the cave and sunlight gleamed from above them. The beach was breathtaking from the viewpoint of the cliff—it was even more so up close.

"They were discussing the smugglers. Edward was explaining them to Dominic." She paused. "They were making plans to stop them. Not long after that, Edward died in a carriage accident."

"So you don't think they were stopped?"

Rosanna remained quiet. Her gaze fixated on the waves hitting the shore. Alys didn't want to push her. When she was ready to speak, she'd explain what was on her mind. She'd only known the girl for a few days, but she'd learned rather fast she didn't hold back. Words floated out her as quickly as they entered her mind—but these might be harder for her because they involved her deceased brother.

"Edward spent a lot of time here at Weston Manor. He loved it more than London. I was actually quite surprised to see him. I was there because it was my duty to land a husband, to make an advantageous match. Edward had given my care to my elderly aunt. She chaperoned me to all the necessary soirees, balls, picnics, musicals...whatever we were invited to. There was no reason for him to come to London."

Where is she going with this?

"When Dominic came to see him shortly after his arrival, I knew something was wrong. They didn't know I was listening outside the door. Dom came to see him because of what he does, who he works for. They believed the smugglers had another function."

Her gaze met Rosanna's. "What did they believe they were doing?"

"Spying. They were smuggling more valuable information than brandy. They were trading sensitive information to the French."

"So if they are still operating here..." Alys gasped.

"Then we could very well be in danger and not

know it." Rosanna paused and looked her in the eyes. "I don't believe Edward's death was an accident."

If her supposition was correct what did that mean for their safety? Wasn't the war over? Did it matter still if there were spies? Alys had a bad feeling about the whole thing. James fought in the war. He'd want to punish those responsible, and if Edward's death wasn't an accident...he'd want to see them punished.

"What do you think I should do?" Rosanna frowned. "I wanted to tell James, but I'm afraid. I've already lost one brother."

"What about the Marquess?" she asked. "Can you contact him?"

"I considered that before I left London. He was nowhere to be found. I'm afraid he found a bad end too."

Alys grimaced. More and more bad news—how was she supposed to give advice when there was no easy solution?

"I think, as much as you want to protect him, James wouldn't thank you for it. Sometimes telling the truth is the hardest thing you can do. You're going to have to talk to him when he gets home."

Rosanna nodded. "I was afraid you were going to

say that." She sighed. "All right. I will tell him immediately upon his return."

It looked like James was going to have to deal
with quite a bit when he deigned to grace them with
his presence. A sad story filled with intrigue from his
sister—and Alys's wrath at his high-handedness.

CHAPTER 8

JAMES AND DOMINIC TRAVELED ON HORSEBACK along the path toward Weston Manor. They'd been on the road for many hours heading to the ducal estate. All James wanted to do was relax and have a drink by a warm fire. He was bone tired.

"James," Dominic called. "Isn't that your sister walking along the cliff? Who's the blonde chit she's with?"

James scrunched up his eyes and stared at the two figures. Bloody hell, it was Alys and Rosanna. What had possessed them to walk along the cliff? Alys especially—she'd explained what had happened to her in her time. Falling to uncertain death should be a major deterrent, yet there she was strolling along the edge without a care in the world. What if she fell off again? Would it take her home, or would he find her body crumpled and broken at the bottom? James shuddered at the image passing through his mind. No, it wouldn't happen—ever. He'd have a discussion with her. He would make it clear she wasn't to put herself into danger of any kind. It was for her own safety. She'd understand his reservations.

He couldn't lose her. Not when there was so much he still had to learn about her. James couldn't watch her leave him. When he looked toward the future, he saw her clearly at his side. Fate hadn't dropped her into his life only to snatch her away.

"Those two will be the death of me."

"The blonde is rather lovely." Dominic grinned wickedly. "Please tell me she's not your intended."

James glared at his best friend. "If you don't want a bloody nose you will quit staring at her with lascivious intentions."

Dominic laughed. "Relax, I have no designs on your bride-to-be."

James wasn't sure if he believed him or not, but it was no matter. He had more important things to deal with. Rosanna knew better than to get so close to the cliffs and the tunnels. He'd have a discussion with her in private too. They didn't seem to have the sense

God gave them not to tread where ladies shouldn't go.

"Let's stable the horses," James said, hopping down from his saddle. "I have much to do and two ladies in need of scolding."

They headed into the stable. The stable master greeted them, took the reins from James, and then prepared the stallion for his stall.

"Be careful, James," Dominic warned. "Ladies don't much care for lectures on proper behavior. Though they sure don't have issue with delivering them on occasion. Your sister has a barbed tongue."

James whipped his head around and stared Dominic in the eye. "How would you know how barbed Rosanna's tongue is? When have you had the opportunity to spend time in her company?"

James wasn't sure he liked how familiar Dominic sounded. Rosanna was his baby sister, and the idea of Dom having an interest in her bothered him. He knew his friend, and he didn't see him settling for one woman. He liked the chase too much. As much as he respected Dom, he wasn't good enough for his sister. Hell, he didn't like any man getting close to her if he were honest. Not one was trustworthy enough to be alone with her. They all ultimately had lecherous intentions.

"I spent a lot of time in London with your brother when he happened to come to town. Rosanna would interrupt us whenever the opportunity presented itself. I think she was rather bored with all that the ton had to offer for suitors. It's probably why she rushed home to Weston manor as soon as she could. With Edward's death, she was given a reprieve from the tediousness." Dom shrugged. "I can't really blame her. I find society rather dull myself. All those matrons trying to pawn off their daughters on the marriage mart, no thanks."

James, at one time, would have completely agreed. Well, if he were to be honest, he still did. He was looking forward to marrying Alys. Something about her drew him, and he wasn't going to fight it. She may have traveled through time to him, but he wasn't about to find a way to send her back. She fell into his life for a reason, one he happily accepted.

"Rosanna never did have much patience for idiots. I'm sure the fops drove her mad."

Dominic nodded. "I witnessed her cut a young dandy with her tongue. It was so precise I kept looking for the signs of blood. You might want to tell her that it isn't done. She won't find a husband if she can't learn to curb her words. No man wants a harridan for a wife."

He sighed. Dominic did have a point, but James didn't want to deal with it... At least, not any time soon. Since they were in mourning, Rosanna could deal with her life as she chose. She wouldn't be going back to London for the season again until after the year of mourning was up.

"I'm sure she has her reasons, I don't want her to change who she is. The man she marries should be well aware of what he is getting into. Rosanna needs a man strong enough to see past her faults and love her anyway."

"Love?" Dominic gasped. "Who said anything about that trivial emotion? Since when did you start spouting off that nonsense? That nonsense has no place in marriage. It's a business arrangement, simple and binding. That's why I'm putting it off for as long as possible." He shuddered. "I can't see myself shackled to one woman for the rest of my days."

They exited the stables and stood outside the entrance. James stopped to consider Dom's words. When had he started to believe in love? James pondered his own beliefs. He had never spouted nonsense about love, not until he'd found Alys. She said love was something you willingly jumped into. James wasn't about to admit he loved her. How could he? They'd just met. He was, at the very least, honest enough to acknowledge he was willing to try, to see if they could have it all. If they couldn't, then at least James knew he provided her safety and protection as her husband. That had to count for something. It was, in a sense, the business arrangement Dom considered marriage. They would both get something out of it. He'd get a wife and mother to his future children, and Alys would have the protection of his name.

"I'm not sure if love is attainable... I still have my doubts, but females seem to want it these days. I think that is what Rosanna is after, and her barbed tongue is her way of testing her would-be suitor's mettle. When she finds the man she wants, it will most likely soften a little." James laughed. "Rosanna's choices are of little concern to me right now. I'm more interested in Alys."

Dominic nodded. "I can see why."

"Come on, let's go meet the ladies. They have to be heading back to the manor by now. I'd like to tell her of my news."

They strolled out of the stable and made a beeline for the two ladies. Rosanna looked up and saw them heading their way. She halted, grabbed Alys's wrist, and pointed. Alys's gaze met his across the distance. She looked upset. What could have her looking at him with displeasure? James hastened his stride so he could get to their side faster. Dominic matched his pace and soon they were standing in front of them.

"Alys. Rosanna," he greeted them. "Why were you at the cliffs?" The words spilled out before he could stop himself.

Alys shrugged. "We felt like going for a walk. The cliffs were only part of our excursion."

Her tone was filled with ice. If James thought she was unhappy at a distance, up close he could tell she was livid. "It's dangerous. I don't want you near the edge." He pinned her with a stare, layering it with the words he didn't want to express in front of an audience. James hoped she got the message.

"I see." Alys was quiet for a few moments. "So you don't think I have enough intelligence to see to my own safety?"

James stood straighter. "Do I need to point out your previous experience?"

She had to see he didn't forbid it to be difficult. It truly was the best course of action. He couldn't find her broken at the bottom of the cliff—or, he gulped—disappear before his eyes and return to her own time.

"James." Alys seethed. "I'm a grown woman. If I choose to throw myself off a cliff, it's my choice to make. I do know what is best for me and don't need a man condescending to me."

"Good grief, James. What's the big deal?" Rosanna stomped her foot. "We were perfectly safe. Leave Alys alone."

"Sweet, perhaps you should let them work it out on their own," Dominic urged. "They can find a compromise that works for both of them."

Dominic gazed at Rosanna with a bemused smile. Usually his soothing tone and feigned sweetness drew women in. James didn't like the idea of his friend using his methods on his sister. His friend was overstepping by interfering.

Rosanna turned to glare at him. "Oh? Forgive me. The great and powerful Marquess of Seabrook knows all. How dare I have an opinion?"

Rosanna stormed away from them. Good for her. She wasn't easily swayed by Dom's charms.

"Rose..." Dominic called. "Wait, let me escort you inside."

Rosanna stopped suddenly, and spun around. Dominic ran right into her, knocking her to the ground. "You oaf, what is wrong with you?"

"I'm sorry. I didn't expect you to stop. You never do what I ask."

Rosanna brushed her skirts down and tried to stand, only to fall back down again.

"Just help me up, you birdwit."

Dom's usual allure must have disappeared. He fumbled to help Rosanna to her feet. His sister seemed to throw the marquess off his game. Was there more between them than his friend had let on? No there couldn't be. She didn't appear to like him much, and Dom said more than once he didn't believe in love.

Alys rolled her eyes. "Nice. Remind me to steer clear of your friend."

"Dominic didn't mean her harm," James said, quietly. "He'd give his life to protect her."

"Clearly." Her voice was filled with sarcasm. "Please tell me he wouldn't bungle that too."

James shook his head. This wasn't going as he'd expected it too. He would have to steer the conversation in a different direction. "Did you miss me?"

Alys lifted her head upward, her gaze landing with his. "Miss you?" She stomped forward. "Did you actually ask me if I missed you? I can't have heard you correctly."

No, most definitely not going well. "So I take it that's a no?"

"Why would I miss James Kendall, His Grace,

the biggest jerk, also known as the Duke of Weston?" Alys jabbed her finger into his stomach. "The one who leaped up upon hearing my story and ran to London for business."

"It was important," James explained. "I had to act with all due haste."

Alys raised an eyebrow. "Oh? And what was so important? Was it a life of death situation? You couldn't stop for five seconds and explain it to me?" She tilted her head. "No? Just throw Alys to the wolves. Why not? It's not like she knew anyone in the mausoleum you left me in or what was likely to happen. Let's not forget the butcher you sent to look at poor pitiful mad me."

When she put it in those terms, he was a bloody arse. "I'm sorry. I didn't think..."

"Well, I already knew that. You didn't stop to think at all. You acted." Her hands were on her hips as she lectured him.

Oh hell, Dom was right, the ladies sure did like a good dressing down, as long as it wasn't them on the receiving end.

"So, out with it already. What was so important in London?"

Maybe if he kissed her. If her lips were occupied then she'd not have any room left to scream at him.

Now, that was a fine idea, and he wanted to feel her lips moving beneath his. It was a furious need building up inside him with each word that left her mouth. James pulled her into his arms and acted on that desire.

Alys moaned as he explored her lips with his. She was so sweet and pliant in his arms. Not the shrew lashing out at him. This was the Alys he wanted. The woman, warm and willing, who would grace his bed each night and maybe some of the days too. Fire burned through him, his manhood growing hard with need. James deepened the kiss. Alys opened her mouth, giving him the opportunity to push his tongue inside. Hers dueled with his for control, spiking his desire even higher. Her hand ran through his hair, tugging him closer.

If he didn't stop, he'd take her on the grassy knoll behind the manor. This wasn't the place to fulfill the need blazing through every inch of him. James had to stop. With every ounce of self-control he could muster, he took a step back. Gads, Alys was lovely. Her pink lips were plump and moist. Her hair a mussed mess of blonde curls, he must have loosened her pins.

"Sorry, I couldn't resist."

"Try a little harder next time," she demanded.

"I didn't hear you complaining." A cocky half-smile formed on his face.

Alys's hand hit his cheek, a sting filling it where it landed.

"Damn. Was that necessary?"

Alys smiled. "Yes, you were getting too full of yourself. Now tell me why you went to London?"

"To get a special license so we can marry."

Alys shook her head. "Fuck." She threw her hands up in the air. "Damn it all to hell. Why would you do something so silly?"

Where had she learned such profane language?

"Because you need the protection of my name if you're to remain in my time."

"That's too bad. I'm not marrying you, James. You can throw that license on the fire tonight. It's useless as is; might as well get something out of it."

With those words, she spun on her heels and left him staring after her. That hadn't gone as he'd planned either. When would he learn that Alys never once acted as he'd expected since he found her on the beach. James frowned. One thing at a time, he would obtain her agreement to be his wife. She'd see that it was the best option. He only needed a different approach.

CHAPTER 9

STUPID. JUST PLAIN STUPID, RIDICULOUS, OLD-fashioned man. How dare he think she'd marry him because he thought it was a good idea? Alys was more than capable of taking care of herself. She didn't need a man to provide for her. So what if she was in a throwback era where it was the man's job to take care of the female.

That did not mean she suddenly backpedaled herself into a state of dependency. She'd been taking care of herself perfectly fine for too many years. This idea that she'd be classified as helpless and in need of protection, it was plain wrong.

Alys stomped inside the manor and slammed the door behind her. She was done with the manor and its lofty duke. She had better things to do, like maybe finding a way back to where she belonged. A time when women were not looked down on as useless humans. Okay, perhaps there were a few that still saw them as inferior, but it wasn't the norm. Years of studying to be a doctor, and scrambling through the hierarchy at the hospital, had taught her a lot. She knew how to deal with male egos and how to knock them down a few pegs on the totem pole. Just because they were born with a penis did not make them superior.

A penis could be removed, and then where would the male population be? Nowhere. They'd be less than female then. Useless, penisless asswipes. An evil grin formed on her face. Not that she'd ever do that. The oath and all—do no harm—so she wouldn't, really.

"Alys will you please stop and listen to reason."

Alys spun on her heals and glared at James. "Excuse me?" She marched over to his side. "Did you imply that I'm not acting rationally? As in a fit of hysterics?"

James took a step back. "I didn't say that..."

"But you did, maybe not in so many words, but it was implied."

Alys clenched her fists at her side, suppressing the urge to slap him.

"I'm asking you to please listen to me," James pleaded. "I don't want anything to happen to you. This seemed like the most logical solution to ensure your protection. You don't have any family here. Who would you turn to?"

Alys narrowed her eyes and studied him. She didn't want to admit it, but he did have a valid point. The only people she knew in this time were his friends and family. Where would she go and what would she do if she left? Sailing to America was certainly an option—it was the land of opportunity. With her knowledge of the future, she could make a life there.

"I have options." Alys shook her head. "You might not like them, but I do not have to stay here and marry you. Why would I? You don't love me, and quite frankly, I don't love you. That's no basis for a marriage."

James sucked in a breath. "So what are these options?"

He completely ignored the part about love. Alys had to recognize a part of her was disappointed. What did she expect? Him to fall at her feet and profess undying love? This was not a fairy tale and a happy ending was nowhere in sight. She had to accept reality as it was. She was staying at Weston

Manor by his good graces. If she kept saying no, he could very well throw her out on her own.

"I can sell my jewelry and sail to America. New York would be a good place to start over. I know that prices these days are less exorbitant. If I'm lucky enough, I can get a relatively nice home and make a living there."

"Doing what?"

She would be laughed out onto the streets if she started practicing as a doctor—still she could try. "I'm a doctor. I have skills that most people these days know nothing about."

James snorted. "You think anyone would trust your skills? What kind of doctor are you?"

"I'm a surgeon"

"Really?" James raised an eyebrow. "So you know how to cut into someone. To what end? No one is going to trust your skills enough to let you anywhere near them with a knife."

"I'm very good, James. Top of my field. I was one of the few hand-selected for a fellowship at a prestigious hospital. It would be a waste not to use my talents." Alys sighed. "It would be an uphill battle, but I think in time people would come to me willingly. If I might be able to save their wretched hide, they will give in to their own pride."

James picked up her hand and stroked her wrist with his forefinger. "You may be right. They would eventually seek you out, but what would you do until then. How would you survive? Who would protect you?"

Tingles shot up her arm where his finger trailed. Alys tried to jerk her hand free from his, but he pulled tighter. "Let me go."

"Why?"

"Because I'm asking you to."

James shook his head. He slid his hands around her waist and pulled her closer. His breath warm against her cheek he whispered in her ear, "I don't think I can. You see, I've got this intense craving for you I can't resist any longer. I've tried and tried, and I gave into it earlier. I find I want to feel your lips against mine again."

"Please, James..."

Alys didn't know if she was begging him to let her go or kiss her. She held her breath in anticipation. What would he do? Would he give them what they both needed? As much as he infuriated her, Alys wanted him on a deeper level. She'd never desired a man as much as she did James. Her whole body lit up with eagerness.

He skimmed his lips across her cheeks. Butterfly

light as he pressed them over and over against her face, not leaving an inch uncovered. When he was done, he sought her lips in a searing kiss. Desire pooled deep inside of her. Alys wound her hands around his neck, pulling him closer, as close as they could be with a thousand layers of clothes between them. The kiss went on and on until their breaths mingled so much she didn't know if they were his or hers.

He lifted the palm of his hand and cupped her breast. Her bodice dipped lower as he untied the ribbons in front. He reached in and used his warm fingers to pinch her nipples. Alys moaned as the tingling between her thighs began to ravage her. She clenched her legs tightly together to alleviate the ache building. The more James played with her breasts, the more she wanted to feel him sliding deep inside of her.

She had to stop him. No, she had to beg him to take her upstairs. She needed...

James took a step back. His breath came out in rapid pants. "We can't do this here."

Alys nodded. "You're right."

"You must see it could be good between us. Please, marry me, Alys."

They were right back where they started. Why

did he think he needed to marry her so damned bad. Alys didn't follow his line of logic. They didn't have to get married to be together. An epiphany presented itself to her. Maybe if she explained to him that she wasn't a virgin, maybe he'd give up on this ridiculous notion they had to be husband and wife.

"James, there really is no need."

"Yes, there is. I desire you. I want you in my bed every night. There is no other woman I'd want to spend my life with, to make my duchess." James lifted her hand and kissed her palm. "Only you will do."

"I'm not a virgin," Alys blurted out.

James nodded. "I suspected as much. It matters not."

Alys may have misjudged him and how much of a true gentleman he was. His honor and belief was ingrained. He wasn't a rogue, at least not in the sense she'd read in so many romance novels. In her fantasies she had wanted one. James would never take advantage of her. He desired her yes, but he was too much of a gentleman to fully give into that passion. The little bit they'd done skated a line of impropriety. If he'd been a rogue, rake, or a scoundrel, he'd have already bedded her. James wouldn't fall easily to any seduction.

She'd wanted a man to want her, to love her, and essentially rock her world. Maybe she could settle for two out of three. James certainly wanted her. He had the potential to send her life completely off balance —the little taste she'd gotten of him had shown her that much.

If only he loved her...

"How can you say that? In these times virginity equaled purity. No man wanted an unchaste woman as their wife."

At least that was how Alys understood this time to be. Had she been wrong?

"Some men do feel that way. I'm not one of them. If you promise to not take other men to your bed once we're wed, that is all that matters to me." James stroked her hair softly. "You're beautiful, enchanting, spirited, and intelligent. I would be honored to have you. Say yes."

"I want to say yes. You're definitely making it hard to say no." Alys bit her lip. "Can I think about it a little while?"

James nodded. "I will give you a week." He pulled her tight against him. His hardness pressed against her belly. "After that, I make no promises. I will form a siege the likes of which you've never experienced before." He leaned in closer and pressed his lips against her ear, whispering, "You won't say no; you'll be begging me to take you any way and every way imaginable."

"James, I'm ready to do that now. Lead the way, and we can explore all the possibilities."

He took a step back and laughed. A wicked grin filled his handsome face, leaving a thousand flutters floating around her midsection.

"No, not until you agree to marry me. If I have to wait for your assent, you have to wait for the pleasures we can find together."

"You're evil." Alys glared. A hiss of breath fell between her parted lips. "You deny yourself as much as you do me."

"The difference is I want so much more than one night. I want every night. If I give in to you now, I won't get them." He crossed his arms over his chest. "The best things are worth waiting for, and you, my dear, are more than worth the wait."

Alys stuck her tongue out at him. "You're a fool."

"Maybe, but I'm willing to play one for you."

Alys didn't know what to say to that. What had she gotten herself into? A week he said, how was she going to resist him for a whole damned week? Maybe she should give in and give him what he wanted—no, that was a horrible idea.

Once she gave in...

He'd think he could get his way in everything. She might cave and marry him, but she'd not do it sooner than the week allotted. If she wanted to start the marriage off right, she'd have to stick to her guns, and live through a hellish week of constant arousal.

"Do you have any clue what that is going to entail?" Alys asked. "What a whole week will be like? You won't be able to touch me, pull me close, press your lips anywhere on my body. If you're going to make me wait, you will have to give me the distance promised."

"As long as you, in return, agree to take my offer seriously and consider all the benefits, I can manage to keep my hands to myself."

Alys smirked. "Oh, I can do that." She'd also make him miserable the entire time. He'd rue the day he ever denied her anything. "It will be an interesting week, Your Grace."

James raised an eyebrow. "Why do I not like the sound of that?"

Alys laughed. "Why, I don't know what you mean." She batted her eyelashes. "I cross my heart, I will do exactly as I promised. I will think about what it will be like to be your duchess every waking hour." Probably in her naughty dreams too.

James looked at her skeptically. "All right, I will leave you to your reflections."

Oh, James, you poor sod. You don't know what I have planned, but you will soon enough. If Alys would be in agony of unrequited desire, James would be writhing in it.

Alys watched him stroll away. His perfect ass right in her line of sight—she licked her lips. Soon she'd have him naked and begging. A week he said, it would be a fascinating experiment to see how long his resolve lasted.

CHAPTER 10

JAMES RODE HIS STALLION ACROSS A NEARBY field. The wind whipped through his hair as he led his horse in a full gallop. He'd needed the exercise. Escape was the only solution, as Alys continued to drive him insane.

To think he'd believed she might be mad at first.

No, she had much more nefarious plans afoot. Alys was a temptress leading him down a path of enticement, the likes of which he'd never experienced in his entire life. They'd made a devil's bargain, and he was getting the raw end of it. He'd given her his word, never taking into consideration her brand of thinking might be testing him. And oh, how she'd tested him.

But he was determined. He would win her.

James played for keeps, and the prize was worth everything to him. In the end, one week was nothing compared to the lifetime he had planned. Alys would see he was a solid, steady, dependable option. Once he secured her consent to marry him though, he'd not hold back the desire raging through him.

Instead of finding peace in his study, he left his home and sought relief in the only way he'd allow himself. Exhausting, brutal, and mind-numbing exercise. Once he returned home, he'd be too exhausted to be tempted by a fair lass with golden locks trailing down her back in enticing curls.

A rider approached in the distance. James slowed his stallion as they neared. He recognized Dom as he came nearer. His friend slowed down as he brought his horse along side of his.

"Is there a problem?" James asked.

Dom shook his head. "Not unless you consider the two harridans taking siege to your home something of a concern."

James snorted. Dominic had no idea—or maybe he did. He narrowed his eyes and studied his best friend. "What did I miss?"

"Nothing of import. Rosanna is driving me mad." Dom looked away, not meeting James eyes.

"Why is my sister making a nuisance of herself?"

James was rather confused. "What has she done now?"

"She is just being her usual impetuous self. I caught her spying on me earlier. Have no idea what she thought to discover. Don't worry though. I set her straight." Dominic shrugged. "As to why she's being difficult... I'm not certain, maybe it's your reluctant bride-to-be's influence."

James didn't doubt Alys had some influence on Rosanna's actions. It might be a good thing, might not. Only time would tell. "Alys is very opinionated." What an understatement. "She has no problems voicing them either."

"I've noticed. This is why you found me out riding. I needed to escape."

"Me too," James agreed. "I have been in need of exercise often these days."

Dominic laughed. "Miss Alys is leading you astray?"

She was trying. Oh Lord, was she trying. "Not at all. Things are going rather well with us. Soon she will agree to marry me, and I *will* have exactly what I want."

A woman full of fire and passion in his bed every night.

"So you say." Dominic chuckled. "What does the lady want?"

To go home. James frowned. Even if he could give her the option, would he let her go? He didn't know if he could. In a short time, Alys had come to mean so much to him. She was a breath of fresh air he didn't know he needed, not until he found her on his beach. No, she was his. Soon, she'd see it too. They belonged together. Alys could never leave him.

"I have no doubts. She wants the same thing, but she's playing hard to get." James smiled. "You know how a lady is. They have to pretend as if they don't want you so they can attempt to gain the upper hand. I won't allow it. I have plans, and they don't include caving before her."

"I don't know, James. Sometimes caving is the only option you have."

James tilted his head. "How so?"

"If, in the end, it gets you what you want most, why not give in? It could mean you can have it that much sooner, and think of how glorious it would be."

"No." James shook his head. "It wouldn't work with Alys. She's got a stubborn streak. This is a battle of wills I intend to win. If it requires breaking or bending, I will...as a last resort."

"You know her better than I do, but I think you might be making a mistake."

James didn't believe so. He may not have known Alys long, but it was enough to understand her motivation. She was an open book and spoke her mind. Her pursuit of him was her way of seeing how serious he was. Well, she was about to find out he kept his word. Thank God, he only had one more day, and then he could demand her answer. The past six had been excruciating on his libido.

"Have you ever been in love, Dom?" James shook his head. "Never mind, I know the answer."

Dominic pulled up short and stared at him. "Do you believe you love your Alys?"

Did he? How was he to know? Love wasn't something he understood or knew anything about. His family was...difficult. They didn't show affection easily. When they were boys, he and Edward had been close. At least until his father started to groom Edward to take over the estate. James had to fend for himself after that. It'd been quite lonely. Rosanna was ten years younger than him. They didn't have as close of a relationship, but he adored her nonetheless. But loving a woman? James didn't know if he even knew how. Passion he knew about in spades, but it wasn't the same thing. He did know that much.

"I don't know what I feel for her." Simple, the truth, and the only answer he could give. He had other reasons for asking Dominic about love though. He spoke as if he knew something about giving in and accepting your fate. "I'm wondering where your words of wisdom are coming from."

"I am not, nor have I ever been, in love." Dom smiled, but it didn't reach his eyes. "I'm not sure I'm capable of it."

James nodded. It was one of the reasons he and Dom had become close at Eton. They'd had a lonely childhood and latched onto each other once they met. James's father had been indifferent, but Dom's had been abusive; it hardened him early on.

"Then, by all means, explain this push to give in to Alys?" James didn't understand it. "If you don't think it's about love, what do you believe is going on?"

"Alys is driving your relationship now, whether you believe it or not. She drove you out of your own home. You are growling at everyone in the household. The servants are cowering in corners. I haven't eaten a decent meal in days. I saw a maid drop a whole tray of lemon cakes the other day and cringed —they looked so tasty. Not to mention, none of them are in the mood to speak."

James pinned him with a glare. "So, what you're really saying is my frustrations have also transferred to you, and you want to put both of us out of our misery." He wanted to laugh, he really did, but he couldn't. Dom was complaining because he couldn't seduce his servants. Something he should not condone. Servants talked, and the last thing he needed was any sort of unrest with his staff, which meant he'd have to talk to them and assure them he'd be less difficult soon. He didn't want to lose good help over his own temperament.

"Exactly." Dom snapped his fingers. "You're going to be a good chap and help me out right?"

"Dom," James said.

"Yes?"

"Go to the devil."

James flicked the reins and set the horse on a canter toward home, leaving his friend behind. He could sort his own problems out. His talk with Dom made one thing abundantly clear. He would need to deal with Alys, and maybe one day early didn't make a difference. It was time to turn the tables a bit on her and see if he could get what he wanted a little sooner. He reached the stable and hopped off his horse. He handed the reins to a groom, then turned on his heels, and headed back to the manor. He entered and found the woman running through his thoughts in the sitting room.

"Did you have a good ride?"

"Yes," he said. His lips tilted into a cocky grin as he studied her lush frame. "Not the ride I desire, but I'm sure you'll accommodate me soon."

Her cheeks tinged a bright pink at his words. She licked her lips and stared into his eyes. "Well, cowboy, there are rides, and then there are *rides*." Alys stood up and sashayed over to his side, stopping mere inches in front of him. She lifted her hand and trailed her fingers across his chest. "Just say the word, and I'm more than happy to demonstrate the difference."

"Cowboy?" Where did she get these words from?

Alys's laughter echoed through the room. "I keep forgetting. Even that is too far into the future for you."

"What is a cowboy?"

"A man who is a wicked horse rider, can rustle cattle, work rope like nobody's business, and lives for the danger of ranch life." Alys grinned. "To put it simply, they will revolutionize an industry in the western states of America, a little south too, I guess."

"I can ride a horse." James didn't like how she

talked about these cowboys. She seemed attracted to them. "Why would I want to do the rest?"

"Because it's dangerous?" Alys shrugged. "Why does a man do anything?"

Hmm... Maybe she had a point. "Fair enough. Now back to the riding." James hated to admit it, but he only had one thing on his mind. "If I were willing..."

Alys interrupted, "You want to see if I can put my money where my mouth is?"

Suddenly James couldn't stop staring at her mouth. What did that have to do with money? "I have better things you can do with your mouth."

"I'm sure you do." Alys smirked. "In fact, I have a few in mind that you can do with yours."

He groaned. Images assaulted his mind. He wanted to do so many things to her he ached. "We have some things to settle first." He moved closer, and pulled her against his chest. "As much as I'd like to carry you upstairs and ravish you," James said. Oh Lord, did he want to. "It's not that simple. We made a bargain. I refuse to go back on my word."

"So, big guy, what is your solution?"

"Say yes, I'm begging you."

Alys shook her head. "No deal. I have one more day."

She lifted her hands and wound them around his neck. Her fingers trailed along his neck and played with the strands of his hair.

"You're determined to see this through?" He leaned in closer. Their lips so close they almost touched. "You would deny what we both want?"

"You're doing the same," she said, her tone raspy with desire.

So stubborn, and beautiful. James could give her the extra day. She was right. They were both aching with need. He was doing to her as much as she was to him. It was a give and take—just not the one they both craved.

Maybe a little taste to get by. *Why not?*

Because he said he'd not touch her for a week? Wait, he was touching her now. He'd already broken a part of his oath. Bloody hell.

"Then why don't we do something about that?" he asked.

Alys met his lips with hers, pushing her sweet tongue inside his mouth. James groaned and gave in, letting himself enjoy the thrill of having her body pressed fully against his. The kiss went on and on, neither one of them getting enough of each other. The self-imposed ban on touching had an effect they'd not bargained on. They would surely combust if they kept going.

James let her go and took a step back, their breathing ragged.

"That was amazing," Alys said, her lips full and puffy from their kiss.

"Think how good it will be once you agree to be my wife."

James nodded and spun on his heels, leaving her with her mouth gaping open in shock.

He had to put distance between them and fast. She didn't know how close he'd come to taking her on the floor of the sitting room. One more second, and he'd have stripped all of her clothes off and tasted every inch of her delectable body.

One more day—he could do it.

James wanted to win, and in order to win sacrifices sometimes had to be made. Being hard as a rock for a week was one he'd been willing to endure. And the pain now coursing through him was worth it too. He'd sate his need in the only way allowed to him, at least until Alys was his.

ALYS ROLLED OVER ONTO HER SIDE AND HIT *something warm and solid. Her eyes fluttered open, and she met the deep blue gaze of the man she couldn't get off her mind. James stared back at her, resting his head in the palm of his hand while digging his elbow into the bed.*

"Why are you in my bed?"

"Didn't you invite me to join you?" His half-smile filled with cockiness as he ran his hand through her unbound hair. "I believe you said anytime I wanted—and I've never wanted anything more."

Alys groaned as heat spread through her belly and desire flared red-hot in her blood. "You said you wouldn't come to me. You wanted marriage first."

He trailed kisses over her cheeks and settled his

lips against hers. A soft kiss filled with a promise of more. "In time, you will give me all I want. For now, I will take everything you're willing to give."

Alys ran her hand across his naked chest and dug her fingers deep into his muscled torso. "It's about damn time you saw the brilliance of my offer."

James laughed. "Darling, I always knew you were brilliant. As to your offer, I'd be lying if I said I hadn't been tempted from the start."

A cold breeze traveled up her legs and hips, cooling her heated skin—Alys's nightgown pooled around her waist. With light strokes, he reached down and grazed her flesh with his fingertips. He stroked her center, building her desire to a breaking point.

"Please, James."

"I will and can give you so much, Alys."

"I know, don't stop," she begged.

The pressure built up inside of her. She was so close. Finally, she would have James on her terms and not his. The pleasure of him bending to her will had been her goal all along. She wanted to prove a point to him, and now—oh yes, now she would feel him ride her into ecstasy.

Just when her orgasm was about to hit its peak and shatter her into a million shards—he stopped.

Her eyes flew open and his gaze pinned her in

place. Something wasn't right. He didn't seem himself. Why would he build her up only to deny her? Again. This was becoming common between them. They would parlay back and forth, dance into each other's arms, and yank back as if being too close would destroy something deep inside of them.

"James?"

"You know this isn't right, Alys."

The look he gave her was so forlorn it broke her heart. What was she doing to him? This was part of who he was. James was a good, honorable man. She was asking him to change and bend to her will. How selfish was she? When had she started to emulate her sister Regina? This was something she would do, put her needs first.

"I'm so sorry James."

He caressed her hair with his hand, his fingers treading through the strands. "I know."

"Will you forgive me?"

"Always," he promised. "But it's time for me to go. I can't be here."

Go? He couldn't go. She wanted him to understand. He had to know why she was acting so horridly. She'd been pushed aside her whole life in favor of Regina. Just once, she wanted someone to see her and love her. How could she promise him forever when *she didn't know if it was hers to offer him? What if she left him alone and returned back to her time? Where would that leave him? Not to mention, he hadn't once claimed to love her. There had to be more. Otherwise, why should she even begin to contemplate marriage?*

"No, wait don't go—"

Alys reached out for him, but he disintegrated right before her eyes. He had been so solid in front of her, and then poof *he was gone. What the hell?*

She woke up with a gasp. Her heart pounded hard in her chest. Her gaze flew to the spot on the bed where she could have sworn James had lain.

It was only a dream. A very erotic, sensual dream.

But it also told her something very important. She couldn't ask James to give her something that would destroy something inside of him. He wanted to marry her. That was his way of making sure she was protected. He never once denied he wanted more, or how much he desired her. If that was all he wanted from her, he'd had plenty of opportunities. It was oh so wrong of her to ask him to bend his ethics and values because she didn't think marriage was the best choice.

If she couldn't marry him, she'd have to leave. It

was for the best. James deserved more than she could offer him.

A door slammed shut, echoing through her room.

What the hell? Who was up and moving around at this late hour?

She slid off her bed and tiptoed over to the door. Maybe someone was up to no good. Wouldn't it be fun to catch them? Alys grabbed her wrapper that hung by the door and put it over her nightgown.

She eased her door open and peeked through the slit. A tall, imposing figure, most likely male, walked past her door. It could be James, or Dominic. Hell, it could be a servant for all she could see in the dark. Alys opened the door wider and slipped out. She watched his movements as he strolled down the hallway. As he turned the corner to head toward the stairs, she could make out his face in profile from moonlight streaming through a nearby window.

It was Dominic. Where could he be heading?

She hurried after him to find out. One day, her curiosity would get the better of her.

When she reached the bottom of the stairs, she couldn't find him. Where could he have gone? She went to James's study to see if that is where he might be. When she entered the room, no one appeared to be inside. She went farther in and looked out the window that overlooked the cliffs. She squinted and could make out someone moving in the distance.

Was it Dominic?

Even if it was, she couldn't do anything about it. She wasn't dressed to chase a man down the cliff tunnels. She would have to ask him about it in the morning—well, later. Technically, it was morning, even though it was the middle of the night.

She couldn't help wondering if the information that Rosanna told her about Edward had something to do with Dominic's late night visit to the cliffs. Was he still investigating the smugglers? Maybe she should tell James about Rosanna's suspicions. She didn't know much about this time period. While she enjoyed history, facts got muddled a bit sometimes inside her head. The actual dates for significant events anyway—she had more important things to remember.

Nothing would get solved staring out the window. Dominic could be down by the cliffs for hours. Alys needed to go back to her room and attempt to get more sleep. If luck was on her side, she'd have restful dreams. James had haunted them enough for one evening.

Alys sighed and left James's study to go back to her bedroom. She shuffled her feet across the soft carpet trailing the hallway to her room, her head down to watch her steps in the dark, lost in her own thoughts.

"What are you doing awake?"

Alys started. "Good grief, James. Are you trying to give me a heart attack?"

"A what?" he asked, puzzled.

"Never mind, it doesn't matter. You scared me."

When had he come out of his room? Why did the man move so infernally quietly? He could sneak up on anyone and get the drop on them. Why was he skulking outside her door? Did he ever sleep? He still wore his breeches and white linen shirt. Surely he had something he wore as nightclothes. *I wonder if he sleeps naked...* Alys dropped that line of thought as quick as it entered her mind. She would not let herself imagine him sleeping nude.

"My apologies, I didn't mean to frighten you." He pressed his lips together as he studied her. The moonlight illuminated the hallway enough for her to make out his features in the shadows.

"Don't worry about it. I was lost in my own thoughts and easily startled."

James nodded. "Are you having trouble sleeping?"

Wouldn't he like to know? He probably

wondered if thoughts of him kept her awake—he'd be right in assuming it. He was the reason she'd woken up from one of the most erotic dreams she'd ever had in her life. Too bad it also illustrated how selfish she was being with him.

"Something woke me up, and I couldn't go back to sleep afterward."

"Oh?" James frowned. "What was it?"

Why was he so damned curious? Alys wasn't used to be on the receiving end of a constant bombardment of questions. Usually she was the one pestering someone for answers.

Alys rubbed her hands across her face. "It doesn't matter. Did you need something from me?"

Whatever Dom was doing she could figure it out later. It wasn't important and could wait. Her heart still pounded rapidly in her chest. The excitement level had risen considerably in a short time.

"No." He shook his head. "Why do you ask?"

"You're standing in front of my door. In fact, you are almost inside the door frame as if you just exited my chambers."

"I saw it open. It concerned me, so I went inside to check on you." He looked back into her room. "It worried me that you were not there. I'm relieved to find you standing before me."

Alys chewed on her bottom lip. He didn't seem at all affected by her. He was standing in front of her, all cool and collected, no passion in sight. Her "dream James" had been hot and ready. If she needed any further signs, this was a blaring one before her. It made her feel rather small and inconsequential in the grand scheme of things.

"Right. I wouldn't want to worry you." She let her gaze fall, disappointment evident in her voice. Leaving James was the only decision she could make.

"Something *is* bothering you. Tell me what it is."

"I'm fine."

James stared at her and folded his arms across his chest. He didn't say a word for several seconds. When Alys didn't either, he raised an eyebrow expectantly.

"I'm serious. You don't have to stress about anything concerning me."

In the morning, after they both got some more rest, she'd tell him her decision to leave. The act of returning to her own time was lost to her, so she'd do the only thing she could. She'd go home to the country she belonged in at least. There she might have a fighting chance.

"I don't believe you."

James wasn't going to leave this alone. She'd have

to tell him something, so he'd drop the protective alpha male stance he had going on. Although—she trailed her eyes up and down his body—it did look rather well on him.

"I saw Dominic go outside. He was heading toward the cliffs."

His head turned toward the window. "It's not safe at night, but I'm sure he's fine."

Alys rolled her eyes. How like a man. It was fine because Dominic was male. "Did Rosanna ever tell you about the conversation she overheard between Edward and Dominic?"

His gaze landed on hers. "No, why should it matter what my brother and best friend spoke about. I'm sure it was nothing of importance."

It was Alys's turn to raise an eyebrow. "Seriously? You are not even remotely curious?"

He shrugged. "Don't see any reason I should be."

Alys narrowed her eyes in disbelief. Why had she thought she'd like men from this time period? She must have lost some important brain cells somewhere along the line. Maybe studying the human anatomy too much left her deficient to understand the male brain.

"I'll do you a favor and tell you anyway." She held up her hand when he opened his mouth to interrupt her. "No, let me finish before you tell me all the reasons you don't want to know. Edward went to Dominic because there was smuggling here in the cliffs. I don't know why he thought Dominic would care—but not long after, Edward died."

"One doesn't necessarily have to do with the other."

"Sometimes a coincidence is just that, yes, I agree. Other times, it is far more complicated and convoluted than you first thought. Otherwise, how would I be here?"

She really hated pointing out the obvious. James needed to realize he should at least ask Dominic about Edward's concerns.

"I concede your point. Some things are simply not explainable. This, however is. Dominic is my friend. If he knew something concerning Edward's death he would have already told me."

"I suppose you know him better than I do." Alys shrugged. "I'd still ask him. But that's just me."

"Don't concern yourself with it. I will handle the matter."

Alys didn't have it in her to argue with him. In the long run, the outcome didn't impact her decision. James would handle it the way he saw fit. The little jaunt downstairs and the remnants of her dream left her too drained to care. Maybe she'd muster up the energy before she departed and said goodbye. For now, she'd let him think she let it go.

"Whatever, James. It's late, and I'm going to try to get some more sleep."

He bowed his head in agreement. "It is. Sleep well, Alys."

That was it? He wasn't even going to attempt to kiss her? Disappointment filled her heart.

"Right, you too," she said and brushed past him to go into her chambers. Once she was in her room he called out to her.

"Oh, one other thing."

She looked over her shoulder, her gaze meeting his.

"I will have an answer from you at daybreak." He crossed his arms over his chest. "And it will be the one I want to hear."

She raised an eyebrow. "And if it isn't?"

His smile was full of cockiness that shown bright in the moonlit hallway. "I am afraid you will have to wait and find out because, my dear," wickedness filled his voice, "I intend to win, and the first rule of battle is not to let the opponent know your plan. It's the best guarantee of success."

He took two quick strides into her room and

pulled her into his embrace. His lips landed on hers in a searing kiss. It was so quick Alys thought she might have imagined it. James spun on his heels and left the room, shutting the door with a soft click.

Oh hell, the man sure knew how to leave a girl on pins and needles.

CHAPTER 12

JAMES HADN'T SLEPT AT ALL. ALYS INVADED HIS dreams and didn't leave much room for a peaceful night's rest. In fact, it had been anything but restful. He'd tossed and turned the entire night. Something bothered him, but he couldn't figure out what. So he'd given up and went in search for the woman who haunted his every waking moment—and those he'd managed to be asleep.

Only to find she was not in her room.

Panic seized him, the likes of which he'd never experienced before. It had never crossed his mind she might leave. The relief that flooded him at the sight of her returning to her room washed over him in waves.

His Alys was entirely too curious for her own good.

It didn't help she'd managed to evade him the entire day. So, not only was he tired, but he was beyond frustrated. There was one thing he could take care of...her concerns about Dominic's jaunt in the middle of the night. James doubted there was much to worry about on that front. Dominic was a grown man and could take care of himself. He wouldn't bother to interrogate his friend. It was odd, but Dominic could act rather strange at times. He had no doubts about his best friend, there was no cause to.

Dominic would tell him what he was doing down at the cliffs in the middle of the night. It could have been for any reason. James didn't know what, but he'd find out. Maybe the information Alys had departed held an ounce of truth. James didn't doubt that Edward discussed something with his friend; he doubted it had resulted in his brother's death. Nothing nefarious could be happening near his home. He'd have gotten wind of it when he returned.

Smuggling was a way of life for those who lived along the coast. During the war with France, it helped provide for the community. He didn't have to like it to understand the motivation behind it. As long as it didn't involve him in any way, he turned a blind eye to it. Edward would have done the same. If he'd had a concern, it was far more serious than mere smuggling.

He wanted to hear Alys say she agreed to marry him. He had to pin her down long enough for her to do so. She would soon....

But he'd have to let it go for a brief time because Dominic needed to answer some niggling questions that wouldn't stop rolling through his thoughts. So instead of searching out the woman he couldn't stop thinking about, he went to find his best friend and found him lounging in the library—or rather passed out on a settee against the back of the room, near an open window.

James shook his head and crossed the room. He stopped in front of Dominic and shoved him off the settee. He hit the floor with a loud thud.

"What the..." Dominic sputtered the words as he sat up. His glimpsed up at James and swore. "Bloody hell, was that necessary, James?"

"Yes. Why are you sleeping here when you have a perfectly good bed in your chamber?" He frowned. "Why are you resting at all? It's rather late in the day for a nap."

"I was up a good part of the night. I didn't mean

to slumber here." Dominic scrubbed his hands over his face. "I didn't get much sleep, and I don't appreciate being shoved onto the floor. What's got you in such a foul mood?"

"Alys saw you walking toward the cliffs last night."

James didn't like that she was disturbed in any way. He wanted her happy. More importantly, he wanted her sleeping in his arms each night. If he were being honest, he wanted a lot more than that from her.

"Why in the blazes was she up so late?"

Deflection—Dom was rather good at it. Answering a question with another one. He'd not get away with it so easily this time. James would demand to be told what he'd been up to in the middle of the night.

"Doesn't matter. Where were you heading at such a later hour?"

With a smug grin on his face, Dom stood and looked James in the eyes. "You want the details of the tryst I had scheduled? Never did take you for one who liked to gossip and hear scandalous details, but if you want to know, I can tell..."

"No." James held up his hand. "Don't say any more. I do not want to be privy to your depravity."

Dominic wiggled his eyebrows and scooted back up onto the settee. "You sure? You're missing out. The chit I had..."

"Enough, Dom." James glared at him. "I said I didn't want to know. Please refrain from giving me any unnecessary details."

"Was just answering your question." He shrugged. "No reason to be so surly."

This is what he got for listening to Alys's concerns in the early morning hours. He loved Dom, but he was a bit of a rakehell. James didn't hold it against him, but he wanted more than a different lady each night in his bed. He only wanted one woman, and that woman was Alys. Now he needed to secure her agreement. He'd not take any answer but yes from her pretty pink lips.

"Pardon me. I've not been sleeping well."

And understatement if there ever was one—sleep had evaded him near on a week.

"You should give in and take Miss Alys to your bed. You know you want to."

James shook his head. Dominic didn't understand his motivations. How was he to explain it to him when he saw women as nothing but sport? "I will not take her to bed until she is my wife in truth."

"Then maybe you should find something to

occupy your mind. It's not my fault she keeps saying no."

"I'll have an answer from her before this day ends," James said firmly. "She promised me one."

"What if it's not the answer you're hoping for?"

She wouldn't say no. Alys wanted him just as much as he wanted her.

"It won't be."

"I hope so. I really do, but you should prepare for all possibilities." Dominic looked past James. "Rosanna, I thought you were above skulking around and eavesdropping. Ladies have better things to do with their time."

"You know nothing about *ladies*," Rosanna sneered. "You keep company with common trollops."

His sister stepped into the room her skirts rustling with each movement. Her eyes blazed with fury at she scowled at Dominic. When had Rosanna started to hate him with such passion? James thought they had gotten along. When had it changed? What had Dom done to her to create the animosity? She was so kind with everyone. It had to have been something awful to make her loathe him so.

"Rosanna, did you need something?"

"I was hoping to have a word with you, but

every time I come anywhere in your immediate vicinity you run away and disappear for hours on end."

"The Duke of Weston does not run."

Rosanna rolled her eyes. "I apologize. Gallop across the fields like hellhounds are on your tail."

Dominic laughed; it echoed through the room and grated on his eardrums.

"Damned if she doesn't have a point, James."

He glared at his friend. "I don't need you encouraging her."

"I don't need him around at all." His sister shot daggers in Dominic's direction. "When are you leaving?"

"You wound me, Ros." Dom flashed her a wicked grin. "Why would you want me to leave?"

James had to suppress the urge to wipe the grin off Dominic's too pretty face. If Rosanna hadn't appeared unaffected by it, he might have. He didn't like his best friend flirting with his baby sister.

Ignoring Dominic, Rosanna turned her attention back to James. "As soon as Lord Seabrook departs, there is something I wish to discuss with you in private."

James sighed. "Dominic, can you give me some privacy with my sister?"

"Certainly. Ros and I can resume our pleas-antries at another time."

"Please, don't hold your breath." She tossed the words at him with an evil glint shining in her eyes. "Or rather, please do. It might save me the trouble of having to listen to your rambling idiocy in the future."

"Oh, sweet, I do love your thorny side." Dominic wiggled his eyebrows. "Such fire." He blew her a kiss as he strolled out of the room.

"What a—" She stomped her foot and paced around the room in a rant. "That man is insufferable."

"Dominic is harmless," James said soothingly. "What did you want to discuss with me?"

She glared at the door Dominic had exited.

"Rosanna," James said her name again to gain her attention.

"What?" She turned to him. "Oh, yeah. It's about Alys."

Fear seized his heart. What did she have to tell him about his intended?

"Yes?" he encouraged.

"I think she might be planning on leaving us."

No, he wouldn't let her. James needed her. She was more important than everything...even his own life. He'd do anything for her. Alys would not leave him. She had come to mean a lot to him in a short time. The idea of not having her in his life scared him. If she could find a way back to her time... It would devastate him. He'd come to believe they'd be together forever. As much as he would love to keep her by his side, a part of him knew that he might have to let her go. James hoped that, if left with a choice, she would decide to remain with him.

After the war, he'd almost given up on finding happiness. Then he'd stumbled onto a beautiful woman passed out on his beach and suddenly everything made sense to him. Alys wasn't misplaced in time—she'd been sent to save his soul. The horror of war had tainted him. The things he had needed to do to survive... He never wanted to relive that again. She was a breath of fresh air he hadn't realized he needed.

"Alys isn't leaving me."

Rosanna bit her lip. "I saw her a few minutes ago. She looked so sad and resolved."

At least she wasn't avoiding everyone—only him.

Maybe she missed her family. James could understand that. She had no one in this time. He'd go to her and make her understand once and for all that she belonged with him.

"Did she say something to make you think she planned on leaving?"

Rosanna shook her head. "No, not exactly. I mean she didn't come out and say she was. It's more of a feeling I had." She stared at him. "She said she doesn't truly belong here. That she's—how did she say it—something about a fish out of water. Nothing and no one is familiar, and she couldn't figure out her place in this world."

"I see," James muttered.

"Do you? Because I don't. What does she mean she doesn't know her place?" Rosanna shrugged. "The whole fish thing was just...odd."

James smiled. Alys did say the strangest things at times. It was one of the things he found endearing about her—what had drawn him to her from the start. Everything about her called out to him. She soothed his unruly soul.

"Alys is one of a kind."

"Are you going to speak with her?" Rosanna asked. "I like her, and I don't want her to leave."

"I rather like her myself." James kissed his sister on the forehead. "Don't worry about Alys. I will ensure she doesn't go anywhere."

Rosanna frowned. "You're in love with her, aren't you?"

Was he? Maybe he did love Alys. He didn't know for sure. He knew that he couldn't go on living without her. That very well could be what it meant to love someone. How was he to know when he'd never been in love before?

"I don't know how I feel about Alys, but I do know she makes everything in my life better."

Rosanna smiled. "Sounds like love to me. At least, the love Alys speaks about. She said love is something you willingly leap into."

That was exactly something Alys would say. She'd said something similar to him once—*"Love is a dream, a whimsical journey constantly surprising you. It's not meant for fools. At least, not in the way you believe. True love is a journey you willingly leap into. You'll see one day. I will help you."*

Maybe that is what she needed from him, she'd promised to help him, and James intended to ensure she kept it. He would willingly give his heart over into her care. He could do that if it kept her with him forever.

Because James would not accept anything less than that.

"Do you know where Alys is now?"

Rosanna looked toward the window that over-looked the cliffs in the distance. They were beautiful and treacherous. The estate was built alongside of them for their defensive position. James had a very bad feeling about where Alys had gone.

"I think she said something about a walk to clear her thoughts," Rosanna said. "She was heading toward the cliffs last I saw her."

"She wouldn't..."

"Wouldn't what?" Rosanna asked. "James what do you think Alys is about to do?"

The cliffs? No, she wouldn't try to jump off and return home. James wouldn't allow it. He ran out the door, leaving Rosanna with her mouth gaping open. He had no time to explain. He had to stop Alys before she did something they'd both regret.

Alys was not going to leave him—ever.

CHAPTER 13

ALYS WALKED DOWN THE TUNNELS TOWARD THE beach below. She'd had a lot to think about when she awoke. It had taken her quite a while to fall asleep after James had left her. After she dreamed about him, she'd thought her course was clear. But maybe—just possibly—it wasn't.

The sun was low on the horizon as she stepped onto the beach—a brilliant orange against the water. Waves crashed against the shoreline. Alys took a deep breath and closed her eyes as the wind blew across her face.

"Well, what do we have here?"

Alys spun around, her gaze falling on a man with long brown hair. It was pulled back behind his head.

His face boasted a full beard that had seen better days.

"Who are you?" Alys asked.

She'd never seen him before, and rather wished she didn't have to look upon him at all. He was covered in dirt that appeared to blend into his beard. His clothes were nothing better than rags with holes scattered throughout. He was quite disgusting. Alys wondered if he knew what the benefit of a bath would do for him.

"Now, don't be asking questions you don't really want the answers too."

Alys shook her head. "Don't presume to know what is going on inside of my head."

"Little lass like you? Seems I can guess exactly what's going on in that pretty little head of yours." He turned and spit in the sand. "You're looking at me like you would cringe at the very idea of touching me. Not good enough for the likes of you, am I?"

Alys took a step back. This man was deranged. "I don't know you, and no I don't want to. I think you should go. This is private property."

"I can't oblige that request." He took a step toward her and grabbed her arm pulling her against his chest. "You're going to have to come with me."

"No, let me go. Please," Alys begged.

"Too late. You've done got yourself involved in matters that don't concern you."

Alys turned her nose away from him and held her hand across her face to block out the smell. The stench coming from the man turned her stomach. It was a combination of overindulgence in alcohol mixed with foul body odor. If he didn't let go of her soon, she'd lose the contents of her stomach all over him. It would only add to the already grotesque aroma filling her nose. She made one more attempt to free herself from his grasp. Her legs got caught in her skirts and she fell backward, but he prevented her from hitting the sandy beach.

Damn skirts. She'd kill for a pair of jeans. The rotten bastard needed to feel her knee hit him in the balls. Then he'd be cowering before her.

"Fighting will get you nowhere. Be a good lass and do as I say."

"No," Alys declared. "I will do no such thing."

He pulled her against him and rubbed himself all over her. Alys held her breath and elbowed him in the stomach. He hunched over enough for her to punch him in the nose. Blood pooled out of it after she heard a soft crack from the impact. She'd not taken self-defense classes for no reason.

He let her go to hold his nose.

"You're a crazy she-devil," he spat out. "You'll pay for that."

He stood to his full height, pulled a pistol out, and then pointed it right at her.

Alys took a step back and held up her hands.

"Now let's not do anything stupid. Put the gun away before someone gets hurt." Alys took two slow steps back. Maybe he was a horrible shot. "Go about what you were doing and I'll return home."

"I already told you." He held the gun steady he kept it pointed on at her. "It's too late for that."

Alys saw movement out of the corner of her eye, to her right and behind the horrid man with the gun. She didn't know who or what it was, but she hoped it wasn't someone there to help murder her. She was afraid to look away from the present danger.

"It's never too late to stop doing something that is bad," Alys coaxed. "This is very, very bad. Put it away and let me leave."

"Alys, get down," James called.

He jumped the man with the gun and wrestled him for control.

"No, you fool. What are you doing?" she shouted.

She didn't know what to do. The two men struggled for the gun and neither one appeared to be giving up. Then a shot went off, and James fell to the ground.

Alys screamed.

The evil man ran in the opposite direction disappearing into the caves. Alys rushed toward James. He had a gaping wound in his upper left abdomen. She kneeled in the sand to check the abrasion.

"Oh, James, what were you thinking?"

"Had to save you," his voice shook. "I'd do anything for you. I love you."

His head fell back in the sand as he lost consciousness. Tears fell from Alys's eyes. "You bloody fool."

Rosanna emerged from one of the hidden caves in the cliff, Dominic not far behind her. "James," she screamed.

"What happened?" Dominic asked.

"A man with a gun shot him. We need to get him up to the manor. I can help him, but I can't do it here."

The marquess nodded. "Rosanna go and get help. Go fast. We need at least two more men to carry James."

The young woman's face was devoid of all color.

"Rosanna, go," he ordered.

She nodded and disappeared inside the tunnels.

"What can I do?" he asked.

"Do you have an unused handkerchief?"

He nodded and handed it to her. "What will that do?"

"For now, I'm going to hold it against the wound to help stem the bleeding. If he loses too much blood, he could die. The faster we get him to his room so I can remove the bullet, the better."

Dominic scoffed. "You can't remove it."

She raised an eyebrow. "Why the hell not?"

"Well, because..." he trailed off.

"I'm waiting for an answer that makes sense, and you better not say because I'm a woman. I assure you I know more than you do about medical care."

He raised his hand in defeat. "As long as James doesn't die, I don't care who removes the bullet."

"Good." Alys held the handkerchief against James's wound. "Because I wasn't going to argue with you about it. I was going to do whatever I damned well felt necessary."

It seemed to take forever before two burly footmen came out of the tunnel. With Dominic barking orders, they moved James up to his room. Then it was Alys's turn to start telling everyone what to do. James's sister hovered in the background fretting.

"Rosanna," Alys called. "Go to my room and get my purple bag."

She nodded and ran off to retrieve it.

Next she turned to a maid and ordered, "I need hot, clean water. Lots of clean linens and soap. You." She pointed to James's valet. "Get all these clothes off him."

"I can't undress him in front of a lady," the valet scoffed. "'Tis highly improper."

She pinned him with a glare. "So you're going to let His Grace die because it wouldn't be proper to undress him?"

"Not at all, miss. I will get it done." He scurried off to do her bidding.

Alys walked over to a basin and poured water into a bowl. She grabbed soap and began to scrub her hands. She was not going to let James die. He told her he loved her—the idiot.

She'd kill him after she saved him.

"Here's your bag," Rosanna waved it in front of her.

"Good, I need you to bring it over here."

Rosanna walked over to her side.

"Now dump it here." Alys pointed to a nearby table.

Rosanna raised an eyebrow. "The whole thing?"

"Yes, the whole thing. It will be easier to find what I need."

Rosanna shrugged and did what was asked. There was a lot inside that purple purse of hers—more of a tote bag really, it was so huge. Alys scanned the items and pointed. "There, that black pouch. Grab it for me."

Alys turned back to James. There was so much blood. She swallowed back her fear. This was why physicians were not supposed to operate on family members or anyone they cared for. What if she messed up? She had to hold back the apprehension filling her. His life depended on her skills as a doctor.

"Are you done undressing him?" Alys asked the valet.

"Yes, miss."

"Good. Now drape a sheet over the lower half of his body and then come grab this black pouch and lay it on the bed next to him." Alys turned to Rosanna. "I need you to go downstairs and wait now. This isn't where you should be right now."

Rosanna bit her lip and nodded. "Let me know when it's done." She turned on her heels and exited James's chambers.

Dominic strolled into the room. "What do you need me to do?"

"I may need you to hold him down if he awakens. I don't have any anesthesia." She paused to consider how to explain what she meant. "There is no way to guarantee he won't feel any pain. He might awaken while I try to help him."

His face paled slightly, but he nodded.

"Now wash your hands and then join me next to James."

He looked puzzled at her request, but did as she asked. Alys walked over to the bedside. The valet stood by the bed. "Can you unzip that for me?"

"Unzip?"

Alys rolled her eyes. "Pull the metal side until it opens all the way and lay it on the bed next to him."

Once it was done Alys examined the contents. It wasn't ever meant to be used. The items were a gift upon graduation—a token really—but all fully functional. It was a first-class medical kit any surgeon would want by their side—if they operated with solid gold instruments. Not very practical, but her mother had meant well. Alys grabbed an alcohol pad and cleaned her scalpel. If only she'd had gloves, but she'd make do.

Alys turned and looked at everyone. "Out, all of you, except Dominic. I don't want the distraction."

They all scurried to leave the room. Alys let out a sigh of relief. Time to save James.

Then she examined the wound on James's abdomen. The blood had stopped seeping out, making it easier to examine. She felt along the edge to see where the bullet was lodged, planning to cut only if necessary. She skimmed the wound with her fingers. Nothing. A small incision would be necessary to locate the bullet. Alys bit her lip and picked up her scalpel. With quick precision, she opened it wide. With the extra space she could locate the bullet. Blood pooled around her hands as she searched. After what seemed like forever she located it and pulled it out. It had hit his spleen, but the damage—thank God—wasn't extensive. Alys wouldn't have to remove it, she could sew the wound and let it heal.

When she was done she took a step back. James had not awakened the entire time. It concerned her a little bit, but she'd worry about it later. She turned toward Dominic. "Can you pull the sheet up farther? I'm going to wash everything, and well...myself too."

He nodded. "Of course. Can I say I seriously misjudged you? I don't do that very often."

"Most people do. I don't hold it against you." She picked up her black case and walked off. Her whole body shook with relief. Her instincts had kicked in, but now that she was done, it all hit her. What if James died?

No, he will not die.

She washed as quickly as she could and returned to his side. Alys planned on staying with him until he woke. It was for the best. She could also monitor for possible infection and give him something for the pain. Ibuprofen would only go so far, but as he'd never had it, it might be enough to alleviate the discomfort he was guaranteed to feel. She put all the items back into her purple bag, swung it over her shoulder and returned to James.

"I'm going to stay with him. Do me a favor and go check on Rosanna and give her an update."

The marquess stood near the bed staring down at James. He had a serious expression on his face. As many times as she'd performed surgery, it never got easier to deal with their friends and family. With James, it was even more difficult to separate herself. The words to comfort Dominic failed her. She never knew what should be said. James should make it through this ordeal. At least she didn't have to deliver any bad news to anyone.

He lifted his gaze to hers and nodded. "Let me

know if you need anything. James is lucky to have you."

"No, I'm lucky to have him," she corrected him.

Dominic left the room. Alys lay down on the bed beside James. Hopefully she wouldn't have to wait long for him to awaken. They had a lot to discuss... she never had given him her answer.

CHAPTER 14

A BURN RAN UP HIS LEFT SIDE, BUT WARMTH spread through to his right. James turned his head and saw Alys asleep next to him. She was fully clothed—but he was not. So they hadn't done anything improper—or had they? The night before was rather fuzzy in his head.

Alys's eyelids fluttered open. "Oh good, you're awake."

"Is this some kind of strange dream?" he asked.

"If only," she shook her head, "I'm afraid you went and got yourself shot. Though from the looks of it, this isn't the first time you've been wounded."

James's gaze flew down his abdomen. "I was in the war. Wounds tend to happen when you're fighting against an enemy."

"Of course," her voice was devoid of emotion.

"I take it I'm going to be fine," he said.

"That remains to be seen," she replied. "I might kill you and put you out of your misery."

He held back a smile. "I didn't worry you overly much, did I?"

Alys leaned in closer to him and then pinched him in his uninjured side, hard. "You're lucky to be alive. Don't even attempt to make a joke of this."

He nodded. "I wouldn't."

If it had been her lying injured...he repressed a shudder. It wasn't, she was fine.

"Good, now we can discuss your stupidity." She sat up and stared down at him. "What were you thinking?'

"That I couldn't lose you." He frowned as he remembered what happened on the beach. "That man meant to murder you. I'd just found you, and he wasn't going to take you away from me."

"James," Alys shook her head, "I don't need you to protect me. I am capable of taking care of myself. I appreciate it, but you took years off of my life. I thought I was going to be forced to watch you die. I can't ever go through anything like that again. Please tell me you won't be so careless with your life in the future."

"I can't promise you that."

He wished he could, but her safety would always come first for him.

"Why the hell not?" she asked. Her mouth hung open in shock.

James smiled at her and grabbed her hand. He placed a kiss on her palm. "If you're in danger, I will never ever let you die in my stead. So as long as you're safe, so will I be. If you can promise not to court danger, only then can I."

Alys chewed on her bottom lip. "Very well. I can understand that. Why don't we make a mutual pact then? I will do everything in my power not to find danger, and in return you'll do the same."

"Alys, love." He brushed his fingers through her hair. "Don't you know there isn't anything I wouldn't do for you?"

Maybe after they were together for many years to come she'd come to accept that. He would go to the ends of the Earth for her. Nothing—absolutely nothing—was more important to him.

She nodded. "I'm beginning to see that."

"Good. Now that we've settled that, perhaps you can send for the surgeon so I can see when I'll be healthy enough to leave my bed."

He had plans, and they required him to get up

and move around. This lying around like a week invalid would not get any of it accomplished. As soon as he could, he planned on utilizing the special license and making sure she was his forever. He couldn't wait to make her his in truth.

"Why ever would you want to leave your bed now?" Alys asked.

"I can't very well stay in here forever." James gestured toward the door. "Now go fetch him. I assume he stayed to check in on me. I have questions that need answers."

Alys was silent. She seemed to be contemplating how to respond. What could be so bad?

"There is no surgeon to fetch, James."

What? The blasted man had left without knowing if he'd need further care. They would never again use his services. "Are you sure?" It didn't seem feasible they'd leave the care of a duke on a whim.

"I'm sure there is no *man* around who did any surgery on you." Alys stated.

Her tone told him that he wasn't fully understanding something. Her entire attitude was rather puzzling. What could be so dreadful? The surgeon appeared to do a fair job of patching him up. "Why not?" he asked, slowly.

"Because I'm the one who removed the bullet

and stitched you up. If you want to know when you can leave this bed, you need to be speaking to me." She scanned his entire body. "And I'm thinking that you should stay here for a *very* long time."

Alys had performed surgery on him? Wait, she wanted to stay in bed with him if he understood her correctly. He'd oblige once he had her agreement to be his wife. He could compromise under certain circumstances. First, she had some explaining to do. Why would she perform surgery on him instead of calling for a doctor?

"You didn't have one of the servants fetch the surgeon? Why would you handle this on your own?"

Alys rolled her eyes. "James, that was my job in the future. I trained to be a doctor—a heart surgeon to be more precise, but I can do any emergency surgery."

"You can?"

The future must be very progressive to allow her to train as a doctor. It must be a fascinating place to live. How could he convince her to stay with him when she had so much to offer her in her own time?

She nodded. "Yes, and, um, I'm afraid your normal surgeon won't ever return to the manor no matter what you offer him as payment."

"What?" he asked. "Why not?"

"I may have..." She hesitated a moment. "... Threatened to stab him in his carotid artery with a letter opener."

He raised an eyebrow. "Now that would have been interesting to see. What was he going to do to elicit such a response?"

"It doesn't matter." She waved her hand. "His skills were inferior. I'm better trained."

James laughed. He had no doubts that she was. She had the benefit of having lived in a time that knew in length how to minister proper medical care. They'd have an advantage under her supervision. James would probably heal much faster with her as his doctor. It also wouldn't hurt if she kept up her bedside nursing.

"I'm sure you're correct. So are you ready to answer my questions?"

She raised an eyebrow. "About your care and when you can leave this bed?" She nodded. "Yes, ask away, Your Grace. I'm at your command."

Was she now? He'd have to test that a bit. He trailed his fingers across her arm and cupped one of her breasts in his palm. She gasped at his touch. "When can I leave this bed, Alys?"

"Are you sure you really want to leave it?" Her voice was husky as she posed the question.

"Depends on if you're going to stay with me, but yes, at some point I do."

"Have big plans, do you?"

He pulled her on top of him. Her body fully filling his with the warmth he craved. "I know you haven't made up your mind yet, but I promise I'd never do you wrong."

"I know that."

He hoped she did. James wanted her to promise to be with him always. The answer he wanted to hear—he'd been denied it. Now he was aching to demand it. "Good. Now I need to know when I can schedule our wedding."

Alys sat up and straddled his hips. She stared down into his eyes. "I never said I'd marry you."

"Don't you know by now that I'd make every one of your dreams come true? I told you there wasn't anything I wouldn't do for you. You own my heart, Alys. I only hope in time that you will entrust me with yours."

"Oh, James..."

Tears fell from the corners of her eyes. He reached up and wiped them from her cheeks. "Don't cry. I can't stand to see your tears. I want to dry them and hold you close. Please, marry me, Alys. I need you."

"How can you be so sure?"

"I've known from the start where you belong. From the moment I saw you, my heart opened up and filled with happiness. I didn't understand what it all meant," James explained. "Stay with me forever. You don't need to look any further to know your place in this world. It's right here by my side. I love you so much I'm bursting with it. Take the leap with me."

Alys remained silent and studied him. He prayed her answer was yes. He'd played all his cards, and if she said no, he didn't know what he would do. She was his everything. Without her...he didn't even want to consider it a possibility.

She tilted her head. "What if I told you I made up my mind the moment I met you too?"

"I'd want to know why you left me waiting for over a week. We could have been doing much more pleasant things than dancing around each other like two fools."

"Love isn't for fools, James."

"I know that. You already explained it to me. Why don't you tell me what this has all been for?"

"I was trying to make you see what love is."

It all became clear in that moment. She'd loved him from the start too, but they'd both been foolish and hadn't wanted to face it. So instead, she'd tested him and he'd pursued her. That is what she meant when she said love wasn't for fools. When you couldn't or wouldn't admit you loved someone, you gave up on one of the greatest gifts you could have in your life.

"I'm still waiting for an answer." He stared up into her beautiful green eyes. "Will you be my wife, my duchess, and the mother of my children? More importantly will you promise to love me for the rest of our days together?"

"I can do you one better. I will make you feel my love in this life and beyond. I too have known from the moment we met where I belong. If you'll have me, I will hold you forever and wrap you in the warmth of my love."

"It took you far too long to tell me that."

"Ditto," Alys said.

He raised an eyebrow. "Sweetheart, you do realize you say the strangest things."

"It will keep you on your toes for many years to come." Alys laughed, leaned down, and kissed him.

James wrapped his arms around her and whispered in her ear, "I look forward to it."

"I love you." Alys stared deeply into his eyes. "More than words can say. It shouldn't have taken this long for me to tell you. I've always wanted someone to love me as much as I loved them. This all seems impossible somehow."

"Promise me you won't stop saying it. Words may seem inadequate, but they are best not left unsaid." James placed a soft kiss on her lips. "Sometimes even the impossible happens. I never believed in love until you."

"I promise." Alys smiled. "At no time in our life together will you ever doubt how much I love and adore you."

EPILOGUE

ALYS STROLLED INTO THE SITTING ROOM. A toddler trailed behind her. Blonde curls bobbed around her tiny shoulders. Her deep blue eyes matched her father's. Elizabeth had a little of each of them in her features. She was the sweetest, most beautiful daughter—and soon she'd have a brother or sister to follow her around.

Alys couldn't wait to tell James he was going to be a father again. But first she had to ask him to do her a favor. He'd hired someone to paint her and Elizabeth's portrait. When she found out she understood why Bradford had mentioned the family gallery. It was her portrait that hung there, but she had to let her family know in some way she was all right. They had to be worried about her.

"Ah, there my two favorite ladies are." James leaned down and pressed a quick kiss on her lips. "A late start again this morning?"

Morning sickness had been hitting her rather hard during the early hours of the day—much harder than it had been with Elizabeth. James was usually gone well before she became disposed with it. He didn't know how bad it was. She suspected that it would pass soon, but she couldn't help wondering why it was worse this time.

"I have news." She smiled. "But first, I have to ask something of you."

"Anything," he promised. "You know that."

"I need to write a letter and leave it for Bradford."

James scowled. "Why would you want to do that?"

Alys bit back a smile. James didn't like to hear about her past—or rather future— depending on how one looked at it. Bradford was her great-great-great-grandson or something. It hurt her brain to think about it. Thank God, they'd never done anything together. Alys shuddered at the thought. Though she did worry about him—he was so very cynical. She wanted him to find happiness.

"The last time I spoke to him, he mentioned the

painting—the one you commissioned. I want to put a letter behind it for him to find. I'm not sure how to get him to look for it and make sure it stays there until he's meant to find it."

"Oh, I bet he didn't realize it was you." James seemed lost in thought. "I have an idea."

"By all means tell me. I'm open to suggestions."

"Go ahead and write your letter. I will take care of the rest. To be on the safe side, write two copies of it."

"Two? You think that's necessary?"

Alys wanted to make sure someone knew she was all right. Maybe her letter would convince Branford to at least let her sister know. They might not be blood sisters, because Alys had been adopted, but they had bonded growing up. Regina only acted the way she did because their parents indulged her every whim. No doubt, Alys's disappearance had soured her wedding day.

"Yes. I am going to leave one with my solicitor and you can put one behind the painting. I'm going to leave strict instructions with them to give a letter upon each Duke's inheritance. They will receive a letter explaining everything and where to find your letter—with one exception."

"What?" Alys asked.

"Bradford is not to receive his until the day after you disappear. I can't risk you being warned and not coming to me."

Alys smiled. "Greedy, aren't you."

"When it comes to you? Always. Now tell me, what is your news?"

She leaned in close and said. "It's my pleasure to inform you that you're going to be a father—again."

James laughed and swung her around the room. "I love you so much, Alys."

"I love you too, James."

Their journey—the leap they took willingly—it proved thus far to be well worth it. Their love endured and grew each day. They were truly blessed beyond words. Soon, she'd leave proof to her family that she was fine and thriving in the past. She'd finally found someone to love her and for her to love in return—it only took falling two hundred years into the past for it to happen. Some things were worth searching for...

SEDUCTION OF MY RAKE

LINKED ACROSS TIME THREE

DAWN BROWER

USA TODAY BESTSELLING AUTHOR

Dawn Brower

SEDUCTION
OF MY
Rake

Linked Across Time

"Time will explain."

— JANE AUSTEN, PERSUASION

PROLOGUE

"You're seriously leaving?" Regina threw her hands up in exasperation. "I don't understand what the urgency is."

Trenton Quinn, her husband of barely three months, was in the midst of packing his bags to travel to England. He was a man obsessed—with another woman. The sad thing was the woman Trenton obsessed over had disappeared over five years ago. Genevieve, a former girlfriend of his, he couldn't forget about. At least not until her sister Alys vanished on Regina's wedding day. Her sister had been missing the entire length of Regina and Trenton's marriage. It put a serious damper on her wedded bliss. At first she believed Alys disappeared to gain attention and had been pissed at her older sister. Regina should've known better. Alys didn't play games. That sort of thing was more Regina's modus operandi.

"I have to do this." He stopped packing long enough to gaze up at her. "Please understand," Trenton pleaded. "This is important to me."

Regina rolled her eyes and wrapped her arms around her waist. It hurt to think Genevieve was more important than her. *Why does he feel the need to run away from me?* Was this a sign of their future? She would always be brushed aside as insignificant? The idea of being considered inconsequential and not worthy of his respect... She shook her doubts away and steeled herself for battle. The time had come for him to realize the grave mistake he was about to make. No one shoved her in a corner and forgot she existed. She *mattered,* damn it. "You do this and we're done." She glared at him. "I mean it."

Trenton sighed and folded a shirt. He set it inside his suitcase and then turned toward her. He lifted his hand and ran it through his dark blond hair. "I'm sorry, Gina." His gaze met hers and he sighed. "I can't let this go. I wish you would understand and be patient."

Fat chance in hell of that happening... Her temperature hit the boiling point. Heat flushed her cheeks and she clenched her fists at her sides. Be patient? As if. That was tantamount to saying calm down. Her husband had lost his mind. It was the only excuse for his rash actions.

"You expect me to tolerate the fact you're about to go thousands of miles away, across the ocean, *and* to another country—to search for a former lover?" She stared at him with bewilderment. "Did you hit your head? There isn't a woman on this planet that understanding, and you've lost your mind if you think I'm all right with it."

"I thought I had let it go." He shook his head. "But when Alys went missing, it all came rushing back. I have to know why Genevieve disappeared." He closed his eyes and took a deep breath. "Think of what figuring this out could mean for Alys. If we understand what happened to one of them, we could find the other. There's a connection. I know it."

Regina wanted to find her sister. Truly she did. That didn't mean she wanted her husband hunting down his former girlfriend. She was his wife. This Genevieve was his past and she should stay there. "I don't mean to sound heartless, but I don't care what happened to your ex-girlfriend. She probably ran away and didn't bother to tell you where she was going. She doesn't deserve you."

Trenton didn't respond to her. He kept folding clothes and stuffing them inside his suitcase. Irritation set in. Regina picked up a vase and threw it. Her husband flinched when it hit the wall. It shattered into thousands of tiny shards and fell onto the beige carpet.

"Hell, why did you do that?"

"I needed something to catch your attention. You're not listening to me." Patience had never been one of Regina's strong suits. His blatant disregard for her feelings had hit a boiling point and left her no choice. She did what she did best and reacted without thinking.

"Trust me. I have heard every word out of your mouth." He sighed and waved his hand dismissively. "I'm choosing to ignore most of it."

Her mouth fell open in shock. He *was* ignoring her. Regina suspected as much, but to have him openly admit it... "You're an ass."

Trenton shrugged as he zipped his suitcase shut. "It is what it is. This is something I feel I need to do. I hope you understand in time how necessary this trip is. The professor at Oxford has valuable information, and I'm tired of playing phone tag with him. The only choice I have is to go there and track him down."

To think she chose him. She could have had another, but she believed Trenton loved her. That he would always put her first. How wrong she'd been. It hit her hard; a heavy weight filled her belly as she realized what this all meant. The truth stared her in the face. It had always been there, but she'd been too blind to see it. Trenton didn't love her. He never had. If he did he would understand why this upset her. That she needed him to do what was best for their relationship.

He wasn't capable of giving it to her. She needed to accept that and move on. She'd thrown down the gauntlet and issued an ultimatum. Told him that if he left they were done, but at that moment she hadn't meant it. Not really. She still had hope he'd see reason. It was her way of giving him a chance to back down and stay, to fight for their marriage. She hadn't counted on their marriage not being enough for him. That he was willing to sacrifice it to locate his missing ex-girlfriend. There wasn't anything left to say, and it was clear their marriage would crumble into a million pieces. Nothing she said or did would hold it together.

"All right."

His eyes appeared to light up. "You mean it. You're okay with me going?"

"I didn't say that." Regina held up her hand to interrupt him. "I'll never be fine with you going on this hunt for your former girlfriend." Her brows drew together as she thought of how to explain her stance. "This is not something I can ever put my stamp of approval on. It goes against everything I believe in." When she married him, she'd believed they had a shot of making it. Otherwise why bother with commitment? At the same time, she thought love was something worth fighting for. She cared about Trenton, but he wasn't by any means her one true love. Apparently he felt the same way about her. They were in the same boat and it wasn't the stuff of legends by far. They fell short in that department. How could she stand in his way of finding the one he did love with his whole heart? "What I'm saying is I understand why you feel you have to do this."

He remained silent for several moments and studied her. "If you understand, then why are you saying you don't approve?"

How did she explain it to him? He was so damned clueless. She wanted to be someone's true love. The one they would go running to, not away from—his Genevieve was that woman for him. She would never be the one he truly wanted. Regina had been a fool to believe otherwise. This a losing battle, and she knew when to let it go. It was time to accept her marriage was over. They both deserved better, and it was time to let go and find the ones they were both meant to love.

"You don't love me," she said softly.

"Of course I do," he protested.

She shook her head. Maybe he believed he did love her, and he might in his own way. "Not the way you should. She means more to you than I ever will. This is too important to you for me to believe otherwise."

He opened his mouth to disagree, but then snapped it shut. Trenton's gaze went unfocused as he stared at the wall behind her. After what seemed like forever he looked back at her and said, "I do care about you."

That was the thing. They *cared* about each other. There was no love involved. Trenton had bought this large diamond ring and went all out on the proposal. He'd taken her to the place they first met and went on one knee. She'd been taken aback and said yes on reflex. It had been romantic and lovely, but her heart had never been in it. It was funny how things were always much clearer in retrospect. She'd done them both a disservice by saying yes.

"I don't doubt that, but it's not enough. You

shouldn't have married me. It would have made our lives so much easier if you hadn't asked. I had so many hopes for us, and now all I can see is how we were doomed from the start."

Trenton paced. His nervous energy was palpable and saturated the room. It overflowed and Regina could almost feel the waves rush over her. "I wanted to move on, needed to. When we met, I thought I had. I promise I never meant to hurt you. When Alys disappeared..." He turned toward her meeting her gaze with his own. "It all came flooding back. The need to know what happened. I can't let it go. You're right. I love her. I've always loved her, and I can't accept she left me willingly."

Her heart skipped a beat at his words. She'd known—seen what he'd been struggling with. Trenton hadn't wanted to admit how much Genevieve meant to him. Hell, she'd had doubts on her wedding day. Why hadn't she listened to them? Alys had said to close her eyes and picture the man she thought she could see herself with for the rest of her life. What she hadn't admitted was she hadn't seen Trenton. She'd forced his image over the one she'd truly seen.

Regina hadn't wanted to admit what was in her heart. Her parents would have been so disappointed in her if she'd called off her wedding. Her flighty nature led her down some unsavory paths. They'd been so happy she was settling down with someone. Trenton was the stabilizing force they prayed would come into her life. What was she going to tell them? Her marriage was falling apart after such a short interval. It was the disaster she feared, and could have been prevented.

"Then you need to go figure out what happened to her," she said softly. She was resigned her marriage was over. There was no reason to fight anymore. There was nothing there to hold on to. The best thing she could do for them both was to let him go. "I won't stand in your way."

He took a few steps and pulled her into his arms. "I'm sorry. Words can't express how much I mean it. I honestly didn't want to hurt you. I want the best for you." Regina leaned her head against his broad chest and sighed. He'd always been solid and dependable. It was rather depressing to realize he wasn't the one she'd been meant to spend her life with.

The sad thing was Regina believed him. He probably did care about her. The problem was he didn't love her. Nothing they could do to change it either. They'd tried. Both of them to forget about the one they actually wanted. They were both fools.

Maybe it was time to quit running from the truth and face it head on. It might be the only way she ever found happiness. There were a few things she needed to do before she took control of her life again.

"I hope you find the answers you're looking for." She stepped out of his arms. "While you're gone I will take care of dissolving our marriage."

He nodded. "I'll let you know where the paperwork can be sent. I won't contest anything."

There was nothing to contest. They had a solid prenuptial agreement in place. He kept what was his and she did the same. There were no concessions. The New York penthouse they resided in belonged to her family's corporation. They had no joint assets. Depressing when she thought about it—they hadn't bothered to co-mingle their lives. It was probably best their marriage ended before they had.

She nodded absentmindedly. "We might even be able to get an annulment. We haven't been married long. It would look better, you know, as if we were never married at all."

Regina would like to forget this marriage existed. It would be like wiping the slate clean and starting over. She would do things right and choose the one man she loved. Explore the possibility he could be the person meant for her. Time would tell if they were supposed to love one another. She hadn't had time to figure it all out before she was set to marry Trenton. Now a new opportunity presented itself. After she took care of erasing the existence of her marriage she would seek him out and give true love a chance.

"Do what you think is best." He strolled to her side and placed a quick kiss on her forehead. "I wish things could have been different."

Regina wasn't so sure she did. Sometimes things happened for a reason. It might not always be clear what it was, but usually it worked out how it was supposed to. Maybe they had to travel this path to arrive at the exact place they were always meant to be. Trenton sought the woman he'd always loved. Maybe if he went to England he'd finally find the answers he'd been searching for. She wasn't about to stand in his way when everything suddenly seemed so clear to her. She knew what her next move was.

"I wish you well," she said, and then smiled up at him. "Go find Genevieve, and if you manage to figure out what happened to my sister, don't hesitate to call."

Maybe she should consider flying to England and investigating herself. She really did want to know what happened to her sister. Regina could be

selfish, more often than not, but her sister was important to her. They'd been close their entire lives and
even when they fought they were the best of friends.
It was hard to imagine living her life without her
sister's solid presence there whenever she needed it.
She didn't want to think of her as anything but alive
and well. The reason for her staying away—she
couldn't imagine what it was, but Alys was the
dependable sort. There had to be a solid explanation
for it all. When she settled things regarding her
marriage with Trenton she'd start to look into the
matter. They needed answers as much as Trenton
did about Genevieve.

"I won't," he agreed. He spun on his heels,
grabbed his suitcase, and headed out of their
bedroom.

Relief flooded her as he disappeared from sight.
She sent a silent goodbye to the future she thought
she wanted. Regina couldn't wait to see where life
took her next. She wouldn't be too far behind Trenton. First things first—she had a marriage to dissolve.
She picked up her phone and dialed the one person
who would always know what to do. He picked up
after one ring.

"Hello, princess," he said.

"Daddy," Regina replied. "I need your help."

"Anything."

Regina smiled. Her father, Paul Dewitt, was a savvy business man, but a marshmallow when it came to his family. She didn't know what she'd do if anything ever happened to him. Something she refused to consider. Her dad was her rock.

"Trenton left to visit that professor at Oxford," she explained and proceeded to fill him in on all the details. "Can we get our marriage annulled?"

"Are you sure this is what you want? This seems rather sudden." After a brief pause he said, "But if you're certain, I don't see why not. I can handle it for you."

"Yes. We talked about it, and it's the only solution that works for us. If you can help me, I'd appreciate it. It's not what we expected...." An edge of sadness filled her voice. She really hadn't wanted things to go this way with Trenton. "Thank you for always being there for me."

She said goodbye and ended the call. Now that everything was in motion she could make plans for seeking out the man she wanted. While she was there, she could investigate Alys's disappearance. It would give her the perfect excuse to visit him too. "Bradford Kendall, you're not going to know what hit you." Her lips tilted into a wicked smile.

CHAPTER 1

REGINA STARED OUT THE AIRPLANE WINDOW. She'd taken her seat and was getting ready to fly to England. At last. The past year had been one of upheaval, loss, and rebirth. She ended her marriage and worked on improving her life in small ways. When Trenton left it had been a huge wake up call for her. Changes needed to be made, and more importantly it was time for her to finally grow up and accept responsibility for her actions. After much soul searching she decided she didn't like herself very much.

The problem of dissolving her marriage was easy enough to handle thanks to her father. A few short months after they filed for the annulment it had been granted. Most of the past nine months had been

spent finishing her college degree. She'd absentmindedly been going to school for a few years, but with
little to no direction. While she weighed her options,
she maintained a small office at her family's
company. Her father offered her a permanent position, but her heart wasn't fully in it. Her current task
was partly an errand for her father, but mostly a deep
desire to return to England.

Regina tilted her head back and closed her eyes.
She steeled herself for the upcoming interaction with
Bradford. He wasn't going to be happy to see her.
Trenton may or may not have told his stepbrother
about the end of their marriage. Her former husband
was hard to get a hold of these days. He was firmly
entrenched in his search for Genevieve, and he
didn't bother to check in with anyone any more.

"It is a bonny day isn't it?" A woman's voice
infused with an Irish lilt filled her ears.

Regina's eyes fluttered open and she turned
toward the woman. She had fiery red hair streaked
with gold. It fell over her shoulders in waves hitting
the middle of her back. Her ice blue eyes were a little
disconcerting. The blue irises were incredibly light
and dotted with white flecks. She'd never seen eyes
quite like hers, and she didn't know what to make of
them. "Undeniably," she agreed.

The woman took the seat next to her. Regina had begun to think she'd not have to deal with anyone on the flight. The first class passengers boarded first, and when no one sat next to her she'd been happy to have the extra space. She should have known she wouldn't be that lucky. Apparently her seatmate had been running late, as everyone else had already boarded.

"I'm Eve," She held out her hand introducing herself. "It's a pleasure to meet you."

She didn't realize they were already the name exchanging phase of their time together. If she had her way they'd ignore each other the entire flight. Regina had no desire for idle chit-chat. She took a deep breath and reminded herself she was supposed to be working on becoming a better person. "Regina," she replied.

She put her seat belt around her waist and leaned back. "I've been meaning to get back to England for some time. It's been a struggle to find my way home."

Regina frowned. What did that mean? She nodded at the woman not knowing how to respond to her statement. "Um, okay," she mumbled. What did she expect in response? Regina wasn't keen on small talk.

Eve ran her fingers though her curls and sighed. "I don't suppose you would understand. Not having been lost yourself." She tilted her head and studied Regina, appearing to take her measure. After a moment she said, "You have lost someone though, haven't you, lass?"

She scrunched her eyebrows up and narrowed her eyes at the other woman. What did she know about her loss? Did she recognize Regina from the New York society pages and latch onto the opportunity to grill her? She'd had several reporters try to interview her about Alys. She wasn't going to be sucked into answering a shady journalist's questions. She was smart enough to refrain from answering them this long, and wasn't going to crumble at this late juncture.

"Who are you really?" Regina asked. "What game are you playing?"

Her laugh had a musical quality to it. Almost mesmerizing in its beauty, much like her voice. It was exquisite and lyrical to listen to. "This is no game. I promise you that."

Yeah right, as if Regina was going to buy that one. She wasn't the sucker Eve thought she was. She learned early on not to trust strangers. Her family was too high profile to open up to anyone.

"If you are not trying to get information from me, then what are you doing?" She glared at Eve. "How do you know about my losses?"

The other woman studied her in silence. She didn't say anything for several minutes. It was disturbing to be scrutinized by her. The eeriness of her eyes alone made her uncomfortable. Regina squirmed under the pressure of Eve's innate stillness.

"I apologize for alarming you. That was never my intention," she finally replied. "I have a gift." She waved her hand dismissively. "More a burden than anything most of the time. I see things others don't."

Regina wanted to snort at the absurdity of her statement. Gift, her ass. She was certain now the woman was on a fishing expedition for more information.

"A gift?" She raised an eyebrow. "Would it include the skills to do proper research about an individual or subject?"

"Tell me something," Eve said, ignoring the sarcasm latent in Regina's voice. "Have you ever desperately needed someone's help and it was near impossible to obtain it?"

What angle was she going with now? "No." The simplest answer was the best when dealing with sharks. They would bleed you out if you gave them

319

too much. No doubt this was another way to find out what happened to Alys. What every reporter didn't know was she couldn't give them the information they sought. No one, not her parents, not her, and certainly not the authorities around Weston Manor knew what happened to Alys. It was a mystery without a solution. She would love to find her sister. Any news would be good. Her family was frantic for answers. Not desperate enough to feed information to an investigative journalist—yet. There might come a time she would willingly submit to an interview. They hadn't reached that pinnacle point of no return.

"In that I envy you." Sadness filled Eve's unnatural blue eyes. She jerked her head to the side and stared across the aisle. She shuddered as if wracked with pain. "I don't have a lot of time. My strength is waning."

What was she talking about now? The woman was so confusing. Could she be any more cryptic? "Sure." She shrugged and tried to rein in her urge to spout sarcasm, and failed. "I can see how weak you are."

Eve shook her head frantically. "I'm not long for this world. If I don't get home soon I won't survive. I need your help." Her eyes were wild as she pleaded with Regina. "Save me."

Oh, holy hell, the woman was a lunatic. It was clear as day now. Maybe that was why she found her so damned unsettling. Save her? From what? Her seat belt? "I don't know what I could possibly do for you."

Eve's head jerked backward against her seat. She clawed her fingers into the armrest. Her breathing became ragged as she fought for breath. *Shit.* She really did need help. Regina had brushed it off, and now she felt like the biggest jerk alive. Was Eve having some kind of seizure?

"Hold on, I'll get someone to help you."

"No time," she wheezed out. "Must tell you what I came here for."

"Sure, um ... yes. That is... I'm listening." Was the woman dying in front of her? There might be time to help her. The plane still hadn't left the tarmac. "Hold on. Don't let go yet. We can help you."

"I certainly hope so. My life depends on you." Her lilting voice was barely above a whisper. The red-haired woman appeared to be fading. "Tell him he's close. He *can* find me."

"Who?" Regina asked. "Who can find you?"

Her lips tilted into a soft smile. "I see why he liked you."

Sadness permeated off her in waves and crashed over Regina. She could feel Eve's emotions as clear as if they were her own. It scared her a little bit.

"And that is?" She raised an eyebrow questionably. "I can't very well deliver a message to someone if I don't know who they are."

"I'm out of time—Remember."

Her voice faded out of existence before she did. In front of Regina's eyes, Eve disappeared. What the hell had happened?

"Pardon me, miss." A stewardess tapped Regina's shoulder. "Would you like a beverage."

Regina shook her head and rubbed her eyes trying to focus them. The seat next to her remained empty. Her hands shook with the surge of emotion that flooded her. A bead of sweat settled on her upper lip. She lifted her hand and wiped it away. It was a dream. Nothing more. Eve didn't exist. Was she losing her mind?

Regina shook it all from her thoughts. Whatever message her subconscious was trying to send her... Regina didn't want to think about it—she could figure it all out later. She had a long flight ahead of her, so when she arrived in England she'd examine it more. Exhaustion had set in and she found herself too tired to think. Her little mindfuck had drained her of all energy.

"Do you want anything to drink?" the flight attendant repeated.

Regina glanced at her and shook her head. "A pillow would be nice."

The woman nodded, brought her a little pillow, and then left her alone. She vaguely heard them talking about safety for the flight before she drifted off. Maybe this time she wouldn't dream of a strange woman with equally peculiar eyes...

CHAPTER 2

BRADFORD KENDALL, NINTH DUKE OF WESTON paced his study. He stopped by a nearby window and stared across the landscape, and his gaze landed on the cliffs in the distance. A year ago his step-brother Trenton Quinn married Regina Dewitt on his estate. Regina's sister, Alys, had disappeared the same day somewhere along the cliffs. She'd been last seen heading toward their steep edges. No one knew what happened to her. Her family had been devastated, and it had ended the festivities rather abruptly.

He'd been grateful. It pained him to admit it, but Alys's disappearance had ended the farce of a wedding. It was too bad she hadn't had the grace to disappear before Regina and Trenton said their vows. Was it too much to ask for that particular wedding to never have happened?

I was an ass. Bradford couldn't make himself care overly much. Alys seemed like a nice enough woman. She even resembled one of his ancestors... Weddings though, he shuddered, were an abomination. They were useless and ended in divorce more often than not. He should know. His mother had been married so many times he'd lost count. Catherine Quinn flitted from man to man like a butterfly seeking a variety of sweet nectar. Her current husband of the past decade, Marshall Quinn, was happy to let her do it without demanding a divorce. It was enough to leave a sour taste in his mouth.

He wished Trenton all the happiness in the world. Sadly, he didn't believe Regina was going to give him any. No, that woman would end up shredding him to pieces. She was nothing like Trenton's first love. His wife was a socialite of the first order. It was too bad she was also, by far, one of the most beautiful women he'd ever laid eyes on. He closed his eyes and sucked in a deep breath as her image floated through his mind. Yes, Regina Dewitt-Quinn was exquisite in every way, and Bradford lusted after her as he'd never had any other woman in his life.

His brother's wife. He was going to hell.

"Fuck," Bradford swore and crossed the room to the bar near his desk. The nearby brandy decanter glistened with amber liquid. He poured two fingers in a glass and downed it in one swallow. It burned as it traveled down his throat. He set the glass down with a thud and reminded himself he couldn't have her. She wasn't his, and he would never hurt Trenton by trying to take her away from him. The duke didn't want her enough to keep her.

Why couldn't he have found her first? Then he could have erased his infernal craving for her. One night. That was all he'd wanted. Then he could forget about her and move on. Maybe once his step-brother's marriage inevitably ended in divorce he could have it. Regina was attracted to him. Her eyes had lit up when she'd seen him for the first time. He recognized lust in a woman's gaze when he saw it. It wouldn't take much to tumble her into bed and have his wicked way with her.

Yup. He was definitely heading to the fiery pits below.

"Pardon the interruption, Your Grace, but you have a visitor."

Bradford turned toward his butler and asked, "Is

it the courier with the documents I've been waiting for?"

"I'm afraid not." His butler remained stiff inside the door frame. "The courier has yet to arrive."

Brad frowned. Who the hell had dropped by? The estate wasn't exactly on the way to anywhere. He had no desire for company. What he needed was those damn contracts he was waiting on. They were important for expanding the software division of his company. The one good thing that had come out of Regina and Trenton's wedding was meeting Paul Dewitt. He was a genius in the business world, and Bradford wasn't about to let an opportunity slip by. They were working on a special project that would benefit both their companies. Dewitt Enterprises was a world leader in technology, and Bradford wanted a piece of it.

"Call the courier service and figure out what the holdup is. I need those contracts," Bradford ordered the butler. "I can't wait all day for them to arrive."

"Yes, Your Grace." The butler nodded. "What shall I do with your guest?"

Bloody hell. He'd already forgotten about the visitor. He had other priorities, and his impromptu guest wasn't at the top of his list. "Get rid of them. I'm not in the mood for company."

"But," the butler sputtered and walked into the room. He stopped in front of Bradford and said, "I implore you to reconsider."

When had his butler become so cheeky and questioned his requests? Bradford glared down at him and said with an edge of steel skimming his voice, "Do as I asked, Ashton. I am not in the mood to make small talk with anyone."

"Your Grace..." he started again.

"Damn it. Don't even attempt to argue with me." He threw his hand up in the air. Heat filled his face. He pursed his lips in displeasure and clenched his fists at his side. It took every bit of his control to rein in his temper. "Inform them I'm not at home to callers."

A soft laugh filled the room. Bradford spun around and met the gaze of the woman who'd been haunting his dreams for over a year. Platinum blonde hair fell down her shoulder in soft waves, and her dark blue eyes were filled with amusement. Her lips tilted into a sultry smile. Hell. He should have known it was her that was disturbing him. She'd been doing it rather well for months.

"I think he was trying to tell you who was here." Regina waltzed into the room. "You shouldn't be so rude to your staff."

Bradford closed his eyes and counted to ten. He was on edge and about to explode. It wouldn't help his cause to lose it now. Regina had to go. Her very presence shattered his control. He might very well do something they would both regret later. He'd been good and kept his hands to himself this long. Betrayal wasn't something he did. He'd not give in to his urges to pull his brother's wife into his arms and ravage her. No matter how beautiful or enticing she was to him.

He opened his eyes and glared at Regina. "What are you doing here?" And where the hell was Trenton?

The butler nodded toward Bradford and quietly exited the room.

"Is that anyway to greet a guest?" She pouted. "I don't know why I'm surprised considering how brutish you are with your servants." She shook her head and frowned. "Why they remain loyal to such a beast of a man is a mystery."

Bradford scrunched his eyebrows together and continued to glare at her. He was not falling into her trap. "I don't have time for your histrionics. Do us both a favor and go back where you came from."

Regina smiled and it lit her whole face up. She was rather perverse that way. He insulted her and pushed her away and she found it amusing. If Bradford were being honest with himself, and he hated when he was forced to—he rather liked that side of her. Perhaps he was a little perverse himself.

"Trust me. I'm as far from hysterical as any woman can be." She kept walking toward him. He took a step back. Her laugher echoed through the room. "Are you afraid of me?"

Why the bloody hell did she have to be so gorgeous? Even in jeans and a simple white shirt. He wanted to rip her clothes off and see if she was as exquisite naked. "Don't be ridiculous." He snorted. "Why would I be afraid of you?"

She shrugged. Regina waved her hand nonchalantly. "I have no clue. You're the one retreating."

Bradford narrowed his gaze and studied her left hand. Where was her wedding rings? He wouldn't ask her about it. He didn't want to have any discussion with her at all. All he wanted was for her to leave, and encouraging her wouldn't gain him any recourse. He couldn't give her anything to dig her heels in about. "I don't want you here." He kept repeating it to himself, but he failed to come up with a good excuse to make her leave.

Besides, it wasn't entirely the truth. He wanted her. But he couldn't have her. At least not yet. Not until Trenton threw her aside. Then he could give in to his baser instincts. One day, he had no doubt, she would be his. That day, unfortunately, was not this one.

Her eyes gleamed with something he couldn't identify. She lifted her chin with a hint of defiance. "I hate to break it to you, but you don't have a choice."

Hell if he didn't. Weston Manor was his home. He wasn't required to let anyone in he didn't want to. She had no idea who she was dealing with, but she was about to find out. In the past he'd been— nice—for lack of a better word. Now though, he didn't have to be. There was no one around whose feelings he needed to protect. Regina meant nothing to him. "I don't have to do anything." He stared at her with a mulish expression. "If I don't want you here, then it is my right to send you packing."

He should probably be concerned about offending her. Trenton might become irate if he knew Bradford had kicked his wife out. He would deal with that downfall if or when it came. It was much better his step-brother believed him rude then the alternative. He didn't trust himself to be alone with her.

"True," she said and stepped even closer to him.

He could see the rise and fall of her breasts. He itched to feel them in the palm of his hands. Restraint was becoming harder and harder to maintain. Regina had to go and fast.

"Then do what I asked and leave."

She raised an eyebrow. "I didn't realize you'd actually asked. You demanded." Regina licked her lips and flashed him a sinful smile. "And I *so* hoped we could get to know each other better."

Lord save him, he wasn't strong enough to handle her. Why was she flirting so much with him? Was she already bored with her marriage to Trenton? The little hussy didn't deserve to be a part of Trenton's life. He'd be much better off if he kicked her out of it. "As is my right. This is my home. Please leave." He ignored the second part of her statement. It wouldn't do any good to address her innuendo. Bradford wasn't a fool and was aware she baited him.

The wicked gleam in her eyes put him even further on edge. His body tightened into a mass of nerves as she raised her hand and trailed her fingers down his chest. "Then you don't want to go into business with my father?"

What game was she playing now? He took a deep breath, and with every inch of what remained of his control he kept his arms at his sides. "I didn't say that."

"Oh, good. Then I can stay."

He opened his mouth and closed it into a firm line. She was blackmailing him to allow her to stay in his home. How bad did he want to do business with Paul Dewitt? Could he risk letting her stay near him to gain what he needed from her father? It was a conundrum, and Bradford didn't like it one bit. The little minx was going to get her way. She'd pay for boxing him into this corner.

"Why are you so adamant about staying?" He had to know what she wanted. If he did, he could work with it. Maybe make sure she left sooner rather than later. The first chance he could manage, he planned on calling Trenton. There was more to Regina's story than she was telling him. He needed information if he hoped to beat her at her own game. Maybe if he was lucky enough Trenton would retrieve her and take her away from Weston Manor. That was the most optimal outcome.

"I have many reasons for being here." She walked over to his brandy decanter and poured herself a glass. She took a sip of the amber liquid and then turned to face him. "There are two things you need to know."

"Those are?" he raised an eyebrow.

"One, I am my father's business liaison. I'll be negotiating the contracts for the software merger you are working on." She grinned. "I've brought the documents with me for you to look over."

"Are you even qualified to do that? What experience do you have with contracts or business?" Paul Dewitt was damned good at business. How could he allow his flighty unorganized daughter anywhere near it?

She laughed. "You have so little faith in me. But to answer your question—yes, I am. I've been learning about Dewitt Enterprises since I was a child on my father's knee. There is no one more qualified than I am. Well," she tilted her head to the side and said, "other than my father that is."

Bradford gritted his teeth. He would concede her point. Paul Dewitt had to groom someone to take over the company. With Alys studying to be a doctor prior to her disappearance, Regina was the logical choice. He hadn't considered the possibility because of her unreliable nature. "You don't seem the type to enjoy business."

"I don't," she agreed. She reached inside a bag

and pulled out a file. Regina crossed the room and handed it to him. "But I am good at it. Father needed my help, and as I'm at a crossroad in my life, I volunteered. Take a look at the contracts. Let me know if you'd like to make any changes. If not sign them and return them to me. I'll make sure they are sent to my father either way—for changes or not."

The contract was important to him. It would help to build one of the divisions in his company sorely in need of growth. Bradford couldn't afford to alienate Paul Dewitt. He'd have to play nice, at least for a little while. It sat like a bitter pill at the bottom of his stomach, but he could handle it. He still didn't understand Regina's motives, but he'd let it go for the moment. "What is your other purpose?"

"I intend to find out exactly what happened to my sister while I'm here."

Great. She was never leaving.

CHAPTER 3

REGINA SETTLED INTO HER ROOM AT WESTON Manor. Had it really been over a year ago she'd last been on the estate? It was all still fresh in her mind. She recalled that day with almost perfect clarity. Alys helping her find her lost shoes and preparing to marry Trenton. It had been a fairy tale ending without the happily ever after.

"Oh, Alys, what happened to you?" She stared out the window and the cliffs in the distance. "I'll find you. I promise." It was one she intended to keep. Even if she had to deal with the prickly owner of the lovely home she now resided in. "No matter how long it takes."

Her sister was and always would be important to

her. Regina had some rather selfish moments in her life, but Alys never seemed to hold them against her. No matter what, they'd supported and loved each other. If she needed someone to talk to or hell, anything, she always ran to her sister first. Alys was the voice of reason when there didn't seem like there was any to be found.

Right now she could use some of Alys's sisterly advice where the resident duke was concerned. Maybe she should have talked to her about it on her wedding day instead of dismissing her feelings so lightly. The resulting chaos may have been avoided, and perhaps Alys would never have disappeared. She bit her lip as a small tear fell from the corner of her eye. Damn it, why did everything seem so reasonable when she looked back on it? She couldn't change the past, and it was best she accept it. All she could do was move forward and continue her search. As far as her feelings for Bradford and how to handle him—she'd figure that out herself too.

Bradford was acting like a veritable beast. She wasn't sure if it was because he knew of the dissolution of her marriage to his brother or if he hated the sight of her. Either way it hadn't been a pleasant arrival. Not once had he mentioned Trenton. She had no idea what was going on through his brain. Maybe he didn't know any more than she did. Perhaps he wasn't aware of the status of her relationship with his brother. He was rather adamant about her leaving at first—it had been borderline rude. Hell, it wasn't even that...he'd been a complete ass. At least she had some leverage to deal with him. It had been her father's idea for her to deliver the contracts in person, so he must have known Bradford would be difficult. Her father had amazing insight to what made a person tick. She'd been at Weston Manor a week now and had found little to no progress on either front.

Bad decisions... She'd made more than her fair share in her short lifetime. This was her time for redemption and to prove to herself, and the world, that she was more than a pretty face. Without her sister to fall back on she was lost. Never had she been so alone in her life. Why did life have to be so complicated?

She took the stairs two at a time and headed toward the library. It had a massive amount of books. Alys would be in heaven. Regina smiled at the thought. Her sister loved books—something she'd never fully understood. What she expected to find in this particular room she didn't know, but she had to start somewhere. She stared at the numerous book-shelves and frowned. Where to start? A bookcase filled with old, worn-out, leather-bound tomes called to her. Before she realized it, she was standing in front of them, skimming each one with her fingers. A Bible at the end of the shelf caught her eye. Regina yanked it free and carried it over to a nearby settee. Once she was settled, she flipped open the cover and read the names inscribed.

Elizabeth Regina Evelyn Kendall born 5 September 1816

Christian William James Kendall born 28 June 1818

Nicholas Edward Paul Kendall born 28 June 1818

REGINA'S FINGERS FLOATED ACROSS THE NAMES. The first name had both her mother's name as well as hers in it. It was weird... She didn't know why, but she felt a connection to these people. They'd been born almost two centuries ago. Why would she believe she knew them? Elizabeth had been born on the day her sister disappeared, albeit almost two hundred years earlier... What did she know? Nothing. "A little girl born September 5, 1816 didn't mean a damn thing." She tilted her head back and closed her eyes. It helped her concentrate.

"Are you sure about that, lass?"

Regina jerked her head toward the sound of the Irish lilt. "You. Why are you here?"

Eve floated through the room as if walking on air. Her golden red hair floated down her back. Regina frowned as she studied the woman. When she'd seen her on the plane, she hadn't paid much attention to her attire. Now though, she couldn't help but notice it. She was draped in an ice-blue gown that almost matched her eyes—it was ancient. Nothing like any modern woman would have worn. Eve stopped and looked outside the window. Her gaze fell toward the cliffs in the distance. She didn't answer Regina's question. Did she even hear her?

"The cliffs are beautiful. I've always thought so."

Regina frowned. She wasn't much for heights and avoided the cliffs. That and her sister's disappearance had been enough for her to steer clear. Someone had mentioned seeing her sister heading toward the cliffs. Then she had not been seen since. She may have fallen off... Regina didn't know either way, but it was enough to make her uneasy. "I don't especially like them."

Eve turned, her eerie eyes filled with sadness. "I understand more than you realize."

"You didn't answer me." Regina reminded her. "What did you mean? Why are you here?"

Her soft pink lips titled upward. The smile didn't reach her eyes. She radiated sorrow that spilled over onto Regina. "The names in the Bible. They do relate to you."

"I don't see how..."

"You will in time." Eve's head jerked toward the window. "I can't stay. Did you give him my message?"

"Who?" Regina asked, puzzled.

"Please tell him. I need... Time to go." She faded before Regina's eyes.

Regina jerked forward. A bead of sweat trickled down her forehead as pain shot forward above her eyes. She winced and held her head to help stabilize the ache. What the hell was happening to her? Why did she keep having visions of that woman? She didn't know her and didn't want to. Was she right though? Did the names she'd read in the Bible have something to do with her? If so, what?

"What are you doing with my family's Bible?" Bradford snatched it from her hands.

She hadn't even heard him enter the room. Showed how much pain she was in that she failed to recognize his presence. Regina lifted her hand and tapped the Bible. "I found some of the names interesting."

"This is a priceless antique. It belonged to the fifth Duke of Weston. His wife wrote down the names." Bradford frowned. "They didn't keep up with the tradition. I'm not sure why."

Of course it was his ancestors. The Bible had been in the Weston library. Who else could they have been? That meant the children couldn't possibly have anything to do with Regina. It was a coincidence, nothing more. Why did she listen to the figment of her imagination? Eve, or whoever she was, didn't know what she was talking about. Regina started to laugh hysterically. She was losing her fucking mind.

"I don't understand what you find so hilarious." He glared at her and then headed over to the shelf she'd found the Bible on. "Stop laughing. Don't touch the books on this shelf again."

Regina wiped the tears from her eyes and shook her head. He didn't understand because nothing made sense. She wasn't about to explain it to him either. No doubt he'd help them lock her away with the insane. "Tell me about the fifth Duke."

He turned to study her. "I don't know much. I wasn't one to study my family's history."

Regina sighed. Why was he being so difficult? "I think there might be a clue in your history that will explain what happened to Alys." And Trenton's ex-girlfriend. She wasn't going to divulge that part yet. She wasn't sure how much Trenton had told Bradford. Eve's hints were enough to make her wonder and search more. She'd not have thought about doing so without the woman's weird clues. What did the names in the Bible mean and how could they possibly be connected to her? She hadn't given her much to go on. So she'd have to dig in other ways in hope of finding the answer. It seemed rather silly to consider a few children's names in a Bible might be important to her. They were born almost a couple centuries ago. For the life of her, Regina couldn't fathom how discovering more about them would help her find Alys. She didn't have much to go on though. So why not dig deeper and to discover for herself it they were the lead she'd been hoping to find? It wouldn't hurt and Regina was desperate for answers.

Bradford didn't say a word. He continued to stare at her as if she'd lost her mind. He didn't know how close he was in that assumption. Regina fully believed she was going crazy. Why else was she dreaming about a woman dressed as if she belonged in the eighteenth century? Eve kept saying to tell *him*. When would she realize she didn't know what man she spoke of? The only male she was around was Bradford. Did she mean to tell the duke? That didn't seem right, but she couldn't explain why. She'd hold it to herself until she was certain what the eerie Irish woman wanted. It was better if she didn't come off as a lunatic without having full knowledge to deliver to the mysterious *him*. Although, in Regina's opinion, the woman should know she couldn't depend on a man to save her. She'd need to do that herself. Men were too unreliable.

Finally, Bradford sighed and nodded. "What do you want to know?"

"Whatever you can think of." Her eyes rested on a chessboard on the other side of the room. It gave her an idea. He was on edge and perhaps a game would help ease some of the tension. "Do you play chess?" She gestured toward the game.

His gaze followed her movements. Bradford shook his head. "I've some experience. I didn't take you for the chess type." Then he tilted his head and stared at her. "On second thought, it is something you'd excel at. You can be quite clever at times."

Unsure how to take that statement, Regina chose to take it as a compliment. "Thanks. So do you want to play?"

"Why not." He waved his hand toward the board. "We can discuss some things as we play."

That had been her thoughts exactly. She stood and strolled over to the set and sat in the chair across from the white pieces. "You don't mind do you? I always liked the white ones." It reminded her of the games she'd played with her father growing up. She didn't know why, but they'd always chosen the same color. It was more of a habit than anything. Regina had learned strategy by watching her father play. She didn't need to use the white chest pieces to play, but she'd prefer to do so. A small part of her was also superstitious and believed she'd play better if she used them. It was silly, but considering how things had gone in the past year, she didn't like taking anything for chance.

"Not at all." He grinned. "I look forward to watching you play."

He probably thought he'd beat her. Regina grinned. "Likewise." She moved one of her pawns on the board. "Now, about the fifth duke and his family."

"It's funny you asked about them." He made his move and glanced up at her. "I may have mentioned them somewhat to your sister on your wedding day."

Regina stopped short. She'd been about to pick up a rook and slide it over, but stopped when he spoke. "What do you mean?" The chess game was already forgotten before it had even begun. "Why would you mention them to Alys?"

When had Bradford and Alys been alone long enough to have a detailed conversation about his family? A small sting of jealousy filled her and she couldn't brush it away so easily. The only time she'd ever seen them talk was when they headed toward the church before her wedding. They had stood up together for her and Trenton. Alys hadn't seemed to like Bradford much, but looks could be deceiving. Maybe they got on a lot better than she'd thought.

Bradford sat back in his chair. "I didn't in so many words. She reminded me of someone in one of the portraits in the family gallery. As we walked to the church, I asked if she'd seen any of them."

How odd. What did it mean? "And that related to the fifth Duke?" Her forehead creased.

346

"His wife, actually." He shrugged. "Are you going to move?" He gestured toward the board.

She gritted her teeth and glared at him. He seemed more intent on focusing on the game than telling her what he'd discussed with her sister. It was rather irritating, but when wasn't the damn man frustrating her? Regina completed her turn. "What was her name?"

"Whom?" Bradford studied the board. "Oh, the fifth Duchess of Weston. After meeting your sister, I got a little curious. Not right away, mind you. It was sometime after your wedding I looked into it."

"Meeting my sister made you look into your family history?" Regina raised a brow. "Kind of lazy of you not to be curious before then."

Bradford smiled. "I've found other ways to amuse myself."

Regina bet he did. His smile was pure sin. If she wanted to, she could reach out and wipe it off his face. Whatever was making him skittish around her was frustrating. Gazing at him now though, she believed he was completely capable of making her forget everything with one touch.

"So what did you discover?" Regina asked again, a little breathlessly. "What was the Duchess's name?"

"I don't know." He shrugged. "I hit a snag. The information I sought was taken by one of my other ancestors when she married."

"Why would she do that?" It seemed a little odd to Regina. What reason could his ancestor possibly have for taking the information with her? "Is that normal?"

Bradford ignored her and continued to study the chessboard. After a moment he made his move and looked up at her with a victorious grin. "Checkmate."

Her gaze flew to the board. *Damn it.* He'd managed to fully block her king in from all angles. How had she allowed that to happen? Regina grimaced and conceded the win. "We'll have to do a rematch later when I'm not so distracted." She hated losing.

He leaned back in his chair and smirked at her. "Why bother? You will lose no matter what you try."

She rolled her eyes and bit back the retort about to roll off her tongue. Volleying digs back and forth wouldn't get her the answers she sought. She had this niggling feeling the duchess's name was important. Why else was it so hard to obtain? She wasn't sure what it would lead to, and it may be nothing, but she wanted the information so she could decide for herself. So she ignored his arrogant grin and said, "You never answered me."

He raised an eyebrow. "I didn't realize you asked anything worth responding to."

Conceited prick. "Why would your ancestor take the information about the fifth Duchess?"

"Oh, that." He waved it off. "She was the last of my family to be married in the vicarage on the estate. They decided to hold weddings in more prestigious locales, but kept the vicarage intact." Bradford stared at her with a hint of distain. "Your marriage to Trenton doesn't count. He's not a Kendall."

Ignoring his pointed barbs was proving to be more and more difficult the more he opened his damned mouth. She clenched the side of the table and shook off the need to punch him in the nose. "Did no one plan on marrying there after her? Is that why she took the record book?"

"I don't have a clue." He stood up and paced the room. "Why does this matter anyway?"

How to answer that? She hadn't a damned clue. It did matter, and she couldn't let it go without digging out all the details. "I'm curious and bored. I've hit a dead end. Tell me about this ancestor. What was her name? Do you know that much?"

"She was the fifth Duke's sister. All I know for

certain is that she married the Marquess of Seabrook. That's where my information ended. I suspect if we want more answers we might have to go to Seabrook and ask if they'll play nice and share."

Regina perked up at his words. "Is that possible?"

She got up and headed toward him. She placed a hand on his arm. His gaze shot down to her movement. Bradford froze in place and slowly turned to meet her gaze. Heat shot through her in that instant. *Deep breath in, exhale slowly.* Regina fought for control. When he stared at her like that...

"Anything is possible if you're willing to work for it." He lifted his hand and trailed his fingers across her cheek. She shivered involuntarily. "How bad do you want it."

So bad she could almost taste it. *Down, Regina. Bradford will chew you up and spit you out.* If she fell into his arms, she wanted no regrets. She closed her eyes and held her breath. Her eyelids fluttered open and met his intense gaze. He wanted her too, and had been aware of their mutual attractions since the moment they met. Too bad she went and grew up in the past year and didn't give into those urges anymore. She wanted love, and at this point there wasn't a chance in hell Bradford would give it to her.

"If you're speaking about visiting Seabrook, then I want to go as soon as possible." She quirked an eyebrow up and asked, "When can you arrange it?"

"The good news is they are having a charity ball in a few days and I have tickets for it." He winked. "You can go as my date."

Date? Regina wasn't sure how she felt about being his date, but shrugged the concerns away. This was important and could lead her to the answers she sought. "Black tie?"

"Of course." He replied. "Balls are the best places for dressing...and undressing in dark corners. If you want to have more fun, wear something easily...accessible."

Her mouth fell open in shock. Regina blinked and realized they were still standing close together. Distance was needed and fast. His beautiful blue eyes were so mesmerizing. Why did he have to be so gorgeous? He grinned mischievously. Arrogant bastard could tell how much she wanted him. Maybe it was time to play with him a little bit. Regina had an intense urge to wipe that cocky grin off his pretty face.

She stepped closer so there wasn't any room separating their bodies. She lifted her hand and skimmed it at the bottom edge of his shirt, snaking it underneath. Her fingers danced across his hot flesh. It was his turn to suck in a breath. Need crashed into her, but she reined it in. This was a game she intended to win. Regina wrapped her arms around his waist, leaving one hand underneath his shirt, scraping her fingernails across the bare flesh of his back.

"Kitty has her claws out." He leaned in close. "How wicked."

Regina didn't say a word. She unwound her arms and let her hand trail down to the bulge growing in his pants. She cupped him in the palm of her hand. He hissed a breath. Regina took that moment to lean in and kiss him lightly on the lips and then bit his bottom lip, hard. He swore and took a step back. A small bead of blood formed on his lip.

"Bloody hell." He wiped his mouth. "Was that necessary."

"More than you know." Her hands shook so she kept them close to her sides. She didn't want to show any weakness. "I'm not a plaything. I'm not *yours* to fuck and leave out like yesterday's trash. I'll never be for you."

His eyes gleamed dangerously. "Darling, I can assure this isn't over."

"No," she disagreed. "It's not even starting. Keep

your paws to yourself." Regina spun on her heels and stormed out of the room before she did something she'd regret. Like strip naked and find out how wicked they could truly be. That would be disastrous. Bradford Kendall was her weakness, and Regina refused to give in to it. No matter how bad she wanted to drown herself in his drug induced kisses.

CHAPTER 4

BRADFORD CURSED AND PACED THE ROOM. HE stopped and stared at the chess game. Images of Regina wouldn't leave him and it had been hours since she left. It wasn't a good sign of what was to come that he couldn't let it go. Her touch still lingered over his skin. The cut on his lip hadn't bled long, but her bite left a throbbing ache in more than one place. His desire wouldn't ebb, and he couldn't think of anything but her. What the hell was wrong with him?

He shouldn't have allowed things to go as far as they had. At least she'd held herself in check. If she'd kept going, he'd have had her on the floor of the library. The urge to go after her still flowed through him. Trenton was the sole reason he managed to restrain himself. He had to keep reminding himself why keeping his hands to himself was a good idea. Something or someone should do the same for his brother's wife. Regina put on a good show, but her desire equaled his in strength. If she continued to stay at Weston Manor in a mere matter of time she'd give in. Pure and simple, she had to leave, and it was up to him to make sure she did. He had one problem —he didn't want her to go.

Why did she tease him incessantly? Did Trenton mean so little to her? Bradford scrubbed his hands over his face. The frustration was starting to get to him, and he was beginning to wonder why the hell he fought Regina so damned hard. Why should he when she wasn't? Playing the better man had never sat well on him. If not for his step-brother he'd have given in without a moment's thought. "Oh, bugger it," he shot out. "This isn't worth overanalyzing." What he needed was a drink. Maybe if he imbibed enough he could control his raging need and forget what was driving it.

He cursed again and swiped his hand across a nearby table, knocking almost everything on it to the floor with a loud crash. A piece of porcelain nicked his palm, causing a tiny drop of blood to pool across the cut. Bradford stared at it for a while, struck dumb. This is the exact foolishness he'd been trying to avoid. That woman drove him to distraction and made him do things he'd normally not even consider doing. He fished his mobile phone out of his pocket and dialed the one person who could save him from himself.

It rang several times with no answer. He swore when voicemail clicked over. Why the hell was Trenton so bloody hard to get a hold of? It had been months since he'd last spoken to his step-brother. "It's Bradford. Call me as soon as you get this voice-mail. Regina is driving me insane. You have to make her leave."

He clenched the phone in his palm. Where was Trenton? Something was off. Trenton should have come with her. It had been a year ago when they'd married. Shouldn't they be celebrating their first anniversary? Trenton wouldn't have missed the opportunity to visit.

"You won't get a hold of him."

Bradford spun around and faced Regina. She had a solemn expression over her beautiful face. It was disconcerting. He'd never seen her look so sad before. "You were eavesdropping."

"I couldn't help overhearing." She shrugged. "It's not the same thing, but the results are."

Why did she have to disturb him? Her presence was what drove him to call Trenton in the first place. She couldn't leave well enough alone. His desire to pull her into his arms was so strong it was near impossible to fight. He clenched his teeth together and fought it with everything inside of him. Instead of calling her out on her intrusion, he decided it was time to ask her all those infernal questions he'd failed to ask previously. "Why isn't Trenton with you?"

She ignored and brushed past him. Regina stopped at the window and gazed out at the cliffs. He'd often done the same. Stood there and stared at their stark beauty. After a few moments, she turned to him and said, "Trenton has more pressing concerns."

"More pressing than his wife?" What could be more important? Bradford was growing concerned. His brother wasn't usually so inconsiderate. "What am I missing?"

A small smile filled her face, an attempt to make light of the situation, before it fell into a bland expression. Her eyes were dull, almost glazed over. "Apparently you're very much in the dark."

Oh hell, this couldn't be good. He shook his head

as something seized his heart—fear, worry, he wasn't sure, but it sank its claws in deep. "Why don't you enlighten me?"

She returned to staring out the window. "Do you remember Genevieve?"

Genevieve was lovely and ethereal. She was everything that Regina wasn't. Which was why he'd been so surprised when Trenton had introduced Regina as his fiancée. Bradford didn't think his step-brother would ever get over his former girlfriend. Had Regina come to the same conclusion? Was Trenton's first love the problem?

"I remember her quite well. She was a lovely woman."

She turned to him and smiled. "Unlike me."

He scrunched his eyebrows up and frowned. "I didn't say that."

She shook her head and headed toward the shelf she'd borrowed the Bible from. Regina lifted her hand and skimmed across the spine, and then dropped her hand to her side. Her back remained to him. He couldn't see her face, and he desperately wanted to.

"You're thinking it," she said softly. "I have an inkling of what you believe me to be."

An ache settled deep into his soul. Every breath he took made it burn brighter. Her sadness—he didn't like it. He only wanted her body. Didn't he? He shook the doubts away. Of course he did. Her feelings didn't matter to him.

"Why should my beliefs have any impact on anything?" He crossed over to her and then lifted his hand to rest on her shoulder. She peeked back at him. A small tear settled in the corner of her eye. The ache inside him intensified, and he was mystified that her agony affected him at all. "What does Genevieve have to do with anything? She's been gone for some time now."

With a wobbly smile she stared up at him. She turned to gaze up at him. The tear had begun to trail down her cheek. He lifted his hand and wiped it away. Bradford couldn't take it anymore. He had to erase the misery before it engulfed them both. With a need more potent than desire he leaned down and placed his lips to hers. Later, when he was alone, he'd examine his motives. For now, it was enough that he wanted to give her something—anything—to focus on other than whatever made her so disheartened.

He coaxed her soothingly until she opened up to him. The kiss was soft and sweet. Something Bradford didn't do as a rule. It led to expectations. It was different with her. It filled him with a warm feeling so good he'd never have enough. Their tongues touched lightly and repeatedly. His hand curled around her waist almost involuntarily as he deepened the kiss. She tasted so good. It was intoxicating, thrilling, and almost like coming home. For the first time he believed he'd found something that was meant for him. Something worth fighting for, if he was willing to reach out and take it.

A memory floated through his mind. He could hear Alys laughing, no mocking him. Her golden blonde hair had gleamed in the sunlight as she gazed at him with green eyes filled with mischievousness. What had she said?

"Someday you will meet someone who takes your breath away. Your very existence moot without them by your side—every breath, every heartbeat, will be only for them. If you're lucky enough, they will feel the same."

Bradford took a step back. His hands shook as the realization set in. Had that blasted woman cursed him? What would she think if she knew she made him question everything? No. Regina wasn't for him—it was a fluke. A mere moment of weakness... He didn't love her. He'd been right when he told Alys it was lust and nothing more he felt for her sister.

Regina licked her lips, her gaze never leaving his. He wanted to kiss her again but resisted. He needed some distance to think. This thing between them couldn't go any further than this room. Even if her marriage was potentially over, he wasn't ready to face the tumultuous rollercoaster flowing through him.

"Genevieve is the reason you won't get a hold of Trenton. She's his reason for everything, but you already knew that. It's why you never accepted me, isn't it?"

He shook his head. "She has nothing to do with how I feel about you."

That was the truth. He liked Genevieve well enough, but he'd never lusted after her. Regina was a different story altogether. It was something he didn't like very much. He almost hated himself for it.

"I see." She turned away from him. "Trenton is trying to figure out what happened to her. He's holed up who-knows-where in deep research with a professor from Oxford. I haven't spoken to him in quite a while."

That explained a lot. Why he hadn't been able to reach his step-brother and Regina showing up unannounced. She was lost with nowhere to turn. Maybe she had ulterior motives for coming to Bradford's estate. He wasn't yet sure what those reasons were, but he'd uncover every last one of them. Whatever game Regina was playing he intended to come out on top. He didn't play the fool for anyone, especially a vixen like her.

Sometimes comfort was needed and anyone would do. Bradford was there and readily available to help with her *needs*. Bitterness filled him at the idea of being used. No wonder she'd bit him and made him bleed. No one wanted to be tossed aside and considered worthless. The idea of her doing that to him didn't sit well. He found he did want more from her, and he wasn't certain he could have it.

"Why are you really here, Regina?"

"I told you already. Those reasons are the same as the day I arrived." She turned back to him. "I'm going to find out what happened to Alys with or without your help."

Regina may or may not want to find out what happened to her sister. He had his doubts about the veracity of that claim. If she was so concerned, why hadn't she started her search sooner? What changed? From his point of view, not a damn thing. She was still as frustrating and equally gut-wrenchingly beautiful as she always had been. Was she any less selfish than a year ago? He mentally shook his head...doubtful. He hadn't seen any evidence to the contrary. To him, Alys was an excuse to come to his estate and torment him on a daily basis. If Regina found out her sister's whereabouts in the process she'd see it as a bonus. Maybe it was a bit narcissistic, but he was starting to believe he was the true reason she'd come to England.

"That may be one reason why you're here, but it's not the only one." His voice had a steely edge. He was steaming with rage. "And I'm not talking about those bloody contracts you gave me to look at. What game are you playing?"

"No games. I'm not the same person you met over a year ago. I've had to grow up and see things for what they are." She smiled softly. "I don't expect you to believe me, but it's the truth."

He didn't believe her, but he wanted to. An idea took root and he found it suited his purposes. A test was in order, and he knew exactly how to go about achieving one. The charity ball at Seabrook was actually a weekend event. Outside of Weston Manor he could see how she interacted with the world. It was time for the blinders to come off.

"If you say so." He shrugged. "We leave for

Seabrook this evening. Pack for an entire weekend of activities," he said and walked out of the room. Soon he'd have the answers he needed. Then he'd know how to handle the situation. Until then, he'd not make any decisions.

CHAPTER 5

Regina stared out the car window. They had been driving for about an hour headed toward Seabrook. She hadn't thought to ask where the estate was located when Bradford told her about the charity ball. He'd also failed to mention it was a weekend long event set up like house parties in a bygone era. With a modern touch, of course; there was no gas lights, candles, or lack of plumbing to contend with. They were modern creatures, and not too many enjoyed roughing it. However, there was riding, card games, and other such frivolities to enjoy while they spent their time on the estate. She had to admit she rather looked forward to it all. She had a fascination with the Regency and Victorian eras of English history. It was why she'd designed her wedding in a similar style. She was supposed to only get one wedding, right? Why not do it in style? Well, that showed exactly how foolish she was. Her marriage didn't last and now she had no husband. What she had was his prickly brother who was constantly surprising her.

"Where is Seabrook again?" Regina felt like a petulant child stuck in a car for hours upon hours. She couldn't help it. It was suffocating being stuck with him with the strained silence. After that kiss... She didn't know how to react or if she could trust her own instincts anymore.

"It's in Hampshire county, Southhampton to be exact. It's along the coast, similar to my estate, and a little over a hundred miles separates us. We should be there in less than an hour," Bradford replied drily. "I'm sure once we get there you will find something to entertain yourself with."

Regina didn't want to find entertainment. The weight on her chest was making it hard for her to breathe. Distance would surely help ease the discomfort. That Bradford was the cause of it didn't go unnoticed by her. She'd been attracted to him, always had been, but now she was drawn to him for different reasons. He'd been so tender in the library, made her want things she thought she'd never have after Trenton's abandonment. She didn't fault her ex-husband for wanting to find Genevieve. She'd come to terms with it all and understood it. "I'm sure I can find something to do," she muttered under her breath. "So this event... Everyone who attends stays the whole weekend?"

"No." He shook his head. "There are not enough rooms to accommodate everyone. A select group of people have the privilege of attending the entire weekend."

Probably cost a pretty penny too. "What charity does this event support?"

She liked the idea of helping people—Something she'd tossed aside as not worth her time. Now she wanted to do something good for the world. Leave her mark on it and not have everyone remember the selfish vain girl she'd been in the past.

"It changes every year. It's part of the surprise. At the ball they announce how much was raised and what charity will benefit from the efforts." His fingers stroked the steering wheel. Regina bit her lip as she watched his nimble fingers tap it almost lovingly. "They take suggestions all year long and narrow it down to a few, and then the attendees vote on which one they think they should support."

"That's a very democratic approach." She rather

liked the idea, and her mind spun on how she could do something similar in New York when she returned. Her mother would love it, and she couldn't wait to tell her about it. "When do the attendees vote?"

He studied the road and didn't answer her question right away. She waited patiently, as she had no other choice. Bradford would tell her when he was ready. Why he held that back she didn't know. It irritated her slightly, but where he was concerned she'd learned to bite her tongue. He didn't do anything until he was ready.

"Packets on the charities were sent out to those who purchased tickets."

That didn't answer her question. Yes, it was good to know what charities were involved, but when did they vote. "So voting is?" She raised an eyebrow.

He chuckled lightly. "You can cast your vote anytime before the ball. There is a website set up and with the results hidden until the end of the event."

She scrunched her eyebrows together and considered what he said. "But then anyone can vote. How does that even work?" It couldn't be as simple as that. If so, she could log in on her phone and vote as they drove.

"You are given a code to vote with."

Regina gritted her teeth together. Why was it so damned difficult to get him to talk to her? Information was not something he gave out willingly. She glared at him and considered punching him, but dismissed it as foolish. She didn't want to die if he lost control of his vehicle. Maybe once they stopped though. Yeah, that idea had merit.

"Am I going to be able to vote?" She really wanted to have a hand in picking a charity. She was curious which ones were contenders. Maybe she'd donate to one of the losers. No doubt they were all worthy charities if they were being considered. "Do you have your packet of information on them for me to look at?"

He sighed. "Why are you so curious? Since when do you care about charities?"

His words stung. Would she ever live down her past mistakes? "It matters to me now." She stared at him mulishly. "Do you have them?"

"I do."

Good. Then she could look them over and decide. Wait, he never said if she'd be able to vote. "Am I able to participate?"

"I'll give you the information so you can." His

voice had an edge of steal to it. "Now can you please be quiet? I want to concentrate on driving."

She revisited the idea of punching him. He was being an ass again. It was his go-to mood. Regina didn't know what was bothering him and wasn't sure if she cared. She sighed. Yeah, she did unfortunately. Being tuned into his mercurial moods didn't help her own peace of mind. He ran hot and cold more than anyone she knew and gave her constant whiplash.

They sat in silence for another thirty minutes. It drove her insane. Finally, she couldn't stand it anymore. "Why do you always feel it necessary to be a total ass?"

He turned his head slightly and glared at her. "Why do you feel the need to be a bitch?"

She opened her mouth and closed it several times. How dare he? She'd been nice, mostly. So she'd bitten him once. That didn't count. He'd deserved it because, well, he'd been a jerk at the time. He thought he could use her and toss her aside. Maybe he hadn't said so out loud, but she could tell. It unnerved her, these different sides of him. In the library he'd been gentle, and now... Well, now he was a total dick.

"Have you ever considered people react to the way you treat them?" She decided to take the higher ground and not call him an ass to his face. Again. Oh hell, she *was* being bitchy. "I'm sorry. I should take my own words to heart."

He pulled into a long driveway and maneuvered his vehicle around until it was in front of the Seabrook Manor. There was an ornate fountain on one side of the circular driveway, and on the other laid the estate in all its glory. The fountain was a nice touch, but the inlaid brick and marble of the entrance was breathtaking.

Once he had the car in park he turned to her and said, "Regina dear, you constantly surprise me." His lips quirked upward into an amused smirk. "I apologize for being an ass. Why don't we go in and meet our host?"

Her, surprise him? She stared at him, startled. He was running hot again. He'd give Doctor Jekyll and Mr. Hyde a run for their money at this rate. She didn't know what version of Bradford she'd get at any given moment. "You drive me crazy." She shook her head. "But, by all means, lead the way, Your Grace."

"I could say the same about you." He exited the vehicle and was opening her door before she'd had time to react. He bowed before her and held out his hand. "May I be of assistance, my lady?"

She didn't trust this helpful side of him. He was

up to something. "What are you trying to accomplish?" She narrowed her eyes at him, but held her hand out to him anyway. He helped her out of the car. She gazed up at him and said, "You don't have to act the gentleman for me."

"Oh, he does." An amused laugh filled Regina's ears. She turned to see one of the most gorgeous men she'd ever laid eyes on. He had golden blond hair and steel gray eyes. He was breathtaking. "It's all part of the festivities. Everyone must be on their best behavior."

"Zane Rossington, the Marquess of Seabrook," Bradford turned to the man and said stiffly, "May I introduce Mrs. Regina Dewitt-Quinn."

"Lose the Quinn," Regina replied, "and it's only Miss."

Bradford's head spun toward her. Shock was evident on his face as he stared at her dumbfounded. She'd suspected he hadn't known about the dissolution of her marriage. His reaction confirmed it. He'd asked her before about Trenton when she'd mentioned Genevieve. She hadn't wanted to explain then the reason for Trenton's absence from her life. It had felt—hell, it was plain embarrassing. She'd accepted her ex-husband needed to find his former love, but she'd not wanted to have Bradford mocking her at every turn. He already looked at her unfavorably. He'd no doubt blame her for the end of the marriage. In his mind she was evil incarnate and of course she'd be the reason things failed. It couldn't have had anything to do with his sainted brother. A part of her was bitter, and it bled through into her thoughts. She'd like for him to see her in a better light, but it was starting to become apparent he wouldn't. This was going to be one more thing he would have to hold over her.

"It's a pleasure to meet you, Miss Dewitt. I hope you will enjoy your stay in my home," Seabrook said smoothly.

She smiled up at him. Her pleasure was hard to hide. "I'm sure I will, my lord."

"Let me escort you inside." Seabrook held out his arm to her. "I can show you to your room if you like."

She laughed lightly. "Don't you have servants for that?"

"Yes, he does." Bradford's voice held barely restrained fury. "Go see to your other guests. I can help Regina."

Seabrook studied Bradford for a few moments. What he saw, Regina wasn't certain, but he acquiesced quickly. "If you need anything let me know." He nodded and left them alone.

"Now, please explain that nonsense you told Seabrook." He glared down at her.

It took everything she had inside to not stick her tongue out at him. He was being such an ass. *Hell, when isn't he?* Instead, she glanced up at him and said innocently, "I don't know what you mean." The need to goad him was too hard to resist.

"Don't act the fool. You know exactly what I'm talking about." He folded his arms across his chest and waited for her to answer. When she didn't, he added through gritted teeth, "Your marriage."

"Oh, that." she waved her hand. "It's nothing. Trenton and I had our marriage annulled months ago. I've been plain ole' Regina Dewitt for..." She tapped her chin as if thinking hard about the time line. "I think six months now."

With that pronouncement, she shrugged and headed inside Seabrook Manor. She didn't bother to check to see if he followed. Let him stew on that information for a while. Maybe it was her bitchy side coming out, but it felt damned good to put him in his place.

CHAPTER 6

BRADFORD NURSED A BRANDY AND GLARED across the room. Regina flitted around, lightheartedly laughing at everything and anything. At the moment, she appeared enthralled with no doubt a bit of nonsense Zane was spouting. Cocky bastard probably thought he had her right where he wanted her. Something he didn't want to admit could be possible.

Zane was not going to step into Regina's life and take over. She was free. That meant Bradford could have her if he played things right. He couldn't act on it without more information. Unfortunately, he hadn't been able to pin her down long enough to obtain any. She'd been avoiding him ever since she dropped the news that she and Trenton were no longer married. Something he should have been aware of. Why hadn't his step-brother mentioned it? Come to think of it, Trenton hadn't called him in months.

The more he thought about it the more irritated he became. There was so much wasted time... He could have had Regina a lot sooner, and he'd have pursued her much sooner. She'd not have had to come to Weston Manor for him to seek her out. He was already doing business with her father, and wouldn't need to search for an excuse to visit the States. But she had come to him, and it was time to ramp up the seduction. He'd already had ample time to seduce her that he'd not utilized because of his ignorance of the situation. He'd not wanted to compromise his relationship with Trenton, and where had that gotten him? Nothing but blue balls for over a week, well, no more. He'd not let her have control over him or the situation any longer.

He stole a glance across the room through hooded eyes. Regina licked her lips and leaned into Seabrook, her hand resting against his chest. A bubble of laughter filled the room again. Bradford sucked in a breath and tried to regain control, and lost. He swallowed the contents of his glass and set it down with a hard thud. He couldn't take it anymore.

"Weston," Zane acknowledged him. "I trust you're enjoying your time here at Seabrook."

Bradford reined in the urge to punch his pretty face. "It's been wonderful. I love visiting." He hated every minute of it. Seabrook had always been a rival of his. They always went after the same things. Now the bastard wanted the one woman he craved more than anything, and he'd be damned before he let Zane have her. "What activities do you have planned for us this weekend?"

Zane's lipped twitched in amusement. "The same as usual. I didn't see the point of messing with what works."

Regina's gaze bobbed between them. Bradford suspected she had no idea the rivalry she'd unwitting stepped in to. She'd find out soon enough. "So I have boring charades and card games to look forward to after dinner?" He raised an eyebrow mockingly.

"Cards sounds fun to me," Regina piped in. "What games will we play?"

"How good are you at Whist?"

She chewed on her bottom lip, tilted her head, and frowned. "I've never had the pleasure of playing. To be honest, I'm not sure how."

"I'd be happy to teach you," Zane offered.

Bradford clenched his fists at his side and

reminded himself it wouldn't do to punch the marquess. They were friends of a sort. "You won't have time," he reminded him. "Someone is always demanding your attention at this event. I'd hate for you have to leave in the middle of instructing her the proper way to play. I can handle her tutelage."

Zane narrowed his eyes and studied Bradford. What was going through his mind? "I have a better idea. We can both teach her."

"That won't do. We can't play Whist with three players." Bradford shook his head. "It isn't done."

"Two isn't enough either." Zane glared mulishly.

He reminded himself again it was most definitely not a good idea to punch Zane, although he could use a little imperfection on his face. No, it would probably aid him more. Ladies seemed drawn to him no matter what he did. Bradford had hated him a little for that in school. Bradford was tired of it all, not that he had trouble with women. He'd had his fair share, but Zane didn't even have to try and they were his. Regina wouldn't be added to the marquess's conquests.

"Now boys," Regina placed a hand on each of their arms, "I'm willing to let you both teach me. No reason to fight over it."

"Who's fighting?" Bradford raised an eyebrow. "And, darling, there are no boys in this room."

"Indeed," Zane agreed. "We British are civilized. You can't fault us for our impeccable manners."

Bradford almost winced at Zane's words. He *had* been itching to pummel him. Best not mention that part.

"I give up. I'll leave you two to duke it out with words." Regina threw up her hands. "I didn't really want to learn anyway." She stormed across the room and grabbed a glass of champagne from a nearby waiter. Bradford watched her down the glass and set it on the tray before grabbing another glass. At least she was no longer fawning over Zane.

"What are you after, Bradford?"

He turned to Zane and shrugged. "I don't know what you mean."

Bradford didn't owe Zane any explanations. He wasn't about to start giving him any either. What was between him and Regina wasn't for public consumption.

"Do you want to know what I've always liked about you?" Zane asked.

"No," Bradford replied, "and frankly I don't care."

Zane shook his head and laughed. "Too bad. I'm

going to tell you anyway." He gestured toward a waiter and grabbed a glass of champagne. "You're unflappable. Nothing ever gets to you, and I've always admired that."

Bradford narrowed his eyes and remained silent. When Zane got on a roll he was hard to stop. It was best to ride it out until the end and walk away with his body intact.

"How long have we known each other?"

Why was he asking questions he already knew the answer to? Bradford glared at him and pursed his lips into a thin line. He wasn't going to bother responding to such nonsense.

"Twenty years?" Turned out Zane didn't require a response; he kept going without even bothering to give Bradford a chance to speak. "A long time, anyway. So I know you. Perhaps better than anyone, save Trenton. I know how close the two of you became after his father married your mother."

"What the fuck is your point?" Bradford asked frustrated.

Zane laughed. "My point is I've never seen you like this, and don't bother to pretend you don't know what I'm talking about. You're gone for that woman. She has you tied up in knots, and she's not even trying." He shook his head. "What I would like to know is how long you've been carrying a torch for the woman your brother used to be married to. More importantly is he aware of it?" He glanced up, amusement flashing through his eyes. "I happened to notice your surprise at her newly minted single status. Figurative fireworks were going off over your head as you gawked with amazement."

Bradford didn't have a clue how to respond to him. He never believed he was an easy person to read, but Zane was right. He *did* know him better than anyone else. They'd grown up together and went to the same schools. They used to go everywhere together. Yes, they were rivals, but they'd always been friends first.

He was more than aware how he reacted to Regina. His whole body radiated with need whenever she was near. All he had to do was think about her and his desire became evident. He was a walking, talking disaster where she was concerned. "I was unaware, as I'm sure you know, that Trenton and Regina had ended things."

Zane took a long drink of his champagne. He didn't say a word. After a few moments he shook his head and said, "Nice way of side-stepping my question. You don't have to answer me if you don't want to. Although I can guess the answer, and I'm probably right. You'd have hidden your feelings from Trenton because he means so much to you. Now that she's free, what are you going to do with those pent-up emotions you're carrying around?"

"I have no idea." Bradford was lost in a way he'd never been before. With no direction and no plan, he was walking around reacting instead of acting. It was time to change that and figure out what his next step should be.

"I gathered that at your introduction." Zane studied him. "Why is she here with you if you're not privy to the details in her life?"

A good question. "She claims she is seeking information on her sister's disappearance." He had to wonder if that was the only reason she was in England. Was she trying to use him to make Trenton jealous? She was playing some game. Bradford was certain of that much. It was a matter of time until he figured out what it was. She had to know that.

"You don't believe her?" Zane raised an eyebrow. "You think she's too vain to care about her sister?"

He shook his head. "No. I don't doubt she wonders what happened to Alys. It's why I brought her here. She'd got some notion that the fifth Duchess of Weston will give her a clue."

Although he failed to understand Regina's logic,

he was willing to humor her. He was curious for a different reason. He had started to research his family history and hit a snag with the duchess. He'd wanted to know who she was after he'd mentioned the portrait to Alys, but it remained a niggling curiosity left satisfied. So, he could find out who she was and then give Regina something in return. It was a total win-win in his estimation.

Zane scrunched up his eyebrows and frowned. "Wouldn't that information be found at your estate? Mine seems an unlikely place to find it."

Bradford laughed. He would have thought the same thing. "It appears that the fifth duke's sister, our mutual ancestor, absconded with the details. The ledger containing her name is missing and all the clues point them to being brought here."

"I'm not sure if they are or not." He rubbed his chin in concentration. "A lot of the antiques and journals were put in storage years ago. I'll have to look into it and let you know."

"I appreciate it." Bradford turned his head and searched for Regina. "The sooner I can get answers, the quicker I can deal with Miss Dewitt."

Although he might deal with her before he got the information she sought. Regina didn't know it yet, but she was about to be claimed. He was tired of fighting his desire. It was a craving that was a part of him and burned with every breath he took. Why fight it anymore?

Where the hell had she disappeared to? He scanned the room again and couldn't spot her flawless figure anywhere. Damn it. He'd have to go in search for her. He grinned at the idea. Maybe a hunt was exactly what they both needed.

"I can see you're looking for her." Zane interrupted Bradford's thoughts. "She slipped out several minutes ago."

Bradford whipped around to meet his gaze. "Why didn't you say so sooner?"

He shrugged. "Didn't see the point, and we were in the middle of a discussion."

Bradford growled in frustration. "You're being so helpful tonight." He glared at him. "Next time, maybe try not being a wanker."

Zane laughed and clutched his chest. "I never thought I'd see the day. I mean, I suspected, but man, now I know."

"Bloody hell," Bradford snarled. "Keep your damn suppositions to yourself. Better yet, stuff 'em up your arse."

Zane laughed even harder at Bradford's heated response. "Priceless. It's going to be an entertaining weekend." He tilted his champagne glass toward him. "I should have paid you for the pleasure of watching you make a fool of yourself. I can't wait to see what you do next."

Bradford swore under his breath and spun on his heels to leave. He was done listening to Zane. Besides, he had to find Regina and figure out what she was still hiding from him.

CHAPTER 7

REGINA STROLLED THROUGH THE CONSERVATORY trailing her fingers across lush vegetation. She stared up and could see stars twinkling through the domed window. The aroma of the flowers filling the room sent a wave of relaxation deep inside. She took a deep breath and allowed it to settle over her. It was peaceful and inviting after witnessing the mental chest-pounding match between Zane and Bradford. They could keep each other company, as the conservatory's beauty held more fascination.

She sighed and leaned down to smell a nearby rose. This was a little slice of heaven. The idea of a conservatory had always appealed to her. So much so she wished to have one of her own. Maybe one day she would, but until that happened she enjoyed the benefits of knowing people who did.

"Those blooms are almost as beautiful as you are."

Regina spun on her heel and turned to stare into the steel gray eyes of Zane Rossington. One of the annoying men she'd been set to escape earlier. Why couldn't they leave her alone? While she found both attractive, Zane didn't make her heart go pitter-patter. Bradford was the one her body craved. Unfortunately, the one she wanted wasn't standing in front of her. No, she couldn't be that lucky. Zane had to go bug someone else.

"Does that line actually work?" She raised an eyebrow mockingly.

His lips twitched with amusement. "I don't know. You tell me." He sauntered over to her side.

"If your gauge is my reaction, I'd say it's a dud." She took a step closer to him and raised her hand to trail her fingers down his impressive chest. Regina leaned up her lips brushing against the side of his cheek. His breath hitched as she and whispered. "I hate to tell you this, but you do nothing for me."

Regina stepped back to put some distance between them. He stared down at her with a cocky smile. He chuckled lightly. "I definitely see the appeal."

"Appeal?" She quirked an eyebrow.

"You're an exquisite woman." He grinned. "You would be interesting to have around."

"I'm not here for your entertainment." She rolled her eyes. "I believe you arranged for fun and games the entire weekend. Find something else to do."

"Such as?"

Good grief, he was an ass. "I really don't care as long as it's not me."

He laughed. "The things you say. You're amazing. We could have a lot of fun together. Say the word and I can make it happen."

"I'll pass." What game was he playing now? How clueless could one man be? Regina was tired of it all. Messing with Zane had been a spot of fun, but now she was tired of it. "As interesting as this little interlude's been, I think I'm going to call it a night."

"Don't go on my account." He bowed. "Enjoy the conservatory. I'll leave you in peace."

She frowned. Zane was as mercurial as Bradford. No wonder they butted heads so damn much. He could be as moody as he wanted to be. She didn't really care. All she wanted to do was have some peace and quiet. She wasn't going to be a bone they fought over. Although, from her observations, they didn't seem to need a reason to disagree. It was a part of the dynamic of their relationship. She had no desire to dig deeper into it or help them to come to an understanding. They'd probably not welcome her interference any way.

All she was certain of was she didn't give one fig and she'd not add fuel to their already brimming fire. The best way to eradicate her involvement was to remover herself from the situation. At first, it had seemed like a fun idea to pit them against each other. That was her old way of thinking, and she'd thought she'd grown past such theatrics. Some habits die hard and she'd fallen into one of her usual patterns with too much ease. It had sickened her a little to realize how easy it was for her to revert to her old self. Now that she did though she couldn't let it go. Regina had to let it go and walk away with as much dignity as she could muster.

"Am I interrupting a tête-à-tête?"

Regina glanced up and met Bradford's gaze. Great now they were going to have another pissing match. She wouldn't be lucky enough to un-entangle herself from this particular melee. She should have left before he strolled in. Then she could've avoided this nonsense altogether.

"Not at all. I was just leaving." Zane nodded at Regina. "Have a good evening." He left the room without saying another word.

"What do you want?" Regina asked belligerently.

Bradford moved toward her. "I can't be out for a stroll?"

She narrowed her eyes at him and frowned. No he couldn't. Bradford didn't do anything without a purpose. His blasé attitude didn't fool her for a moment. He was up to something. She lifted her chin defiantly. "In that case, I'll leave you to your solitude." She brushed past him to depart. He snaked out his arm and latched his hand onto her wrist.

"Don't leave."

Regina yanked her arm back and glared up at him, but couldn't shake his grip. "Let me go."

She gritted her teeth and waited for him to release her. When it wasn't forthcoming, she realized she would have to make him. *Thank you, Alys, for making me take some self-defense classes.* Regina leaned into him and then wrapped her leg around the back of his knees and yanked. It worked, but not in the way she'd hoped. He fell backward and took her down with him. Her body was fully sprawled over him, draped in an enticing fashion.

"If you wanted to have your way with me, all you had to do was ask."

Insufferable bastard. It was almost as if he had a line to her pulse and could feel her body's reaction to his presence. She wouldn't give him the satisfaction of knowing how much he affected her. She tilted her head and studied him. On the other hand, she could use it to her advantage. "Asking has never been my strong suit." She leaned down and pressed her lips to his.

His reaction was immediate and evident with his hardness brushing across her. He wrapped his arms around her waist and took what she offered. Bradford's lips rolled over hers smoothly and oh so effectively. Her body sang with tension and need. Regina hadn't realized how much she craved his touch until she had it. His hand trailed down her ass and rested at the hem of her short black cocktail dress. When she felt his nimble fingers working their way upward once again beneath her dress she deepened the kiss. She reached up and ran her fingers through his hair and wound them around his dark strands, holding his head in place.

Both of his hands were now under her dress, caressing her. He cupped her ass cheeks in the palm of his hands and then twisted her body around so he was on top. Bradford kissed down her throat and licked the top of her breasts. She shivered with a need so strong it overtook her. He'd taken control. What a fool she'd been to think she'd been the one leading him into a seduction. The duke was more skilled than she realized.

"This isn't how I wanted to do this," he said huskily. "I can't resist you."

She was as much a goner as he was. Stopping what was happening between them was futile, and damned if she wanted to anyway. He'd been in her mind and heart for longer than she'd been willing to admit. His presence set her on fire. Bradford did things to her no man ever had. Why had she thought to fight what was between them? She'd been a fool to think she could let it go. Trenton had deserved better, and she never should have married him with her desire for Bradford coursing through her veins.

"Shut up and kiss me," Regina demanded.

"As the lady wishes."

He didn't kiss her the way she thought he would. She expected another scorching mind numbing lip lock. Instead, he pushed up her dress and kissed the inside of her thigh. His lips trailed feather light kisses until he reached her panties. He slid them down with excruciating slowness until Regina squirmed with desire. She was past thinking. All she could see in her haze was him and what he did to her.

"Bradford," she moaned his name. "Please."

"Patience, sweet."

He kissed his way back up her thighs and pressed his lips to her core. She screamed as his tongue swirled around her sensitive nub, and his fingers stroked inside her. Bradford kept licking and sucking as she wiggled under his assault. Regina didn't know how much more she could take. She was on the brink of an explosion. She'd never experienced anything like his magic tongue.

"Yes," she moaned. Regina opened her eyes and gazed up at the stars through the domed ceiling. They exploded before her eyes as she peaked into the best orgasm she'd ever had. She screamed his name as he continued to lick her into more pleasure. Why had she resisted him so long? This was exactly what she wanted. Him. Always. Bradford could give her this, and she intended to do what she could to keep him. "That was amazing."

Bradford moved upward, trailing kisses along the way. He kissed each cheek as he reached her face. "Darling." He sucked her earlobe into his hot mouth. "This is just the beginning."

She didn't know if she could take anymore. He

had incredibly nimble fingers and one hell of way with his mouth. Did she really want him to stop now? Hell no. She reached down and cupped his cock in her hands. "What are you waiting for?"

He hitched a breath and ravaged her mouth with his. Regina kept her hand rested over his erection and caressed it through his pants. Bradford squirmed under her touch. It was his turn to moan in pleasure. She wanted to get her mouth on him and show him no mercy. She lifted both her arms and curved them around his neck. With careful precision she wrapped her legs around his waist and flipped him while he was distracted. She grinned down at his shock.

"It's my turn." Regina scooted down his hard body and unzipped his pants. She freed his hard cock from the constraint caressing it firmly. Bradford sucked in a breath and held it as she stroked him several times. Up. Down. Repeat.

"Regina," he begged.

She had an idea of what he wanted. He didn't even have to ask. Although she considered making him. This was power, and she enjoyed having him exactly where she wanted him. She leaned down and licked the side. He moaned louder.

"Inside," he demanded. "Take me inside."

She would. When she was ready. He needed to

be tortured more first. She sucked the tip between her lips and rolled her tongue over it. Bradford writhed beneath her ministrations. He mumbled nonsense. She thought she heard a, "Please," and, "Yes, that's so good," but couldn't be sure. She stopped and glanced up at him.

"No, keep going." A muscle in his jaw twitched as he stared at her through a hooded gaze.

"I don't know. I don't think you're enjoying this." She suppressed an amused smile. "I don't want to do something you don't like."

He cursed. Bradford reached for her and clasped his hand around one of her wrists. He tugged at her while his gaze flickered with desire. "I fucking love it. *Please.*"

Regina decided to stop messing with him and show him how wicked her mouth was. He'd suffered enough for his earlier cockiness. She took him fully inside her mouth and cupped his balls in her palm. She licked, sucked, and kissed him until he exploded in her mouth. She sat up and stared down at him. His eyes were closed and his mouth hung open. "Darling, I think we need to take this upstairs."

She grinned. "Afraid we might be caught?"

"Not at all," he replied. "I'm afraid we might get

interrupted." His eyelids fluttered open and met her gaze. "I'm tired of fighting this."

They were both on the same page. It was about damn time. They'd been dancing around each other too long. There was something here, and Regina wanted to explore it to see where it led them.

"Who's fighting?"

"Not me." He reached up and cupped her cheek in his hands. "I'm going to explore every inch of you. Be prepared for one hell of a sleepless night."

Regina tilted her head and laughed. "Babe, I'm willing to bet you'll fall before I do." She didn't know what would happen after they had each other in every way possible, but she didn't want to think too hard on it. If things were meant to work between them they would. For now, she intended to enjoy what he had to offer. The rest could wait.

"That's a bet I'm willing to take." He found her lips with his and turned her mind to mush once again. Regina could become addicted to his kisses if she didn't watch herself.

CHAPTER 8

Bradford held Regina's hand in his as they exited the conservatory. He'd truly gone and fallen down the path to hell. What's more, he didn't give a damn. This was what he wanted, and he didn't see any reason not to reach out and take it. He'd been fighting himself too long. Regina was no longer married to his step-brother. There was no real reason not to have her in every way possible. Maybe he should stop and consider what Trenton would think, but at that moment, with her warm in his arms, he couldn't bring himself to care. Regina had mentioned he'd gone to search for Genevieve. Maybe he'd already forgotten about his failed marriage and his priorities lie elsewhere. Of course, it was a certainty Bradford was making excuses for his own behavior and desires. He'd deal with the consequences—whatever they may be—later.

"Pardon me, Your Grace," a servant said, stopping them in the hallway. "I don't mean to interrupt, but you have a message."

He scrunched his eyebrows up and frowned. Who would be trying to contact him? "Thank you," Bradford said and picked up the note. After he read it he cursed. Trenton had finally contacted him. His step-brother had the worst timing. His libido had been squashed faster than if he'd taken a cold shower. *Damn it, Trenton!* He'd had plans. Wicked, diabolical and so decadent he'd have been riding a pleasure high for months.

"What is it?" Regina curled in closer to him. "You look irritated."

"I'm sorry." She wouldn't have a clue how much. "Something's come up that needs my attention." He kissed her quickly. "Why don't you go upstairs. I'll join you when I'm done."

He wasn't going anywhere near her that night. Guilt was an ugly emotion, one Bradford hated experiencing. After he talked to Trenton, he'd confront his feelings for Regina. Until then, he couldn't continue as if none of it mattered. Unfortunately it all mattered far more than he'd been willing to admit to himself. Trenton was important to him. Regina was fast becoming equally as much. He wanted her more than he'd ever wanted another woman. He had to do things right. This was entirely new territory for him. He didn't—he gulped down a lump in his throat —do relationships. Was that what he wanted with her? These feelings he had rolling through him...he had trouble understanding them. A part of him refused to examine them too closely either.

"Don't keep me waiting long." She lifted her hand and trailed her fingers across his arm. "I'm not a patient woman."

Lucky for him, he could be patient enough for the both of them. "Trust me, the wait will be worth it."

He had a lot at stake, and he wouldn't take any of it lightly. When he figured out how to proceed Regina would be the first to know. Until then, he had to take things one step at a time. He'd been under the influence of pleasure when he'd suggested they go upstairs and continue. It'd been a heady experience that drugged him beyond reason.

"I'm going to hold you to that." She smiled coyly. Regina spun on her heels and headed toward the stairs. She stopped on the third one and turned back to him. "Oh, and if you disappoint me, I promise you will live to regret it." With a quick wink, pressed her lips to her palm, and blew him a kiss. Then she turned and headed up the stairs.

No doubt about it, she would give him hell of the worst kind. He'd have to make it up to her, in some way. Bradford suspected he'd need all the assistance he could get. She wouldn't let him off lightly, but it couldn't be helped. He stared up the stairs until he could no longer see her. With a sigh, he headed to the study. There shouldn't be anyone around to disturb him when he made his call.

Bradford was right. The room was empty. He reached inside his jacket and pulled out his phone. Bradford didn't understand why Trenton hadn't called, but then realized he had. There were several missed calls. He'd been so wrapped up in Regina he hadn't felt the vibrations alerting him. She was dangerous to be around. He'd never been so involved he didn't notice his surroundings.

He grimaced and clicked Trenton's name in his contact list. After several rings the voicemail clicked on. Bradford cursed under his breath. "I'm sorry I missed your calls earlier. I'm going to head back to Weston Manor in the morning. Meet me there when you can. We need to talk. Don't disappear again, Trent. This is important."

"Trouble in paradise already?"

Bradford closed his eyes and took a deep breath. Zane was turning out to be a bad penny. One he couldn't avoid and couldn't get rid of either. If he wasn't one of his oldest friends he'd have knocked him out already. "No one around who was willing to put up with you for the evening?" Bradford raised an eyebrow mockingly at him. "Poor Zane. What are you going to do with yourself now?"

"That's rich coming from you." Zane smirked. "Where's the lovely Regina at? I thought you'd have been busy with her for the rest of the night."

Why was Zane so interested in his interactions with Regina? Bradford narrowed his eyes and studied him. Did he stick around to witness what happened between them in the conservatory? He wouldn't put it past him. Zane could, and would, listen at the door to gather information. Bradford wanted to call him out on it, but if he was wrong he didn't want to bring it to his attention either. It was a conundrum and entirely his fault. He'd been too careless in his haze of desire. He'd thought he'd be loving Regina all night long. This turn of events was definitely not how he'd seen the rest of the evening going. He'd be damned if he admitted that to Zane

though. The marquess was too smug to give him
more ammunition to throw back at him.

"Who says I won't be?" He grinned. "The night
is still young."

"Touché, my friend." Zane nodded. "Don't let
me keep you then."

Damn, he was stuck. He couldn't admit he
wasn't going after Regina, but it would look bad if he
stuck around. How to steer the conversation away
from his potential bed partner though?

"Did you find any more information on our
mutual ancestor?"

That should do it. Bradford doubted that Zane
would have had much luck locating the documents that
would help him, but it would at least change the direction of their exchange to a more business-like tone.

"Actually, I did."

Bradford glanced up at him. Surprise filled him
at his words. "You did?"

"You didn't expect that answer did you?" Zane
laughed. "It's good to know I can still shock you."

As if he'd lost that skill. Zane kept things too
close to the vest to do otherwise. He could shock his
own mother if he wanted to. Although it probably
wouldn't be in a good way—the marchioness was a

stern lady and extremely prudish. Zane's mother should have been born in another era.

"Don't hold out on me. What did you find?"

"I didn't find any of the documents or books you said she brought here with her." He paused and gazed up at Bradford. "I *did* find a journal of hers in the library. Strangely, it was lying on my desk. I haven't a clue how it ended up there."

That was odd, but Bradford didn't want to look at it too closely. It was another gift. Not the same as Trenton's untimely interruption earlier, but a present nonetheless. "You're sure it's the former marchioness's journal?"

"I didn't read the entire thing to ascertain the contents, but I did read enough to know it is hers." He reached inside his jacket pocket and dangled it for him to see. It was a small booklet no bigger than a large mobile phone. Bradford gauged it to be around six inches in length and four or five inches across, less than an inch in thickness. "I think it's the first one she wrote after she married and moved into Seabrook."

"Give it to me." Bradford lunged forward attempting to snatch it from him.

"Not so fast." Zane held it out of Bradford's

reach, a smirk settling over his face. "What do I get if I give it to you?"

Zane had a death wish. His oldest friend had suddenly lost his mind. There was no other explanation for his behavior. "What do you want?"

"I want Regina."

Bradford blanched at his demand. He schooled his features as best as he could. The desire to strike was at the forefront and one wrong step from Zane and Bradford would blow. He had to play this right or he'd do something he'd regret. One thing was certain: he didn't give a bloody fig what Zane wanted. He'd not give in for anything. Zane wasn't going anywhere near Regina. He didn't need the journal that bad. "She's not mine to give."

"Isn't she?"

He'd like her to be his, but even then it wouldn't be his decision to make. This wasn't the dark ages when women were owned by the men in their life. Regina was free to do as she chose. It might grate on his nerves in the worst way, but if she wanted Zane he'd step back and leave her be. He didn't think it would come to that. He hoped so anyway. It wouldn't be pleasant to see her with his friend.

"Regina makes her own decisions." Bradford

gritted his teeth together. "What is this really about, Zane?"

The man tucked the journal into his pocket and crossed his arms across his chest. "I'm trying to figure out what is so special about her. I've never seen you this way over a woman."

It wasn't anything he'd ever thought he'd see himself. Regina was different. He couldn't completely understand it. It was a realization that was hard for him to accept. She'd always been there in the back of his mind. Her sister had called him out on it when Regina was about to marry Trenton. He'd brushed it aside then, and if he'd had to he would have kept doing it. Now he didn't have to. She was there and he could have her, but not without a cost to his soul, and perhaps his relationship with Trenton.

"Why do you care?"

He needed a damn drink. This night wasn't going well. It had started out bad, with a little plea-sure in the middle, and now was on the brink of completely falling apart. Bradford crossed the room and snatched the brandy decanter off a shelf. He poured some into a crystal goblet and downed it. He refilled the glass again and turned toward Zane. The marquess studied him with a blank expression.

"You're one of my best friends," he replied. "I don't want to see you make a mistake over a woman."

Bradford snickered. That was rich coming from him. "How many women have you fallen for? How many mistakes have you made?"

"That's different and you know it. I enjoy women, and they equally return that sentiment. I don't make commitments. It's easier that way. But you..." He paused and stared at him. "You don't fall for anything or anyone. Everything is carefully planned out to the nth degree. With Regina you're a loose cannon, and I'm afraid for you."

Bradford shook his head. His laugher echoed through the room. It was the God's honest truth. This was all new to him. He didn't know up from down and he was on a yo-yo course of destruction. He'd go one step forward and three steps back. There was no progress. He'd taken a giant leap with Regina only to find himself in the company of Zane regretting it. What was wrong with him? Why couldn't he make a decision and stick with it. He wanted her. Lord did he want her. It was a longing so deep it had embedded itself into his soul.

"Bradford?" Zane asked. "Are you all right?"

Was he? He doubted he'd ever be all right again. He lifted his glass and swallowed the remaining brandy in one drink. "So your solution to your fears is to demand I give Regina to you? In what world does that make sense?" He slammed the glass on the shelf. "If you think she means that much to me, why would you even suggest something so ridiculously outlandish? What kind of friend would do that?"

Zane sighed. "I admit it was wrong. I shouldn't have taken it that far. I was testing your commitment to her. I should have known it wasn't the way to play it."

Maybe he should be grateful Zane was willing to go the extra mile to make sure he wasn't taken for a ride—albeit a pleasurable one—but it was his choice to make. He'd not been pleased by his way of assessing the situation. Zane did appear a little... deflated. There was no other way to describe his friend's forlorn expression. Maybe he should go easier on him, but he couldn't yet. Not until his blood cooled a little.

"Damned right it wasn't. Now give me the bloody journal so I can read it. Maybe this can all be solved tonight and Regina can go back to New York tomorrow."

"Do you really want her to go?" He pulled the book from his pocket and held it toward Bradford.

No. He didn't want her to leave him, but it

wasn't up to him what she did. She wanted to find out what happened to her sister. The marchioness's journal might hold all the answers she sought. He'd not deny her for his own selfish reasons.

"What I want doesn't matter." Bradford snatched the journal out of Zane's hands and left him alone in the study. He had a long night ahead of him.

CHAPTER 9

"Regina," a female called out to her. "Wake up."

She opened her eyes and met Eve's eerie gaze. Great, just what she needed. Why wouldn't she leave her alone? "What do you want?" She hadn't been helpful thus far, and Regina didn't see this visit being any different. "I'm too tired to deal with you."

"He has the book."

Like she cared? She'd rather keep her eyes closed and enjoy the comfort of her bed. Sleep was so wonderful. Regina waved her hand. "Go away. I don't care about any damn book."

"Are you always this difficult?" Eve sighed. "I'm trying to help you."

Please, as if...Eve wasn't doing anything for

Regina. This was all about what the damned woman needed not what Regina did. She was done running around looking like an idiot. Nothing Eve told her had given her any solid answers thus far. Whatever news she had to depart, it could be dealt with later.

"No, you're not." Regina mumbled. "Your motives have everything to do with what you need, and nothing to do with me. I'm not inclined to roll out of bed and jump to do your bidding."

"You're right," she agreed. "I need you, but you should know that this also has to do with your sister."

"What?" Regina sat up abruptly. The room started to spin. She leaned down and put her head between her knees and took a deep breath. "Explain yourself," Regina demanded.

What did Eve know about Alys? She kept alluding to her, but had yet to give her any real information. She was sick and tired of the cat and mouse game. Why couldn't she come out and tell her what she knew. She wanted to know where her sister was. If Alys needed her she wanted to do everything in her power to assist her.

"The answers are in the book. Go find it and you will know everything—or most of it any way."

Regina glanced up at Eve and rolled her eyes. "Are you serious? What's with all the cryptic bullshit? Why don't you tell me what you know and put us both out of our misery?"

Eve stared at Regina and remained silent. Her eyes held a tinge of sadness. Regina almost felt sorry for the other woman, but squashed it as fast as it entered her mind. She didn't owe Eve anything. All the woman had done was freak her out several times. She was over it already. She wanted a clue as to what happened to Alys. Eve wasn't helping, and Regina was tired of it.

"I can't tell you."

Of course she couldn't. Probably because she was a figment of her imagination—answers didn't jump out just because you wanted them bad enough. They had to be researched and discovered through normal means. Yet she couldn't help carrying on a conversation with Eve as if she'd suddenly disclose all.

"Why the hell not?" Regina crawled off the bed and stalked toward Eve. "This is the last time you come to me with this crap. I don't have time to deal with you and your secrets. If you can't tell me, then quit popping into my head."

"I'm not inside your head," Eve explained. "I'm here in the only way I can be."

"Again with the mysteriousness you impart every

time you come to see me. I don't want to know how you're here." Regina glared. "What I do want is for you to leave. I didn't manage much sleep last night."

"I know." Eve nodded. "You were waiting for him, and he didn't show up."

Did she have to remind Regina of her stupidity? Yes, Bradford never showed up as he promised. He'd left her waiting. It'd left her with a sickness pooling in her stomach. She'd been a fool to think he'd finally changed. Bradford wasn't ready to see where they were heading. No, the dense man had played her. He was acting like a rakish jerk. Maybe seducing him had been the bad idea to begin with. The rat bastard didn't deserve her. If she said it often enough to herself, perhaps she'd believe it too.

"I don't need your commentary on my night. I was there, thank you very much." How creepy was it that Eve knew she'd spent the night waiting for Bradford? Did she watch her often? Had she witnessed their encounter in the conservatory? "Do you see everything I do?"

"No." Eve glanced away quickly.

"You're lying," Regina accused. "What did you see?"

Now she was pissed off. She didn't appreciate Eve's voyeurism. Even if it was inside her head, thoughts and a person's deepest desires—her desires —should remain private.

"I don't see everything you do. That wasn't a lie." Eve met Regina's gaze. "I did perhaps witness a part of your more, um, erotic dreams. I bowed out before I got an eyeful."

Regina clenched her hand into a fist. "Erotic Dreams?" What was she talking about now? *Oh... that. Damn it.* She couldn't exactly help what her subconscious conjured up. "I knew I didn't like you."

"I'm sorry." Eve glanced down. "I had to speak to you, but my timing was off. I'm not infallible. My gifts are limited."

Regina didn't give one iota about her damned gifts or their limits. "Why don't you tell me why you're here and do me a favor and not pop in ever again."

If she was lucky enough Eve would heed her request and leave her alone. She didn't need her kind of help. All it did was irritate her. Yes, she'd given her some decent clues, but full on answers would have been better. Regina wasn't one to appreciate mysteries. Never had liked them as they usually left her with a headache—something she tried to avoid as much as possible.

"I told you he has the book. It should tell you

what you need to know. She promised me she'd leave a clue in there for you to find."

"Who did?" Regina rubbed her temples. Speaking of headaches... "Why can't you speak like a normal person?"

"Dreams are funny things. You can only manipulate so much." She waved her hands. "I can tell you certain things, but you may or may not believe me. The mysterious makes you think and want to find the answers."

"So you're purposely being obtuse?"

Wouldn't that figure? This was all a dream so it had to be weaved in vagueness to make sense. It didn't surprise her that Eve's explanation made sense. If this was a dream, anything was possible. The impossible was possible and the blurred was crystal clear—the yin and yang of the dream world.

"Oh, you understand. Good." Eve glanced over her shoulder. "I'm out of time. Don't forget to ask him about the book."

"Who do I ask about the stupid book?" Regina yelled, but it was futile. Eve disappeared before she could get an answer. Damn it, how was she supposed to solve a mystery without all the clues?

"Darling, wake up."

"Go away. I already had this conversation."

Bradford's light chuckle filled her ears. "I assure you we did not have this particular discussion."

Regina opened one eye and found him sitting on the edge of her bed. "I don't want you here. Please leave, you missed your chance. Now I'm too tired to do anything fun."

She was still pissed at him for not showing up when he'd promised. Regina didn't forgive and forget easily. He'd have to do a lot of begging to get back into her good graces. As far as she was concerned, it would also have to include gifts, expensive ones.

"I'll make it up to you." He kissed her forehead. "Quit being difficult. It's not becoming."

She turned to stare at him. Who was this creature and what had he done with Bradford? Not becoming? Who said that kind of nonsense anyway? "I don't care what you think." All right, maybe she did a little bit, but he didn't need to know that.

"I don't have time for this." Bradford sighed. "We have to head back to Weston Manor. Pack your things and meet me downstairs in thirty minutes."

Her mouth fell open at his dictatorial manner. It took her several minutes for his words to fully sink in. He got up to leave as if his command was the end of their discussion. She was not a dog he could order around. She didn't care what his reasons were or why he had to go back to his estate. So what if his plans had changed? They didn't have to have an impact on what she wanted to do. The blasted man could leave and never look back. The way he bounced back and forth was grating on every last one of her nerves. "By all means, go back to your estate. I don't need to follow you back. I rather like Seabrook, and the company it provides."

She let that settle into the room before she hopped off the bed and rummaged through her travel bag. Let him suck on that for a little while. His little competition with Zane was sure to make him rethink his plans. He hadn't liked her interlude with him. At the time, she'd rather enjoyed his jealousy and had taken it as a sign of his interest. Afterward, it led her to believe he wanted to be with her. What a joke. Bradford had wanted to win; it'd had nothing to do with Regina.

"I'm afraid I can't allow that."

"Allow it?" She turned toward him and raised an eyebrow. "Please explain when I started answering to you?"

He stalked forward, stopping directly in front of her. "Don't be like this. Last night was unavoidable."

She would not cave. Not at all. Nope. Damn it, she was going to be mush and she couldn't stop herself. Why did this man affect her so? "I don't care. I deserve to be treated right. So far, you're doing a shoddy job of it."

"I told you I'd make it up to you," he exclaimed, and ran his fingers through his dark hair. "Please just do as I asked. I need to go home, and I don't want to leave you behind."

"Why do you have to go back? Maybe if you explain it to me I won't be so difficult." Was it too much to ask to be included in what was going on? She hadn't thought so. Regina hated being the last one to know anything.

"I'll tell you everything on the way."

"No deal." She turned back to her bag and pulled out an outfit for the day and set it on the bed. "I'm going to take a shower and prepare for the day of fun I was promised. Not stupid traveling that will exhaust me further."

He crossed the room and stood directly behind her. She flinched as his hands came up to her arms holding her in place. Bradford leaned in, his hot breath caressing her ear. "What will it take to convince you to come back with me?"

"Nothing. I already tried talking with you" She turned around and faced him. "You're the one who doesn't feel like sharing." Regina took a step back and shrugged. "That's your prerogative. Kind of like how mine is to ignore your demands and do what I want. See how that works?"

"You want to do this the hard way then?" He grinned wickedly. "We can do that."

Oh hell, what had she goaded him into? A tingle pooled in her stomach and spread through her whole body. She would never admit it to him, but she was excited at the prospect of what he considered the "hard way." Regina licked her lips seductively and winked at him. "Do your worst, Your Grace."

Then she spun on her heels and sprinted. He caught her before she was able to exit the room. He turned her in his arms and pinned her against the closed door. "That wasn't very sporting of you."

"I never said I played fair." Heat consumed her from the inside out. He always did this to her. She wanted him beyond reason.

He leaned down and touched her neck with his lips. "Some of the best things in life are that much better when you're the victor." Bradford trailed light kisses across her chin and cheek. "I play to win, and when I'm serious, nothing stands in my way. Not even stubborn females who should know better than to tempt the beast."

She was going to combust. There was no stopping it now. He hadn't even done more than kiss her lightly, and she was about to come apart. What would happen when he did so in earnest?

"Can I wave my white flag and surrender?" He was right. She should have known what would happen when she baited him. Perhaps she had on some level. This was what she wanted. Him giving her his full attention—the true master of seduction. "We can skip to what we both want."

"What is it you want?"

"You," she whispered. She'd never wanted anything as badly as she did him.

"If you're good and do as I asked." He nipped her ear. "We might arrive at Weston Manor in time to seize what we both desire."

That sounded lovely. Wait a minute, she had to remain frustrated all the way to his estate and even then, there was no guarantee he'd give in to the pleasure they both craved? "You're not serious?"

"I promise you I am." He cupped one of her breasts in his hand. "Quit fighting the inevitable and prepare for our journey."

"Fine." She sighed and pushed him away. "You win." She should give him more of a hard time, but she didn't have the energy. "At least for now, but be prepared for a siege of epic proportions once we arrive at Weston Manor."

"I look forward to it." He saluted her with three fingers. "I expect nothing less from you." He exited the room with those words, and he was lucky he'd escaped so quickly. Otherwise, he'd have been maimed by a nearby candelabra.

"Cocky bastard."

Maybe it was time to knock him down a peg or two for real. A blindfold and rope would be a good start...

CHAPTER 10

"I STILL DON'T UNDERSTAND WHY WE HAD TO leave." Regina said for the hundredth time.

All right, that might be an exaggeration, but it felt like it. Why did she have to keep stating that as if it would change things? Bradford didn't want to tell her he was expecting Trenton, but he might have to break down and do it. He couldn't predict her reaction to the news, and avoiding it seemed like the best idea. She'd already been difficult about leaving. Every so often she'd glance over at him with a look that made him uneasy. She was planning something, but he had no idea what it was. He twitched uneasily every time she glanced in his direction. The way she stared at him... A shiver ran through him as he remembered the last time he dared to look at her.

"I'm not explaining myself again." He'd already done it more than he was used to. Bradford didn't feel the need to tell anyone why he did anything. That was his business. That he afforded her that respect should have said a lot. "Something has come up and it is imperative I return."

She folded her arms across her chest and stared out the window. "You're a jerk."

"But you like me anyway."

"Not even close, you clueless prick." She shook her head. "Like has nothing to do with what I feel about you."

He didn't want to examine what she meant by that statement. She glared at him at regular intervals and he was afraid it had turned to hate. What she may or may not have felt before that—he hoped to go back to it at some point. She meant something to him, and he wanted to figure out exactly what that was once he settled things with his brother. His conscience wouldn't allow him to do anything differently. For now, he'd deal with her constant disapproval and continued hostility. He didn't blame her for her displeasure. In her shoes, he'd feel the same way.

"Pardon me, Your Grace, but your vehicle has

been brought around. Do you require assistance with your bags?"

His mind kept wandering to Regina's words. Why couldn't he let it go? He wanted to, yet he couldn't. Bradford wanted to push the butler aside. He hadn't appreciated the interruption. What had Regina meant by she didn't like him? Was it only lust on her side? Would she disappear on him once she sated her need? It wouldn't do good to assume anything. She was angry and probably saying things she didn't actually mean.

One thing was certain though. The more he dissected her statement, the less he liked the conclusions he was coming to. It left him rather unsettled to believe she might not feel the same way about him as he did for her. He was turning into a maudlin woman, and he hated it. The bloody Duke of Weston didn't act like a pansy over a woman. He steeled himself and forced himself to deal with the situation with as much pretense as possible. There was no reason to let her know how much her rancor affected him.

"No, we can manage. Please give Lord Seabrook our thanks for his hospitality."

"Very well, Your Grace." He bowed and then turned on his heels to leave.

Bradford glanced at Regina and sucked in a breath. She was staring at him with such open appraisal he almost forgot his reasons for leaving. What was the rush anyway? He could throw her over his shoulder and take her back upstairs... He shook the idea away and nodded toward her. "Come, it's time to leave."

"Fine," she agreed. "But I'm not happy about it."

She didn't have to state the obvious. Bradford was more than aware of how upset she was, but they had to go. After they were on the road she'd either get over it, or not. He didn't bloody care as long as she got in the damn car. They walked outside in silence, not a word spoken as they loaded their luggage, or when they got inside. Bradford put the car into drive and started the journey back to Weston Manor.

The silence was almost deafening, but he didn't believe she'd stay quiet long. It wasn't Regina's strong suit. She liked everyone around her to hear what she had to say. An hour into their journey she still wasn't speaking to him. Something he found rather surprising. Maybe he should do something to shake her up a tiny bit. There had to be a way to bring her out of her decision to remain mute and driving him stark raving mad. He'd become used to her constant chatter and this—silence—had grown to be more than he could take. Insulting her was the only thing he could think of to shake her out of it.

"I don't particularly like you much either." He kept his focus on the road, and didn't turn even slightly to look at her. "Doesn't mean we can't find some common ground and continue to enjoy each other.

"I have no words." Her voice dripped with disdain.

At least she'd spoken. That was a start. "Who says you need any? There are plenty of things you can do with your mouth that doesn't require them."

That was crass, and he couldn't believe he'd uttered it. Where Regina was concerned, he had no control of the nonsense he spouted. Although they were true words, he'd not really meant to tell her that. He was turning into a complete wanker.

"Something you'll never experience from me again." She snorted. "Of course a handsome bloke such as yourself should have no problem finding a trollop to satisfy your needs. If you're lucky, she might even be willing to use her *mouth* too." She held her fingers up and used air quotes as she said the word mouth.

"Don't make threats you don't have any intention

of carrying out." He glanced over at her. His lips twitched into a smug smile. He had her going, and exactly where he wanted her. "We both know you'd never let anyone else near me."

"You keep on believing that," she replied with sarcasm. "You'll see how much that theory holds up."

Damn, she was cheeky, but he bloody well adored her. "Oh, it'll hold up, down, and in every position we find ourselves."

She would murder him if he kept this up. They'd be back at Weston Manor shortly and they'd not be stuck in a car together. No telling what she'd do when they arrived. If the little glances she kept throwing at him gave him any indication it wouldn't be good. Nope, it would be an all out war, and he couldn't wait to start it.

"What game are you playing?" she asked. "You're the most confusing man I've ever met."

"And you're not?" He paused, and rephrased, "Confusing that is." She most definitely *wasn't* male.

He pulled his car along the drive to Weston Manor and parked by the front entrance. It was time for a reckoning. She'd been steaming mad before they left; now she was past the boiling point. Was it wrong he was excited. Bradford exited the car and slowly sauntered inside. They had plenty of time to continue sharing barbs with each other. When he stepped inside, he stopped short when he realized Regina hadn't advanced any further than the foyer. He was surprised to see her standing stock still. Why wasn't she moving? He turned his head and there is brother stood a few feet in front of him.

"It's about damn time you found your way home," Trenton said. "I've been waiting all night for you."

"What are you doing here?" Regina asked. "Have you found her?"

Bradford tilted his head and studied them both. She was shocked to see him at Weston Manor. They didn't seem to be on the same wavelength at all. They were both staring at each other like two people out of place, and no direction to speak of. Regina didn't seem to be happy to see Trenton, and neither did the feeling appear to be reciprocated. What was going on between them? Was there more to the story that Regina hadn't bothered to tell him? Hell, it wasn't as if she'd been overly forthcoming with details. He didn't know a damn thing except they were divorced and Trenton was searching for Genevieve.

Trenton glanced at Regina and shook his head. "No, but I think the answers are here."

"Really?" She frowned. "I think you may be wasting your time."

Everything they said went completely around him. Regina appeared to be aware of what Trenton was looking for though. Was this about his search for Genevieve? If so, he had to agree with her. There were no clues to her whereabouts at Weston Manor. Their reserved manner with each other bothered him, and he didn't understand why. It should make him feel better. This had to mean there was no chance of a reconciliation. Maybe it was because she hadn't bothered to mention they'd ended their marriage until the day before. Bradford was sick of being the one without a clue.

"Why don't you two tell me what the hell is going on?"

Trenton turned toward Bradford. "It's a long story. Why don't we go sit down and discuss this in comfort?"

"No," Bradford said mulishly. "I want answers now."

He didn't like the camaraderie between Regina and Trenton. Yes, he fully realized they'd been married, but he hated seeing her even remotely close to anyone. He'd started to think of her as his, and none of this exchange sat well inside his gut. It churned and twisted, sickening him with each glance they shared.

"Well, you two can continue this conversation amongst yourselves. I've spent way too much time already with him." Regina pointed at Bradford and rolled her eyes. "He's all yours Trent, good luck."

"Where are you going?" Bradford demanded. "I'm not done talking to you."

"Too bad, because I'm beyond done with you." She stomped away and headed up the stairs.

Trenton glanced toward Regina and back to Bradford. "What's Gina doing here anyway? I thought she was still in New York."

Bradford shook his head and said, "I need a drink."

He brushed past Trenton and headed toward his study, not once checking to see if his brother followed. None of this made a lick of sense. Regina had turned him into a raving lunatic, and his brother was being a mysterious oaf.

"When did you start drinking in the middle of the day?"

"Oh, about the time your wife showed up on my doorstop demanding to negotiate the contract with her father's company, and being allowed to search for clues on her lost sister."

"She's not my wife." There was no emotion evident in his voice and his face was expressionless.

Trenton imparted the statement as if he was delivering a set of facts that should have been obvious to the world. It wasn't as if Bradford said the world was flat, and not round. If he'd bothered to tell Bradford what was going on in his life he'd have known things had fallen apart with him and Regina. There was one thing he could cling to.

Regina hadn't lied. Relief flooded through him. He hadn't realized he'd been holding his breath waiting for Trenton to verify what she'd said. Yes, he'd grabbed a hold of the idea of their separation with both hands and clung to it as a beacon of hope, but he also hadn't fully believed her. He wanted to, but he couldn't risk it.

"Yeah, she may have mentioned that." He poured brandy into two crystal goblets and handed one to Trenton. "Why'd you get divorced?"

Trenton took the glass and sipped the amber liquid. "Annulment actually—we realized we made a mistake early on. I never fully got over Genevieve, and I wanted to come back to England to search for her."

"I see." And he did as everything clicked into place. Of course Trenton would be searching for the love of his life. Regina couldn't have been happy to realize she came in second place. Bradford understood that well, as he now was firmly in that place next to his step-brother. She'd married him, and that meant she must have *loved* him, perhaps still did. Bradford wouldn't measure up to that, so why should he even try? He swallowed all the brandy in his glass and poured another one. Why not get completely drunk—no reason to stay sober.

"We care about each other a great deal, but neither one of us are each other's true love."

What the hell was he blabbering on about now? "No, I could've told you that. Genevieve was your everything; although, I'd hoped you moved on. There is no indication she can be found or is even still alive."

Could Regina let go and love someone else? She already said she didn't like him. What could he do to change her mind? There had to be something. He almost snorted at the absurdity of his thought process. Their journey from Seabrook hadn't endeared him to her. He'd been a bloody arse.

"I've been looking into it for months now. I honestly believe the answer is here. I've been working with a professor at Oxford. We've gone through every clue and the last set indicated there might be something here at Weston Manor that would indicate what happened to her. It might be a long shot, but I have to follow every lead."

Bradford didn't understand it, and maybe he didn't want to. It might even be wrong to encourage Trenton to continue his search, but he couldn't do that to his brother. If he wanted to find out what happened to Genevieve, Bradford wouldn't stand in his way. How could he? *He* wouldn't stop searching if the woman he loved disappeared. Nothing and no one would stop him from searching for her.

"Well, you're welcome to look, but I don't see how there would be anything here for you to find. I've had a long day and night, so if you'll excuse me, I'm going to retire to my chambers."

Bradford turned to walk out of the study and leave Trenton to his searching. Pain was shooting though his chest, and he didn't quit understand why. He rubbed his hand over it trying to ease the constant ache.

"She loves you."

"Pardon me?" Bradford turned toward him.

"I didn't miss the way you were looking at her." He smiled. "I know why you're so irritated. You think she's emotionally unavailable, and I'm telling you, you're wrong. Regina never loved me. Oh, she cares, and probably always will, but she didn't fight too hard for our marriage. She accepted the end quite amicably. I think she always loved you, but thought she had to honor her commitment to me."

Bradford scrunched his eyebrows together and stared at him. He didn't think he was that obvious with how he felt about Regina. He prided himself on his poker face, and here his step-brother read him like an open book. "I don't know why you're saying this."

"Of course you do." Trenton crossed over to him and placed his hand on Bradford's shoulder. "You don't need my permission, or approval, but it's yours. Don't hold back. I wouldn't in your place. When I find Genevieve, she won't doubt for a minute I love her."

Bradford was living in some other dimension. It was the only conclusion he could arrive at listening to Trenton speak. "Right. I'm leaving."

"Don't wait too long to make your claim." Trenton laughed. "Or she will make it for you."

He shook his head as he exited. Trenton was

433

right. He had to do something or Regina would. She'd had an evil glint in her eye earlier, and no doubt had a plan designed to terrify him, as well as put him in his place.

It showed how insane he'd become that he looked forward to whatever she'd concocted.

CHAPTER 11

Regina slowly opened the door and crept inside. Moonlight glowed through the window and fell across the burgundy bedspread, and she smiled. It couldn't be more perfect if she'd planned it. The headboard had wide posts with an array of smaller ones carved inside the middle. It would be easy to slide a rope through to secure someone's—the dastardly duke's to be precise—hands.

She slid the silk rope through her fingers and studied his sleeping form. He hadn't moved since she sneaked inside his chambers. It had been too easy to avoid him the rest of the day as she planned her revenge, but it was time to begin enacting her plan. As quietly as she could manage, she prepared the ropes into loops on each side of the bed. Bradford stretched his arm up to one side, causing alarm to shoot through her. *Don't wake up.* She sighed when he didn't open his eyes and slid the rope around his wrist and secured it. One down, one to go, and then the fun will begin. She tiptoed across to the other side and quickly slid his wrist inside the ties. As she was about to fasten the knot his eyes fluttered open.

"Regina?"

She swiftly pulled the cord and smiled down at him. "Are you nice and comfy?"

He yanked on the ties, but they didn't budge. "What the hell is going on?" His voice was still hoarse and groggy from sleep.

Regina rolled her tongue over her teeth and stared at her handiwork. So far so good, and she was pleased to find he slept nude. That made things much easier.

"You look a little warm. Why don't I remove this pesky quilt?" She yanked it off him, and then reached over and turned on the bedside lamp. "Oh yeah, that's much better."

He glared at her. His blue eyes rivaled ice; they were that cold. "Untie me, now."

"I can't do that." She tapped her finger on her chin. "I feel like I'm forgetting something."

"Regina."

"I know what I didn't do." She strolled over to the other side of the bed and grabbed the blindfold she'd set down on the pillow. With careful precision she slid it over his eyes. "There. We can't forget that important detail."

"Untie me, now," he exclaimed, yanking hard on the ropes. "This isn't funny."

She held her hands over her stomach and suppressed laughter from bubbling out. He couldn't know how much his predicament amused her. "If you're not quiet, I'll be forced to gag you. That would be a tragedy. I have a lot of things planned for that mouth of yours." See how he liked being told he could do a lot with his mouth that didn't involve words. "Talking is *not* allowed."

"I promise you," he said with steel in his tone, "if you don't stop this game you're playing now I'll make sure you regret it."

That was a chance she was willing to take. He had to understand she was tired of his attitude and derogatory implications. She would not be a play thing for him to toss aside and forget. This farce was about to end. She wasn't just done—she was fucking angry. No one messed with her the way Bradford had over the past several days. Regrets? She had many, but tonight wouldn't be among them.

"You stay comfy there. I have to get a few things for our festivities." She leaned down and kissed his cheek. "Miss me while I'm gone."

"Regina," he bellowed. "Get your pretty ass back here and I'll be lenient in your punishment."

She grinned down at him. He was adorable in his frustration. "Right, I'll bring the ball gag back with me. These demands won't be tolerated."

Several curses flew from his mouth. Damn, he could be so inventive with swear words. It was fascinating to listen to them all, and she took note of them all for future use. Then she slid out of the room to gather a few things. The ball gag had been a joke, mostly. As much as she'd like to use the device, she'd not had time to acquire one earlier. She could make do with something else, but it wouldn't be as fun. Maybe she could find a few things in the kitchen to use. It would be even more fun to keep him stewing for a while. He'd be steaming mad by the time she returned.

Regina skipped down the stairs, joy filling her with each step. She made her way to the kitchen, stopping short when she found Trenton staring into the refrigerator. "Find anything interesting in there?"

"No." He shook his head. "I'm looking more out of boredom than anything."

"Well, if you don't mind, I'd like to take a gander inside." She looked over his arm and peered at the contents. Oh, there were several things she could use. She grabbed the whip cream and then debated on the chocolate syrup. No, that might prove to be too sticky.

"Midnight snack?" Trenton raised an eyebrow questioningly.

"Something like that." Regina was suddenly uncomfortable discussing her current relationship with her ex-husband. It was rather—weird.

"What is Bradford up to?"

She shrugged and looked into his eyes. With a straight face she said, "I don't have the foggiest idea. Whatever it is, I'm sure it has him all tied up." Literally, she wanted to laugh at her little joke, but it would bring even more questions.

"I need some ice." An idea forming in her head, she grabbed a glass and filled it to the top with the frozen cubes. She grabbed all her items and started to leave the room.

"Don't you want something to drink to go with your ice?" Trenton asked.

"Nah, I like to suck on the ice. It's more effective."

Trenton wasn't an idiot. He had to know she was

gathering these items for a very naughty reason. Her desire for ice had nothing to do with thirst and everything to do with pleasure so torturous it was amazing. She'd never got in touch with her freaky side with Trenton. He didn't have a clue she had these crazy ideas. Bradford was about to get a front row seat to it all. Either it would scare him away for good, or rope him in nice and tight. She was betting it would be the latter.

"Before you go, I want to say something to you."

Damn it. She'd almost made a clean getaway. The last thing she wanted was a little heart-to-heart with Trenton. They'd made their peace with each other. It was enough for her, and it should be for him too.

"Oh?"

"I know there is something going on between you and my step-brother."

"So?" She scrunched her mouth to her side in displeasure. "I don't see how that's any of your business." Regina mentally cringed at how waspish she sounded. Trenton meant well... But their marriage was over. She'd wished him happiness in his search for Genevieve. The way she saw it, she deserved to find something for herself.

"I want you both to be happy." He sighed. "Be

careful with him. He might seem like he's cold and hard inside, but deep down he's a marshmallow. It's because he cares so deeply that he has trouble showing his emotions."

Why did he have to be so—nice? He wasn't a bad guy. Regina deflated a little bit at his statement. He did want her to find someone to love. Wherever Genevieve was, she was an idiot. Why had she left a man so obviously crazy over her?

"I know that." She did. But that didn't mean he could stomp all over her and get away with it. He would know that before the night was over. "But if it's all the same to you, I'm going to tread my own path. If, and I'm not saying there is, anything going on between me and Bradford, that is our business. We will work through it in our own way."

He held up his hands and shook his head. "I'm not going to stand in your way. Like I said, I want you both to be happy."

Regina nodded and left the room. She was done with that impromptu discussion, and she'd left Bradford alone longer than she'd planned. She entered the room to find him thrashing on the bed attempting to get loose. "Now what did I tell you before I left?"

Bradford stilled at her words and turned his head toward the sound of her voice. "To miss you while you were gone?" He licked his lips. "I promise I missed you so much I had to try to get free so I could go find you.'

"Tsk tsk," She waved her finger at him. If he could see her, he'd be glaring at her with evil intent. "I actually said I'd bring back a ball gag."

"Don't you dare," he warned.

She laughed, unable to hold it in any longer. "Oh, don't you know there's not much I'd not dare to do?"

If he doubted her, he wouldn't when she was done. Whatever was between them was worth fighting for. He'd not push her away ever again. She wanted someone she could depend on, and who would do everything in his power to be with her. She would matter above anything else. The man she allowed into her life would cherish her and know how lucky he was to have her by his side. Regina wanted that man to be Bradford. She believed he could be her one and only, and all she had to do was convince him of the error of his ways.

"Darling, trust me, I know exactly what you're capable of." He yanked on the bindings to prove his point. "Untie me now so we can have an enjoyable night together."

"Who said it wasn't pleasant?" she asked. "This

is the most entertaining evening I've had in a very long time."

Sadly, it honestly was. Seeing him trussed up in all his naked glory was pleasure at its finest. He was magnificent, and she couldn't wait to run her hands all over his glorious physique. She strolled over to the bed and set down her items on the bedside table. Regina hopped onto the bed and licked her lips. No time like the present to begin her exploration. She lifted her hand and danced her fingers lightly across his chest and stopped at his lower stomach.

He hissed out a breath. "Touch me now, damn it."

"Do I need to retrieve the gag?"

"No," he ground out. "Don't make me beg."

"Honey, that's the whole point of this exercise." She leaned over and picked up an ice cube and sucked it into her mouth. The coolness melted inside her hot mouth. She pulled it out and trailed it down his chest.

"Fuck me," he swore.

"Not tonight, but maybe soon."

He thrashed underneath her ministrations. His cock hardened with each touch. It was pointing up in all its glory, begging her to wrap her lips around it. Regina wanted to taste him again, and didn't see any reason to deny herself. She wrapped her fingers around the base and leaned down to slide her tongue down the side.

"Yes," he said. "Take me inside your mouth."

He liked that too much, and she wasn't about to let him enjoy his confinement yet. At the end, when he realized he'd been wrong to treat her like a tart, she would take pity on him, but not a moment before. "I don't think so."

He strung together an even more inventive list of curse words. This was truly educational.

"Do you know why I'm doing this?"

He shook his head. "No, please stop."

Was he really that dense? She hadn't thought so, but she'd been wrong before. "Do you know how frustrated I was last night? Lying in my bed, anxiously waiting for you—how disappointed I was when you failed to show up?"

"I wanted to. I needed to."

"Then why didn't you?" This was all so baffling to her. "What was preventing you from being with me?"

He remained silent for a few moments before responding, "I was a damned fool. I've never wanted anyone more."

Regina had a hard time believing him. He didn't

act like someone who had trouble resisting her charms. He'd left her hot and bothered, with no way to ease her ache. "Do you want me? Do you need me beyond all reason?"

"Yes!"

"Then prove it."

He was quiet for several moments. She didn't know what he was thinking, and was almost afraid to find out. "Untie me and I'll show you."

"No." She had something else entirely in mind.

"Please untie me," he said softly. "I want to hold you."

Regina sighed. He sounded so earnest, but she had to be strong. "You're not holding me tonight, or for several more to come. I had to show you, make you understand what you're doing to me."

"I promise I do. What do I have to do to prove it to you?"

"Let's start with no sex." She lifted the blindfold off his eyes and stared into them. "We've done a lot of damage to each other. It's time to undo it and move on."

He studied her. His blue eyes were filled with an emotion Regina couldn't identify. Whatever it was, it undid her. She wanted to believe she'd finally reached him, and things would be different between them. There was so much between them and most of it was riddled with uncertainty.

"I'm not sure I know how to do that," he finally said.

"We need ground rules." Lots of them or why bother? Although, if she knew Bradford, and she believed she did, he'd try to break every one of them. He liked rules, but he hated when others imposed theirs on him.

"But..." He started to protest, but she held up her hand to stop him.

"You're going to court me. No touching, kissing, or crudeness. Pretend I'm a lady you respect above all others." She was pushing him too far, but what fun would it be to give in to easily. He had to work for her or he'd never appreciate her properly.

"I don't have to pretend. You are the only woman I've ever wanted to be better for." His voice was full of conviction as he spoke.

He sounded almost—sincere. Should she believe him? Warmth had spread through her at his words. This was the side of Bradford she'd started to fall in love with. He was so good at saying the right things when he wanted to. She believed he meant them too, but he was up to something. She wasn't so foolish as to believe otherwise. She'd tied him up, of course he wouldn't let that go. He had to insinuate his dominance on her.

A thrill of anticipation flooded her senses. Damn if she couldn't wait for him to show her what he had in mind. In truth, it had been her ultimate goal. "Good. We begin again tomorrow. I'm going to untie you now, but I want your assurances you'll keep your hands to yourself." What she really wanted to say was, "*If you don't touch me, I'll gut you.*"

He nodded. "You have them."

Yeah, she had no doubts now. Bradford was going to do his best to show her who he believed was boss. He didn't realize he was going to do exactly what she planned for. Regina wanted him, all he had to offer, no holds barred. In order to get that, she had to stir the beast inside. She smiled and undid the knots. After the last one was loosened he reached up and wrapped his arms around her waist and flipped her over

"Darling, I told you I'd make you regret tying me up." He pinned her to the mattress with one hand leaving the other free to undress her. Bradford grinned down at her wickedly. "I made you some promises, and I do intend to keep them." His gaze roamed over her. She'd made sure to put on a sexy piece of lingerie comprised of little more than a slip of black satin trimmed effectively with lace. His eyes darkened with desire as he slipped a strap down her shoulder. "Just not tonight."

She should be scared, but instead she was excited as hell. "Bring it." The night was young, after all. Who knew what they might discover about each other before morning?

"Oh, I plan to," he said as he started to undress her. "When I'm done with you there will be no question where you belong."

The last thought she had was...*damn, he's good with words—his tongue—and hands, hell he's simply freaking talented.*

CHAPTER 12

Bradford sat in his study staring at contracts he was supposed to sign. They were a blur of nothingness in front of him. He couldn't make out what any of them meant, why he should approve them, or why they were even important. All he could think about was the glorious night he'd had the night before. He'd finally had Regina in every way possible and it had been as glorious as he'd imagined it. No, it had been a million times better. She'd surprised him in a way no one had ever been able to. At first, when he'd woken up tied to his bed he'd been blazing mad. After she left him to his own thoughts he decided to take advantage of the situation. She'd thought she had the upper hand, and it was up to him to show her otherwise. She wanted to be cherished? He planned on doing so for the rest of his days, but he wouldn't be a weak-kneed fool in the process.

"Pardon me, Your Grace," his butler said. "But there is a gentleman here to see you. He says it's most urgent."

Who the hell could it be? "Send him in." Might as well get it over with. He had plans with Regina later and he didn't want to be disturbed.

His butler led a man into the room he'd not seen before. He had sandy blond hair and light brown eyes obscured by wire rimmed glasses. His suit was dark and professional in appearance, and he carried a brown leather satchel in his hand.

"My firm owes you an apology, Your Grace."

He didn't know him or his firm, to demand anything from them, let alone an apology. "For what?" He was curious what it was all concerning though.

The man didn't say much. He crossed the room and stopped in front of Bradford. He placed his satchel on his desk and clicked the latches open. "We were dispatched with delivering a letter to you a very long time ago. There has been a lot of upheaval at our London offices, and it was overlooked until now."

A letter? This was about some bloody correspondence. That didn't seem so dire as to make the man apologize. "Well, give it over."

"Again, I apologize. This should have been delivered to you over a year ago."

Bradford tilted his head, startled by his statement. "A year ago, you say?" That was around the time Regina and Trenton married on his estate, and when Alys disappeared. It couldn't be related to that event. *Could it?*

"Yes, Your Grace."

The man pulled out a parchment that was a weathered yellow and sealed with a red candle wax and handed it to Bradford. The Weston crest was imbedded inside the wax. Was this from one of his ancestors? Why would they have given this man's firm a letter to hold on to for so long? "What is this pertaining to?"

"I'm not at liberty to say." He held his head high. "I've not been privy to the details of the document. I've been dispatched with its delivery."

Somehow Bradford didn't believe the man was being entirely truthful. He knew more than he was letting on. It didn't matter as he'd soon know all there was about it once he read the contents. He picked up a letter opener from his desk and slid it under the wax to loosen it. He unfolded the letter and read it.

It wasn't long, but was too the point. It was from James Kendall, the fifth Duke of Weston. It included instructions on how to locate a letter that had been hidden behind the portrait of his wife and daughter. What the letter contained, Bradford didn't know. What distressed him was the correspondence was addressed directly to him: Bradford Kendall, the ninth Duke of Weston. He shouldn't have known his name, as Bradford was born almost two centuries in the future.

He turned toward the man and asked harshly, "Is this a prank of some sort?"

"Certainly not, Your Grace," the man replied. "I assure you our firm is highly respectable and we would not do anything unsavory."

Bradford didn't know what to make of it. There was only one way to find out if what the man said was the truth or not. Without sparing the man a second glance, Bradford stood up abruptly and headed toward the portrait gallery. Why had he never looked behind any of the paintings? Hell, why would he? Who hid letters behind family portraits? Apparently his ancestors did; no wonder he was screwed up, considering who he was descended from.

"Bradford," Regina called out to him as he rushed down the hall. "Damn it, wait up. I can't walk as fast as you."

He ignored her and went into the portrait gallery, heading toward the portrait the letter directed him to. Bradford stopped in front of it and stared at it for several moments. The fifth Duchess of Weston was lovely, and a complete replica of Alys, Regina's sister. The duke and duchess's daughter was a mini version of the lady. She had golden blonde hair and sparkling green eyes.

"Why are you in here?" Regina finally caught up to him. "What are you...?" She gasped. "Oh. My. God. That looks just like Alys."

"I realize that." Bradford replied. "I mentioned the portrait to your sister once." The day Regina married Trenton—the day she disappeared. It still bothered him to think about that day and what it represented.

"I forgot about that. You distracted me that day if I recall correctly." She nibbled on her bottom lip and studied it. "Did she ever see it?"

"No, I didn't get a chance to show it to her." He had his suspicions that she'd had a part in its creation though. Why else would the fifth duke known his name? The only explanation he could think of was Alys. She had a part in all of this, but what it was he hadn't quite figured out yet. None of it made a lick of sense. He couldn't wrap his mind around the uncanny resemblance between the duchess and Alys. Maybe he was losing his mind. Regina certainly did her share of driving him crazy.

"Who is she?" Regina moved closer to the picture. "The little girl in the picture must be her daughter? She's adorable."

"It's strange, but I don't know the duchess's name. It was never mentioned in any of the Weston family archives. The children, though, are talked about often."

"So she's a member of your family?" Regina asked as she studied the portrait. "I wonder why she looks so similar to my sister. Alys was adopted, did you know that? Maybe she is an ancestor of hers."

Bradford hadn't known Alys was adopted. Could she be a relative of his? It would make more sense than where his thoughts had been going. For a moment he thought the duchess *was* Alys, but that was ridiculous. It would mean she time traveled, and as far as he knew that wasn't possible. Maybe he'd have to do a little research on Alys and how she'd come to be adopted.

"The woman is the fifth Duchess of Weston, and Lady Elizabeth was her daughter."

"Elizabeth?" Regina scrunched her nose up and frowned. "I saw that name somewhere." She snapped her fingers and replied. "I remember. It was in the Bible you took from me. The first name listed was: Elizabeth Regina Evelyn Kendall. I remember finding it interesting she had both my name and my mother's."

Bradford jerked his head toward her. "What did you say?"

"Hmm...oh, you mean about Elizabeth. Her middle names are Regina and Evelyn, you know mine and..."

"I heard you," he interrupted her. "I hadn't made the connection before..."

Damn it, now he was back to thinking the portrait *was* of Alys and her daughter, but how could that be?" There was one way to find out. He had to get the letter from behind the portrait and find out what it was all about. Maybe it was good that Regina was with him. If it had something to do with her sister, she'd finally know what happened to her.

"Why are you in here staring at this portrait?"

Regina asked. "You were in such a hurry to get here you wouldn't stop to wait for me."

How to answer that? The truth seemed like the best option, but he feared she'd think him insane. Maybe part of it would suffice for now. "I got a weird letter from a solicitor to check behind the painting."

"That is odd." She studied it, and frowned. "What are you waiting for? Look to see if there is something of interest for us to find."

He nodded. "Yes, you're right." He pulled back the frame and peeked behind it. Stuck inside the edge of the frame was a parchment similar to the one he'd received earlier, sealed with red wax. No doubt he'd find the Weston seal on it as well. He lifted it and pulled it from behind the painting.

"Open it already!" Regina bounced on her feet. "Give it to me, I will."

He yanked it out of her reach. "Patience is not one of your virtues, is it?"

"Not really." She bit her lip. "But can you please open it. I'm dying of curiosity."

He shook his head at her and grinned. Was it any wonder why he'd fallen in love with her? He froze as it hit him, damn if he hadn't realized it before. When had he fallen for Regina? An exact moment in time didn't stand out for him. It was almost as he'd always loved her. An overwhelming need to tell her filled him. It was squashed down by the equally unnerving fear that settled inside his gut. What if she rejected him? He'd never laid his heart out to another and left himself vulnerable to hurt before. It might prove to be his undoing if she tossed him aside. Could he risk it?

Instead, he decided to put off his confessions and concentrate on the moment at hand. The mysterious letter and what it could mean for them both. He slid his finger under the wax seal and broke the letter open. He slowly unfolded it and perused the contents. The letter was yellowed and some of the writing was hard to decipher, but most of it was surprisingly legible. If handled improperly the paper would probably tear easily. How had they not noticed this letter hidden behind the portrait before? It was amazing it had survived intact.

Bradford,

If you're reading this, then you know I'm gone. Something crazy wonderful happened to me that I'm still baffled over years later. Yes, you read that correctly—years. It's been a while since I fell off the cliff near your estate and found myself living in the year 1815, a few months after the battle of Waterloo. You might remember that your ancestor, James

Kendall, fought in that battle. He was lucky to survive, but I digress. There is another purpose for this missive.

James and I married, and have started a family. My daughter, Elizabeth, is a couple years old, and I recently discovered I'm pregnant again. It's crazy to think that my children are your ancestors. Truly, it boggles the mind. Please tell my family I'm all right, and I love them. Make sure they understand how happy I am. This is where I believe I've always belonged.

With much love,

Alys Dewitt Kendall,
   The fifth Duchess of Weston

Bradford stared at the letter and still couldn't wrap his mind around what he'd just finished reading. The duchess in the portrait was indeed Alys Dewitt, and she'd married one of his ancestors. She was his family; he carried her blood in his veins... Boggled the mind? Bradford snorted, talk about an understatement. A part of him still didn't want to believe it even with the evidence staring him in the face. It could still be one big joke, but deep down he didn't really believe that. Alys hadn't been the type to play games. She had been whimsical and romantic, but never one to hurt those who'd cared about her. This was her way of letting her family know she was all right and to be happy for her.

"What is it?" Regina asked. "You look like you've seen a ghost."

In a way he had. The portrait was a ghost of the woman he'd known briefly. How would Regina react to the news? She'd never get her sister back, and even if he could, he wouldn't find a way to bring her back to the twentieth century. Alys was where she belonged. She'd said she was happy. Why would he willingly take that away from her?

Alys's words on Regina's wedding day still haunted him. *"Someday you will meet someone who takes your breath away. Your very existence moot without them by your side—every breath, every heartbeat, will be only for them. If you're lucky enough, they will feel the same."* Except she'd never be here to see it—what would she say if she realized he'd fallen for Regina in truth? He'd denied it vehemently that day, but having her was beyond the realm of possibilities then. Now though, she was his, all he had to do was tell her how he felt. Could he do it? Was he brave enough to offer her his heart?

Bradford sunk to his knees and stared up at her. His heart beat rapidly inside his chest. There was one way to find out if she'd have him. He had to do the one thing he swore he'd never do. Beg a woman to be his forever... "Regina, will you marry me?"

CHAPTER 13

"What the hell is in that letter?" Regina reached for it, but Bradford kept it firmly in his grasp.

"Answer me," he demanded

How could she when she didn't know what led up to his proposal? She looked over his shoulder and stared at the wall. Think, think, there had to be a way to stall him. Regina wanted to say yes. But she couldn't, not without knowing why. If it was any answer other than he loved her, she'd have to decline. Bradford hadn't once told her he'd loved her, and she hadn't spoken her feelings aloud either. She hadn't wanted to think too heavily about it. They'd had amazing sex, but that wasn't enough to build a marriage on. Who was she kidding? She did love him, but she was too afraid of what it all meant. Marriage was serious, and she didn't want to do it without being certain this time it had a chance of lasting. She needed more from him before she could make that kind of commitment.

"I can't..." she stumbled over the word.

His smile fell. Complete dejection filled every inch of his face. Oh hell, what had she done? He stood up and stared at her blankly. "I see. Then we will forget this ever happened." He handed her the letter. "Here's the answers you were seeking. Please leave my estate today."

"Bradford, wait," she called to him, but he kept walking.

Her heart broke into a million pieces. She had to make him understand. If he'd listen, she'd explain why she answered as she did. She wasn't against marriage, but she had to know his reasons. Tears flooded her eyes and fell down her cheeks. She couldn't see two inches in front of her. The misery inside her was overwhelming, and all she could allow inside. Regina slid to the floor and let it all out, until she didn't have any tears left.

Bradford had asked her to marry him, and she'd

crushed her chance with him in one final blow. It didn't matter anymore that she loved him, and wouldn't love anyone as much as she did him. She should have said yes. What had she done? Maybe she could still fix it. They weren't broken yet, at least she hoped so. It was so sudden for him to propose, and whatever was in that letter had prompted it.

She unfolded it and scanned the contents. Her heart skipped a beat as she read it. Alys wasn't missing anymore. No wonder he demanded she leave. There was no reason for her to stay. They both knew where he sister was, and she was perfectly content to stay there. Regina glanced over at the portrait and smiled. The little girl was her niece. No wonder her middle name was Regina Evelyn, Alys had wanted to honor her family. The evidence was hard to believe, but it was her sister's handwriting. She'd recognize the familiar scrawl anywhere. Alys wouldn't have left willingly, and it wasn't in her nature to lie.

"I'm glad you found the love of your life," she whispered. "Now help me find mine."

Something in this note spurred Bradford into action. Was it reading how Alys was happy? Hell, Alys was his family too. She was a direct link in his bloodline. Maybe that had been enough to make him want more in his life, but he still hadn't mentioned love. Regina needed more from him if she was going to take that leap. What would her sister do?

Alys believed in love more than anyone she knew. She would probably tell Regina to take a chance, and to have faith it would all work out. It might be too late, but if she loved him, she'd have to open herself up to hurt. That's what love meant, she had to trust Bradford with her heart. It was a gift, one that didn't always protect like it should. The good news was little hurts could heal.

"Regina?"

That sounded like her mother, but that couldn't be. What the hell was she doing at Weston Manor? She had to be hearing things, or maybe it was wishful thinking. She needed a shoulder to lean on, and Alys wasn't available. "Mom?" Regina lifted her head off the gallery floor and called out to her.

Her mother strolled into the portrait gallery and smiled. "The butler thought you might be in this wing. I'm glad I found you."

Evelyn Dewitt was dressed in the highest fashion, her blonde hair perfectly coiled into a chignon. Her mother believed in putting every effort into presenting herself right. As children, she and Alys had rebelled against it whenever they could. Now, Regina appreciated it in a way she couldn't explain. Her mother was a comfort she never thought she'd crave.

"Were you crying?" Her mother asked, studying her carefully.

"I was," Regina admitted. "I have news."

She didn't want to admit she'd broken her own heart by denying Bradford. When she had the chance, she'd correct that mistake. For now, she'd give her mother something else to focus on.

"What is it, dear?" Her mother reached out to her. "Let me help you off the floor."

Regina slipped her hand into her mother's and stood. "I know where Alys is."

Her mother smiled. Evelyn Dewitt's whole face lit up with happiness. "You do? That's wonderful. Where is she?"

This was the hard part, telling her she'd never see her adopted daughter again. Not that it mattered that Alys wasn't her biological daughter. Evelyn Dewitt loved her as much as she'd loved Regina. She treated them both as cherished individuals who deserved all the love she had to give.

"She's not here."

"Of course not, silly. I can see that. When can I see her?"

Regina bit her lip. She hated hurting her mother, but it had to be done. It was best to get it over with as quickly as possible. She turned and pointed to the portrait behind her. Evelyn followed her direction and froze.

"Is that Alys? Who's the little girl?" All the questions she'd asked when she first saw the portrait spilled out of her mother's mouth. She'd not assumed the portrait was of Alys at first though, but it could've been a woman who resembled her.

"How do you know that's Alys?" Regina asked.

"It's obvious." Her mother pointed at the portrait. "Do you see the little scar above her left eyebrow? She had stitches when she was three. She climbed up on a counter trying to get cookies, and well, it didn't go well. The person who painted this was brilliant. The artist captured her perfectly." Her mother's voice hitched a little as she spoke.

Regina stared at the portrait as if seeing it for the first time. This time she saw what her mother meant. This was Alys as she remembered her. Perhaps a few years older, as she was with her daughter, but it was a reminder of the sister she'd missed over the past year. Through the haze of Bradford's proposal, she hadn't stopped to appreciate it. Alys had married and had children. Three if she remembered the Bible listing correctly, one daughter and twin boys.

"I admit I am confused about her attire," her mother finally said. "Her dress is a nice replica of what a woman in the 1800s might wear."

Her mother's comment shouldn't surprise her, but for some reason it did. She was a fashion icon herself, why wouldn't she know about the fashion in another era? "What do you know about that time period?"

Her mother shook her head. "More than I'd like to sometimes, but even that time isn't something I'm too familiar with. Too far into the future from my expertise—I did read a little about those years."

It was the day for odd statements apparently. "Alys is living in the 1800s." Time to snap her mother to the present. "This painting isn't the only proof I have." She handed her mother Alys's letter.

Her mother snatched it and read it quickly. "Well, I'll be."

Regina studied her mother. She'd expected disbelief, not quiet acceptance. Her mother stared back up at the portrait. "So this is my granddaughter? Oh, I wish I could have met her." She started to walk around the room and stopped by another portrait and gasped. "It can't be."

"What is it?" Regina asked concerned.

"Why, it's Captain Jack."

Regina stared at the portrait. A handsome man with golden-blond hair and sea green eyes filled her vision. His smile held a wicked gleam to it, and the woman next to him looked like a grown up version of Elizabeth. She still resembled Alys, but she wasn't an exact replica. "The mythical Captain Jack you used to tell us stories about?"

"The very one." She smiled. "I'm so happy he survived."

"I thought he was fictional," Regina replied. How had her mother known a rakish pirate? "I think there's a lot you're not telling me. You're accepting all of this too easily."

Regina didn't know what to make of her mother's acceptance of Alys's jaunt to the past. She expected disbelief—not whatever the hell this was. Her mother seemed so blasé about the entire thing, as if time travel was an everyday sort of thing. Who was this creature and what happened to her mother?

"As it happens, I know a little about time travel."

Regina's mouth fell open. Her mother held back a lot. So much that she was beginning to wonder if she ever knew her mother at all. What did she know about time travel, and more importantly how had she come by the information? "Tell me everything," she demanded.

"Another time," her mother said. "All you need to know right now is that your sister is happy."

She narrowed her eyes and studied her mother. How could she be so dismissive? Regina was bubbly with excitement. She wanted as much information as her mother had inside her pretty head. There had to be a way to make her mother talk about it.

"No. I want details."

Yes, she was acting like a spoiled child, but this was huge. Her mother could explain about time travel and tell her so much, and she was holding it back. That was wrong. She wanted to know it all.

"Fine. I'll tell you a tiny bit," she said. "But we don't have time for more. Your father is meeting with Bradford and then we have to go back to the states. This is what your father refers to as a pit stop."

If Bradford wouldn't listen to her, she'd at least have a way to escape. She'd have to stall her parents long enough to have a heart-to-heart with him. "Tell me." For now, she could forget her own woes and get lost in a fantastical tale.

"I was born at the start of the eighteenth century," she explained. "Your father, with a little help from Captain Jack, saved me in 1722."

Of all the things she thought her mother might admit to, that wasn't at the top of her list. She'd traveled through time, the same as Alys. Why hadn't she gotten that lucky? It would be amazing to visit another time.

"I believe that, in some instances, we're able to time travel so we meet our one true love." She stared at the portrait of Jack and Elizabeth. "I'd love to have been there to see Jack fall. He was such an arrogant man."

Her mother's theory made sense. Alys found her James and the love of her life. Regina hadn't time traveled because her soul mate was in her own time. That meant she had to do everything in her power to fight for him. She'd been a fool to let her uncertainty stand in the way of happiness.

"One day you're going to sit down and tell me everything, but right now I have a few things to take care of."

"It will be a pleasure to finally share it with you." Her mother smiled at Regina. "Go do what you need to. I'm going to go through all these portraits and familiarize myself with them all. They're our family too now." She gasped. "It just hit me that makes Bradford family too. I'll have to let your father in on that. He's incredibly hard on the duke."

Regina scrunched her nose up. "I don't think of him in that way."

He might be distantly related to Alys, but that didn't make him her family, at least not the way her mother referred to him. She loved the damn man and intended to spend the rest of her life with him. Nothing was going to stand in the way of that.

Her mother laughed. "He'll be family regardless soon enough."

"What's that supposed to mean?"

Her mother made way too many cryptic statements for her liking.

"I'm not blind," she replied. "I know you're in love with him, but you had to realize that for yourself."

Regina shook her head and frowned. She'd always done things the hard way. Falling in love wouldn't be any different. Her mother knew her too well. It was a little eerie how much her mother managed to figure out. It made for rather difficult teenage years. Her mother always seemed aware of what she had planned before she did. Perhaps that was the way of mothers though.

"Then you won't mind me taking off to tell him that."

She didn't wait around to hear what her mother had to say. Bradford was going to listen to her, and then she'd tell him that he was going to marry her. He'd asked, damn it, and she wasn't going to let him take that back. They belonged together.

CHAPTER 14

BRADFORD HAD BEEN SURPRISED TO FIND PAUL Dewitt waiting for him in his study. The solicitor must have seen himself out, not that he'd care to find out. The last thing he wanted was to deal with Regina's father. He'd laid it all out to her and she'd pushed him away. Regina said she couldn't marry him. What the hell did that mean? It was either yes or no, not "I can't." After her rejection he couldn't stay. If he remained in her presence, he would've started begging. He loved her, and she clearly didn't feel the same. It was much better to make a clean break.

"Hello, Paul." He crossed the room and greeted the older man. "I wasn't expecting you."

"I stopped to pick up the contracts. Regina said

you were going over them. I hope they met with your approval."

The damn contracts—they'd been so important to him at one time, and he'd forgotten their existence. He'd signed them ages ago and left them in a folder on his desk. "I've already read through them and signed them. I was going to give them to Regina to take back with her when she left later today."

Not the entire truth. He'd probably not have realized they were still on his desk for quite a while, but it sounded good to say he'd been prepared to send them off. Paul's appearance might even be to his benefit. He could take his daughter with him when he left. Then Bradford could get back to the normalness of his life, and do everything in his power to forget about the blonde vixen that'd disrupted his life.

"Excellent," Paul said. "I didn't realize Regina planned on flying home today."

Bradford couldn't very well admit the reason behind her sudden departure. It might disrupt their future as business partners. It was best to keep the peace as much as possible. The contracts were important to his company's future.

"It's a sudden decision. She accomplished everything she came here for."

He wondered if breaking his heart was one of the goals she'd sent out to achieve. If so, she'd done a damn good job of it. No one had the power to destroy him quite like she did. She'd had him fooled. He thought they had something, but he'd been wrong.

"She found Alys?"

So her father had known about Regina's other project. At least she didn't lie to one male in her life. She'd been brilliantly good at it where he was concerned. Her father must hold her respect more than Bradford did. "Not exactly, I'll let her explain it to you." He glanced up and found Regina standing inside the doorway. He ached inside at the sight of her. Why the hell wasn't she in her room packing? Did she find out her father was here and come to seek him out?

"Hello, Daddy," she said. "Momma can fill you in on Alys. I need to have a conversation with Bradford. Can you give us some privacy?"

Her father studied her a moment and then nodded. Bradford wanted to argue with her proclamation. As far as he was concerned, they'd said everything they needed to. She could go and he'd be fine without her.

"All right," her father said. "Come find me when you're done."

"I will," she agreed.

Once her father was gone Regina turned to him. She was quiet as she crossed the room to stand beside him. "You didn't let me explain before you rushed away from me. You do that a lot, jump to conclusions and think you're right. News flash, that isn't always the case."

What could she possibly have had to say that would've made a difference? "I can't" had seemed pretty damn clear to him. That was all he'd needed to hear to walk away and not look back. Why stay behind and let her rip him to shreds?

"There was nothing left to discuss," he said in a clipped tone. "I trust you've packed and are ready to leave? You're parents' arrival was rather serendipitous to your departure. You can now travel with them."

He turned away from her and sat down at his desk. The journal Zane had given him sat nearby. It was unnecessary to finding Alys now. He could return it to Seabrook the next time he traveled there. Bradford picked it up and flipped it open in an attempt to ignore Regina. He read the first line and froze.

My brother married Alys today.

If he'd opened it sooner he might have gotten the

answers quicker, and Regina would already be gone. Why had he avoided opening it before now? Maybe he'd been hoping for a better outcome between them. Now he knew better. He glanced up and met Regina's gaze. "Why are you still here?"

"I told you we needed to talk. I'm not leaving until you hear what I have to say."

Regina stared at him with purpose shining within her beautiful blue eyes. He wanted to reach out and pull her into his arms, but that would end up in a torment he didn't want to succumb to. She had to leave, the sooner the better.

"Nothing you could possibly spout out of your mouth would be worth hearing."

She glared at him and tapped her foot impatiently. Why did she have to be so bloody beautiful? He wanted to pull her into his arms and kiss her senseless, but he had to resist the urge. It would just extend the inevitable. She was leaving him, why give her more ammunition to hurt him?

"Why are you so stubborn?"

He had to be strong, and as obstinate as possible. It was the only way he'd survived in his mother's household. Weakness wasn't tolerated. He raised an eyebrow mockingly, and snorted. "You have no room to criticize, my dear."

She smiled. "We're two peas in a pod then."

"Fine. Say your piece so I can be rid of you."

It would be easier to give in to her now. He knew her well enough to realize she wouldn't let this go. Whatever it was, he could dismiss it after she was done. Then after she left he could drown his sorrows in a bottle of his favorite brandy.

She placed her hands on his desk and leaned in. Their faces were so close he could incline his head a little and kiss her. He refrained from doing it, but oh he wanted to. He craved her taste, the touch of her lips against his, and the smell of her sweet skin. Why was she torturing him?

"Yes," she said.

He scrunched his eyebrows together and frowned. "Yes what?"

"I'll marry you."

He had to be hearing her wrong. She'd already said no. Hadn't she? He heard her say she couldn't...

"I believe that discussion has already ended. I've moved on."

She laughed. "As if you could."

Hell, she was right. He'd never be able to forget her. Why was she toying with his emotions? Bradford clenched his hand into a fist and pounded it on the desk. "Go. Now."

The smile fell from her face. She didn't move for several seconds. Then when she did he was afraid she'd listen and walk away from him. He stood to stop her, but she met him halfway. Bradford pulled her into his arms and crushed his mouth over hers. She'd said yes. What was wrong with him? He should've pulled her into his arms sooner. He was such a fool.

He lifted his head and stared into her beautiful blue eyes. A small tear was falling down her cheek. "Why are you crying?" he kissed her cheeks trying to erase the hurt. Had he done that to her? Regina didn't cry, at least not that he'd ever witnessed.

"I was afraid it was too late. That you'd truly send me away."

Bradford had been ready to do exactly that. He'd started to build the walls around his heart. If she'd left him he'd have reinforced them so no one could get past them ever again. It was amazing she'd been able to breach his defenses.

"I'm sorry," he said softly. "When you said you couldn't marry me—I have no excuse. I was totally gutted and lashed out."

She lifted her hand and caressed his cheek. "I want to spend the rest of my life with you. I love you more than words can say, but I can't live with all these doubts. Please tell me that, from this point on, we're going to talk things through. We'll never make it if we don't learn to communicate better."

Regina loved him. She'd admitted it, finally. He'd thought he would never hear those words from her lips. Relief filled his heart, and a lightness that he'd never felt before. His future suddenly looked a whole lot brighter. Mere moments ago he'd been planning to drink away the rest of the day—hell maybe even the week. Who knows where his drunken stupor would have led him.

"I love you, my darling incredible woman," he said as he trailed kisses over her face. "I promise from this moment on we will discuss everything. I don't want there to be any doubts between us either."

She laughed. "Thank God. I thought you were going to be unreasonable."

"You have to forgive me. I can be a total arse sometimes."

"I know, but I love you anyway."

He laughed and pulled her closer to him. "I want to get married right away. None of that fancy nonsense." He couldn't bring himself to say the words, *"like your other wedding."* That first one didn't matter. The one they would have was the one that would count as far as he was concerned. Regina would be his wife.

"That sounds reasonable to me." She grinned. "My parents are even here. We can get married as soon as you can arrange it."

Yesterday wasn't soon enough for him, but even he couldn't work that kind of magic. It would take several days, maybe even weeks, to plan even the smallest of ceremonies in England. "Maybe we should fly to the states for the ceremony. I hear Las Vegas is lovely."

Regina laughed. "Yeah, if you're partial to bright, flashy lights."

"As long as you're there the rest are minor details."

"In that case," she said as she leaned her head on his shoulder. "Let's go to Vegas, baby."

This was a moment he would remember for the rest of his life. The beginning of their life together, and when she finally told him she loved him. He'd not been joking. The wedding itself wasn't important, as long as the end gave him what he wanted. Regina as his wife, his duchess, and the only woman he'd ever love.

EPILOGUE

Regina flipped through the journal Bradford had brought back from Seabrook. They were on their way to Las Vegas for a spur of the moment wedding. She still couldn't believe she'd agreed to the impromptu wedding, but she didn't regret it. Bradford was her future and her home. She didn't want to be anywhere he wasn't.

He'd given her the journal as a wedding gift. She laughed at him. It wasn't his to give away, and she'd reminded him of that fact. To which he'd said, "Zane can kiss my behind. He's not getting it back."

She didn't want to upset him, but once she was done reading it she fully intended to return it to its rightful owner. Regina didn't believe in keeping something that didn't belong to her. The journal was a Seabrook heirloom and belonged at the estate. She'd read a good portion of it. The marchioness had begun an amazing adventure and she wanted to see what happened to her. This journal told the tale of how she'd fallen in love with her husband, and the path that led to their coming together. It was terribly romantic, and fully of so much love.

She glanced next to her and smiled, it wasn't unlike her and Bradford really. They'd both fought their love every step of the way. Regina wondered if a lot of couples did the same thing. Love was a scary thing, but incredible with the right person.

"I'm so glad you'll be my last first kiss." Regina told him.

"Ditto, darling, but where's this coming from?"

She'd read about Rosanna's first kiss with her Dom. He'd been the only man that had ever kissed the lady. Regina couldn't be Bradford's first kiss, but she could be his last.

"I love you, and sometimes I wish I'd have met you before I made all the mistakes of my past."

"They made you who you are. Don't regret what's made you the woman I love." He lifted her hand and kissed her palm.

When he said things like that she wondered why she fought so hard to keep him at a distance. They had been attracted to each other from the very beginning, but lust wasn't love. They had to spend time together to build that emotion into what it had become. Regina leaned her head back and closed her eyes. The trip to Nevada would take a while, and she was tired.

"It's about bloody time," Eve exclaimed.

"I thought I was done with you." Regina glared at her. Eve sat in the seat next to her. She didn't question how she'd come to be there. At this point she was used to the woman invading her thoughts. "Didn't I tell you to stay out of my head?"

The other woman frowned. Her eerie eyes held a hint of sadness in them. What was going on with her? Why wouldn't she leave her alone?

"You have the journal now. Read it and make sure you get it to Trenton."

"Oh, now you're ready to spill it all are you?" She shook her head. "I'm sorry to tell you this, but I have no clue where he went. He left Weston Manor the same time we did, and didn't bother giving us a forwarding address. Why is this journal so important anyway?"

She sighed. "Find him. He has to know where to locate me."

Regina studied her and everything clicked into

place. It all made sense now. Why couldn't she have just told her sooner? Maybe she could have been more help. "Eve. You're the one he's searching for?"

No wonder she was so damned sad all the time. Genevieve was an ethereal beauty and Regina could understand why Trenton had been drawn toward her. She was lovely, when she wasn't being annoying.

"The journal is the key. I'm sorry I couldn't tell you sooner. I told you there are limitations to my gift. I was weak, and couldn't hold onto the thread long enough to tell you what you needed to know." She shook her head. "You're the most obstinate woman I've ever met, and let me tell you, I've met a lot."

"I've been told that before." By her future husband to be exact. "This journal will help Trenton find you?" Regina wanted Trenton to find happiness. After her wedding, she'd track him down and give him the journal. She didn't fully understand how this dream world worked, but she was glad Eve had been able to reach out to her. "Why don't you contact him? Wouldn't it have been easier than going through me?"

"He doesn't have the same gifts you do. His mind isn't open to them. In time, he could learn, but not in time for me to reach him." She smiled. "Your innate psychic abilities gave me something to work with."

Great, she was a freak like the rest of her family, she'd just not gotten the time travel gene. "I have no words."

"It's a lot to take in," Eve said. "Are you going to help me?"

"I will." She held up her hand when Eve opened her mouth to speak. "But I'm not tracking Trenton down until after my wedding. Bradford and I deserve happiness too."

Eve nodded. "I don't blame you. He loves you a great deal. Hold on to it and never let go."

She didn't intend to. They'd not come this far to lose each other now. "Go away, Eve. I'm done talking to you." She'd never get any rest with the other woman talking her ear off.

"I'm going," she replied. "I hope you have a lovely wedding."

Regina smiled as the other woman disappeared. She'd make sure Trenton got the journal, and the information he needed to find his true love. So much for returning it to Seabrook...

"Regina, dear," Bradford whispered in her ear. "Wake up, the plane's about to land."

Her eyes fluttered open and met his gaze. "Already?"

"Well, time flies when you sleep it away."

"It feels like I've been asleep for a few moments." How long had Eve been talking to her? The dream world must work a lot differently than the real one.

"You were sleeping so peacefully I hated to disturb you. It must have been quite a dream you were having."

That was an understatement. She laughed. "I'll tell you about it sometime. Right now, I can't wait to get off this plane and marry you."

"I couldn't have said it better myself," he said. "I love you."

"I love you more," she said.

"Debatable." He laughed. "It's best to admit that it's impossible to prove. It's enough that we love each other and make each other happier than words can express."

"How much?"

"Pardon me?" he raised an eyebrow questioningly.

"Do you love me?"

She sat back and waited for his answer. He had such a way with words despite his comment about mere words not being enough. She loved how he weaved them.

"You take my breath away. My very existence wouldn't be the same if I didn't have you. Every breath and heartbeat is for you alone. I'm lucky to have your love and the ability to shower you with adoration."

He was fucking perfect, at least for her. She leaned over and kissed him. They may have taken the road less traveled to find each other, but it had been worth it because it brought them to where they belonged—in each other's arms.

EXCERPT: WHEN AN EARL TURNS WICKED

BLUESTOCKINGS DEFYING ROGUES
BOOK ONE

DAWN BROWER

USA TODAY
BESTSELLING AUTHOR
Dawn
Brower
When an Earl
Turns Wicked

Southington Castle, England, 1808

THE DAY WAS LIKE ANY OTHER ONE IN ENGLAND. Rainfall had become a normal enough occurrence that Jonas didn't notice it—even as it dripped down his face, drenching him completely. He stared at the chiseled stones in the cemetery near Southington's chapel. Only members of his family were buried there—many he never met personally. Pictures of them filled the great hall, but they were history to him, and he'd been able to distance himself from their stories. This, however, was far different.

His life would never be the same. The death of his father had marked an unchangeable truth. The duke now had control over Jonas's life. His grandfather was a tyrant and had always attempted to brow-beat his will into him. His father had been the one person he'd been able to count on. A buffer the duke couldn't break through, and he'd tried often.

So, no, the cold didn't matter because he was numb through and through. Rain? Paltry in compar-ison to what he had yet to face. The Duke of Southington, his grandfather, hadn't started yet—mainly because he couldn't. There were people around, and he dared not cause a scene. Once all the mourners departed, things would start to unravel ever further around him. Would his grandfather allow him to return to Eton? What about his mother? Would she have it in her to fight him? Somehow, he doubted everything and yet prayed for anything resembling his life before his father's death.

"Lord Harrington," a man said as he rested his hand on Jonas's shoulder. How could *he* be the earl now? That was his father's name, and he doubted he'd ever become accustomed to it. "It's time to head back."

He glanced up at the man as the rain continued to drip down his face. His hair was black, but had already started to turn to gray along the sides. Jonas barely knew him, but Lord Coventry had been a friend of his father's. "I'm not ready," he told him.

"George was a good man," Lord Coventry said. "He loved you."

"I know," Jonas replied woodenly. He'd long ago stopped feeling and now went through the motions. What else could he do? Lord Coventry was correct—it was long past time to go, yet he couldn't move. Once he left, it would all become too real for him. His grandfather would start barking orders, and he had years before he could be free of him. Three long years to be exact—once he turned eighteen he could seize control of his inheritance. As long as his grandfather didn't find a way to break the will. "But that doesn't change anything."

"No," Lord Coventry agreed. "He's still gone, and nothing will ever bring him back."

If Jonas were capable of crying, he'd have done so days ago. It was probably a good thing he hadn't. Any sign of weakness would have set his grandfather off. He had to be brave, and somehow find the strength to move on sooner than he'd like. His father deserved to be mourned, but he'd understand why Jonas couldn't openly do it. "I'm ready now." Jonas didn't look at Lord Coventry. He spun on his heels and began the long trek back to Southington Castle. He hated his grandfather's home—it was as cold as he was. There wasn't anything welcoming about it.

"Lord Harrington—"

"Don't call me that," Jonas interrupted. The sound of his father's title shot pain through his already aching heart. He didn't want to think or feel. Everything reminded him of his father and the loss that he couldn't escape. The title... That was more than he could bear.

Lord Coventry cleared his throat. "It's who you are now."

"That may be." Jonas swallowed hard. "But filling my father's shoes is something I'm not yet prepared for. I can't hear his title without thinking of him and what I've lost."

"I understand," Coventry said and sighed. "You're too young to have lost your father already. If I had a son..." He shook his head. "That doesn't matter. You have a long road ahead of you, and there's probably no one you feel you can trust. You might not know it yet, but you can trust me." He paused for a moment before continuing, "What would you like me to call you?"

"Nothing," Jonas said. "I doubt we will see each other again after today."

The older man laughed. It was a foreign sound, considering their surroundings. Sadness permeated everything around them, yet the earl had found something humorous. Coventry seemed like a likeable sort and in another time, Jonas may have liked him. Somehow, he doubted he'd find anything appealing or even joyous for a long time.

Coventry gestured toward the castle in the distance. "We shall see. Come, let's get out of this rain."

The earl followed behind Jonas as they entered the castle. He didn't stay long after that. He'd spoken to the duke quietly before his departure, and the duke didn't argue or order the earl around. That alone made Jonas wonder what they'd discussed.

"Now that everyone is gone we have some things to discuss, boy." His grandfather stormed across the room and glared down at him. "Starting with your education... I was going to keep you here, but Coventry made a good point. You'll need to make connections, and those are rooted in school. So, I'll allow you to return to Eton—at least for the rest of this school year. We'll revisit that idea before the next term."

He owed the earl far more than he realized. Never had he truly believed his grandfather would allow him to return to school. "Thank you."

"Don't thank me yet," his grandfather said

gruffly. "We have a lot of work ahead of us to prepare you for the dukedom."

He was barely an earl, and now he had to worry about grandfather's title? Jonas wanted to curl up into a ball and sleep for days—no, weeks. That was the cowardly way though, and he refused to give in to it. "Where is Mother?"

"She's gone to live with her sister," he replied. "Your mother is too delicate for Southington. Don't worry. Your father made sure she'd be provided for."

His mother had abandoned him? He'd always been closer to his father, but still... She left him alone with the duke, and she was well aware of his brutish nature. He had no problems using his fists to make a point. The Harrington title was prestigious, but he wouldn't have control of the estate for many years. They had plenty of funds as long as they did what the duke wanted. His father had decided to cut as many ties as possible with Southington. They lived in a small townhouse in London, and his father had invested in a profitable shipping company with the income he had available. They didn't live in splendor, but they'd been comfortable.

None of it had made the duke happy, but then nothing could. He liked having control over his family, and losing it had made him cut them out of his life. That was until his father died and he saw a way to wiggle his way back in. Now, Jonas was his ward until he gained full access to his inheritance. It was not a huge sum, but it would be enough for him to break free.

"May I be excused?" The duke hit Jonas's mouth with his fist before he was fully prepared for its impact. Jonas jerked backward involuntarily, but then gained control as quick as possible. He lifted his gaze and stared the duke in the eye, repeating his request, "May I be excused now?" Leaving without permission would prolong the torture, and he didn't want another punch to the face, or anywhere else.

The duke nodded, and Jonas left as fast as his feet would carry him. He didn't run as he wanted to because he would not give in to the duke's bullying. If he darted out of the room, his grandfather would find a reason to make him stay. Instead, he walked briskly and steadily until he reached his chambers. Only then, once the door was closed and he had privacy, did he give in to the emotions raging through him. The tears he'd held in finally flowed freely, and he grieved for his father.

London, 1812

JONAS PICKED UP THE GLASS OF BRANDY ON THE table and took a drink. He set it back down and stared at the cards in his hand. So far, luck hadn't been on his side, and he was steadily losing what funds he had. He should have given up a long time ago but stupidly thought he'd win if he kept playing. Freedom had led him astray when it should have brought him happiness. He learned fast that the latter was an elusive emotion not meant for him.

"I think it's time to call it a night," announced Jason Thompson, Earl of Asthey. He ran his fingers through his dark blond hair and grinned like a cat that'd caught the prize mouse. "It's been a productive night."

At least it was going well for one of them. "I'm ready too." He threw his cards on the table. "I've lost too much as it is." And he had very little he could afford to lose. His grandfather still held onto most of the purse strings. Somehow, the duke had found a way to gain control over a large part of his inheritance. Jonas had won his independence a year ago, but he wasn't truly free. The one thing he had left that the duke couldn't touch was a tiny sum his maternal grandmother had left him. It barely gave him enough to live on. He needed to figure out how to raise his income, but he was at a loss on how.

"That's a shame," Asthey said. "Winning big would solve a lot of your woes."

Jonas rolled his eyes. "I need more than I'd win in a few hands of cards to solve all that." It might help if his grandfather decided to roll over and die, but no, that wouldn't happen. The old man was too bullheaded to do anything as congenial as save the world from his type of meanness. "Where is Shelby?" Gregory Cain, the Earl of Shelby, was the other member of their trio. Jonas scanned the room for Shelby's midnight locks. They were his trademark. No one else had hair quite as sinfully dark as his. His friend was nowhere to be seen in the gaming hell.

"He found a light-skirt to his liking and appropriated a room for a bit of sport."

Of course he did... Shelby was quite the rake, and relished in ravishing any willing female in his vicinity. "Should we wait?"

"He knows his way home," Asthey replied. "I rather not wait on him to finish. He might take all night, or he could come out in an hour. It's hard to say with him."

"You're right," Jonas agreed. He stood and pulled

on his jacket and buttoned it over his waistcoat. "I'm tired and would rather sleep in my own bed."

They both headed to the front door and exited the gaming hell. It was still quite dark, and for once it was a rather clear night in London. The rain had been dreadful for days. The streets were filled with puddles and mud. They walked in silence for a few moments as they headed for a nearby hackney. As they stepped onto the road to cross over to the carriage, Jonas was yanked backward. He fell to the ground, his head smacking against the hard surface.

"Bloody hell," he said with a groan. "Why'd you do that?"

"I have a message for you." A big, burly man loomed over Jonas.

Jonas lifted a brow. "You might want to work on your delivery. I won't be recommending your service to anyone."

"Don't need it," the burly man replied. Jonas couldn't make out his features in the dark, but felt the sting of a fist hitting his jaw. "The message isn't the verbal kind."

Jonas was poised to throw another punch, but was jerked backward before he could land it. The man hit the ground in much the same manner as Jonas had. Served the bastard right... Jonas leapt to his feet before the other man could get up. He rubbed his hand over his sore jaw. "Took you long enough." He turned to whom he'd thought was Asthey, but was shocked to find Lord Coventry instead.

"Where's Asthey?"

"There." Coventry pointed in the distance. He was battling a ruffian of his own. He landed a solid blow, and the man fell to the ground. "What is going on?"

"Unfortunately, this is the work of your grandfather," he replied. A hint of sadness echoed through his voice. "I heard a rumor and came to investigate the veracity of it."

"And?" Jonas didn't like where this conversation was going. His grandfather could do a lot of damage if he wanted to, and it appeared as if he'd decided to employ his power. He had to have all the information Coventry possessed so he could form a plan of his own. His grandfather's contacts were extensive and his reach even farther. In order to beat him at his own game Jonas might have to fight dirty.

"I'm afraid it was correct by the looks of things," Coventry answered.

Asthey joined them, shaking his hand in the air as he walked. "That hurts more than I want to admit.

I might need to learn a thing or two about throwing a proper punch."

Coventry nodded. "I might be able to help you both." He turned to Asthey. "Go inside and fetch your friend, Shelby. I have a proposition for you all."

Asthey didn't question Coventry's order. He nodded and headed back into the gaming hell. Jonas watched him until he disappeared inside, and then turned back to Coventry. "What do you know?"

"Far more than you do," he replied cryptically. "The duke has plans for you, and he's not happy with your reluctance to follow them."

"That's something I know far too well." He wished the old man would leave him alone already. "Was this his way of forcing me to go to Southington?"

"I'm not entirely sure what he hoped to accomplish tonight," Coventry admitted. "I know he arranged it, and I'm here to help if you'll allow it."

Jonas was so tired of constantly fighting with his grandfather. There had to be a way to stop him from coming after him again and again. "What do you have in mind?"

Asthey and Shelby came out of the gaming hell and joined them. Shelby carried his cravat in his hand and was straightening his jacket. "This better be important," Shelby muttered. "The chit was..."

"We don't need to know," Asthey said, interrupting him.

Coventry smiled. "I believe you boys will fit right in."

"I don't follow," Jonas said, then frowned. "Fit in where?"

"A very special club," he replied. "Come along. I'll explain everything and how it'll help you with Southington, your social life, and even financially, if you like."

He didn't understand how a club could do all that, but he was willing to hear Coventry out. He had saved him from being beaten, and as long as Jonas had his two friends with him, he didn't see the harm. They could decide together if it was something worth doing. They'd stuck together this long.

They followed Coventry to a nearby carriage and climbed inside. It rolled across the cobbled street with ease. The interior was plush, and the seats rather comfortable. Jonas had never ridden in a carriage so fine. After a short drive, the carriage stopped. They all got outside to find an elegant townhouse with a W emblazoned near the door. Where were they? What had Coventry said earlier? Something about a club.

"Where are we?" Asthey asked vocalizing Jonas's thoughts.

"Doesn't look like much," Shelby replied. "Why'd I leave that lovely lass again?"

Coventry pulled a key out of his pocket that had the same W on the top of it. He pushed it into the lock and opened the door." "Gentleman, please come inside." He led them from the foyer into the main part of the house.

The outside expertly disguised the decadence found inside. Rich velvet draped the windows. The settees, chaise lounge, and every chair in the place had similar color scheme of dark red and burnished brown. To the side was a long cherry banister that wound around an elaborate staircase. To the side was a large room with a blazing fireplace. Several men sat at one of the tables as they played cards. Each one had a beautiful, scantily clad woman on their lap. Jonas's mouth fell open at everything he saw, and he couldn't believe he didn't know the place existed. He turned to Coventry and said, "You have our attention. Want to explain this to us now?" He continued to stare at the luxuriousness of his surroundings.

Coventry smiled. "Welcome to the club. You

have been nominated for admission—if you want to join. There are rules, of course," Coventry told them. "Nothing too extreme, but you should all find them reasonable. Keep the club a secret, and you forfeit your membership once you marry—only the leader of the group is allowed to have a wife and retain his membership. If you're wondering who that is—I am the currently in charge of the club and its members." He glanced at each one of them and asked, "Do you wish to be a part of all this?" He held his arms out wide.

They all nodded immediately. Jonas didn't give it much thought, and figured the other two hadn't either. The sheer excess of the place had won them over. The rest he could figure out later.

It was a decision he never regretted...

CHAPTER 1

London, 1823

DARK GRAY CLOUDS FLOATED IN THE SKY ABOVE, threatening to unleash rain upon everyone who dared to walk the streets of London. Lady Marian Lindsay stared up at them as she chewed her bottom lip. It was not a good sign, and she hoped the bad omen didn't lead to a disastrous meeting with Sir Anthony Davis. Not that rain wasn't commonplace in England—because it most certainly graced the country with regularity; however, Marian's luck never held when it deigned to fall from the sky. So her meeting with Sir Anthony would surely be doomed.

Nonetheless, she fully intended to go through with it. She had plans, and Sir Anthony stood in the way of them. Without his permission, she'd never become a part of the Royal Medical Society. They had this misbegotten notion medicine and women didn't mix. She hoped to change his mind and have him recommend her for admission.

She'd been studying medicine and herbs her entire life. All right, maybe not that long, but it felt like it. Her interest started almost a decade ago after her aunt and uncle's death. They'd both been in a terrible carriage accident near her family estate. Her father was the Earl of Coventry. Her uncle, the Earl of Frossly, married her Aunt Belinda and became a part of the family. After their death, Marian's mother had been desperate with grief and the loss of her beloved younger sister.

Everything in Marian's life changed after that. Her two cousins came to live with them, and her mother became sick following their arrival—leaving her launch into society, as well as her cousin's, forgotten. Not that she had minded especially once her mother succumbed to her illness and they lost her forever. Her grief had been too great, and she'd decided she wanted more in life. Marian didn't want to marry and have children. She had much loftier goals—like becoming an actual physician and making a living helping people.

Which brought her back to Sir Anthony—he had to let her into the society. This was the next step to gaining the knowledge she needed to become a doctor. She glanced up at the sky once more.

"Please hold off until I'm done," she begged. "I need a little bit of time." She quickened her pace until she reached Sir Anthony's building and pushed the door open. Marian entered as the rain started to fall. It pounded against the street, creating puddles almost instantly. She shut the door and blew out a relieved breath.

Someone cleared their throat. She turned and found two men standing inside, staring at her with a modicum of surprise etched on their faces. The older gentleman must have been Sir Anthony. He had dark hair streaked with gray. The other gentleman was rather handsome—dashing even. He had dark hair and devilish blue eyes. Much to her chagrin, she'd always found him enticing, and not because he was the most gorgeous male she'd ever seen. There was something about him that made the heart inside her chest beat heavily. Marian's whole body hummed with some unnamable energy. Jonas Parker, the esteemable Earl of Harrington, would always put her at a disadvantage, and sometimes she believed he knew it too. *Damn him.* "Hello, my lord," Marian greeted him and then turned to the older man. "Sir Anthony." She hoped her presumption was correct and he was the man she thought, or wouldn't that be embarrassing...

"Lady Marian," Lord Harrington said in a slow drawl. "Does your father know you're in this part of town?"

Drat. Of course that would be the first thing he'd ask—at least he hadn't corrected her about Sir Anthony. "My father is well aware of my activities." That wasn't entirely a lie. He did know she hoped to be a doctor and humored her. He didn't really believe she'd succeed, but she planned on proving him wrong. Men had all the advantages in society and women were given little say in their lives. Something she hated to the depths of her soul. "You needn't worry about me."

"What may we assist you with?" Sir Anthony asked. "Did the rain drive you inside?"

Lord Harrington lifted a brow. "I don't think that's it at all." He kept his gaze on Marian, unnerving her. He saw too much, and she rather disliked the scrutiny. "You're here because of your little project, aren't you?"

Anyone acquainted with her father, and therefore her, was aware of her desire to be a doctor. Her father boasted of her hobby even though he doubted her. It was his way of giving her his support. Not that it was a lot or even a stamp of approval, but it had managed to aid her in her quest thus far. "What if I am?" She jutted out her chin. "You aim to prevent me from taking the next step?"

He held out his hands in front of him. "Far be it from me to step in front of a bluestocking on a mission. By all means, say your piece and see if Sir Anthony is willing to assist you."

Sir Anthony glanced back and forth between them, but Marian barely noticed. She was irritated more than she should be. Lord Harrington was being nice by allowing her to speak—a sardonic, arrogant, and presumptuous...*man*. Rolling her eyes would not help her convince Sir Anthony she should be a part of the Royal Medical Society. She took a deep breath to calm herself. Calling him names inside her head would not further her goals. She had to pull herself together and try to present herself in the best light to Sir Anthony.

"You require something from me?" Anthony asked as he gave her his full attention. "What is it?"

"Well," she started. This was much harder than she thought it would be. "I have a request I hope you'll agree to."

"Oh?"

That was it. Nothing else from him or any encouragement for her to go on. Lord Harrington, the rogue, leaned against a nearby table and crossed his arms over his chest. He had a wicked grin on his too handsome face. If Marian wasn't a lady, she'd do something to wipe that knowing smile away. Someone should put him in his place, and maybe then he wouldn't be so condescending.

"I've been studying for a while to be a physician..."

"You have?" Sir Anthony scrunched his eyebrows together. "Your father knows you're doing this?"

"Well, yes," she said. "I did mention he was aware of my activities..."

"She's a bluestocking," Lord Harrington added. "You know how they are when they get an idea in their head. It's why I didn't stop her when she came in, if you'll recall."

Marian gave in and rolled her eyes. She couldn't

help herself any longer. Why did she have to be attracted to him? He drove her mad in more ways than she could count, yet he was the one man her body became alive near. She hated him for it. "Thank you, my lord." She pasted a cheerful smile on her face. "You give glowing recommendations."

"It's the least I can do," he replied with that sinful voice of his. It sent shivers down her spine. "As you can see, Sir Anthony is quite scandalized with your chosen hobby. He's gone mute with the shock of it."

Damn him, he was right. Sir Anthony stared at her as if she were a bug to be studied in length. He hadn't said a word in several heartbeats. "I had hoped you'd foster my admission into the Royal—"

"Absolutely not," he responded with vehemence. "Ladies do not become doctors or study anything. I don't understand this generation and their need to poke their noses in things they best not be a part of."

"Some ladies find science and knowledge enticing," Marian said as she lifted her head in defiance. "Intelligence is quite an attractive asset to inspire to."

"Touché," Lord Harrington agreed. "But I'd take it a step further and suggest there are things a gentleman finds more attractive in a lady than what's inside their head."

She shook her head. "I didn't come here to debate the qualities one looks for in a potential spouse. I want to become an active member of the Royal Medical Society."

"That's not going to happen, my dear. I'm afraid women are not allowed and never will be." Sir Anthony squared his shoulders, preparing for battle. Good, she planned on giving him something to fight about.

"Never is a long time to adhere to," Lady Marian replied. "Do you want to limit yourself when there are infinite possibilities if you'd open yourself up to them?"

"It's not up to me," Sir Anthony told her. "Society has rules for a reason. Go home and do something more ladylike. It truly is for the best."

She narrowed her gaze and pursed her lips together. *Ladylike?* He was much worse than Lord Harrington. At least the earl pretended to give her the space to argue her stance. Sir Anthony was an old-fashioned sycophant. He thought playing up to her feminine tributes would make her abandon her calling and do a bit of embroidery instead. Why could a man do anything he wanted, but a woman had inadequate options? If she decided to take up water colors or the pianoforte, they'd encourage her.

Being a doctor though? That was a ridiculous notion.

"Thank you for your sage advice," Marian replied with false sweetness. "I'll leave you gentleman to whatever you were discussing. It's time for me to return home. Good day." She curtsied and turned to the door.

"Wait," Lord Harrington demanded as he stepped forward. "I'll escort you."

"There's no need," she explained. Marian did not want him following her home. If he spoke to her father, then much more than a failed attempt to gain entry into the Royal Medical Society would befall her. "I managed to arrive here safely without an escort. I don't need one to see I find my way home."

"Perhaps," he replied cordially. "But I will be by your side every step of the way regardless. I'd never forgive myself if something happened to you and I could have prevented it." The corner of his mouth lifted enticingly. "I admire your father, and for that alone I'd see you safely to the ends of the Earth. Nothing you can say will talk me out of this."

Damn him. She cursed him for the thousandth time in the space of a half hour. At that rate, she'd start saying it aloud. There was no way she'd win in an argument with him. The easiest way would be to agree, but that irritated her nonetheless.

"Fine," she replied. "Have it your way."

"I always do," he retorted. "Good of you to see that." His blue eyes practically twinkled with mischief. He was a conceited scoundrel.

She ground her teeth together and refrained from responding. Instead, she spun on her heels and exited the building and Sir Anthony's misogyny. She would not give up on her dream. There had to be another way, and if there was, she'd find it.

The rain hadn't stopped while she was inside the shop. It beat against her in a rapid staccato, making her wish she'd stayed inside a bit longer, or procured a carriage. Why hadn't she planned this a little better? Because that would have made sense... She'd been blinded by her ambition and the need to be a part of something much bigger than herself. One day she'd learn the benefit of a well laid plan. Unfortunately, that day was not this one.

"Come with me," Lord Harrington leaned down and spoke directly into her ear. His heat enveloped her, making her forget where she was for a moment. He picked up her hand and rested it on his arm to lead her in the direction of his choosing. "My carriage is around the corner."

She blinked several times as rain continued to drown out the sound of the London Street. What was happening to her? She shook her head and did as Lord Harrington said. A carriage in this kind of weather was desirable, and for the first time since she saw him inside Sir Anthony's place, she was happy to have him near.

Thankfully, Lord Harrington's carriage wasn't far away. He helped her inside, but unfortunately, she was already soaked through. She couldn't wait to return home and put some distance between them. Uncomfortable wasn't a strong enough word to describe how he made her feel, and it didn't help that she was drenched from head to toe. She had to look a fright... What nonsense.

Why did she care if she looked less than desirable? Lord Harrington wasn't a potential suitor even if she was looking for a husband. He was one of the biggest rogues of the ton, and she was firmly on the shelf. Marian was a bluestocking and a spinster in the making, as untouchable as possible and quite content with that fate. Her pent up wantonness could dwindle down to nothing. She didn't need a man to find happiness.

Maybe she'd found a spot of luck in a sea of bad fortune. So, she'd taken a couple steps backward from her main goal. That didn't mean she couldn't find a way to move forward. For now, she'd allow Lord Harrington to see her home, and then she'd meet with her two closest friends to make a new plan. This was not the end of anything. Marian chose to see to it as a beginning. The likes of Sir Anthony and Lord Harrington would not discourage her.

EXCERPT: SURRENDERING TO MY SPY

LINKED ACROSS TIME FOUR

DAWN BROWER

DAWN BROWER

SURRENDERING
TO MY
Spy

Linked Across Time

PROLOGUE

June 1815

Lady Rosanna Kendall strolled down the hall of her family's townhouse. Her brother, Edward, was the current Duke of Weston. He'd inherited the title when their father passed on. An echo of voices came through the walls. Rosanna stopped short when she recognized who was speaking with Edward in his study. Lord Seabrook was in there. "Dom," she whispered to herself.

Dominic Rossington, the Marquess of Seabrook. She'd loved him from afar most of her life, and he was now a breath away. If she dared to go into the study and interrupt she'd be able to see him, and if she was lucky enough maybe a touch as well.

Did she dare?

Rosanna inched closer to the room. The door was slightly ajar. She peeked inside and a movement caught her attention. A blur of dark fabric, a slight hint of blond hair, and then nothing more. She wanted the full view of Dom's perfection. He had to be the most handsome man in creation—glorious golden hair, eyes the color of a stormy gray sky, and the face of an angel. That is if an angel could master the wicked glances the marquess threw out with regularity.

Rosanna was no fool. He was a rogue of the highest accord, and made no secret he wasn't seeking a wife. Dom found what he desired in the arms of many other women. Her heart hurt to realize he'd never love her the same way she did him. Unrequited love would be her lot in life. She shook her melancholy away and focused on their discussion. It wouldn't do to fall into that particular line of thought. Dom would never be hers, and it was time to let the fantasy go. She'd had suitors aplenty, but not one of them measured up to her dream.

"I wish you wouldn't involve yourself in this," Dom said. "James..."

"I don't bloody care what my brother would say,"

Edward spat out. "I'm the Duke of Weston, and I can do whatever I want."

What were they arguing about? What did it have to do with James? Rosanna hadn't seen her other brother, Edward's twin, in a couple of years. He'd joined a Calvary regiment and went off to fight in the war against Napoleon. She was terrified they'd receive horrible news about him one day. It was hard to sit with the knowledge he could be gravely injured or—she gulped—die fighting. Dom was James's best friend. If not for their friendship, she'd not have had the opportunity to become acquainted with Dom. She saw a side of him none of his chosen lovers did. He was funny, protective, and loyal to those he cared for. That was the man she'd fallen in love with. Rosanna was vain enough to realize she'd noticed his face first, but once she'd seen past his blinding beauty and into his soul everything changed.

A loud crash brought her back to reality. It echoed through the room as something thudded against the wall. Rosanna jerked back and clenched her arms against herself.

"You're a fool," Dom shouted. "What you've done..."

"I've done nothing you haven't."

"There is a difference and you better well realize

it before you make a mistake you can't return from." Dom's voice was edged with a hardness Rosanna had never heard before, and involuntarily flinched. She raised her hand to her chest and placed it against the rapid beat of her heart. What had Edward done? "Tell me what your reckless plan uncovered."

"Not here," Edward said. "You never know who's listening."

She took a step back and hugged the wall. What if he'd seen her through the crack in the door? They would both chastise her for eavesdropping if she were to be caught. What was Edward hiding? What made him so nervous? Should she be worried? Dom appeared to be angry at her brother, and Dom never even remotely raised his voice. He was always care-free and congenial. If Edward didn't want to discuss it at their home—it must be serious. She should leave before they exited the study. They'd both turn their ire on discovering her hovering nearby.

"Something you should have considered before you followed a trail that could lead to your death."

"Don't be so dramatic, Dom. That's unlikely to happen."

Was Dom right? Had Edward done something that could get him killed? She'd been worried for so long about James's safety and perhaps she'd been praying for the wrong brother. Rosanna backed away from the study and headed to the library. It was close enough to Edward's study she'd be able to hear when they left—it was only a few doors down the hall.

She stopped short when she realized the library wasn't empty as she'd assumed. Lady Callista Lyon, the Countess of Marin sat, reading a book, on a nearby settee. She glanced up as Rosanna entered. Her dark green eyes brightened when she met Rosanna's gaze. Callista was betrothed to her brother, Edward. They were set to be married in a sennight, and the wedding was to take place at Weston Manor. Everyone was scheduled to travel there by midweek.

"I'm sorry to disrupt you," Rosanna said. "I thought the library was unoccupied."

"I welcome the intrusion," Lady Callista said and set her book down. "I sent my maid to fetch my cloak. It's past time I went home."

It was rather unusual for her brother's intended to be lounging in their library. There were still proprieties that should be met. The countess was skirting the edge of what was acceptable by remaining alone. She'd not been so bold in the past. What had the lady been thinking? Perhaps the upcoming wedding was making her take risks she'd not have otherwise taken. She was rather independent, and a widow, but that didn't mean she should ignore what it her actions might mean to her reputation.

Rosanna didn't know Lady Callista well. She'd married the elderly Earl of Marin when she was nine and ten, and then the earl had died a mere six months after the marriage. She'd been out of mourning no more than a month before she caught Edward's eye. It was no surprise why. Lady Callista was a beauty. She had beautiful mahogany hair, the greenest eyes she'd ever seen, and her heart-shaped face was exquisite. Rosanna wished she could be as graceful and poised. She didn't feel as if she could truly become close to her as one would with a member of the family.

"I have your cloak, milady," Lady Callista's maid said as she entered the room. "Do you wish to depart now?"

"You're leaving?" Edward entered the room. "I didn't realize how late it was. I'm sorry I left you alone."

"It's all right. I entertained myself. We can discuss the wedding plans on the way to your estate in a couple of days." Callista nodded at her maid.

The young woman draped the cloak over her with care. "I'll take your leave until then."

Edward nodded. He didn't even spare Rosanna a glance. "I'll see you out."

It was brief and over before she'd even realized what happened. Lady Callista and Edward left the library without a by your leave. Edward's relationship with Lady Callista was so...odd. She wasn't sure what it was that bothered her. Perhaps she never would. In her experience, it was hard to truly understand what went on between two people. Only those inside it were truly aware of all the nuances. Maybe one day she'd share that wonder with another.

"What are you doing all alone in here?"

Rosanna turned and met Dom's gaze. She repressed a sigh at the sight of him. This had been what she'd wanted—some time to stare at his male beauty and hear his voice in that low tone that sent shivers down her body. She'd never tire of being around him.

"Edward left to escort Lady Callista to the door. I don't rate a glance from my brother these days." She tilted her head and studied him. "What are you doing here?" Perhaps that was insolent, but she couldn't help herself. She'd never stood on formality where Dom was concerned. Why hadn't he left before her brother came into the library?

Did Edward and Dom have plans to go somewhere more private to discuss Edward's discovery after Callista was gone for the evening? Edward could have forgotten his fiancée was lounging in the house while he and Dom disagreed over—well, whatever it was her foolish brother had done. She had no doubts he'd been the one in the wrong; Edward could be rather impulsive.

"I have business with your brother, brat." He strolled into the room. "But I can keep you company until he returns."

"It's not necessary." As much as she loved him, and adored being in his company, Rosanna was afraid she'd confess it all in a blubbery mess of need. He turned her insides to mush, and her thoughts weren't far behind. "I'm capable of spending time by myself."

His eyelids drooped low as he stared down at her. "A beautiful lady shouldn't ever be left to her own devices. What fun would that be?"

Was he? No, he couldn't be. Dom appeared to be flirting with her. What game was he playing? She didn't dare hope he wanted to court her properly. He'd never once indicated an interest in her. He wouldn't start now. There had to be another reason for him speak to her in an overly familiar manner.

"I'm not one of your lightskirts," she said harshly. "Don't speak to me as if I were."

Dom stepped back as if she'd slapped him. Color drained from his face. "I'd never..."

"I'd hope not." Rosanna lifted her chin arrogantly. Her tone was filled with an acerbity she'd been unable to control. Probably because she didn't believe he'd ever consider her as someone other than her brothers' little sister. It was too late to take any of it back, and she continued to speak before she realized her mistake. "I plan on marriage, and the entire ton knows how you feel about taking a wife."

"That they do," he said sardonically. He gave her a once over with slow, excruciating precision. "I assure you, not only do I never intend to marry, but you're the last lady I'd ever consider."

He spun on his heels and left her alone. *Fool— what had she done?* His words shattered her heart into thousands of tiny pain-filled shards. She'd pushed him away forever. Would she ever learn? Apparently, she could be as equally imprudent as her wayward brother when making hasty decisions. She'd been irrational, and she wouldn't blame Dom if he never forgave her. He hadn't done anything untoward. Dom—was well—Dom; there wasn't a mean bone in his body. Rosanna might never recover from her blunder.

ROSANNA WAS SITTING IN THE LIBRARY DOM HAD last seen her in. Had it been two days since he'd laid eyes on her? She was as beautiful as he remembered, and equally as untouchable. Her dark tresses were coiled on top of her head in an elaborate chignon, and her violet eyes drew him in as she observed him with cool efficiency.

"Lady Rosanna," Dominic Rossington, the Marquess of Seabrook said, with a bow. The discord between them remained palpable whenever they were near each other. She'd been so warm and welcoming in the past, but that changed with one flicker of thoughtless words flung in her direction. He should regret them, and in a way he did. It didn't change the circumstances. Rosanna needed to understand he would never marry. He wasn't a fool, and was very much aware of her growing attachment. In a different world, he'd have been pleased and delighted at the prospect of having her as a wife, but his life didn't leave room for one. "I apologize for intruding, but I have news I must share with you."

"I won't keep you. Tell me what you must, as I'm sure my company disgusts you." Her voice was hoarse with an unidentifiable emotion. She met his gaze with unrepentant defiance. "I believe I'm the last person you wish to have any sort of discourse with."

This had to be about his parting remark—her being the last lady he'd ever marry. No young lady liked to hear those words thrown at them. Dom had been the worst kind of swine to say them aloud to her. He meant them though, but not for the reasons she assumed. Lady Rosanna Kendall was too good for him. He would taint her by spending any amount of time in her company. She deserved a husband who would cherish and adore her. Someone who didn't have the reputation he'd carefully cultivated over the past few years.

"I promise you—I don't disdain you in the slightest." His forehead creased. She was the one woman he'd always felt more for than he should. He couldn't tell her that though. It was better if she hated him. "You're to go to Weston Manor in the morning, and I had to tell you..."

How could he say it? She'd be devastated once

she learned of the news. The whole family would be. What about James? How was he to tell his best friend he was responsible for what happened to Edward. If he'd been able to stop him in his foolhardy inquiries...

"What is it?" Rosanna leaned forward and studied him. "You're not usually at a loss for word."

Dom didn't want to hurt her, had never wanted to do her any kind of harm. The words currently lodged in his throat would surely cause her no small amount of pain, but he had to tell her before someone else did. She should hear the news from someone who cared about her and her family.

"There was an accident..."

Rosanna leapt up and strode toward him. "Is it James?"

Of course she'd jump to that conclusion. Why wouldn't she? He was at war and on the front lines. Dom shook his head. "It isn't James."

"Who is it?" she demanded. "You're scaring me."

Dom closed his eyes and prayed for strength. Rosanna was the one woman he'd always admired and vowed to take care of. No other had ever mattered as much to him. He'd lay down his life to protect her, and here he was about to destroy a part of her. It had to be done. "Edward's carriage hit something in the road. A wheel broke and it tipped over the side of a bridge. He—didn't make it." He stared into her violet eyes and said morosely, "It's with greatest sympathy I must tell you that your brother, Edward, the fourth Duke of Weston, has died."

Rosanna's screams filled his ears. Tears streamed down her face as she beat her fists against his chest. He took every bit of her ire as he believed was his due. Dom hadn't protected Edward from his reckless behavior, and now the people he cared about most would pay that price. After a short while, he helped her back onto the settee and called for a maid to see to her care. He turned, exited the room, and left her alone—not once glancing back.

Rosanna wasn't his, and never would be...

CHAPTER 1

June 1818

DOMINIC STROLLED INTO THE WAR OFFICE. THE war hadn't ended everything as it should have at Waterloo three years ago. Napoleon's supporters still sneaked around trying to free the man. Espionage always seemed to run rampant within the government. When he signed up to be an agent for the crown it had sounded like jolly good fun. What a fool he'd been. His younger self had been an idiot; not that he wasn't inclined to make imprudent mistakes these days either. The difference was he stopped and considered the best option hoping he'd not regret the choice in the end.

This spy business had become old years ago. He

was ready to step aside and leave it to other ambitious gentlemen. All Dom wanted to do was retire to his Seabrook Manor and ignore society. He was becoming maudlin and it wasn't a good state to be in. He was three and thirty and, as his mother liked to point out, well past the time to wed and continue the line. Something he'd been profusely avoiding most of his adult life. Dom didn't believe he'd make a good husband or father, but leaving the family's fate in his dimwitted cousin's hands didn't sit well with him either. He knocked on his superior's door and grimaced.

"Enter," a deep booming voice called out.

Dom opened the door and stepped to the side. He waited for the Duke of Branterberry to acknowledge his presence. The older gentleman was a genius in plotting and developed strategies that boggled the mind. Dom often wondered where he came up with his diabolical schemes. Under the duke's tutelage he'd learned a lot. It had become apparent rather fast he'd signed up for more than he'd bargained for. The life he'd lived previously was superfluous and filled with every luxury imaginable. Being a marquess and one of the esteemed peerage offered him every opportunity to indulge in all the vices known to man —and Dom had partaken whenever possible.

And it left him completely jaded...

"You requested my presence," Dom said, growing impatient. "Are you going to leave me standing here all day?" He quirked an eyebrow.

The Duke tapped his fingers together. He stared over Dom's shoulder, apparently lost in thought. After a moment, he shook his head and then waved at Dom. "Come in and shut the door behind you. We've quite a bit to discuss."

Dom did as he was instructed and sat down in the chair near the duke's desk. He'd become weary watching the duke—who was still lost in his own thoughts. What was bothering him? It had to be something bad for it to weigh on the Duke of Branterberry. There wasn't much that fazed him and he took everything by storm. Nothing and no one stood in his way. Dom had always admired that trait in him.

"I'm sure you're aware that Bonaparte has been secluded on the isle of St. Helena successfully for years now." The Duke frowned. "Something we'd like to continue for the unforeseeable future."

Dom nodded. "I take it there has been a development in that area for you to be concerned."

The duke waved a hand. "I don't doubt that Napoleon will die on that island. It's a matter of when." He leaned back in his chair. "That being said..." He paused a moment and studied Dom. "There is something I believe could be an issue if we don't handle it."

Dom leaned forward and asked, "What is it?"

"It's rumors and speculation at this juncture, but as we both know sometimes there is a whiff of truth to be found in those whispers." The duke sighed. "I'd rather not ignore it and regret it later."

Dom agreed with him on that. It was better to investigate and find naught than to pretend it was insignificant. Something of that nature could result in bloodshed or an economic collapse they'd never recover from. Even if it was small they couldn't afford to sit idly by while someone attempted to undermine their king and country. "What do you require from me? Tell me what these whispers are."

"When is the last time you visited the Duke of Weston?"

Dom blanched at his words. It had been a while since he'd been to Kent and visited his friend. It hurt him too much to be around him. It wasn't anything James had done—more Dom's own feelings of inadequacy. James had everything Dom didn't believe he deserved. When he married and started a family it had changed the dynamic of their relationship. Dom was perpetually single and had no plans to change it. Even if his mother harassed him on a regular basis, in his mind he had plenty of time to marry and sire a child to inherit the Seabrook title. It was recently that he'd begun to question why he waited.

"I saw him several months past." It was a chance meeting in town. James had come in for some business matter but hadn't stayed long. They had a drink together to celebrate his upcoming fatherhood—again. He already had a daughter and hoped this time to have a son. Weston hadn't stayed long—he didn't like leaving his family. The man adored his wife, Alys, and suffered separation anxiety. "He doesn't often come to town."

"But you're still in contact with him?"

What did this have to do with James? Dom was instantly on alert. He should have been immediately after the duke inquired about his relationship. Surely he didn't believe James would have anything to do with smuggling Napoleon off of St. Helena. James had taken a saber to the gut and carried the scars of battle with him. Waterloo had almost ended his life, and James wouldn't take lightly the accusation he was a traitor. He had to do everything he could to protect his friend. He'd failed him once with Edward's death, and Dom refused to do so again.

"What is this about?" Dom's jaw hardened. "James is one of the best men I know, and yes we still keep in contact."

The Duke of Branterberry nodded. "Good. I need you to go to his estate and keep an eye on things."

Dom raised a brow. "What exactly am I to keep a look out for?"

The longer he sat without answers the more surly Dom was becoming. He didn't like the way the conversation was going and had no clue how to handle it properly.

"Don't worry about your friend," the duke said, and then paused briefly. "He isn't a traitor, but someone on his estate is. There is information being smuggled out and across to France. I don't know what is going on, only that there is a ring running in full force there."

A band had operated there in the past. Dom had witnessed it when he visited after James's return from Waterloo. After James was shot by smugglers, Dom took care of them—or at least he thought he had. Alys handled removing the bullet and seeing to James's medical care. Dom took care of the rest, and had done it without complaint. He'd considered his duty complete, but now it appeared as if he'd been wrong or foolish in believing that the end of the situation.

"I see."

"I thought you might. You have the best reason for being in the area. Your estate isn't too far from Weston Manor. You can visit for a while, investigate, and handle the matter before returning home."

Dom's mouth twitched. "I didn't realize I was going to return to Seabrook for any amount of time."

The duke smiled. "Don't you think you should? I'm not young or stupid. I know you want to stop this life style and go home. Do this one last assignment for me and then you can. I won't fight you on it."

It was the last thing he expected the Duke of Branterberry to say. Dom thought he'd hidden his feelings well. How wrong he'd been... Though, to be fair, the duke wasn't the usual sort and saw far more than the average person. It shouldn't have surprised him he'd uncovered Dom's secret desires. Although the duke didn't know his biggest secret, the one thing —no, the one person—he craved above all. Did he dare claim her? His life was dangerous and he'd not have her in harm's way for anything. Maybe after he was fully un-entangled from the war office he could. The problem was he didn't think he could wait until he was fully decommissioned. His desire for her was too strong.

He hated hurting her and pushing her away. His life was rife with danger, and he shouldn't bring her anywhere near it. That was the main reason he'd pushed her away so many years ago. She deserved better than he could offer, but if he could free himself from his obligations to the crown... That changed everything. He'd carefully crafted his reputation so no one expected him to marry. That way, if his status as an agent were ever to be found out, no one would be harmed because of him. It didn't make his feelings go away though. He'd always wanted Rosanna, but didn't believe he could ever have her.

Dom tapped his fingers on the arm of his chair and considered the duke's words in silence. He would be free, but the price was he had to invite himself to stay at Weston Manor until he closed the case. The duke didn't know what he was asking of him. She was there—and still unwed. The mourning period after Edward's death should have stalled the inevitable, but now three years later... She should have married.

Why is she still not married? Were these young lords all nitwits and unable to see the diamond they had in front of their eyes? But *he* could claim her, and he would, once this last mission was completed. The duke had given him the one thing he didn't think he'd ever be able to attain. He'd be a fool not to take it and run. Dom shook his thoughts away. Their loss would be his gain. But first he had to take care of a few things. Like unraveling a smuggling ring and ending it once and for all.

"I'm not going to admit or deny anything," Dom said carefully. "But I will take on this assignment and pay a call on my good friend. As luck would have it, if my calculations are correct—I believe his wife is due to give birth soon. I'm sure James would appreciate the company."

"Good," the duke said. "Then it should be fairly easy for you to stay for an extended period of time."

James would never turn him away. They'd been the best of friend since the early days at Eton. The Duke of Branterberry realized fully what he was asking of him, and that he was the only one of his operatives who could handle the situation. He would, and could, visit Weston Manor for any length of time. The problem would be Rosanna. The last time he'd seen her she'd been a veritable harpy. His fault of course—he encouraged her to let her claws out. When she drew blood though... Sometimes he wondered if he'd survive her thorny nature.

"I can leave on the morrow," Dom said. "I will report when I know more."

He hoped he could wrap it up rather quickly. As much as he adored Rosanna he didn't trust himself in her company for long. She was the one woman he'd always wanted, but refused to have. He'd always believed she deserved more than him. She should have married someone more worthy of her. She hadn't, and that meant she was his for the taking. Once the assignment was over, he'd make plans to woo and win her. It would be no easy task because, unfortunately, Rosanna hated him; something he thought was best when he'd cultivated it. Now though, he wished he would have handled her fledgling emotions with better care. If he'd seen a way out he'd never have treated her so haphazardly.

"Perfect," the duke said. "Keep me updated on your progress."

"What if there isn't much to report?" Dom asked.

The duke leaned back further in his chair. "Give me a report in a sennight regardless of information. I want to know what you find, even if it's the most minute detail. That way if you fail to report in I'll know if something untoward may have happened to you."

Dominic understood his reasoning. It was what

made him the perfect person to head up the war department. He made sure he was aware of what all his operatives were doing at any given moment. "I'll make sure you hear from me by the end of the week."

"I hope you end this swiftly," the duke said. "I'll miss having you around. I also realize you have a duty to your title. Not too many lords working for me, and I admit I was pleasantly surprised at how you adapted to the field. There's no one quite like you, and you will be rather hard to replace." The duke paused a moment before speaking again. "Don't let anyone stand in the way of your happiness. You deserve to find some after all you've done for king and country."

Dominic wasn't so sure about his assessment, but he knew what he wanted. Lady Rosanna Kendall was everything good in the world, while he, Lord Dominic Rossington, the Marquess of Seabrook, was the complete opposite. Maybe she would make him better. He wasn't sure one way or the other. Dom did want her, and after he finished this last assignment— he'd do everything in his power to make her his.

He nodded at the duke and left the room. There was much to be done if he were to journey to Weston Manor the next day. James would be surprised to see him, and Dom had to admit to himself he was rather glad to have the opportunity to spend some time with his friend. He missed him. His best friend might not be so happy to see him once he realized how much Dom lusted after his sister. James had bricks he called fists. Dom feared at some point he might use them on his face, and he'd hate to allow his friend the opportunity to mark up perfection.

Oh, but it would be worth it in the end...

Thank you so much for taking the time to read my book.

Your opinion matters!

Please take a moment to review this book on your favorite review site and share your opinion with fellow readers.

www.authordawnbrower.com

USA TODAY Bestselling author, DAWN BROWER writes both historical and contemporary romance. There are always stories inside her head; she just never thought she could make them come to life. That creativity has finally found an outlet.

Growing up she was the only girl out of six children. She is a single mother of two teenage boys; there is never a dull moment in her life. Reading books is her favorite hobby and she loves all genres.

BB bookbub.com/authors/dawn-brower

f facebook.com/AuthorDawnBrower

twitter.com/1DawnBrower

instagram.com/1DawnBrower

g goodreads.com/DawnBrower

Odds of Love (Dawn Brower)

Bluestockings Defying Rogues

When An Earl Turns Wicked

A Lady Hoyden's Secret

One Wicked Kiss

Earl In Trouble

All the Ladies Love Coventry

Marsden Descendants

Rebellious Angel

Tempting An American Princess

Marsden Romances

A Flawed Jewel

A Crystal Angel

A Treasured Lily

A Sanguine Gem

A Hidden Ruby

A Discarded Pearl

Novak Springs

Cowgirl Fever